Denial of
Conscience

Cat Gardiner

Denial of Conscience

© Copyright by Cat Gardiner
Publisher: Vanity & Pride Press
ISBN-13: 978-1508790877
ISBN-10: 1508790876

Denial of Conscience is a work of fiction. Names, characters, businesses, places, events and incidents are either the products of the author's imagination, Jane Austen's novel, *Pride and Prejudice,* or used in a fictitious manner. Any resemblance to actual persons, living or dead, or actual events is purely coincidental.

Denial of Conscience Spotify Playlist
Denial of Conscience Pinterest Inspiration

Cover design and formatting: JDSmith Designs

Dedicated to Sheryl and Pam
Two fabulous women who appreciate
a hot Mr. Darcy on a Harley

Prologue

It was early yet, and the assassin's target wasn't due to arrive until the sun was hot and high and the mosquitoes and humidity became annoying. Elevated upon his perch in one of the lush trees of the Yungas tropical rainforest in Bolivia, Fitzwilliam Darcy had become a branch. No, he became an epiphyte—a tree within a tree. He was so still, so lifeless that his heartbeat regulated below normal as he waited.

It was the way of the sniper—hiding, blending, and deceiving—and many considered Darcy the best of them, and as the best, he knew that even the most organized, strategic plans changed on a dime.

Nine hundred yards away, the growl and lurch of four heavily laden trucks ceased, and their cargo unloaded men, women, and children who began the duties of harvesting the coca leaves of Bolivia's largest planta-tion in the Yungas Valley.

The last truck in the caravan stopped just as the sun crested above the eastern mountain range and the blue and yellow macaws and light-green parakeets came alive to greet the day. Unexpectedly early, the devil himself, the target, exited the cab of the truck. Dressed in his white suit and Panama hat, he looked like a tourist amidst all the laborers while he surveyed his vast plantation.

Ricardo Morales, the biggest cocaine producer and trafficker south of the Peruvian border, was about to meet his demise. Referred to as the

Lord of the Jungle, he had created an empire that exceeded even Colombia's market in cocaine production. His plantations and cultivation produced some of the most toxic, unrefined cocaine currently shipping into Europe and America. Untouchable by the government of Bolivia as well as US Drug Enforcement Administration officials, Morales was the target of the CIA's next hit. Or rather, the CIA's hired henchmen, the covert, four-agent civilian contract group named, Obsidian.

Morales raised his hands in frustration at a woman laborer whose infant clung tightly to her back in a traditional sling. His anger echoed throughout the valley, competing for airspace with the roaring river some three thousand meters below him.

The adrenaline within the assassin's body and mind began to escalate. He was about to rid the world of another evil son of a bitch. He despised drug lords, cartels, dealers, and pushers, all of whom preyed upon the weak, wounded, compulsive, and especially the youth.

With steady hands and superb accuracy, he looked through his scope, made concessions for wind, distance, and bullet velocity, and then aimed his rifle four inches above his target's head. With his kill shot ready, he emotionlessly mouthed the words, "*Adios,* mother fucker."

The ex-Navy SEAL breathed out and, holding his lungs empty, placed his mind in time with his heartbeat. Between beats, he squeezed the trigger with the ball of his finger.

Bolivia's drug kingpin, the Lord of the Jungle, fell dead from the bullet's sudden impact directly between his eyes—Fitzwilliam Darcy's trademark sniper hit.

As all hell broke loose down the mountainside, he slid deeper into his hide sight, patiently waiting the precise moment for extraction. It was only a matter of time before Operation Samba came to its conclusion and he could go back to his home in the States.

Now rising over the eastern ridge of the Andes Mountains, the sun cast hues of purple and grey into the Yungas Valley. The air hung still in the cool fog clinging to the side of the buttress. From Darcy's lone perch, he focused on the shouts of chaos, ignoring the rushing whitewater from the river below him. His dark eyes blended into the background, unseen by the fauna as well as the armed and dangerous drug cartel security forces now hurrying and shouting around him and in the valley below.

"¡alli!" ¡apúrate!"

"Él *está muerto!*"

As the sun rose higher, Darcy could make out the corded rope zip lines that extended from one side of the narrow, deep gorge to the other side. Their final destination lay hidden in the lush, dense jungle, ready to carry the coca leaves away to safety.

He looked at his own well-concealed zip line, seeing it at the ready for his undetected escape, ready to carry him over two thousand yards to the south through the Amazon basin with speed rivaling any of his Harleys at full tilt.

Movement was impossible when Darcy suddenly felt the pressure and coil of a long, slender, Amazonian snake slither up his muscular leg. The *Chironius carinatus* crawled over his inert body, not even realizing that the surface below wasn't authentic.

Nine feet of powerful scales crept up his six-foot-two, 220-pound body until it stopped. Its pointed head stilled, poised just below his shoulder. Its moist tongue flicked near the jungle interloper's ear to smell danger and any possible prey.

The panicked voices of Morales's men below the sniper became clearer, louder, and closer in search of the assassin.

Killing the snake would be a mistake, but Darcy would if he had to. With one eye still trained through his rifle scope, ready to fire at cartel sentries if necessary, his left hand hovered over his razor-edged tactical knife, waiting for the snake to make its move.

Long seconds passed until the reptile finally continued slowly into the canopy of leaves above. The stilled sniper released his breath.

Vipers, snakes, and serpents—he hated them all. They came in many different forms but were all the same. The key to survival was recognizing them and crushing them below the sole of his motorcycle boot. For example, the venomous woman—she was the most dangerous and deadly type of snake. The sharp forked tongue and deceptive nature of a woman usually came with a killer body and eyes of fire. That combination was the worst kind of trouble, but he considered every woman a viper. His mother's betrayal had set that precedence. Then there was the toxic horned viper, spawn of the devil scumbags whom he killed on an op, and lastly, was the actual reptile itself. Each slithery, each intently destructive and each, if left unchecked, could render a man incapacitated or even dead.

Yes, the stone-cold sniper hated snakes, each and every one of them, but he knew that while danger was real, fear was never an option. He feared no man, woman, or experience. The only thing the assassin feared were his own demons—or rather, facing them.

Darcy was thankful the unwelcome visitor wasn't dangerous, unlike the jaguar that visited the night before. Its light green eyes flickered from the beam of moonlight casting down through the tree canopy. He was sure the stealthy, deadly big cat had smelled him through the human-scent-blocker camouflage applied to his body. Fearless and ready as he was for the fight of his life, it never happened. The jaguar began to mew instead, sending its mating call throughout the jungle. Its sinewy body moved on, and the jungle's interloper breathed easy and settled in for a long night's sleep.

In the far distance, the trucks departed, including the one carrying Morales's dead body. Each one precariously traversed the mountainside along La Paz's dangerously rocky and narrow "death road," kicking up the dry dirt for the wind to carry away to heaven. Heaven seemed so close at that altitude, but that wouldn't be the final destination for the Lord of the Jungle.

Extraction was still impossible. Darcy waited. It didn't matter; he was a patient man. He had to be in his line of work. As a rule, he used the passage of time to meditate and quiet his breath. Usually, his daydreams took him to memories of laughter of long ago. He would ruminate about thrilling rides on his Harley through North Carolina's Blue Ridge Parkway, or he would recite passages from classic books locked within his memory. Sometimes, like now, he tapped the button on the stock of his camouflaged semi-automatic sniper rifle so he could listen to the messages stored on his specially designed Bluetooth, now blackened, concealed, and buried well into his ear canal.

"Hello, brother dear. Just touching base since I haven't heard from you since you arrived in Tokyo. Maybe you finally met the girl of your dreams, and that's why you haven't called me back."

He heard Georgiana giggle.

"Anyway, I just wanted to let you know that Justin invited me up to his cabin near Grandfather's Mountain on the Blue Ridge for the week. I've given Mrs. Reynolds all the information, so don't worry." She snorted. "Like you won't anyway. Just so you know, you *are* going to have to stop treating your twenty-two-year-old sister like she's fifteen, at some point. Yes, I know; it makes you feel better. So just to make you further happy, I called Aunt Catherine to let her know I was traveling. By the way, she's still pissed off at you for not going to see her.

"Ok … so I gotta go, and don't forget to pick me up a silk kimono when you're making the purchases for DBI.

"You know, brother, I do have a bone to pick with you; you never mentioned when you'd be coming home. You and I have tickets for the symphony at the end of the month. Just let me know…*please*. Because if you're going to bail on me again, I'll ask Justin in your place.

"Be safe. Enjoy the sushi. Love you. *Sayonara*, brother-san."

Darcy smiled ever so slightly, the scope of his rifle concealing the movement of his lips. Hearing Georgiana's sing-song voice had such power over him and confirmed his reason for continuing on in his profession and staying focused. He could deal with the isolation and the days-on-end cramping. He had long mastered his bodily functions and the need for food. His body had become immune to the abuse it took: jungle rot, insect bites, inflammation, spasms. None of that mattered. He looked at each operation as a means of keeping his sister comfortable and safe—no matter how old she was—while ridding the world of evil men and women who would bring harm to her and so many others. No, he had yet to have any compunction about what he did.

With the chaos fading and all but the laborers below him cutting and sorting, Darcy again tapped the button on the stock of his rifle to listen to the next message.

It was *her,* the bane of his existence, and he cringed at her feigned sickly sweet voice. Now there was a viper if he ever knew one. Yes, *she* was a viper like none other, and her talents extended into the most venomous, deadly kind, but she knew not to mess with him. He had crushed her below his boot long ago. The two might be on the same team and fighting for the same cause, but he'd never again give her an inch, any inch of his for that matter, or she would take a yard for sure.

"This is Caroline from the Bingley Dance Studio. I'm just calling to let you know that your next dance class is scheduled to commence upon your successful completion of the samba. Your next lesson will be the Virginia Reel. So please give us a call or stop in."

Christ, another job. He needed a break after this one. A Bolivian rainforest was the last fucking place he wanted to be, but Virginia … now that was tempting. He would be going back to his home, not the place where he currently lived—that was in Asheville, North Carolina—but home, the place of his birth. Darcy wondered how he could have stayed away from Virginia for so long, away from Pemberley, with its peaceful landscape and towering oaks.

Had it really been five years since he last checked on the empty estate? He didn't realize just how much he missed the essence of his family home despite all the pain associated with it. Nevertheless, he made his choice long ago. The cold, hard-edged man left abruptly, seeking a new life and new surroundings. Pemberley and its once staid, comfortable life of money, polo, and thoroughbreds wasn't his ideal any longer. Now he lived balls to the wall. He was a different man. Experience, pain, and revenge did that to him.

The assassin's curiosity was piqued. Who the hell would be the target of a CIA-commissioned hit in Virginia? Was it a government official? Enemy spy? Al-Qaeda near the Capitol? Rogue agent? Terrorist cell?

"Virginia, here I come," Darcy whispered as his body slowly came alive from within the tree.

With two swift moves, he hooked himself to the zip line and hit the button on his Bluetooth, sending chords of AC/DC's electric guitars coursing through his body as it played "Shoot to Thrill."

A catapulting push broke the branch and sent the assassin soaring through the air. Rocking to his signature song, Darcy disappeared like the ghost he was. He was headed home for Operation Virginia Reel.

~♠~

1
Longbourn

Standing beside the weather-beaten mailbox at the end of a dusty road, Lizzy Bennet shielded her eyes from the bright sun while looking toward her family home. Situated below the towering pines in the southwestern corner of the family estate, Longbourn Plantation house's graying white façade and newly-broken black shutter stared back at her like a winking taunt. She swore the house conspired against her, having just fixed the shutter on the *opposite* side of that same window two days prior. *Darn it.*

Before opening the mailbox, Lizzy surveyed the vast, overgrown field of weeds and wildflowers beside her. Strangling pieces of Spanish moss eerily hung from the massive oak before the house, and a broken wood-slat fence fell in disrepair along the perimeter. She shook her head and opened the rusty door to the mailbox.

"Please, oh, please ... no bills today," she pleaded, reaching in for the stack of letters.

"Thank God." She breathed in a sigh of relief, knowing that every day brought more invoices requesting payment for the never-ending repairs the house required.

In spite of the estate's poor condition, it didn't matter what the land or plantation house looked like to her. Since childhood, Lizzy considered the former tobacco plantation her most favorite place. Longbourn held a magical air about it. For seven generations, the family homestead embodied the quiet, peaceful mystique of her ancestors, who had helped to form and build a nation.

Once a three-thousand-acre plantation located just outside of Mount Vernon in Alexandria, Virginia, Longbourn now totaled three hundred acres nestled alongside the banks of the Potomac River. In its day, locals and visitors considered it one of the most beautifully situated, simplistically appealing, architectural designs of the early nineteenth century. From its construction in 1813, women of refinement and culture flourished within its bright and airy two stories. From cone-shaped to hoop to miniskirts, the plantation witnessed and survived each generation's changes of both lifestyle and architectural design preferences.

Now, two hundred years later, the neighboring beautifully restored estates, former plantations, and historical societies surrounding George Washington's stately Mount Vernon were all calling for either Longbourn's sale, destruction, or complete restoration. Longbourn was an eyesore and an insult to the first president's neighboring homestead.

With the hot sun beating down upon her, Lizzy felt the perspiration bead above her upper lip as she sorted through the letters. Her eyes finally settled upon the last one. Its anticipated arrival from the state's Historic Preservation Office had been awaited with apprehension for three months. The moment of truth lay at hand: Longbourn Plantation's acceptance—or not—for National Register of Historic Places designation. If accepted, it entitled the Bennets to apply for grant funding to cover the expense of the necessary renovations and upkeep. This was their final hope. All other options and funding had sadly been exhausted.

Lizzy fanned herself with the all-important, unopened letter. Her straight, long brown hair moved slightly from the fast infusion of air. It was too hot for any comfort in or out of the house, and the humidity had settled fast upon Virginia. June was turning out to be one hell of a month. Hot as blazes and with no air conditioning in Longbourn, she swore she would be better off either staying at her sister Jane's small apartment in DC or volunteering to teach summer school. Neither was appealing. Besides, there was so much work to do at home; her father needed her here. His depression was growing, and his distracted attitude had become increasingly obvious.

Passing the cherry trees, now void of their lovely pink blossoms, she continued to wave the letter back and forth before her. "Well, Daddy, you'll know what to do with Longbourn once you open this letter." Her skirt blew in the much appreciated breeze, baring long, slender legs above dirty Timberland work boots.

Skirts were her thing, and even though her sister insisted that given their sexiness every man enjoyed them, she didn't believe her. In her opinion, she was nothing special. Jane also insisted that Lizzy would look great in a pair of blue jeans, but Lizzy, who was all things proper and feminine, neither owned a pair nor would be caught dead in them. No, she thought her hips were curvy enough. The last thing she wanted to do was draw attention to them. Besides, blue jeans were meant for other women, women who dreamed large and played larger. That wasn't her—oh no—not the Lizzy of today. *That* Lizzy was long gone. The Lizzy of today played it safe, sound, and demure.

She playfully and deliberately kicked up the dust and pebbles along the dirt road, creating a sandy fog about her feet and spoke out toward the overgrown field of tall weeds beside her. "We should sell down Longbourn. If only he'd take my advice. We don't need three hundred acres that we can't maintain."

It was a crazy idea to think her father would make the right decision no matter what the contents of the letter were. In fact, he refused to do the inevitable: sell the entire estate or sell off land. He insisted that Longbourn was the "Bennet ancestral home" and that its legacy should pass from "generation to generation of Bennet heirs." He felt passionately that Longbourn was Jane and Lizzy's home and would be home to their children and grandchildren one day. Selling was not an option.

As she neared Bennet Oak, the tree her great-great-grandfather planted in honor of Virginia's succession from the Union in 1861, she shook her head in amazement at how she and her father had been able to hold onto Longbourn for as long as they had.

In spite of Thomas's lackluster experiments, free-lance computer programming jobs, and a respectable government career with the Department of Defense, his income enabled them just to make ends meet. Her salary as a Kindergarten teacher hardly made any difference in the grand scheme of things.

She hesitated before the black front door, neither turning the knob nor retreating down the walkway. Tilting her head from side to side, Lizzy sighed. The brass knocker was loose again. *Darn it.*

Thomas sat comfortably settled in his wobbly desk chair watching his favorite daughter from the study window at the front of the house. It was where every brainchild of invention and light-bulb idea emanated from, and it was the one place he was sure to find enough distraction from the pressures and demands that plagued his mind, particularly of late.

After removing his reading glasses, he placed the temple tip between his lips and watched Lizzy acutely. He noticed the white envelope in her hand and how she vacillated on whether or not to enter the house. What a mess he had created, he thought, feeling extremely regretful of oh so many things: divorce, apathy, too many bookish hobbies, long hours at the Pentagon's computer lab. His chickens were now coming home to roost, and his options had run out.

He knew the blame of Longbourn's ruin rested upon his shoulders. He should have prepared by saving, acknowledging that it was sinful the way he had allowed the landscape to become overgrown and the trees to grow wildly untamed. Even the outbuildings were left neglected, becoming more dilapidated each year. The plantation house … oh, the plantation house's needs were way beyond even attempting to itemize. The only good thing it had going for it was the new roof, recently replaced when the existing ninety-year-old slate roof had come to its end. Replacing it to its historic grandeur wasn't cheap. They could not maintain that elegant splendor of days gone by, and that was what he hoped for above all things. This estate was his life's blood and his family's legacy.

As soon as Lizzy opened the door and stepped into the foyer, he cleared his throat, shoved his eyeglasses back on his face, and quickly attempted to go back to the book lying upon his desk—a book that had called to him earlier in the morning as if begging to be read because it had a message to impart.

The familiar smell of musty history along with her great-grandmother's portrait welcomed Lizzy. A stack of bills and receipts rested upon the antique pier table against the wall below the charcoal rendering.

Expecting her exuberance, which Thomas knew she always put on for his benefit, he closed the book.

"Daddy!"

"In my study."

Straightening her posture and smoothing her hair, she entered the dusty, book-filled, computer-laden room cluttered with a ragout of schematics and parchment documents. She announced as positively and brightly as possible, "It came. The letter came."

"And...did you open it?"

"I waited for you. I thought we could open it together. I'm sure it's good news. How can it not be, right?"

Thomas stood, placed his book on the only open space on his desk, and held out his hand. It was a small hand. He wasn't a tall man, not quite five foot seven, the same height as Lizzy and his older daughter, Jane. However, unlike his daughters, he was unremarkable. He often wondered where their beauty came from, certainly not his ex-wife.

Lizzy looked down at the book and furrowed her brow. "Dostoyevsky? Why are you reading *Crime and Punishment*? You hate that book. *I* hate that book. It's a totally depressing piece of work. You should keep away from it."

Her father shrugged his shoulders, ignoring her question and opinion and temporarily zoning out, remembering something that he read minutes earlier.

If he has a conscience he will suffer for his mistake. That will be his punishment.

He knew exactly why he gravitated to the book. He felt like the main character, Raskolnikov.

Lizzy snapped him from his deep thoughts of compunction. "Daddy?"

"Well! Let's see what the preservation office has to say shall we?" Thomas cheerfully replied. His letter opener, the one with the Pentagon's emblem on the handle, sliced through the top with precision. In spite of the mess surrounding him, he was ordinarily a scrupulous man.

With reading glasses resting at the tip of his nose, he read aloud, his face growing darker by the second. Lizzy knew. She didn't need to hear him say the words, but he did anyway.

We regret to inform you that although Longbourn Plantation House is steeped in the history of the great plantations of the nineteenth century, too many structural changes have been made to both the interior and exterior of the main estate. Unfortunately, we find that it does not meet the criteria to be listed as a property on the National Register of Historic Places...

Thomas looked up from the letter. "Would you care for me to go on?"

"No, they've made their decision." Lizzy felt sad—sad for him, sad for the estate, and sad that her father would need to face the facts.

As though it would make a difference and although he knew it truly would not, Thomas spoke in almost pleading tones.

"Lizzy, you may want to re-consider that marriage proposal from Bill Collins. I know school principals don't make a lot of money, but certainly his income could help us substantially. He and I have talked at length about his net worth. He's quite diligent in his investments and has a tidy sum waiting to be put to good use. I think you and I would be foolish to pass up the opportunity, not to mention the fact that he has repeatedly expressed to me how much he cares for you."

In truth, it wasn't the money at all—well, maybe just a little—but mostly, it was the security he hoped that his youngest daughter would find. Thomas grew increasingly afraid of what the future would hold for *him*, and he needed assurance that Lizzy would be safe and taken care of as she remained at the estate to care for it. Although he thought Bill a ridiculous man, he was stable and did profess feelings for Lizzy, and that was enough for any father. The fact that Bill had a keen desire to live at Longbourn and a willingness to provide the necessary cash to restore it made the union even more appealing to a father in need.

"I'm not telling you what to do, of course, but it would mean you could remain at Longbourn. I've already discussed this with Bill, and he would like nothing more than to remain here after the wedding. You know how happy that would make me." Thomas seemed to beg.

Unconsciously mimicking her father, Lizzy shrugged with no intention of commenting in reply. She, too, zoned out, remembering sitting across from Bill at Madison's restaurant on their date last week.

Is he really still talking about his new Italian shoes? He has got to be the most boring man I have ever met. Like this food—white rice and broiled skinless chicken. God, what I wouldn't give just to run out of here, get in my Jeep, and ... and ... keep driving ... out of Virginia. Of course, the Jeep would probably break down and Lizzy Bennet, the Lizzy that everyone knows—school teacher, hospice volunteer, inner-city illiteracy tutor— wouldn't do that. Would she?

No, she really didn't want to address the possibility that she might consider marriage to such a self-absorbed, boring, vain man. Her pragmatic self was leaning toward agreement with the prompting from both her father and Aunt Elinor, but lately, her inner voice cautioned her almost violently.

"Lizzy? Are you okay? You didn't really expect that we would get registry approval and a grant did you?"

As usual, she lied because it was what she thought he needed to hear at that moment. "I did. Don't worry. Something else will come through."

"I have no doubt that something else will fund Longbourn. Don't *you* worry. We won't be thrown into the street. We own this land lock, stock, and barrel."

Truly, he didn't have any doubt now where the money would come from. He had already committed to an unthinkable, heinous act, and like Dostoyevsky's Raskolnikov, the desperate man in him would hide within his rationalization while ignoring whatever second thoughts might attempt to surface.

Lizzy swallowed hard. "Perhaps we can sell some of the land. That alone should give us more than enough funds to make the necessary renovations to bring the house up to historical standards. We could remove that hideous 1960s sunroom built onto the sitting room. I think selling at least fifty acres on the northeast corner of the estate would be very profitable."

"Never! Generations before have sold enough land from the fine plantation that our Longbourn once was before the war. The land and this estate are who we Bennets are. You travel down a dark road when you sell your history and legacy for a profit. It's as good as selling a man's soul; nothing good ever comes from it."

A knock upon the study door interrupted father and daughter.

Thomas's good friend and co-worker in the IT Development Division for the Department of Defense poked his head around the door frame.

"Excuse me. Sorry to interrupt, but the front door was open, so I let myself in," Henry Crawford greeted.

"Come in, Henry. No worries. Lizzy and I were just reading the letter that finally came today from Virginia's Historic Preservation Office."

"Good news, I trust. I hope I'm not intruding."

"Intruding? Nonsense. It's good to see you, my friend. You're a balm to the disappointment Lizzy and I feel right now."

"Oh, I'm sorry to hear that," Crawford offered, although he didn't give a shit.

"We're not scheduled to work on our software project until Saturday. What brings you by Longbourn?"

Lizzy smiled tightly at Crawford, not really greeting him welcome or dismissing her father's one and only friend. Fact was, she couldn't help the uncomfortable feeling that always came over her whenever the man was near. He came to visit her father once a week, sometimes staying late into the night as they worked on various computer projects. Unfortunately, with his arrival, always came his sickening aura. His smarmy ways sent a chill up her spine.

Crawford was one of those men who clearly thought himself superior in every way, but in truth, he was completely average: average intelligence, average height, average build, and average looks. His only redeeming feature of vibrant blue eyes resembled azure vinyl-lined swimming pools that one just wanted to dive within. Then he'd smile that crooked, smirky smile of his, and the desire to take swimming lessons disappeared immediately.

Not to mention Crawford spoke in tones he thought agreeable and charming, trying to convince the listener that he was someone other than who he really was. Lizzy knew his true character by the simple fact that, whenever he came to Longbourn, he would seek her out when far from Thomas's earshot—a pinch here, an innuendo there. Six months of repeated rebuffs and rejections never deterred his persistence. He came back for more, always with the intent of intimidating his prey into submission—to do anything or everything—whether it was a date, a one-night stand, or a friend with benefits.

Lizzy hated him. Henry Crawford, with his blond, wind-tunnel-tested hair and smooth words, was definitely not her type. She was partial to tall, dark, and handsome. She preferred a man who lived by the codes of honesty and forthrightness, someone she could trust with her life.

"I…um…the deadline has been moved up for completion of the software. They're expecting the final source code by the end of the month. Do you think you can complete it in time?" Crawford said.

Lizzy turned to her father. "Is this one of your freelance programming jobs, Daddy?"

His face turned white as a ghost as he gave Crawford a look of admonishment for his careless disregard to his duplicity and secrecy. "Yes, you know me, just trying to earn a little cash on the side. Lizzy, why don't you prepare us some lunch? Henry and I have some business to attend. Henry, are you staying for lunch?"

Crawford looked in the direction of Lizzy standing off to the side of the room misting a plant with a water bottle. The lecher in him didn't resist his thoughts even if standing before the young woman's father. *Damn sexy legs.*

His eyes traveled their length up Lizzy, stopping on her full breasts. Like a hungry wolf he replied, "Lunch…absolutely."

~♠~

2
Menace

The Jack Daniel's bottle touched the rim of Darcy's rocks glass, clanking before its amber whiskey chugged in a torrent, carelessly sloshing and splattering.

Three days were never enough to recover from a black op. One day for travel, one for the processing and psychological decompression, and one for *attempting* sleep, but sleep always evaded him, and there was such a thing as being over tired. Lack of sleep for days on end did that.

Obsidian's safe house apartment on U Street in Washington, DC usually sat empty and quiet since its four agents technically only used it whenever they arrived inside the Beltway for their debriefings or new assignments. Although specifically designed and stocked with every amenity to assist in the acclimatization process, all Darcy usually needed was a bottle of Jack Daniels. Sleep would come eventually, not to mention a wicked hangover the next morning, but that was the price he expected to pay.

With its distinct caller ID ring, his cell phone rang from the end table beside him. Darcy knew who it was. "You left me only half a bottle," he coldly stated when he answered. His exhaustion was now catching up with him, making him more irritable than his usual darkness.

The fellow Obsidian team member on the other end cheerfully greeted his friend. "Glad you're back, Darce. Just wanted to see that you arrived home without a hitch. Caroline's expecting you tomorrow at four o'clock."

"Yeah, yeah. Tell your sister she can kiss my ass. I'll be there when I'm good and ready."

"I see now why you're itching for the rest of that whiskey bottle," Charlie Bingley joked. "Sorry about that. I tied one on the other night with this Nubian beauty, and well…"

"Spare me the details. Don't worry about the whiskey. Thanks for checking in on me."

"Hey, Darce, go easy on the Jack. Caroline's in rare form, and you won't want to be hung over for your debriefing."

"Rare? I hardly think so, but thanks, buddy."

Darcy turned off his cell phone. No one else would be calling, least of all Georgiana since she was still away on the Blue Ridge with her boyfriend. He was thankful for that. He hated lying to her, although he had done nothing but lie to her since his recruitment by his cousin, Rick Fitzwilliam, to join Obsidian four years earlier.

Sitting in silence in the darkened apartment, he slugged back what was left of the straight Tennessee whiskey and wondered how much longer he would be able to live dual lives. More like *duel* lives, he mused. His sister, not truly believing him, most likely would laugh if he told her what he did for a living. He thought for a moment that she may well be angry, too. She was hip to the ways of the world and was becoming politically opinionated in the process, growing into the idealist that their aunt, Georgiana's guardian, nurtured all through her formative years. He and Georgiana may have had a lot in common, but they were very much on opposite ends of the political spectrum. On her own, she would figure out soon enough that her brother wasn't actually an importer-exporter and that Charlie Bingley wasn't his partner at DBI. He would have to deal with the fallout when it happened.

He sat staring out the window at the street below. It was a relatively busy night in the eclectic Shaw and Dupont sections of DC, so Obsidian's agents usually went unnoticed within the myriad of colorful personages who came and went. Catching his attention as he stared out the window, two men walked along holding hands. They stopped, and the taller of the two turned to admire his reflection in the window of the market, running his hands down the side of his shirt. The other man moved closely beside him and they kissed.

Thankful his keen attention to the men diverted toward the Italian Pizza Kitchen's neon light hanging in the next-door window, Darcy watched it flicker and buzz. He hoped that if he stared at it long enough, it might put him to sleep. His eyes fought the pull as they grew heavier thanks to Jack. He was almost there. Sleep was close, but his mind still whirled from the rush of adrenaline from his last op: the thrilling dangers of the viper and the jaguar, the exhilaration of the zip line escape, the super-fast speedboat down the Amazon. He loved this persona and the powerful rush it gave him. It was the personality best suited for his career as a top-secret professional killer.

There were other words for what he did—government sanctioned sniper, assassin, contract sharpshooter—but those weren't honest enough. He preferred to call a spade a spade. From his perspective, he was, in fact, a stone-cold contract killer.

Pulling out his iPad, he logged into his Swiss account to make sure the two million for Operation Samba had been wired. For some, the money would be the incentive to stay in this line of work, but for Darcy, it had no bearing at all. He knew at some point soon he would leave this chapter of his life behind, much like the two chapters before. It wasn't because he had a conscience. No, he truly believed it was his moral obligation to work for Obsidian and rid the earth of evil, scum, and nefarious beings who would bring harm to others. To do nothing about them would be morally objectionable. That's how the assassin in him rationalized putting his bullet to bone. Thrills or no thrills, reasons or not, his days of deception were ending. He felt it in his gut.

Darcy wouldn't lie about the real reason for leaving. He had another job to do, a personal one that would require all of his focus and attention. He clicked his countdown calendar. Eight months and eleven days until George Wickham's release from the Halifax Correctional facility. In Darcy's mind, doing the time didn't negate the crime. Retribution, an eye for an eye, revenge—it was all the same, and it would finally be his. He would see to it that Wickham paid for the crimes he perpetrated against the Darcy family.

After tugging off his black motorcycle boots, he propped his feet up on the ottoman before him. He stripped off his black T-shirt and, raising his arms above his head, stretched cat-like, long and lean. The dark hair under his arms contrasted to the smoothness of his solid, broad chest and six-pack abs.

He rested his head against the back of the leather club chair and looked up at the ceiling to watch the sleek titanium fan go round and round, attempting to lull him to sleep. Running his hands through his grown-out hair, he wondered if it was time for a cut. Nah, long was starting to grow on him.

From the Bose, the soothing piano of Debussy's "Claire de Lune" began to overtake him, and within three minutes, Fitzwilliam Darcy was dead to the world, dreaming of nothing, just blackness.

~ ♠ ~

Charlie Bingley's loose blond curls bounced with his cha-cha-cha dance steps to Tom Jones's "Sex Bomb" as he held another lonely housewife in his arms for her weekly dance class with him. Big breasts, low cut shirt, and a warm, welcoming smile was all it took for Charlie to mix business with pleasure.

His hips rotated along with hers. "One, two, three, and four..." he said, moving with her to the powerful beat and provocative lyrics. "Good, good, you're getting it."

"Do you think I'm getting good at it, Charlie?"

"Oh yeah, Priscilla, you're gonna get it real good."

She stepped on his toes, and they stopped dancing, breathing heavily, the result of the fast tempo and innuendo.

Outside the Bingley Dance Studio in Georgetown, the forbidding sound of one of Darcy's hogs rolled down the street, alerting both Caroline and her brother that Obsidian's top agent and his hung-over, tired, black mood were expected at any moment. Darcy was never a delight to be around following an op.

Thunderous dual exhaust pipes bellowed behind him until the imposing silver and black motorcycle finally came to rest. He cut the motor in the angled parking spot directly facing the plate glass window of the dance studio.

Charlie walked to the music and turned it off. "That should be it for today, Priscilla. I'll see you Saturday for our extended lesson in rhythmic body movement."

"Yes...I'm looking forward to seeing what new moves you have in store for me."

"Make sure you book next week's appointment with Fanny at the desk. She'll take care of you."

Priscilla pouted. "I rather like when you take care of me."

Yeah, he did, too and thought of doing so as he watched her perfect, tight ass saunter to the side of the studio before he turned, highly aroused, to enter the business office. Man, he loved his jobs—both of them. Best thing he ever did was to agree with Caroline to run Obsidian from a ballroom dance school. It was the perfect cover.

Although the idea met much resistance from both Darcy and Fitzwilliam at first, it turned out to be a brilliant idea. Naming each op after a dance style based on the location of the hit was absolutely brilliant.

Priscilla dropped the small leopard print towel she held when she noticed the biker through the window. Her eyes fixed upon the perfect male specimen as he removed his black helmet and dismounted the Harley. What truly caught her attention was that strong, muscular thigh when it rose over the bike to get off the sleek beast below him. One word came to her mind: vigorous.

The biker was tall, dark, and imposing. With a strong jaw and nose, he looked incredibly handsome, and his tight body was clearly hard to the touch. Dressed in his signature black jeans, black T-shirt, and black leather jacket. Danger emanated from his every pore. Yeah, she wanted to ride that beast for sure…vigorously.

The cheerful bell above the door of the studio jingled when he entered. His presence filled the mirrored room, and his reflection in the glass created four more Darcys.

Biker god appeared everywhere, teasing and tempting Priscilla, overpowering her with his palpable virility.

Even the studio's part-time receptionist, Fanny Price, a preacher's daughter, gazed in awe upon his raw, bad-boy perfection. Of course, he brought about that reaction in her every time he came into the studio.

The hottie removed Ray Ban sunglasses to reveal eyes as dark as his mood and aura. Ebony pools of ink inspired in Priscilla a desire to scratch pages of lust-filled poetry with her nails across his broad chest and warm sonnets down his thighs with her tongue.

With each resounding step he took toward the back office, it was as though George Thorogood's electric guitar began the chords to "Bad to the Bone" in accompaniment to the heavy sound of those thick, black engineer biker boots. Although "Sex Bomb" was equally appropriate in her opinion. The man was explosive.

As he walked toward the back of the studio, the biker unsnapped his black gloves and bit down on a finger to pull off the tight sheath surrounding his long fingers. Priscilla thought she would die watching his perfect pearly whites tug at the tight leather, revealing strong, large hands.

It wasn't until he stopped before the open office door, unzipped his leather jacket, and removed it that Priscilla's mouth went slack. The wide black tribal tattoo wrapping around his brawny bicep was her instant weakness. Never breaking her line of vision, she squatted, picked up the towel, and ran it down her neck, wiping away the heat he caused in her just from his bad-boy persona and oozing sex appeal.

Caroline watched Priscilla from the other side of the room where she stood teaching her student the Mambo. *Let her look*, she thought. *He's been sworn off women for a long time, and if he won't get it on with me anymore, he sure as hell isn't going to with you, doll. Pay up and get lost. We have business—real business—to attend to.*

Darcy stared Caroline down, resisting the urge to insult her snake-skinned-patterned, tight dress before he entered into the business office.

Charlie sat beside the desk, watching the interplay of all three parties through the office's glass window. Having been a good judge of the ominous look upon Darcy's face, he offered a ready cup of black coffee to his friend.

"New student, Charlie?"

"Oh yeah, heaven on earth. She's an angel with a huge pair of knockers. She can't dance for shit, but she screws like the lambada runs in her veins."

"Nice talk. You kiss your mother with that mouth? There's a reason they call the lambada the forbidden dance. One day, Charlie, your womanizing will catch up with you, ya' know."

"Of course I don't kiss my mother. Like yours, my mother's dead."

Darcy's face darkened, and he raised an eyebrow to alert his friend of the inappropriateness of the joke. Nothing about *his* mother's or father's death was a joking matter, and Charlie knew it. Taboo, off limits.

Charlie coughed. "So…my womanizing ways are going to catch up with me you think?"

Darcy took a seat while they waited for Caroline. After grabbing the coffee, he leaned back and rested his ankle on the opposite knee. "Yeah, I think. Disease, angry husband, pregnancy trap, *Fatal Attraction* stalker—it's just a matter of time, buddy, before your dick gets chopped off one way or another. Women are all cut from the same mold." *Trust me, I know.*

"What are you crazy? I've had sex with some of the most incredible women on the planet: South African, French, Korean, Russian, not to mention that babe in Scandinavia who rocked my world for two straight weeks."

"Your angel out there looks American. Isn't that against one of your new rules of engagement?"

"Yeah, I know, but those tatas are real. That sets her apart. Besides, she's married, less chance of her getting too clingy. She's not looking for a commitment, just an occasional hook up."

Mockingly, Darcy snorted. "I have two words for you: Isabella Thorpe."

"Okay, so she was an isolated example of a psychotic nymphomaniac. How was I to know that she was just released from an institution and that her husband was a cop?" Charlie smiled broadly, "You, my friend, need to get laid. You're becoming way too cynical."

"And you, my friend, need to see the movie *Fatal Attraction*. Among other things, it scared the shit out of me and every other guy on the planet. Getting laid for the sake of getting your rocks off is highly over-rated, especially considering that you have to deal with women like your sister afterward."

"Overrated? Man, it has been a long time for you, hasn't it?"

Darcy smirked and flipped Charlie the bird.

Signifying the departure of the two students, the bell above the entrance door jingled once and then again. The men heard the familiar sound of Caroline bidding good-bye to Fanny then locking the deadbolt and pulling the chord to extinguish the neon "open" sign. She shut down the remaining ballroom lights and entered the office, closing the door behind her.

"Rambo," she greeted Darcy in her usual scorned woman attitude, strained with disdain and insult.

"Medusa," he replied.

Charlie laughed. "That's good, Darce. Oh, that's really good. I thought for sure she was going to turn Priscilla to stone when she couldn't take her eyes off you. Get it Caro, Medusa?"

"I get it, fool." Her eyes tightened to a menacing glare, her lips pursed, and she lifted her chin, retorting, "Very funny, Darcy. Don't forget Medusa sought her revenge on men."

Darcy took a deep drink of coffee, hoping to shake the hangover pounding inside his head. What a price he had to pay for a sound sleep. He should have listened to Charlie's caution the night before. He needed a clear head to deal with the likes of the red spitting cobra before him.

He turned to his ever-smiling friend. "How's business in the studio, Charlie?"

"Excellent, excellent. I've got a full tango group lesson booked for Wednesday nights, and since we started to choreograph wedding dances, I've had an army of warring couples sign up. For Christ's sake, I feel like a marriage counselor, and they haven't even gotten married yet. Case in point why I stay single."

"Now *that* we can agree on."

"You should teach, Darcy," Caroline taunted. "Didn't you grow up learning how to ballroom dance in that high-society world of yours? Weren't you some polo superstar in your youth?"

"That was another life, one I don't ever care to go back to. Hell will freeze over before you catch me on that dance floor of yours."

"Let's get down to business, shall we?" She took her seat behind the desk.

"Aren't we waiting for Rick? He really should be heading up this little meeting of ours unless, of course, you finally disemboweled him in order to take over his position," Darcy asked.

"No, he's in Austria on scouting and recon—learning the Vienna Waltz for an upcoming mission. He asked me to handle the debriefing along with your next assignment." She ignored his comment to her obvious posturing to run Obsidian.

He looked eye to eye with his former lover, a.k.a. the second biggest mistake of his life. Caroline's beauty didn't extend beyond her overall physical image. Sure, she had brilliant copper tresses and porcelain skin, but apart from those, together with her shapely body, high cheek bones, and plump lips, she possessed no other redeeming features: no depth, no spirit, no flame, and no warmth. She was perfect for Obsidian. Hell, she embodied Obsidian: stone-cold and black-hearted. Caroline personified a cobra in every way, and the venom she spat could kill any man, even one made of hard, cold-edged steel.

"How did it go in South America?" she asked.

Darcy tapped his ear in reply.

"Don't worry; Fanny's gone, and we had the entire building swept for security two days ago. We're clean."

"The Amazon was hot. It's a wet, bug-infested, miserable country. Then there was the issue of a *Chironius carinatus*, but in the end, it was worth the time and effort. I successfully completed Operation Samba.

"*Carinatus*? In English, Darcy. Our Latin is restricted to the dance floor here."

"It's a snake, Medusa, like the ones writhing on your head." Darcy smirked.

"Screw you."

"We tried that; it didn't work. Remember?"

"Enough, you two. Let's focus on the important question here." Charlie knew the answer before he asked, but he thought it funny to jerk Darcy's chain a bit. "Was there at least a tempting Brazilian hottie while you were down there? A little uncomplicated cha-cha-cha between the sheets?"

"Bolivia, Charlie, and you know the answer is no. I zipped in, did the job, zipped out, and took the next flight home."

Caroline unlocked and fully extended her desk drawer. After pulling out a slim aluminum briefcase, she spun the numbers of the lock, popping open the case to slide out a razor-thin file. Holding it between her fingertips, she exposed the cover midway before the three of them. It's manila face read "Virginia Reel" above the Obsidian logo, a black, multifaceted stone.

"What do you know about EMPs, Darcy?" she asked with a chill to her voice.

"Electromagnetic Pulse is a burst of electromagnetic radiation, which usually follows nuclear explosions sending out gamma waves—an extremely high-voltage energy field causing an electrical disturbance and the subsequent breakdown of…basically everything electrical, battery, or chip-based. If a nuclear warhead holding an EMP detonates over America, it has the potential to wipe out our nation as we know it, sending us back to the Middle Ages. So I know enough to know that my cell phone will be a worthless piece of crap and your daily supply of pharmacology won't be available to you."

"Yes, all communications, all types of commerce, *including* medications, as well as banking, financial institutions, transportation systems, and basically everything else it takes to live as we know it…gone in two seconds," Caroline said in her straight-forward business demeanor, deliberately ignoring his reference to her training method of acquired poison immunity.

"Has it been proven then that the Iranians have EMP capabilities within their warheads? For the record, I have no desire to travel to the Middle East again. That last job in Bahrain was a real ball-breaker," Darcy stated.

"What if I were to tell you that it is not the Iranians or the Russians or the North Koreans, but an American?"

Charlie became serious for the first time all day. "An American is selling the technology?"

"Not just *any* technology, Charlie, but technology in the advanced stages of development by the Department of Defense these last two years. It is an EMP generated by a *computer virus*. With the proper detonation code, the virus is triggered over the internet, transmitting the electromagnetic pulse from every device that has a specific country code IP address. Utilizing our computers, smart phones, iPads, you name it as conduits, the virus converts every device's non-ionizing electromagnetic radiation into cyclotron radiation so that it projects the gamma wave out, virtually frying and shutting down the targeted country forever.

"That's where you come in, Darcy. Now that you're home, you're taking a little trip south of here."

"This isn't home; Asheville is."

"Whatever."

Caroline's red-tipped fingers threw the file onto the desk before him for his perusal. "Meet your next target. He's the creator of this little ingenious weapon, only he isn't playing on our side any longer. He just sold the first half of the computer programming source code for a song to a terrorist group named Al-Hanash, and the only things the psycho bastards are waiting for are the second half and the detonation code."

Not in four years had Darcy felt doubt about the plausibility and rationale of the hit. Previously, he was never one to ask specifics or to want details. As standard practice, he took the assignment, got his money, and did the job. However, on this day, and maybe it was a residual effect of the Jack Daniels, something niggled in the back of his mind.

"Why not have the FBI or Homeland Security arrest the guy and put him behind bars? A hit seems a bit extreme, doesn't it?"

Caroline folded her arms across her chest. "We haven't been called upon by the CIA to ask questions, just to do the job. This particular assignment comes from the top, from the administration directly. Perhaps you don't understand the magnitude of what can happen if they get that last bit of software code from him. Besides, these extremists are everywhere. They'll get to him in prison, witness protection, anywhere. A man such as this will break under the threat of having his head sliced off. He'll give up that source code in a heartbeat."

"Taking him out means protecting every man, woman, and child in the United States, Darcy. He's a security risk of the worst kind," Charlie said.

Darcy opened up the folder to examine the photographs and review the measly one paragraph bio and intel within.

"This guy? *This* guy's a traitor? He barely looks like he can carry a water bucket for the Redskins. He looks like a bumbling idiot."

"They come in all shapes and sizes. We're talking brains, not brawn, Rambo, and yes, he's a traitor to the United States government. He's a government employee assigned to a top-secret programming job and a turncoat who got greedy. Look, if you don't want the assignment, then I'll have Charlie do it, but two million, Darcy, think about it."

Charlie laughed. "What's your Obsidian account up to now?"

"Forty-six million. And if your sister calls me 'Rambo' again, I'll kill her for free."

Caroline smiled broadly. She loved pushing him to his limits. It did things to her in places that only Darcy could affect. Even if she did currently have a long-term lover, memories of what Darcy had in his pants and what he could do with it always surfaced and exacted their toll on her composure. She hated to compare him to her current lover, but she couldn't help it. He still had a control over her that she never wanted to relinquish.

Standard procedure would normally forestall Darcy from questioning an operation, but for once, his conscience overrode custom, and he resumed his line of questioning. "The dossier is rather thin. Is this the only intel we have on the target? Who did the scouting on this?"

Caroline was exasperated; she hated being questioned. She sighed loudly.

Charlie quickly replied before his sister sounded off. "I did the scouting since it's not very far from here. What's in the file is all I could get from three days of recon. The target's habits are pretty cut and dry. He travels to work and back, and that's it. A young woman lives with him, but she comes and goes frequently. I couldn't get a clear view of her, so I have no photographs. The target spends all his time in what appears to be a study on the first floor. It'll be an easy assignment, no fuck-ups or interferences. Like samba, you'll be able to strike and withdraw undetected."

"Did the agency not even give us the name of the target?" Darcy asked.

"Not on this one. Apparently, our security clearance isn't high enough," Charlie replied.

"That's bullshit. They can tell us to kill the bastard and why we are doing so but not tell us his name? Bureaucratic bullshit."

"Are you satisfied now, Rambo? Will you accept the contract and the two mil?"

Darcy nodded once, closed the file before him, and flung it back to rest before Caroline's open arms.

"Good, you're to leave in three days for Mount Vernon. He lives on a former plantation near the Potomac, so there'll be lots of tree cover to get to your hide site."

"What's the name of it? Can you at least tell me that?"

"The estate? Longbourn Plantation House."

~♠~

3
Personas

The door to DC's Hard Rock Cafe pushed inward as Lizzy and her sister, Jane, entered for their monthly lunch date. The young male host stationed nearby sprinted from the reservation desk to hold open the door and stutter a greeting. Individually, the Bennet girls were beautiful, but together, they could incite any young man's fantasies. Today, he liked his job...a lot.

The blonde, slender beauty, was dressed for attention in the trendiest apparel. Glossy leggings encased the shapely, long limbs perched upon four-inch strappy heels. Her face was classically beautiful and tastefully made up below short bobbed hair. Everything about Jane Bennet said "take notice of me," and men did. If there was one thing to say about her, it was that she lived life large, happy, and free, and it extended into every facet of her life. Every day was enjoyed on her terms and her terms alone and certainly not spent acquiescing to the dictates of her father's selfish expectations or excessive, unrealistic needs.

The second woman, as tall as her sister, with long brunette tresses, glowed with natural and radiant beauty. She didn't need cosmetics or trendy clothing to draw a man's eye. Lizzy Bennet was pure ivory perfection. Everything about her, including her lifestyle, bespoke peaches and cream. However, the vivacity in her hazel-green eyes told any observant admirer that an altogether different enchantress lay below that peachy composure—one itching, *thirsting* to get out.

On that day, Lizzy wore a short yellow sundress and a pair of vintage Candies slip-on heels, and when the hot summer sun hit the dress just right, admirers approved her look even more.

Heads turned as the host escorted the sisters to their booth beside the street window. The only thing missing was ZZ Top's "She's Got Legs" coming from the sound system, orchestrating their approach. A longer stroll around the room would have been greatly appreciated by most of the male diners, but these two had things to discuss, privately.

Sliding into the red vinyl seat, Jane pled, "Don't do it, Lizzy. I'm begging you."

"Too late, it's done. I said yes."

The look on Jane's face vacillated between shock, horror, and disappointment. She couldn't believe what Lizzy just divulged.

Diverting her sister's attention to the menu and waitress, Lizzy motioned to the waitress in her usual avoidance tactic. "Excuse me, miss. We're ready to order."

"I'll have the SOB burger," Jane said between cracks of gum on the side of her mouth. "Extra spicy and also a margarita, extra salt."

Lizzy didn't need to look at the menu; she always ordered the same thing at their luncheon.

"I'll have my usual bacon-cheddar cheeseburger, medium rare with the works, onion rings, and a pint of Amstel to wash down all that sinful goodness."

The burger platter and beer were Lizzy's monthly indulgence and basically the only time she allowed her cravings to surface. The routine meeting with Jane embodied Lizzy's narrow version of living balls to the wall. Here, she even enjoyed the rarely listened to rock music.

Of course, afterward, she always regretted the gastronomic indulgence and swore that living on the edge was much too dangerous. Lizzy immediately went back to her simple fare, simple life, classical music, and accommodating demeanor. In her acceptance of her life's status quo, she thought she was in too deep to change or cut loose, so she simply ignored the promptings of her conscience.

At twenty-five, she already felt that the direction of her life was now irrevocable, her course set. Oftentimes, she found herself envious of Jane's decision to leave Longbourn the year following their parents' divorce.

Apparently, Jane's foresight proved warranted. She once explained to her sister that she refused to get sucked into the needs and selfish whims of their father. That was, after all, the same reason their mother had left eight years ago, never to be heard from again.

Lizzy, however, with a heart full of love for her father remained at Longbourn by choice. She became everything bright and positive for him. Everyone else had bailed on him, and she swore she wasn't going to break his heart further. With great compassion, the dutiful daughter recognized Thomas's depressive tendencies and obsessive, not to mention compulsive, behavior when it came to his work and his hobbies. With the issue of the house, fear immobilized him, and Lizzy became his solace, the calm in his mental storm. Never wanting to upset her father's delicate microcosm, she lived an unassuming, wholesome life, but in the process, her heart and soul yearned for the exact opposite. She had become a prisoner of her own making. Her life and outward persona were the greatest of deceptions, and she assumed that not even Jane knew of her inner struggle and desires. Sure, Jane saw the sarcastic, dry wit and the occasional snarky responses, but since leaving Longbourn, Lizzy believed that Jane never saw the trapped woman lurking below her dove-like exterior.

"What do you mean you said yes?" Jane insisted.

"Just what it sounds like. I said I'd marry Bill. I accepted last night when he stopped by Longbourn with a *Phalaenopsis* orchid. Never mind the fact that I have a whole friggin' greenhouse filled with my own cultured orchids, but it was a nice gesture. He was being thoughtful."

"Let me see the ring. I don't believe you."

With a smug look upon her face, Lizzy held out her left hand and proudly displayed the one-quarter-carat diamond as if it were the largest engagement ring ever.

"You're kidding, right?" Jane asked incredulously.

"Hey, he's watchful of his money. Frugality is important."

"So not only is he ridiculous, but he is also cheap! Why are you settling for this—for him—Lizzy? You can have anyone, do anything! Why are you giving up your life like Mom did? You'll grow to hate him as Mom hated Dad."

"Stop, Jane! And no, I can't have anyone. I haven't had a decent date in a year.

"Besides, we've had this conversation before. I have my reasons for marrying Bill; you know I do. Marrying him will help Longbourn. Daddy is petrified that we will lose the estate, and then our whole Bennet history will be gone. It's the right thing to do. Bill is respectable and has done very well for himself. He has a large bank account and will help us restore Longbourn."

"Then take a loan from him. Don't sell your soul for a house that doesn't care if you come or go. Please start living as you were meant to. You're not Dad's wife or caretaker. You're a vibrant young woman. Start living like the twenty-five-year-old you are. Bill is what, forty-seven?"

"Forty-one." Embarrassed by her admission, she looked away from her sister's glare. From outside the restaurant, the distinct sound of a motorcycle's muffler caught her ear. It sounded exciting—recklessly exciting.

"Think about this for just a moment, Sissy. You're going to have to have *sex* with him. Bet you didn't think about that, did you? He'll talk the whole time...about himself! You'll be the first woman in history to fall asleep while having intercourse. Don't do this."

Lizzy took a sip of her beer, then turned to look at her sister. "Sex is overrated."

"Oh, you are so wrong there."

"It is. Heartless, selfish, passionless copulation where the guy is pumping and sweating until he comes while completely forgetting there is an actual living, breathing woman below him who might actually desire to be caressed or experience *her* own orgasm. I'm telling you, it *is* overrated."

"See! That's exactly what I'm talking about. You haven't *lived*, Lizzy."

"Oh, I've *lived* alright, four times, each time as bad as the next. Men don't need a reason, just a place."

"You just haven't been with the right man. And I assure you that Bill isn't him. Please trust me on this one. The right lover can set your world on fire. I should know. There was this guy in Tulsa who … never mind. All I'm saying is don't settle for Bill's limp biscuit and most likely disinterested and boring repertoire of moves for the rest of your life."

Lizzy rolled her eyes. "Please. I have yet to find a guy out there with a *Chironius carinatus* who knows how to use it to a woman's satisfaction. And why do all our conversations always seem to gravitate back to your fabulous, and I might add overactive, sex life?"

"We are talking about *your* sex life, not mine, and what the hell is a chir … onius … car…?"

"It's a snake, a very long one, and frankly, I think even they're a mythological creature, like the anaconda. Anyway, I don't want to argue this any longer."

Jane snorted a laugh. "Oh, that's right—your love of snakes."

"Only reptilian ones. The other I can do without."

"Ok, so chiro...crinat...aside, I concede; maybe I am going about this all wrong with you. Sex for the sake of sex obviously isn't your thing, but what about sex within a committed monogamous relationship? Love. Let's talk about romance and love; surely you don't think that a man in love would be so selfish in the bedroom?"

"I can't answer that, Jane. I'm not a romantic any longer. You know that. I don't believe in love, but I am convinced that my chance of happiness with Bill is as fair as most people can boast when they decide to get married."

She was lying, and she knew it. Every bit of it was a lie. Lizzy *did* harbor those secret hopes and desires of finding the deepest love, but she was terrified of the realization of those dreams, too. True love usually accompanied a broken heart in the end. At any rate, she didn't want to end up alone. Horrified at the thought of becoming an old-bitty spinster trapped in a decrepit old house with no one but her decrepit old father prompted her decision. At least with Bill, something was better than nothing. He was willing to help save the estate, which meant that her father could have peace of mind. She could settle. After all, she had done so her whole life. She was accustomed to sacrifice in the name of duty and honor for both Longbourn and her father. They were really one and the same.

"Not a romantic? Bullshit," Jane said behind the rim of her margarita glass. "You used to believe in love. You used to have dreams of your knight in shining armor riding in and saving you from Longbourn. Before I left, I distinctly remember you and I talked about our dreams of finding true love."

"That was before you ran off with Steve, the pot-smoking jerk with the unibrow, and before I realized that knights weren't real life and stuff like that only happens in fairy tales. Stop this. You're starting to piss me off. I'm pragmatic now. I don't believe in romantic love, end of story."

"So you *don't* love Bill?

"Good God no!"

"Have you at least kissed him?"

"Yes. It was … it was … nice." Of course Lizzy wouldn't admit that nice meant boring, unaffectionate, lacking spark and flame. In a word: brotherly. But, heck, isn't that what her life had become?

Jane furrowed her brow, meaning to convey confusion to her sister, but she *perfectly* understood why it was a bland kiss. She had been around the block enough to know and trust her instinct and intuition. "Nice? Were there tongues involved, or was it a chaste peck on the lips?"

"Stop it, Jane! It's done. We're getting married Fourth of July weekend since we won't be able to have the wedding once school begins. He has important responsibilities as a school principal, you know."

"Yes, Lizzy. He's an authority figure to six-year-olds."

"It doesn't matter."

"No honeymoon?"

"Why bother?"

"Oh, that's right: he's frugal," Jane sarcastically stated. "Do you want a bridal shower?"

"What's the point?"

"Do I have to be your maid of honor if I don't approve of your decision?"

"Yes," Lizzy smugly said before popping a french fry into her mouth.

"Where will you live once you marry Mr. Personality?

"Longbourn, of course."

Jane's mouth was as full of sarcasm as it was with hamburger. "Naturally, where else would you live? Is there anything else you need to tell me before I slit my wrists?"

"*Naturally*, you have to help me plan this. We'll be marrying on the lawn under the Bennet Oak and having a small reception in a tent."

"Isn't that where Grandpa Andrew and Snowflake the cat are buried?"

"Shut up!"

Jane laughed at her sister's frustration. "Whose brilliant idea was marrying under the oak?"

"Daddy's."

"Of course it was."

~ ♠ ~

Charlie cut the motor on the small fishing boat as it neared the shoreline of the Potomac River bordering the Longbourn estate. The moon was high, but there was thick cloud cover—enough to conceal the boat and the vast array of stars in the pitch-black Virginia country sky. It was three in the morning when Darcy exited the boat to assume his position for his kill shot the next day.

The incessant song of crickets filled the night air around the two men who bid each other good-bye. They planned to rendezvous the next night unless otherwise messaged through the Bluetooth that an earlier extraction was necessary.

Dressed in black stealth apparel and face mask over camo-painted skin, Darcy slung the ghillie suit over his shoulder on top of his high-powered rifle. All other gear was strapped at his waist with the exception of a Camelbak water knapsack that rested behind him between his shoulder blades.

He had a bad feeling about this assignment. He did from the start, but he took the job anyway. The night had an eerie feel to it—a sense of foreboding and bad luck that hung heavy in the air. Darcy had felt this once before in his tenure with Obsidian during Operation Mambo during a daylight hit on a well-known arms dealer on the waters near Cuba. That day, he had come close to capture and being killed in a high-speed boat chase. He should have listened to his conscience then.

That was when Obsidian worked in two-man teams for a hit. His female partner, Lucy Steele, a woman with whom he thought he was in love, had betrayed him. She had all but admitted that she was a double-agent for Castro's government. It was clear to Darcy, when faced with her betrayal, that he didn't love her at all. There was no compunction, or emotion for that matter, when he put a bullet between her eyes and dumped her body overboard for shark bait.

He vowed never again to open the door to betrayal by any woman. Lucy Steele taught him a hard lesson. Twice in a lifetime was more than any man could stand, even for a man whose veins ran cold with ice.

Darcy shook off the memory and the uneasy feeling. He rationalized: *that* was an altogether different bad-luck op; a woman was involved. Such was not the case here.

Stealthily moving from tree to tree, he passed small outbuildings scattered around the property: former slave quarters, a blacksmith's shed, smoke house, and tobacco barn. He didn't overlook their state of disrepair and abandonment. It was his job to notice things. Nothing ever went unnoticed. He had eyes everywhere and was known for his observation skills.

And that was how he came upon it. On a well-tended plot beside the plantation house sat a large, lovingly-restored greenhouse. Not a single pane of glass showed the wear of time through breaks and cracks. Colorful summer perennial flowers blossomed all around the structure.

With his back against the glass perimeter of the hothouse, he twisted his head to peer into the building through the small windows. Whoever was its caretaker obviously had a green thumb. The greenhouse, filled with an abundance of blossoming orchids, beckoned him.

All it took was the rustling movement of an unseen doe beyond the tree line, and within three seconds, Darcy was inside, face-to-face with hundreds of cultivated *Orchidaceae* of various species.

That mistake should have been his first indication that this op was doomed from its start.

From a squatting position within the structure, he gazed around in amazement and delight at the tables and toward the roof where many orchids hung from small wooden-slat baskets. He conjured the Latin names of each colorful plant.

A break in the clouds above allowed the magical splendor of the moon to cast glorious beams through the glass roof and into the building. He could make out the shade cloths loosely pulled back for the night as well as the antique nineteenth-century vent wheel connected to levers to operate the windows on top of the house. As the moon continued to cast its spell, he noted the thickness of the old glass and the waves and ripples within each small pane. Yes, it was enchanting, and for a moment, he allowed himself a few minutes of respite, breathing in the heady fragrant scent of his favorite orchid. With its vibrant white bloom and yellow center, the *Coelogyne ochracea* reminded him of another time, another life—one of fond, happy memories. Pemberley.

One broke through his stony reserve—his mother in her greenhouse. *"And this one, my little man, is called a Dracula gigas orchid."* She handed his six-year-old outstretched palm a cut bloom. *"What do you see."*

"A monkey!" Fitzwilliam beamed.
"Yes, just like the ones we saw at the zoo last week."

Darcy forgot himself, his mission, his target, even his caution, causing him to do the unthinkable. He rose, unsheathed his knife, and sliced half the stem and bloom from the potted white plant, and as he did, he noticed a small open sketchpad on the table. On the pad's open page, a rendering caught his analytical attention. The image and the artist intrigued him, speaking to him of another life, yet hearkening the one he currently lived. The artist's drawing of a horse running with unencumbered freedom, its mane and tail flying in the breeze, tugged at his heart.

He briefly skimmed through all the pages filled with sketches: birds in flight, sail boats, various orchids. He deftly pocketed the book and exited the greenhouse.

Unnoticed under the shifting cloud cover, he passed the three-car barn garage behind the house. Making his way along the perimeter of the building until once again at the tree line, he headed toward the field beside the dirt road that led to the estate. It was so quiet that even the cicadas silenced their chorus in the cooler early morning hours.

The assassin was thankful that Charlie, as operation scout, determined the best hide site for this job. The unlikely position for concealment was out in the open. This field of uncut grass was dry and weedy with an unobstructed view of the full façade of Longbourn Plantation House. Two hundred yards away from the front of the residence, Darcy became part of the neglected grass and brush after donning his ghillie suit; not even a scavenging possum knew the difference when its short legs ran over the back of his long ones. The synthetic camouflage suit covered him completely, giving the appearance of just another mound of grass. Even his rifle lay concealed.

The Army had trained Charlie well. Army sniper school was nothing to sneeze at, but the military operated in two-man sniper teams. Although Rick, Charlie, and Darcy were former military, they now worked for Uncle Sam in a different capacity. Obsidian acted outside the rules of war, and in doing so, they did things their way. After the disastrous Cuba debacle, Obsidian changed its procedure. Now they were only one-man units with a scout surveying ahead of time when possible.

It would be there, near the entrance of the estate's land where only the postal delivery truck traveled on the dirt road, that Darcy would observe, meditate, and attempt to remember every orchid species until the anticipated hour of his kill shot the next day. He was in place, ready to wait and strike.

Looking through the scope of his rifle, he carefully examined the graying house, noting that, similar to the garage and outbuildings, it was also in a sorry state of disrepair. He frowned at the annoying black shutter precariously hanging by just a few nails. Such a waste of history and real estate, he thought. Longbourn was in need of either a bulldozer or a massive amount of cash to restore it to its historic grandeur. He wondered if that was the reason behind the target's traitorous decision. Irrelevant, it wasn't any of his business. The object of his bullet was a pathetic weakling and a traitor to his country. That was all Darcy needed to know in order to do his job effectively.

He took note of the closed heavy curtains in the target's study on the first floor and hoped it was an unusual occurrence. Otherwise, he might have to relocate his position to a more advantageous one, perhaps to the back of the house for a bedroom shot.

It was now five in the morning. Dawn would be breaking shortly. The Bluetooth beeped deep in Darcy's ear canal; he was receiving a voicemail. Silently, he tapped the button on his rifle stock.

"This is Caroline from Bingley Dance Studio. We would like for you to give us a telephone call here in the studio to let us know when you would like to begin you next lessons on the Shag." There was a giggle. "Please call us immediately so we can make arrangements for your private lesson." Another giggle.

He thought to himself, *Over my dead body. Wait ... Isn't the shag a dance from South Carolina? Blood-sucking viper.* Darcy hated this code crap Caroline thought up. Just because she knew his mother sent him for ballroom classes when he was young didn't mean he knew every godforsaken dance on the planet and its geographic origin. He regretted the day he ever told her about dance school. It proved his point about why he never talked about his past to just anyone, but at that time, their relationship was sexed up, and they discussed normally guarded things over pillow talk.

Now Caroline was instructing him to break standard operating procedure to telephone as soon as the kill shot was made. Well she could whistle Dixie before he did that.

Five hours later, with the sun rising high, Darcy was sweltering from the heat of the ghillie suit. He'd already sucked his water pack half empty. His wrist was beginning to swell from a bug bite, and damn if he didn't have to take a leak. Those things were nothing he wasn't equipped to handle, easily in fact, but they were enough to intrude, conjuring back the lingering bad-luck vibe.

Nevertheless, he remained, focusing solely on the house, observant, hidden, and completely motionless, waiting for the curtains to open on his target.

The house remained silent; the study window remained covered, and the land remained deserted. Even the air hung tranquil as the choir of unseen cicada bugs revived in the heat of morning.

Faint operatic music came from the distance down the dirt road. A soprano duet grew louder, drowning out the song of the seven-year locust as the music neared Darcy's hide site. French lyrics sung of gathering flowers at the bank of a river, flowing and rippling under white jasmine.

Darcy knew that piece of music. He knew it well. In his other life, he grew up loving opera.

He waited patiently, hoping to see the vehicle through his riflescope and eyeball the driver when they turned onto the private dirt road. Within seconds, a beat-up, topless, old Jeep flew past him toward the house, traveling down the private road, kicking up a fog of dirt and rocks. The female driver's long brown hair whipped around her head, taking flight as she listened to the "Flower Duet" from the opera *Lakmé*. Through the small aperture of his scope, as the driver's mane blew from the force of the wind upon her face, Darcy instantly recalled the sketch of the horse he had stolen from the greenhouse. The image was imprinted in his mind. Henceforth, he knew that faceless, nameless woman would be called Lakmé whenever he referred to Operation Virginia Reel.

Just as quickly as she came into view, she was gone, having driven toward the back of the house and the garage. He wondered if her presence represented the first sign of good luck all day or was she the portent of bad things to come? He went back to observing and waiting with the sweet smell of the white orchid crushed in the palm of his hand assaulting him.

~♠~

4
Decisions

The screen door slammed behind Lizzy when she entered the hallway at the back of the house. It was a beautiful Monday morning, and she felt fantastic, almost renewed in spirit after sleeping at Jane's tiny apartment in Georgetown the night before.

She immensely loved her sister and, therefore, accepted all of Jane's opinions and misgivings about Lizzy's upcoming marriage in the spirit in which they were given: out of love and concern. However, Lizzy wasn't Jane and never would be. Their lives took separate pathways the moment Jane packed her suitcases and loaded the trunk of her '85 Camaro bound for DC to live with her rocker boyfriend of the time.

Lizzy found herself surprised by the feeling that came over her when she awoke in the carefree, liberating environment of her sister's converted warehouse apartment. For once, she felt free from obligation and free to listen to the banished voice in her soul, if only for a little while. Perhaps it was the burger the day before. She didn't have any regrets later that night when they ate spicy tamales while watching the horror movie *The Hills Have Eyes* until two in the morning. *Heck, that was fun!*

The two sisters awoke with nowhere to go and nothing to do. They laughed over breakfast—coffee and Whitman's chocolate—biting each in half only to put the uneaten half back in the box. They talked about the boys they dated in high school and Snowflake the cat, their childhood pet that seemed to have more than nine lives, many of which Lizzy and Jane took with their own hands. Lizzy reminisced about the time she climbed out Longbourn's widow's walk onto the rooftop and the day she put the firecracker in her fifth-grade teacher's desk drawer.

The euphoria inspired by memories of a younger, audacious Lizzy Bennet continued on the drive homebound. It was a shame that the old Jeep's radio tuner broke years ago. Only the cassette player worked, which was unfortunate because she would have liked to have borrowed some of Jane's CDs: Evanescence or Audioslave but an old cassette of the "Flower Duet" did well enough.

She felt oddly unfettered in spite of her acceptance of Bill's marriage proposal. On this day, she tried not to let her thoughts gravitate there. It felt like the harbinger of death. A strong sense of doom knocked upon her heart, and if she allowed herself the negative thoughts, they would definitely cause her to respond to that ignored voice in her soul and flee far, far away.

Entering the kitchen, she frowned at the mess left for her by her father from the night before. Judging by the amount of dirty dishes, used mugs, and the empty coffee container, Thomas pulled another all-nighter in his study. Most likely, he was still asleep there.

Trying hard not to allow resentment to surface, she left the kitchen and the mess, resolved to deal with it later when she felt more amiable and understanding. Instead, she chose a much happier place to continue her euphoric feeling: the greenhouse.

With bare feet, she almost skipped through the tall grass toward the back of the house. The sun, now sizzling, reflected off the glass roof. It was a good thing she came home when she did. The shades needed pulling to protect the delicate blooms within.

Darcy lay in wait, looking through the scope of his rifle for any movement at all, either inside or surrounding the plantation house. It didn't matter; he had all day to wait. Charlie wasn't scheduled to extract him until eleven that night. The assassin had twelve more hours, but he couldn't hold his urine in that long. With a shallow breath, he let all the air out of his lungs while simultaneously emptying his bladder into the parched earth beneath his body.

Opening the greenhouse door, Lizzy deeply breathed in the pervading welcoming smells of the fragrant orchids. Really, this was where the magic of Longbourn lay. Her greenhouse was the heart of the estate, not the plantation house. In a startling revelation, she acknowledged that within the 30 x 20 glass structure, colorful life cultivated, breathing and growing uninhibited, bringing harmony and peace. It was in such contrast to the rooms within the plantation house, where the memories and lingering auras of the dead "seven generations of Bennets" sucked the life out of its inhabitants.

Lizzy acknowledged that it wasn't the house she loved. It was the greenhouse, the Potomac River, and the towering pines. If she searched her memories, she would add to the enchantment of the estate the tire swing suspended over the small pond at the edge of the plantation. It had been a childhood sanctuary where she spent summer afternoons listening to her mother's transistor radio. She listed among the charms of Longbourn the thousands of stars she gazed up at from the eerie widow's walk at the top of the house as well as the custard apple pawpaw trees that grew along the banks of the river. These beloved things were worth saving in her mind, but the house was what kept her father grounded and alive. Apart from her, it was all he had. Yes, she would do what she had to do for him *and* her greenhouse.

Lizzy drew the sunshades and opened the air vents. Taking the water bottle, she sprayed some of her blooms until she found her way to the white *Coelogyne ochracea*. Fingering the cut stem, she knit her brows. *Henry must have done this.* Furious, she grabbed the potted plant and headed straight for her father's study. Her euphoria was now stripped away, pushed aside by the spirited Lizzy who momentarily resurfaced in what she regarded as a violation of her peaceful sanctuary.

After all, if there was one thing to say about Lizzy Bennet, it was that her courage *attempted* to rise at every endeavor to intimidate her, and that was exactly what Crawford loved trying to do: intimidate *and* get her to acquiesce to his advances.

Once again, the screen door of the house slammed against the frame with a resounding whack that reverberated throughout the house. With long strides, she walked down the narrow hallway to her father's closed study door. She didn't hesitate and didn't knock. That day and that day alone, the "other" Lizzy, the one who everyone saw and loved 365 days of the year, didn't exist.

She flung the door open into the darkness. The thick, drawn curtains still didn't conceal the image of her father asleep on his tattered loveseat, curled under her grandmother's crocheted blanket—the ugly one with all the black, red, and yellow granny squares that screamed "take me to a thrift shop." Nevertheless, Thomas loved that blanket. It had become his trusted friend these past eight years and was the *only* thing keeping him warm at night.

"Lizzy…is that you?"

"Yes, Daddy, it's me, and it's eleven o'clock in the morning. Why didn't you go to work today?" She switched on the floor lamp standing beside her father's loveseat. The light blinded him awake like a vampire exposed to the sun. Although he shielded his eyes, she noted he looked like a bedraggled mess. His salt and pepper hair stood askew, his eyes hooded and puffy with bags. His face revealed deeply marked creases from sleeping cock-eyed on the hard pillow.

The air in the room hung heavy and dank. She walked toward the window and its closed curtain.

"Where were you last night?" asked Thomas through the waking fog of sleep.

Lizzy's reply was abrupt and agitated, taking him by surprise, especially when she put the orchid on his desk with purpose.

"I called you three times and left three messages telling you were I was. I was at Jane's for the night. Why didn't you pick up the phone?"

"I was…I was busy on the programming until the wee hours. I let the office know that I would be working from home today. It's not nearly finished, and I get so much more work done in my study."

Lizzy looked at the large amount of papers strewn on the floor surrounding his desk. *Crime and Punishment* rested on the coffee table before the loveseat. It appeared his "busyness" included reading.

"But going to the office is good for you. That therapist told you so years ago. You have to find some hobbies and get out of this dark house, or the depression will just get worse. Please, Daddy. There is life outside of Longbourn. I can't be here for you every minute of the day," Lizzy stated, hoping something—anything—she said would sink in.

Thomas chuckled. "I know that, but if only you would be here every minute. Ah well, I do have company though. I have all our ancestors in this house, some of whom sit beside me day and night."

Lizzy's head snapped up. That was a first. He never spoke of ghosts before. "Seriously?"

"No, just fooling you, Kitten. I love to see that line form between your eyes when I say something you think is outlandish."

"Whew, you scared me there for a moment."

Thomas put on his black-rimmed eyeglasses and observed his daughter from top to bottom. "That's a pretty dress you have on, Lizzy. Very feminine and ladylike."

"Thank you. You've seen it before."

"Have I? You should always wear dresses. They become you. All good girls wear dresses. I'm sure Bill likes when you wear them."

Lizzy rolled her eyes. She was twenty-five, and her father was attempting to tell her how to dress. Her ire was so pushed to its limits that she couldn't resist musing on what he would say if she went braless. God, how she would love to go braless—just once—if for no other reason to see the look of shock and disapproval on her father's face. *No, Lizzy, you did not just think that!* No matter, she could never go braless anyway. Given her size and the type of sundresses she wore, the combination of the two would have severe ramifications.

She steered the subject away from her apparel. "Daddy, was Henry here last night?"

He furrowed his brow, running a hand through his hair. "Why do you ask?"

The tone in his voice conveyed—she couldn't quite put her finger on it—guilt? "I think he was in my greenhouse and clipped one of the *Coelogyne ochracea.*"

"He likes you. He probably just wanted a memento of you."

Her hand paused upon the closed edge of the curtain. "Tell him the greenhouse is off limits. I don't like him, and I don't trust him. He has lecher written all over his forehead, and I can't help but think he's using you and your intelligence to further his career at the Pentagon."

Thomas rose from the loveseat and exited the room while scratching his backside. He called over his shoulder, "Don't be so judgmental. That's not the Lizzy I know and love."

Turning toward the window, Lizzy placed one hand on each side of the curtain panels and spoke under her breath, "No, that's the other Lizzy, the one who lives life wearing dresses to please her father 24/7 in some alternate pre-Civil War Longbourn universe."

With one big tug, she separated the curtains, exposing and flooding the study with glorious morning sunlight. It was so brilliant that if she paid attention, she would have seen dust particles floating in the air. However, Lizzy was too absorbed by the radiance of the day to notice.

She didn't notice anything, particularly the man whose eye blinked rapidly when her beauty suddenly burst into the aperture of his rifle scope some two hundred yards away.

Darcy's trained eye had remained fixed upon the big pane window at the front of the house, awaiting the moment when the curtains to the target's study pulled back. Never did he expect Lakmé, the girl from the Jeep, to be the one to do so.

Gorgeous wasn't even the word for her—more like heavenly vision. The sun illuminated her porcelain skin and cast brilliance upon her long chestnut hair. Like magical snowflakes, the microscopic particles of dust floated around her. She wore a simple, yellow tank sundress with tiny flowers upon it. The woman was so close to his eye that he felt he could reach out and touch her. The dress's slender shoulder straps caused his finger to twitch as he imagined dropping one side down. Lakmé's breasts beckoned to him with their alluring fullness, appearing to fit perfectly in his hands. When she closed her eyes and lifted her chin to feel the heat of the sun warming her face, he thought he would die. The intoxicating brunette shot so much life into him that, in his visual closeness, he desired nothing more than to kiss her passionately. She was breathtaking, and that was when he knew this job *was* bad luck.

The woman moved from the window and suddenly, in complete surprise, Darcy felt immense disappointment.

Frequently, Darcy's eye automatically returned to the riflescope. There was no point remaining riveted to the view beyond the window of the target's study. For this op, protocol restricted him to making the kill shot in the dark of night anyway. Until then, he lay trapped in the vast field of weeds and grass. Getaway would be obvious, and extraction upon the river would be dangerously impossible in the light of day. Besides, he knew that to see the woman again would no doubt be another sign that this job was going to hell in a hand basket fast. The only things left for him to do were to wait and observe comings and goings and, of course, daydream.

There was always a lot to daydream about, especially on that day. In that one brief moment when that gorgeous woman pulled back the drapes, Lakmé grabbed hold of him in lust. Then she was gone, as were most of his visions of heaven. Those were always elusive and fleeting. It was only the memories and images of hell that continually appeared before his eyes and in his life, in every way, shape, and form. Then he recalled that most realities of hell *always* began as visions of the sublime. That woman in that house, he was sure, was like every other stinkin' woman who passed through his life: bad, fucking luck.

The sky above grew dark and foreboding. The clouds gathered, heavy and oppressive, becoming filled with the rage of a summer storm that threatened tornadic activity. Darcy hunkered down in anticipation of the onslaught when one large raindrop then another pierced the thirsty ground, sucking it down quickly. As much as he hated rain during an op, he knew the mud would further conceal him, even if the ghillie suit made breathing difficult from its weight. His breath remained shallow anyway while awaiting the target's appearance in the window.

The wind kicked up fiercely when heaven's hell broke loose. The violent rain pelted his prone body with such intensity that he was sure he had no breath at all. The downpour beat it out of him. Teeming with vengeance, it fell, assaulting the earth too fast to be absorbed. Water pooled around him, soaking him, drenching his rifle and equipment. Laying motionless two inches deep in hard-fallen rain, he had nowhere to go. Yes, he was certain that this job was not only a bad break but also a bad omen of things to come, a presentiment that the devil was never too far from him, chomping at his heels and waiting to take him down.

Big breasts and a fabulous smile would not be his undoing again. *Wait a minute,* he thought. *I'm not here for the woman. I'm here for one of the devil's own, a traitor to his country, a man who sold his soul for a price, scum who could kill women and children by his deceit and willful terrorism. Why should the woman's presence matter?*

~♠~

Resting upon the sleek chrome desk with smoke-glass top was an empty penholder and an engraved nameplate embossed with the shield and eagle insignia of the CIA. One man, the contract employer to the other, leaned back in his chair, twirling the pen. The repetitive distracting motion annoyed the visitor, who just flew in from Austria and sat near dead with his brain barely functioning. The last thing Rick Fitzwilliam wanted was to sit before Thomas Bertram, Director of the Central Intelligence Agency, in his office at Langley Air Force Base.

"So your man is in place?" Bertram queried, his beady eyes drawing even tighter with the question.

"That's what I have been told by my deputy. Virginia Reel is scheduled between 20:00 and 22:00 hours tonight with immediate extraction to the safe zone. Should be an easy enough dance."

"I'm counting on your team, Fitzwilliam. You have yet to fail the agency, but this one ... this assignment is intensely important. the president as well as the secretaries of defense and state recognize the importance of this operation. They've sanctioned this hit as necessary in the interests of the State Department. There are many reasons for the extreme measures we are taking here, and I need your assurance that this operation will go off without a hitch."

Pissed off by the insinuation, Rick ran his hand through his red hair. He was hard as nails tough with a frankness that pulled no punches. As the director of Obsidian, he barked in incredulous anger. "What kind of organization do you think I'm running? Of course it'll go off without a hitch. That is why you called in Obsidian, isn't it? My men aren't a bunch of inexperienced fuck-ups. Pardon my French. Those three, which *includes* my female operative, have bigger balls than you and I put together. Don't underestimate us, and certainly don't *ever* question our ability to get the job done swiftly and accurately—not to mention cleanly—in the interest of the state."

Bertram sat forward, his mouth in a thin set line. He put the pen back in its holder. "Don't get your balls in an uproar, Fitzwilliam. I don't mean to imply anything of the sort. It's just that this job could blow the lid off terrorist cells operating on the East Coast, and it will lead us to the main strike, the mother lode: Al-Hanash and his current location and, with luck, the worldwide terrorists with whom he does his business. Al-Hanash's contact man has been operating undercover as a level-three programmer in the Department of Defense. He is just the patsy we need to lead us to them. This whole operation has been under the watchful eye of the agency for the past six months. We have our best agent, Rushworth, on top of it and, of course, another agent who is out in the field."

It took every ounce of Rick's willpower not to roll his eyes at the proclamation that Agent Rushworth was one of the agents covering the Al-Hanash case. He was a bumbling, boring jackass.

His face was impassive. "So you are telling me that Virginia Reel's target is *not* the terrorist's inside man; he's *not* the level-three programmer you speak of?"

"No, the target is the actual *creator* of the software. He is just another unsuspecting fool who sold out for money. Al-Hanash's inside man probably believes in his cause. These terrorist extremists are all the same: American religious converts who turn traitor. They are promised the world both before and after death if they blow up their country or themselves in the name of religion. We can assume that the target, Bennet, only wants the money. He's negligible and an unfortunate casualty of both politics and war. His assassination is expected to stir up the hornet's nest, scare the shit out of Al-Hanash's man, Crawford, and send him straight back to the Middle East or wherever to the safety and protection of Al-Hanash's compound. It's what they always do, and we'll be hot on his trail."

Bertram removed the pen from the holder again. "The administration needs both the Virginia Reel kill and the headline news of bringing Al-Hanash to their knees before they set off an EMP. Re-election is a shoo-in after that, and as you well know, when the time is right, I promise you that Obsidian will be the one to reap the financial benefits. You'll be the ones to lead the kill of Al-Hanash, not any SEAL team. Obsidian will be the ones, do you hear? You and I will rise to the top along with everyone else who was instrumental in saving America from disaster."

"Everyone but this Bennet character whose death you say is negligible." Fitzwilliam shook his head. "I don't like it. Obsidian doesn't play politics. We're in the business of killing very bad people who do very bad things. We are *not* in the business of deliberately killing American innocents and on American soil no less, particularly in the name of political ambition or anyone's re-election. We only accepted this contract because it came at the president's directive, and now you are telling me that the target is *negligible,*" Fitzwilliam objected with full conviction.

"Let's be clear about this. Bennet is *not* an innocent. He's a traitor no matter how you spin it. And while we are at it, let's be clear about something else; you don't have to like it. You can either take the money, which you already have, and ride on the coat tails of victory, which will be forthcoming, *or* you and your team can crawl back into that shithole from where you came and where I will bury you so deep that you will never see the light of day again."

Fitzwilliam rose from his chair, his face beet-red from anger and his usually immaculate navy suit now wrinkled from too much travel. His fiery temper below the cool façade of his stylish gentlemanly appearance couldn't help rising to the surface when the reputation and honor of his team lay challenged before him.

He walked to the office door and turned back to the director. Ice-blue eyes bore into Bertram's brown, beady ones as he spoke. "That *shithole* you are referring to is the United States Military where three of us trained and became indoctrinated with the principles of integrity and honor we believe in. You, Director Bertram, shouldn't bite the hand that feeds you."

"And you, Rick Fitzwilliam, better get the job done; because, if this op goes south, we'll pull the plug on you, expose Obsidian, and make your men the fall guys as co-conspirators. The press will believe anything the agency feeds them, and your people will be their next meal."

~ ♠ ~

A bright-yellow Mini Cooper drove down the muddy, washed-out road onto the Longbourn estate. Darcy heard the treads of the tires slosh and splash through the potholes and bumps created by the violent storm.

With the rain now ceased, his camouflage suit began to smell. It didn't just smell like a wet dog. It actually reeked like shit baking in the sun. The smell of the saturated synthetic fabric always repulsed Darcy, and he couldn't wait until this night came to an end and the bad-luck op was over.

Darkness had finally set in, and only one more hour remained until the approximate time of his kill shot. The curtains still lay open, but the study light was off. The rifle's sight zeroed in on the window and the back of the desk chair.

After hitting and driving through a rather deep, water-filled hole, the car stopped in the middle of the road some one hundred yards away from where Darcy laid, its headlights shining brightly down the road in the direction of the house. His head slowly moved as he slid his arm upward in fractional movements to bring his infrared night binoculars to view the person exiting the driver's door.

A man appeared to skip around the front end of the vehicle through the puddles, well maybe not skip, but tiptoe and hop lightly toward the front wheel on the passenger side. Darcy couldn't hear him speak but could see from his expression that he was annoyed. The man kept looking at his shoes, lamely kicked the tire, felt the rubber, then skipped back through the mud, careful not to mess his pant legs as he pulled them up. There was something very familiar about his mannerisms. It niggled in the back of Darcy's mind. For once, he couldn't put the face with the place. He wondered if he knew him. Probably not. It was just familiar behavior.

He silently mouthed "pansy ass" when the car rolled away toward the house, the behavior confirmed, the identity dismissed.

Once Bill Collins arrived and stood before Longbourn's front door, the knocker slammed against the brass on the door then fell off, crashing to the concrete below. He looked down and shrugged, thinking that, too, would become a thing of the past once he was installed as the new owner. Looking up at the house's façade, he thought, *Piece of crap house. The land is worth more than this pitiful structure. Nevertheless, it'll make a fine bed and breakfast once Jared and I are through with it.*

Bill smoothed his sandy-blond hair and dug into the pocket of his pants, pulling out a Burt's Bees lip balm. Gliding it over his lips, he waited patiently. He knew it was late, but he needed to finalize some of the details for the wedding. If he was going to go through with this, it had to be believable. In some small measure, he felt bad about it all. In truth, he had a problem with deceiving such a nice girl as Lizzy Bennet. She was everything his mother wanted for him in a wife. No, he had to marry her. After all, it was growing tiresome hearing his mother's constant badgering about how a man with a sizeable bank account should be in need of a wife. He didn't want a wife, but he did want a bed and breakfast. His conscience told him it was wrong to pretend, not to mention deny and conceal his real urgings, but he lived his whole life in denial. Why change now? He wasn't too dissimilar from so many others. In the end, he rationalized that his deceit was necessary for all parties involved, especially himself.

Lizzy opened the front door, immediately observing Bill's unusually imperfect attire. The wet and muddy cuffs of his slim-fitted chinos clung to his ankles, and his prized new shoes looked dreadful. "What the heck happened? You're six inches deep in mud!"

Entering through the open doorway, Bill replied with exasperated expression, "First thing we are going to do is fix that dirt road. There are potholes everywhere. I am sure the front tire is ruined. Oh, there is probably a slow leak now. I guarantee you that I'll have a flat tire by the time we are through with wedding plans tonight. Look at my shoes, Lizzy. These were my brand new Italian leather loafers." He made a pfft sound and waved his hand when he added, "Ruined."

If Lizzy could have rolled her eyes without notice, she would have. Instead, she smiled with as much compassion as she could garner. "Yes, we'll have to be careful until we can have it paved. Would you like a sweet tea?"

"No, too much sugar. Diabetes runs in my family, you know. I need to be very cautious. Did you know that diabetes affects 8.3 percent of all Americans? Thirteen million of them are men. No, no, I cannot take the risk."

Lizzy smiled again, wishing for a bullet to enter her brain for a quick death. Damn, she tried so hard today not to be reminded of her impending marriage. She led the way to the den where her father sat watching the History Channel.

"Daddy, look who is here."

As the men shook hands and greeted each other like old friends plotting to take over the world, Lizzy looked at her fiancé as though assessing an expensive purchase or keenly watching the behavior of one of her five-year-old students. Her mind traveled as she blocked out the conversation of the two men sitting side by side on the 1970s avocado-green sofa.

Bill was a fairly decent looking man: sandy-blond hair, brown eyes, expensive veneered-teeth. He was certainly someone she could tolerate looking at for the next twenty or so years. His hygiene was impeccable, and he dressed well. He was slender, even if he had a bit of a potbelly, but that was negligible. When noticing the strength—or lack thereof—of his handshake and the size and delicacy of his hands, she grew a bit concerned. Longbourn required hands made for, or at least accustomed to, work. Bill had weekly manicures and pedicures for goodness' sake. His hands appeared small like her father's. Echoes of Jane's argument ran through Lizzy's mind. A chill ran up her spine when she thought of his small hand caressing her body. *Yuck.* She shook it off and regained her focus.

In the men's conversation, Lizzy thought she heard something to the effect of wedding dance lessons. She was probably mistaken. No, no, no. Her two left feet in no way would ever travel down *that* romantic road. *Never!* Those plans are for the weddings of the fairytale dreamers of impractical sentimentality.

"Lizzy, wouldn't that be nice? We could have our first dance choreographed—maybe a nice rumba or a tango. Both are dances of love, are they not? I have just the Elton John song picked out, and I know this lovely little studio in Georgetown that came highly recommended. We can have your sister also learn to dance with the best man. You know my good friend, Jared. He and I have already picked out all the songs together. A nice mix of disco, show tunes, and some pop. Jared is especially fond of Britney Spears, so there is a bit of her in the mix, too."

Like one of Jane's favorite songs for Lizzy, Evanescence's words from "Bring Me to Life" washed over her. Her lips moved, but she couldn't believe what she was saying. "Sure, Bill. It sounds nice. I don't know what a rumba is, but it sounds nice. We only have a couple of weeks until the wedding. Do you think we have enough time?" *Someone please wake me up.*

"Absolutely. They have classes geared just for this sort of thing. Of course, allow me to flatter myself, but I am quite the dancer and a quick learner. We have our first lesson tomorrow night. I've already arranged it, and Jared will meet us there. Hopefully, Jane can meet us as well," Bill passive-aggressively suggested for the second time.

Lizzy found herself nodding silently in agreement with a smile fixed upon her face.

"Well, it sounds as if you kids have a lot to work to do. I'll leave you to it then," Thomas said. "If you need me, I'll be in my study. I've got a long night of work ahead of me."

In the silent black field where only a most observant eye could see the scavenging raccoon's golden ones, Darcy's eye remained unblinking the moment the study's light switched on. The target was right on schedule. Once again, Charlie's recon work confirmed why he was one of the best Army-trained snipers. Darcy regulated his breath and waited until the traitor came into view.

He remained still and itched to pull the trigger so he could be done with the nightmare of Operation Virginia Reel. Operation Shag in South Carolina was going to have to wait if he had anything to say about it. Forget stopping by Pemberley. He needed to get back to the mountains to hit his reset button. In the solitude and beauty of the Blue Ridge Mountains, he would put it all back into perspective, including the memories that this job brought to the forefront of his mind. Those he would process back into their rightful box, hiding them away in the recesses of his subconscious. With only Georgiana and Mrs. Reynolds near him, he would regain his equilibrium. They were the only people he had ever allowed to touch his soul.

The light streamed from the uncovered study window out into the black night. It shone like a lighthouse beacon so bright that even a satellite or drone could zero in on it easily enough. With the storm's cloud cover still lingering, even the moon couldn't compete with the study's brilliance. The night was pitch-dark, except that large picture window at the front of the house. The only thing missing was the target within.

Thomas stood to the left of the room with his fingers touching the binding of *Crime and Punishment*, which Lizzy must have put back into the bookcase. He chuckled. That was her way of saying, "Stop reading this book." She never admonished him, just subtly directed him. His Lizzy was so good to him, and he felt sorry for being such a disappointment to her.

Taking the book from one of the floor-to-ceiling mahogany bookcases covering the entire eastern wall of his study, Thomas walked to his desk. He stood at its corner and fingered the orchid that Lizzy had left in the wake of her well-concealed anger. He knew her ire lay planted below the surface. Thinking he knew her very well, she was as predictable as the sun rising and setting.

Feeling the smooth slice upon the stem, he wondered if Crawford had been so bold as to do it. The man was becoming increasingly belligerent, applying more pressure, dancing around threats and implications for non-compliance. Perhaps the cut stem was a threat, an indication of what would be in store for *him* if he tried to back out of the deal. Thomas was an educated man. He watched CNN, so he knew what terrorists were capable of. As a result, each day made him more fearful that his life would be in jeopardy if he didn't finish the program by the deadline.

He reminded himself to stay focused. It was all about the money, restoring Longbourn, and leaving his daughters a legacy they could be proud of.

His words to Lizzy the day before played repeatedly in his mind like Raskolnikov's guilty conscience.

"You travel down a dark road when you sell your history and legacy for a profit. It's as good as selling a man's soul; nothing good ever comes from it."

Just then, Lizzy and Bill appeared at the study doorway, startling Thomas from his deep, depressive thoughts.

"Is everything alright?" Lizzy asked as her father sat down in his desk chair directly at the center of the window.

Two hundred yards away, Darcy let out all the air from his lungs when his target came into view within his scope. He began to zero in, making adjustment for the storm's wind and his yardage. His finger rested poised when the target turned to face out the window in his direction. It was clear, he was looking out into the black night, and the expression on his face was equally as dark. Darcy's adrenaline kicked in when faced with the perfect opportunity and easy execution of his signature CIA kill shot.

In that millisecond of adjustment, Lakmé also came into the rifle-scope's view. She looked beautiful. Her hair was pinned up with falling tendrils, and the alluring flush to her cheeks from the heat within the house mesmerized him. She wore a formfitting, rose-colored tank top and black shorts, which gave him a full view of her long, bare legs. Lakmé was so close to his line of vision that he imagined reaching out his hand to caress her bare, smooth thigh. It did something to him. It made him feel something he hadn't felt in a long, long time. The blood pulsating through him was a different kind of exhilaration than the adrenaline rush brought about by his career. It was pure and simple desire.

His logical mind commanded him. *Take the shot. Take the damn shot... now!*

Darcy watched as the vision of perfection walked to the man, bent her knees, and kissed his temple with so much concern and affection that the sight of it shot through and penetrated Darcy's stone heart and soul. That, too, was an altogether different feeling: yearning.

His conscience reacted. *Don't take the shot. Walk away from this…now!* Seconds ticked by. His finger remained poised—inactive.

In unexpected empathy, Darcy watched the woman smooth the target's hair at his forehead. He thought of the immense pain she would feel when she found him dead at his desk the next morning or, God forbid, witnessed the kill shot—something he himself had witnessed so long ago.

The duel was over. Withdrawing his finger from the trigger, Darcy released the breath he swore he had previously released, but instead found himself holding. His heart rapidly pounded against his chest. He bowed his head to rest upon the top of the stock of his rifle and closed his eyes in defeat. *Damn!*

There would be no kill shot, no adrenaline rush, and definitely no AC/DC signature song. Moreover, and more surprisingly, he was sure there would be no regret.

Darcy's conscience prevailed. It was confirmed: Operation Virginia Reel was the devil's own luck, and Lakmé was his instrument of torture.

~ ♠ ~

5
Reasons

It was late when Bill finally left for the night after creating list upon list of wedding arrangements needing to be accomplished. Lizzy sat in her darkened second floor bedroom looking out her window from the cushioned window seat. The moon shifted in and out of the clouds. It looked like rain again. She thought she saw a fishing boat at the shoreline behind the pine trees but ignored it. The locals usually went out upon the Potomac at night, especially in inclement weather when the fish were biting. Her eyes traveled across the field to her greenhouse where she could have sworn something moved in front of the door. No, she was just tired.

Bone tired, actually. Weary, and not from physical labor. That was never her problem. She seemed to be able to keep up with most men when it came to home repairs and building. This was a weariness born from the continual struggle between duty and desire, and it was beginning to take its toll on her.

Clutching her father's bulky 1990s cordless phone to her ear, she attempted to listen to Jane detail her newest conquest. "Gorgeous and sculpted like Hercules" was someone whom she met at the International Spy Museum in DC where Jane worked as an exhibition curator.

Lizzy, however, was preoccupied with her own buoying thoughts. *You will go through with this marriage, Lizzy Bennet. You will marry Bill, and you will ignore the irrationality of your heart's promptings. You are an intelligent creature who lives in the real world where caprice and disappointed hopes dwell, not fantasyland where romantic bodice rippers come to life. This is a safe and logical decision.*

"Lizzy? You're really quiet tonight. Is there anything you want to talk about?"

Lizzy shrugged in the moonlight. "Did Mom love Daddy? I mean, do you think they married for love?"

"They did. They were once very much in love. It just became too hard for her. You know Dad can be very trying, and Mom didn't have the patience to put up with his needs and obsessions. He left her to manage everything at Longbourn while he shut himself away in his study. It was unfair and selfish of him to take advantage of her love in such a fashion."

"You always make excuses for her abandonment. Maybe she didn't have *enough* love for him to have overlooked his shortcomings. Perhaps it would have been better had they never loved at all but married for convenience. That way she would have had different expectations for her future, and her disappointment wouldn't have been so great as a result."

"Perhaps, or perhaps you are trying to convince *yourself* of that, given the future you have planned."

"Maybe. But she didn't leave just Daddy. She left us, too. That was pretty damn selfish if you ask me. Not too dissimilar from what she or you blame him for being."

"I agree. I suppose it all became too much and she just wanted to run away from it and we were part of that 'all.' Not everyone has your sense of duty and sacrificial love. I'm the case in point."

"I suppose." Lizzy paused, reflecting on what her sister said, then promptly changed the subject by dropping the bomb, which was the real reason she had telephoned. "Hey, listen, you have to go ballroom dancing with me tomorrow night."

"Whyyy?"

"Because Bill wants our wedding dance choreographed, and he thinks that you and the best man should learn as well. We have our first lesson tomorrow and then we are staying for some sort of tango group lesson. You won't have to go far. The studio is right there in Georgetown."

"Is it Bingley Dance Studio? One of my co-workers at the museum has been dying to take hustle lessons there. She says there's a hot blond instructor who teaches it. That could be enough incentive for me."

Lizzy chuckled. "Yeah, certainly not to help your most beloved sister. Apparently, I *am* the only one who self-sacrifices."

"You know what I mean. If I have to spend time with your fiancé, then there has to be something to sweeten the deal for me. Is the best man at least good looking?"

"Jared? I haven't met him yet. I don't know much about him other than that he lives off Logan Circle."

Jane sighed. "Well, there goes that opportunity. He's gay."

"Just because he lives in the gay section of DC does *not* mean he's gay, Jane."

"Yeah, we'll see. You've never had very good gaydar. Me on the other hand... So, what time do I have to meet you at the dance studio?"

"Be there a little before seven for our private lesson. Eight is the tango group lesson. I'm actually looking forward to doing this with you. Other than our sleepover, it will be the most fun I've had all month."

"I will be there with bells on, Sissy. You can count on me."

"Please, leave the bells at home. I don't want to draw any more attention to my two left feet than I have to."

The fishing boat arrived at the appointed time and sat rocking while waiting for Darcy at the shoreline of the Potomac behind Longbourn. Charlie sharpened his hunting knife on a stone, pushing it away from his body in long, pressured strokes. Every once in a while, the moon peeked out from behind the clouds, casting its beams on the shiny surface, causing the blade to glint in the darkness. He had been waiting for sixty minutes now, and Darcy was nowhere in sight. It was unlike him to be late for a coordinated extraction.

Charlie paused when he heard the bushes rustle at the shoreline. He hoped it was Darcy approaching. He waited another minute in stillness, then resumed his mindless task.

It was another eerie night. The vile mosquitoes bit mercilessly, and the humidity remained oppressive in spite of the torrential rain from earlier in the evening. Charlie itched for a swig of the beer chilling in the

Styrofoam cooler at his feet, but he'd wait. Darcy always appreciated an ice-cold one whenever he entered the safe zone. It was both unusual and fortuitous they were sharing this op, and he thought it would be nice to take advantage of his friend's arrival in town. Maybe they could hit the Cues and Dice bar for a burger and a whiskey afterward.

The shrubbery moved again. This time, Darcy emerged from the tall cattails and surrounding bushes while still wearing his smelly ghillie suit. Charlie signaled for him to remove it and throw it at the front of the fishing craft. He sheathed his long knife, then turned the motor over, quietly bringing the rocking boat back to life.

Twenty feet from the shoreline, like black ghosts gliding over the still water, Charlie asked, "You were late. What happened?"

He couldn't see his friend's expression, which was still camouflaged and as dark as the jet night.

"I couldn't get a clean shot," Darcy lied. Of course he lied. What was he going to say, "I fucked up, and I'm thinking of hiding off the grid, possibly going rogue, leaving Obsidian because of it?" Could he tell Charlie that something was seriously wrong with Virginia Reel, and he needed, not to mention wanted, to investigate this hit, these people, and that woman covertly? Absolutely not. That was not what Obsidian did. They were assassins, not spies.

"Impossible, Darcy. You of all people can get a clean shot from a thousand yards let alone two hundred. Was the target not in his study?"

"I don't want to talk about it." Darcy cracked open two beers and held one out to Charlie. "Is Rick back yet?"

He took a deep swig, not caring that he hadn't eaten in twenty hours. At this stage of the game, he was beyond caring. His wrist was swollen the size of a tree branch. He'd already pissed his pants at his hide site; he smelled like crap, and he was so soaked to the bone that his skin was wrinkling. The last thing he cared about was an alcohol buzz due to lack of food. In fact, he welcomed it.

"Yeah, Rick arrived this afternoon from Austria via Langley. He's at the safe house. You're gonna need to contact Caroline about Operation Shag. I have strict instructions that you should call her immediately. Did you get her message?"

"I got her message. Shag, samba, lambada—it's all the same shit. I need to talk to Rick."

This was a side of Darcy that Charlie hadn't seen in years, not since Cuba. It was an unreadable, indefinable aura he put out. He was too much of an enigma to describe or even to attempt to find rhyme or reason in his actions, let alone his moods. His partner wondered what set him off with this defeatist attitude.

"Anything you want to talk about, Darce? We'll have another shot at this. It's clearly no reflection of your skill. Christ, one-shot, one-kill Darcy can do it with his eyes closed and walk away without the slightest misgiving or emotion. The Iceman rules. The blood in your veins runs so cold that in comparison, even my sister's reptilian blood is warm."

He meant it as a compliment of course, but Darcy was annoyed by the truth of it, neither acknowledging the offer to discuss it or the perceived belief in his cold, calculating indifference. Hell, he didn't have these scars before the brutal murder/suicide of his parents. He was once a man with feelings and briefly wondered if it was the kiss that Lakmé gave to the target that pulled at his heart, causing him to feel and remember familial love. Yes, that was it, and it unnerved him. He was, as Charlie stated, the Iceman.

"We won't be completing Virginia Reel if I have anything to say about it. The CIA can keep their two mil," was his reply.

"Wait a minute. You said you couldn't get a clean shot. Is it that you *couldn't* or that you *didn't* take it?"

Darcy turned, his profile visible to Charlie. He stared out onto the river as the boat created a small rippling wake that split behind them.

The Iceman didn't answer because he didn't *have* an answer. All he knew was that he screwed up an op, deliberately, and it was over a gut feeling. He'd be deceiving himself, which he never did, not to admit that it was over a gorgeous woman and a kiss—her kiss. *What the hell kind of rationale was that?*

"What the hell happened out there?" Charlie persisted.

"Nothing. I need to speak with Rick immediately. Take me to the safe house."

"Yeah sure, of course. What should I tell Caroline? She needs to talk to you about Operation Shag."

"Tell her she can go shag herself. Rick is in charge. Besides, I don't think I'll be taking any more jobs."

Darcy realized that he was treating his friend poorly, acknowledging that it wasn't Charlie's fault that the job went south. "About time you start earning your keep," he joked. "They'll give you all the ops instead, or maybe Rick will finally put Caroline out in the field. Anyway, I want out."

The fishing boat turned left into Gunston Cove where Charlie had parked his Hummer at an abandoned house's fishing dock. He noticed the moonlight shining off the front grill of the truck and knew he was close by.

"Out? Like leave Obsidian out?"

"That's the only out I know. Unless, of course, we're counting on my cousin finally outing that he's been screwing your sister for the past year."

Charlie's mouth went slack. "You know about them?"

Darcy looked at his friend with a humored expression. "Please. I've been in the observation business far too long not to have noticed. Rick's a fool to think he can hide things from me. Isn't that how *you* know about them?"

"When you're right, you're right. Caroline keeps secrets tighter than a clam's ass. She'd bite a cyanide pill before she'd say anything. Hey, do you want to stop for a something to eat at Cues and Dice? We can talk about this decision of yours over a burger."

"No thanks. You'd better just drop me off at the safe house and head on out yourself. What I need to discuss with my cousin is sensitive material, and I'd rather not get you involved if it can be avoided. The less you know about tonight, the better."

Now Charlie really was concerned. Darcy may have been taciturn as well as a moody son of a bitch, and he may have had a temper that flew off the handle with ease, but he never kept secrets from him. In fact, he often asked Charlie for counsel and liked to use him as a sounding board. This was definitely out of character.

"Sure, Darce. Just know I'm here if you need me."

Darcy grabbed his gear and his ghillie suit and stepped onto the shaky dock. "Thanks, buddy. I hope I don't have to."

~ ♠ ~

Rick fingered the thin file in his hand, snapping back the edge of the manila folder below his thumb while he sat in deep thought, oblivious to the jazz music playing from the Bose.

It felt good to be back in Virginia. He never liked traveling abroad and swore he would take all the domestic ops from here on out. Darcy and Charlie didn't mind traveling. One because he never liked to be tied to any one place for too long, and the other because he was hell-bent on shagging women in every corner of the globe.

Caroline was a whole other story. She wanted to be out in the field more. She craved to make the kill shot. Rick reasoned she was more of a behind-the-scenes operative, but he couldn't deny that death and cold blood ran through her veins. His second in command could actually be quite effective as an assassin of a different type: a femme fatale. After all, she was quite beautiful and could disarm even the most skilled target. Caroline's long, straight red hair was mesmerizing in its own right, and her body was as lethal as her other finely honed skills.

He smiled at the thought of her. How on earth had they been able to pull off this one-year-long affair without anyone figuring it out was beyond him. Thankfully, Darcy didn't know. That would be uncomfortable, for sure. Being the rebound lay and subsequent relationship man following his cousin's failed involvement with her wasn't something he was proud of. But, truth be told, Darcy's liaison with Caroline ran hot and fast. The combustive fire of their few sexual encounters burned itself out before anything serious began. That had been Darcy's way back then. He was never going to commit to a woman. His mother saw to that, and then Lucy, who delivered the final *coup de grace* to his heart. No woman was ever going to encourage him to feel much again, let alone love. Darcy had become the Iceman after Lucy's betrayal three years earlier. As such, he was the perfect operative. However, Rick knew that even after all this time, if Darcy found out about Caroline and him, it would only push him further away from ever trusting a woman. And as usual, Rick ignored his conscience's urgings to tell him the truth.

The Director of Obsidian's mind went back to the folder. He didn't like Operation Virginia Reel in the least, even less since Bertram filled him in on the target's "inconsequentialness." Nothing good ever came from taking out an innocent, particularly an American, in the name of politics or ambition, even where terrorism was concerned. Those weren't the principles Obsidian believed in. It was over by now, anyway. He looked at the clock and noted that it was almost midnight. The job was done. Virginia Reel was over, and the target was probably lying face down in his living room or bedroom by now.

Rick took a sip of his Bordeaux and tapped his manicured nails on the marble counter at the bar. Even after a long day of travel and jet lag, topped off by a bullshit meeting down at Langley, Rick tried to remain the epitome of style and sophistication. Caroline joked that he was the original GQ man and could give James Bond a run for his money. Slender, tall, fit, and completely put together, he oozed sex appeal. She always said that his red hair drove every ginger-lover crazy, and his pearly white smile sealed the deal. Even he had to admit that he could have any woman he wanted after a night of dinner and dancing. Only he didn't want just any woman. His heart was already committed to Caroline.

A key slid into the lock, and the door opened wide with a resounding bang against the wall. Darcy and his black mood filled the open door frame. Traces of his camo face paint remained, some concealed by the long hair he'd allowed to grow to his collar. It had been twelve weeks since Rick had last seen his cousin.

He noticed the set scowl and that Darcy had dropped some weight. He was leaner yet still ominously fierce. There was new ink on his inside right forearm but he couldn't quite make out the design. He also noticed the swelling of Darcy's left wrist.

"Don't you knock anymore?" Rick joked. "What if I had a lady in here with me?"

"Sorry. I…um…didn't think about that." Darcy dropped his equipment onto the marble floor beside the door, then rested his rifle case against the wall. He looked Rick up and down. "You look like shit."

"Used to be you could sit nine hours on a plane in an Armani and never get a wrinkle. Oh well, like everything else, they're becoming more cheaply made."

Rick wrinkled his nose. "And you smell like shit."

The dark scowl on his cousin's face said a lot to him, but then again, Iceman was always in a piss-poor mood after a black op.

Darcy barely acknowledged the Armani or the shit comment. Instead, he walked straight to the kitchen bar, pulled down a tumbler from the overhead cabinet, and poured himself a stiff drink from the half-empty Jack Daniels bottle. Finally looking up at his cousin's amused expression, he motioned to the bottle. "Drink?"

"No thanks. You know I don't drink that hard stuff any longer."

"Sorry."

Turning to the freezer, Darcy pulled out the filled ice bin, laid it on the bar, and shoved his left wrist in it. With his right hand, he slugged the whiskey back in one long drink until the glass was empty. He promptly poured another.

"What's up with the wrist?"

"Bite."

"You look like you lost some weight. Getting back to your polo horseman's physique?"

"No."

Rick grabbed his wine glass and sat on the bar stool across from Darcy. With his monosyllabic conversation, something was clearly wrong. "Is something stuck in your craw that you care to talk about?"

"I blew the shot. No, more accurately, I didn't *take* the shot. I could have taken the shot. It was right there before me, a perfect kill shot between the target's eyes, but I flinched."

Rick didn't know what to think— not just about his cousin's confession of deliberate failure, but also about how he himself felt about it, especially in light of Bertram's admission about Operation Virginia Reel. He looked into his cousin's black eyes. There was something behind them tonight: emotion and pain.

"I'm glad that you didn't take the shot. It was the right thing to do."

Darcy's head snapped up. "Am I missing something here? You mean to tell me that I've been laying in my own piss and mud for two days so that you can imply this job was bogus?"

With glass still in hand, he walked around to where Rick sat. His expression was thunderous when he ran his hand through his hair, causing it to settle in disarray.

Rick finally saw the new tattoo in all its beauty. It was a tribal snake. He raised an eyebrow. His cousin hated snakes.

Darcy looked down to follow his cousin's line of vision. "Yeah, I'm trying to get over my aversion to all things with a forked tongue. Never mind my ink. Did you know this op was crap?"

"I only found out today on my way back from Austria. Virginia Reel's target is just a political pawn. Bertram is hoping to flush out the real target, a terrorist group named Al-Hanash, by sending their mole running in fear back to the nest following Bennet's hit."

"Bennet?"

"Yeah, your target tonight. He's the creator of the EMP software, not the end user. Apparently, he sold the source code to this radical group. I told Bertram the op was wrong—that the hit itself was wrong, even unconstitutional—but he insists the end result will win votes and keep the president in office for another term."

Darcy looked out the window at the flickering pizza sign below. The street was barren until a lone car drove past; its red taillights blurred in the rain that had begun again.

"For politics, I was to kill a man and destroy his family," he said, thoughtfully remembering the pain of his past. "I want out, Rick." After slugging back the last of his whiskey, he turned to face his cousin and the shocked expression upon his face. "My time with Obsidian is over."

"Give it a few of weeks before you make that decision. Look, you're always on edge coming off a couple of days of sniping. Mull over what transpired tonight, and don't make a rushed decision. We need you. I need you."

Darcy solemnly shook his head and shut off the jazz. He hated jazz, and tonight it only seemed to grate on his nerves even more.

"Darcy, what *did* happen tonight? What kept you from taking the shot?"

"You won't believe me if I told you, and even if you did believe me, given my track record, you still might not believe I did the right thing."

"Try me."

"I had a gut feeling going into this, a feeling that the hit was extreme. Bad luck unfolded over every damn hour I was out there. It became increasingly clear this op was going all wrong. Then the devil really laughed in my face. There was a beautiful woman at the target's house. The minute she kissed him, I knew I couldn't kill him. She looked like his daughter, and what really messed me up was that I was drawn to her like a bee to a flower. She was as inviting and intoxicating as the orchids in that plantation's greenhouse. When I first saw her, it was as though she filled my lungs with life. I can't explain it. Even I'm confused."

"Interesting analogies. Clearly this woman has touched your base instinct. Try as you might to hide the Fitzwilliam I grew up with, he's still in there and hoping you'll let him come out to play for a little while.

Go to the opera, take a walk in the park, wine and dine a woman like she should be treated, get back on a horse. Shall I continue with the list of things that made up the man I knew for twenty-one years before he went off the deep end and joined the Navy?"

"You've made your point, Cousin. That weak, overly-sensitive sap is long gone. He disappeared the moment my cowardly father shot my cheating mother in the chest and then put the pistol to his own heart. Who he really should have shot was Wickham, who used all of us to make his way to the top. I was big and as blind a fool as my father was not to see she had been fucking Wickham for months. No matter, I've waited a very long time to seek retribution, and it's finally coming."

Rick knit his brows. "Is that why you want to leave Obsidian? Wickham is being released from prison?"

"No, it's time, that's all. The fact I actually listened to my conscience and didn't take the hit on Bennet told me that my time with Obsidian has come to a close. Wickham is another issue altogether, and one kill shot that I *will* be taking in eight months. I *definitely* won't be flinching on that one. Any moments of sympathy or conscience were forever silenced the moment he laughed in my face about destroying my life." Darcy chuckled guiltlessly. "We'll see whose life will be destroyed once he's lying dead, face down in horse shit."

It might have seemed odd to anyone else that something so dangerous and risky would be voiced so coldly and openly between the two men, but such was their relationship, and such was the depth of Darcy's hatred for Wickham. The cousins understood and trusted each other implicitly. Rick would have reacted the same way had he found out that his mother was having an affair with his best friend.

"So Wickham is being released after serving his time for kidnapping Georgiana."

"He should have gotten the chair, if you ask me. I don't want to talk about that. I want to talk about what to do next."

Rick surreptitiously watched him pace the room in front of the large window looking out onto U Street. If he outright stared, Darcy would have noticed and might have clammed up.

As it was, Darcy was speaking to himself while he paced. The red curtains surrounded him, making it look as if he were on stage in a one-man drama, hand running through his hair, furrowing brow, body pacing back and forth as he voiced his thoughts. "I just couldn't do it. I couldn't let her see him dead afterward. I know that pain, and it's not what I wanted for her. I couldn't hurt her like that. It was Mom and Dad all over again. To have her find him dead would have scarred her for life."

"You're scaring me. You don't even know this woman. Shit, you haven't known *any* woman for quite some time. Why should you care what she has to deal with? She's a nameless person who you will never see again. This is what we do. Your quitting Obsidian over an unrealistic obsession is ridiculous."

"I know. I know. I'm getting soft. I'm a sucker. For God's sake, she's a woman. She's bad luck."

"No, you're not getting soft. Your subconscious wants you to feel again, that's all, and a beautiful woman is tempting you out of this half-life you've been living for thirteen years."

Darcy stopped his pacing and turned to Rick. "What should I do, Rick?"

Handing his cousin the remaining bottle of Jack Daniels, he replied, "Get some rest before you make your final decision about Obsidian, and come by the dance studio tomorrow night with your answer. We'll talk after you've had a night to sleep on it and determine if you feel the same way in the light of day."

"And Bertram? What are you going to tell him about tonight?"

"I have got to sleep on that, too. There could be severe fallout from this. The agency has had a long investigation hinging on the Bennet hit. They have been watching one of Al-Hanash's soldiers inside the Pentagon, a guy named Crawford, the one who turned Bennet. I'm afraid that just because Obsidian didn't go through with the hit doesn't mean the agency won't get someone else, or worse, do it themselves. I will stall as long as I can, trying to buy us some time before ol' Berty figures it out. Why they ever appointed him as director is beyond me, not to mention the fact that they put Bozo the Clown on the case."

"Pompous ass Rushworth? See this whole thing stinks. Any op I have ever been on where Rushworth was involved turned to shit. Bahrain was a prime example. A fat white guy with blond hair and a lisp pretending to be an oil sheik from Kuwait hardly lends itself to authenticity."

Rick walked to the Bose and put his jazz music back on. Al di Meola's guitar filled the living room, and Darcy cringed.

"Yeah, I hear that Rushworth was promoted to a field agent because his father-in-law was the former director of the CIA under the previous administration. They are all screwed up at Langley. You know Bertram used to be a low-grade administrator for the Department of Education and now he's running the CIA. Anyway, get some shut eye, and you and I will talk tomorrow."

Darcy grabbed the bottle of Jack—without his glass—and promptly left the living room for the bedroom. "Thanks, Rick."

~ ♠ ~

6
Unexpected

Darcy sat in the dance studio's office, long legs stretched out with his thick black leather motorcycle boots propped on the corner of the desk. He faced the studio window, awaiting Rick's arrival, and as much as he hated to admit it, he was enjoying watching the goings-on on the other side of the glass.

Charlie was flirting with yet another new student, and Caroline was fending off hers while teaching him to cha-cha. It was all quite humorous, and Darcy couldn't help but to smile slightly every time Caroline said with steely sweetness, "Hands go here, not there."

As the lyrics of the pop song "Poker Face" filled the studio, Darcy reflected that he did, in some small measure, miss this part of life—the lightness, the happiness. Instead, he found himself in a covert and dangerous world of his own making. He wanted to laugh at how the song spoke of deceit hidden behind a mask.

The small bell above the studio's entrance door jingled again, diverting his attention from Caroline's intrepid removal of her student's hand from her backside.

The glass Coca-Cola bottle he'd been nursing nearly dropped in his lap the moment he saw that instead of Rick entering the studio, it was *her*: Lakmé! His shocked heart began to pound.

She looked beautiful standing before the receptionist desk, but he could tell she was nervous by the way she scanned the room. Then she smiled. That perfect, white, beguiling smile lit the room when Caroline approached her in greeting. The scene in and of itself was interesting: Lakmé, the elegant, innocent dove, was being welcomed and about to be consumed by the carnivorous viper. Darcy almost smiled, watching the two women put on what he assumed to be their friendliest masks.

The woman who tormented his dreams the night before looked lovely. Though her sleeveless peach dress was nothing special, it clung perfectly to all the right parts of her curvy, incredible figure, stopping just above the knees of the longest, sexiest legs he had ever seen.

With her right hand, she unconsciously swept her long hair away from her bare shoulder, exposing her neck without realizing the impact that small involuntary move made upon onlookers—specifically him.

What is she doing here? What kind of joke is this? Is bad luck following me? He couldn't be sure of any of it. All he knew was that she was here, and he had no need to hide. He could sit here and watch her...openly.

Charlie ended his dance lesson with his newest angel and went to greet the alluring brunette.

Darcy's senses went on hyper alert, and if he had been paying attention to his emotions, he might have sensed extreme jealousy in his maelstrom of thoughts. It was in that moment that he felt as though he sat in a fishbowl looking out. All he could do was observe the happenings beyond the glass. After all, it was what he did best.

When the bell rang again, a blonde woman entered and greeted the object of his admiration with a big hug and a kiss to the cheek. In Darcy's astute observation, it was clear they were sisters. There was a similarity of features, not to mention height. They shared the same glorious smile. Both were beautiful in their own right but very different. One tried too hard to impress while the other—his girl—didn't need to try at all. She had impressed alright, impressed upon him his desire to touch every part of her body—with his tongue. He unconsciously licked his lips at the thought.

His girl kept looking at the door as though waiting for others to join their dance party. He couldn't hear what they were discussing but gathered their lesson was to begin immediately.

Judging from the look on Charlie's face, he had found another angel: the blonde. Darcy leaned back in a sigh of relief, surprised at how relieved he felt seeing that his friend had set his sights on someone other than Lakmé.

He settled in for the show, gripped his soda bottle, put his feet back upon the desk, and watched every move his girl made. He committed every fidget, nervous smile, and thoughtful expression to his memory, and like all subjects of temptation and lustful desire, he knew he would live on those memories in the dark of night and the brilliance of day. He would enjoy those memories when he had time to contemplate why she strummed her fingers on the side of her right thigh or why she bit the corner of her lower lip. And he would savor the remembrance of those spiky heels and well-defined calf muscles. In the loneliness of his solitary life, he would dream they were wrapped around his waist. Yes, the memories made tonight would give him hours of pleasure.

He had to admit that she seemed to lack natural coordination in the smooth dances, and he couldn't help but wonder how she would do in a rhythm dance, something like the cha-cha or the rumba. With hips like hers, she'd feel great in his arms. It was then in a flash of memory that he remembered the rumba was once one of his favorites. The feel of a woman moving with him in such an intimate, exotic dance was something he truly missed. Man, his life had changed.

The women moved closer to the office window, and Darcy reveled in her nearness and close enough proximity to listen to her. Every dulcet tone of her voice and cadence of laughter caused by her uneasiness shot through his heart like a lightning bolt charging it to life.

Charlie left the sisters to put some music on so they could practice the basic tango step, which he had just taught them.

In his absence, the blonde blurted, "We have to talk about this instructor."

Lakmé smiled knowingly. "Incentive enough for coming?"

"Hell yeah."

"I thought you'd feel that way the moment you laid eyes on him. He's definitely your type, but then again, who isn't?"

"Have you noticed the dark, striking hottie staring at *you* from inside the office? He can't keep his eyes off you."

She turned briefly, glancing at him through the glass, giving barely enough time to notice anything beyond his black tee-shirt, tattoo, and motorcycle boots.

"He's alright, not handsome enough to tempt me. I'm getting married, Jane. I don't need to mess around with some Hell's Angel motorcycle creep who stares too much."

Darcy's heart seized. *See, forked tongue like a viper with a body to kill,* and *she's getting married. Retreat! Danger!*

"Maybe a fling with a guy like that is exactly what you need before your final descent into hell." The blonde moved closer toward her sister. "His feet are like size thirteen, Sissy. What was the name of that snake, the long one you mentioned?"

"*Chironius carinatus.* Very large and aggressive with a super-fast tongue."

In reply, this "Jane" put her hand on her heart. "Oh my. I want one."

"Don't we all?"

Darcy's heart seized again. *She* is *a viper, an intelligent one. A serpentine. Stay!*

Jane looked over her sister's shoulder to see if he still watched them. "He's still staring."

Clearly, the beautiful brunette had insecurities, not to mention thought he couldn't hear a word of the conversation when she said, "Probably because he's finding fault with me or my dancing."

Without even realizing what he had done, let alone elicited, Darcy clasped both of his hands and rested his palms at the back of this head, opening his elbows wide as he settled back into the chair.

Lizzy turned at the prompting of Jane's jabbing elbow. She couldn't help but to admire the artistry of the snake-like tribal tattoo inside his forearm. *Ooh … He likes snakes!*

The bell above the door jingled, and in walked two men. Darcy again watched the scene unfold before him. The taller of the two kissed Lakmé upon her cheek although she remained virtually expressionless, offering just a small smile. Jane shook hands with both men and moved closer to her sister. The shorter of the two men moved closer to the other man.

With his usual congeniality and enthusiasm, Charlie greeted the newcomers and demonstrated with the blonde what he had just taught the women.

Two things became clear to Darcy's observant eye: Lakmé certainly was not enthused by the man he assumed was her fiancé, and the other thing…the moment the fiancé looked into the studio's mirror, smoothing his hands down his waist, Darcy recognized the mannerism, having seen it once before. He was the man kissing another man on U Street. Her fiancé was gay.

He smirked. *This is getting interesting.*

Caroline walked into the office and followed his stare. "Find something of interest? And here I thought you had grown immune to women."

"Only redheads."

"That's good to know. There's less chance of that animal in your pants coming near me again."

"If I remember accurately, you weren't complaining about it back then, but our brief affair was so unremarkable, not to mention unmemorable, that I can't be sure."

"Yeah, well, unfortunately, *I* remember, and as much as I hate to admit it, it set a precedent."

Lifting his chin to the women on the other side of the glass window, he motioned, trying to act nonchalant. "New students to the studio?"

"Yes. The brunette is having her wedding dance choreographed, and the other one is her sister, who I think will probably find herself a victim of my brother's womanizing charms before long."

Darcy noted Jane's hand resting upon Charlie's bicep. "A willing victim, it appears."

Caroline motioned with her hand for Darcy to remove himself from her desk chair. "Up, Rambo."

He rose and stretched liked a cat, bringing his arms up and flexing his chest. It was a sudden and entirely inviting movement that did not go unnoticed on the other side of the glass.

Lizzy tried not to stare at the guy with the hard body and five o'clock shadow, but suddenly she couldn't help herself from looking over Bill's narrow shoulder into the office. The biker was smoking hot and dangerous. *Dangerous, Lizzy!* She hated admitting it to herself, but she was attracted to him.

He caught her attention for a fleeting moment until she quickly averted her eyes back toward her fiancé's face.

Bad boy, stone-cold Iceman couldn't help but to smile. It was barely perceptible, but it was there. Actually, at that very moment, a full-blown grin *did* exist—in his soul. He could almost hear the wind rushing through the opening door deep down within him. The covert observer and sniper had been caught in the act, and he rejoiced in it.

"Does she have a name, the brunette?" He bravely asked Caroline, hoping not to be called out by the always-poised and ready-to-strike viper with that acerbic, slithering tongue of hers.

Looking for a nail file, she dug into her Louis Vuitton handbag, replying without making eye contact. "Lizzy, Lizzy Bennet and her sister Jane. Why do you ask?"

He shrugged, rested his bent arm on the window frame above his head, and resumed his stare, replying tonelessly, "Just curious." *Lizzy. Her name is Lizzy. Childish name. However, she is no child. Liz. Bennet... she is his daughter.* Sighing in relief, he knew then that he had done the right thing by not executing the hit. He wondered if he should listen to his conscience more often.

"Do you know anything about her?"

"For a guy who is 'just curious,' you sure ask a lot of questions. I only know she's a kindergarten teacher and has two self-proclaimed left feet."

Kindergarten teacher. Oh God. She is fabulous, he thought.

Caroline pulled the emery board across her broken fingernail. "Listen, Rick called to say he's running late. He wants you to stick around, but shortly, we're going to be starting our tango group class. So you'll have to just make yourself comfortable back here."

"I thought I had done that until you kicked me out of your chair."

"You know what I mean. Comfortable, but don't go messing with my stuff."

It was the perfect opportunity for another insult or at least a back handed one, but he let it slide; his mind was otherwise occupied with the woman dancing in her gay fiancé's arms.

Twenty minutes later, Charlie dimmed the lights, and the guests who had already arrived for the class began to assemble on the dance floor. The disco ball hanging from the center of the ceiling glittered and cascading white lights twinkled from the perimeter walls toward the revolving mirrored globe. The feeling within the studio was romantic and captivating, perfect for the tango.

Lizzy felt nervous. It was one thing to learn to dance in a private setting, but an altogether different thing to learn with strangers. She didn't know what to expect and turned to Bill.

"Have you done this before?"

"Sure, don't worry. They are professionals, and as I mentioned, I'm quite the proficient already, even after one private lesson. Just follow me, and try not to step on anyone's toes. These Gucci loafers cost a fortune, and those spike heels of yours could do some real damage, girlfriend."

Gee, that is reassuring. Did he just call me "girlfriend"? "I'll try, *boyfriend.*"

Charlie stood before the class with his back to the mirrors. "Welcome, everyone. Tonight begins our basic tango class. Throughout the course of these four weeks, we will cover the basic steps and body positioning so that you'll have a solid routine you can use socially."

He counted the men-to-women ratio. They were one man short.

"Please line up facing one another. Men on one side, women on the other. Now, we are one partner short, so when the line rotates, the odd woman out will proceed with the steps, but without a dance partner to lead her."

Holding out his hand, he invited Jane to join him in the center between the two rows of students. "Jane, would you care to demonstrate with me the basic tango step we just learned in your private class?"

After she joined him before all assembled, Charlie held her in the classic tango dance frame to demonstrate the eight-count steps. He counted out loud. "Slow, slow, quick, quick, slow. Walk, walk, tan–go–close."

Jane was unable to force herself to look over her shoulder away from Charlie as he had taught them to do. Instead, she locked her glazed-over gaze onto his big, bright baby blues, imagining nights of passion-filled tan-go-closing between the sheets.

Jared had that same look in his eyes for Bill and vice versa.

And Darcy saw it all from his comfy seat in the office. With his soda long finished, he now needed popcorn for the show taking place before him, and what a show it was. He felt strangely liberated. No ghillie suit, no rifle, and no concealment—he was out in the open, watching and assessing, and no one gave a crap, especially him.

Lizzy turned her head, looking over her shoulder toward the man in the office. He was staring again. She felt as though his dark eyes were stripping her body and soul bare. Her face grew flush, and all of a sudden, she unexpectedly became ashamed of her two left feet as though wishing to dazzle the intense observer and make a good impression through superior dancing skills. Silently, she chastised herself for thinking that way. In less than two weeks, she would be marrying the man standing before her. What did she care whether she impressed someone who was staring at her only to find fault?

Caroline turned on the music, and the moment the first notes of Britney Spears's "Toxic" filled the ballroom, everyone turned to Jared who squealed in delight, clapped his hands, and began bouncing on his toes.

Iceman chuckled for the first time in a long time.

The male dancers took their female partners into awkward dance frames, and the tango commenced. After a few tries, the partners changed, and Charlie taught a second step. The dancing re-commenced, and the partners rotated once more. At last, Lizzy found herself the odd woman out, left to dance by herself without a partner. She bit her lower lip.

Darcy was not happy with her isolation. He saw how nervous and self-conscious she was by the way her fingers bounced on the side of her thigh. It disturbed him that no one, most of all her fiancé, cared to notice the anxiety written upon her face.

In that moment, hell froze over.

With a loud scraping of the office chair's legs on the linoleum tile, everyone turned toward the office to see him push out from behind the desk then walk with purposeful steps directly toward Lizzy.

Again, his reflection filled the room with his six-foot-two powerful frame and commanding presence. He didn't acknowledge the gay fiancé, who unabashedly stared in what he assumed was lust. Nor did he glance at the young woman at the end of the row, fanning herself with her hand. He thought he heard a "hmph" emanating from Caroline in jealousy, but he paid no mind. Darcy didn't even look at the approving, broad smile upon Jane's face. The only thing he focused on when he took Lizzy into his dance frame was the glowing embers in her incredible eyes and the relief that washed over her expression. It was in that second that he knew that although her physical exterior portrayed her to be wholesome and innocent, she hid an entirely different person deep down inside. He knew that look well because he saw it reflected in his own eyes every time he looked into the mirror. She, like him, lived in denial. They were two sides of the same coin.

Lizzy was astounded when the stranger took her into his tight, strong grasp, but she couldn't deny that she felt simultaneously relieved. His right hand rested firmly against her bare shoulder blade, yet it caressed her at the same time, as though trying to know and touch her intimately. Like Jane's reaction to Charlie, she couldn't look away, and, surprisingly, she couldn't pretend to be ambivalent toward his raw, overpowering masculinity. This man did something to her, and Brittany Spears's lyrics were confirming that she, too, felt the danger and loved it.

Her left hand never made it to its final awkward destination behind his shoulder. What her fingers really wanted to do was run through his dark curls. Instead, she found her palm resting upon the black tribal tattoo circling biker god's hard bicep. She noted the smoothness of his skin and the brawn of the massive muscle below it, and both observations caused her to shamelessly think of his other muscles, thrusting and sliding upon her. Her skin grew flushed when she silently admitted to herself, instinctively knowing, that sex with him definitely would *not* be overrated.

Furthermore, she couldn't deny that his presence was bringing her to life.

The man's dark eyes bore into hers as if trying to read and understand her hidden emotions and thoughts. She attempted to look away but couldn't. His magnetic pull kept her eyes riveted upon his. He said nothing, his face remaining expressionless. Lizzy had no idea what he was thinking. She assumed he was looking for flaws and raised her chin in silent defiance as the song's seductive beat vibrated along the wooden dance floor, traveling straight up her legs to her pounding heart. *Boom, boom, boom!*

Darcy had seen her lift that beautiful chin in his direction once before, and at that time, when she sought the sunlight upon her face, it was his undoing. The feeling of her in his arms when she raised her chin again was all the more captivating and equally tormenting. He fought the temptation demanding, *Kiss that proud chin and her graceful neck and that beautiful collarbone.* His body and mind soared the moment his hungry fingers felt the softness of her supple skin upon her back. Lakmé's scent was strawberries, and he desperately desired a taste—everywhere. The moment he took her hand in his, he had to resist entwining his fingers with hers. They fit perfectly.

The spell woven between them during only one short minute broke when Charlie called out for the students to begin the next set of dance steps.

Darcy pulled Lizzy closer to him. Their bodies touched in blazing heat, their chemistry palpable. His thighs brushed against hers with each "slow, slow, quick, quick, slow" of the dance.

It was when he executed the basic corte step, where he dropped his heel back behind him and pulled her forward upon him in a lunge, that she was sure her knees would go weak. It was *very* intimate as his long leg stretched below hers. She felt him. She felt all of him and trembled in his arms. Then it happened. He smiled—ever so slightly—but absolutely in response to the quiver of her body.

Hmmm. Barely tolerable, huh? he mused.

In her mind, Lizzy responded to his smile. *Smug bastard. Gorgeous, smug bastard.*

She finally looked away. The heat from his stare was burning her, cauterizing every frayed nerve that ran through her body. Denial was pointless, impossible. He had lit a flame within her, and the moment his index finger caressed her bare skin, she couldn't help but lean into him more. The hidden Lizzy wanted more. She wanted all he had to give and suddenly found herself looking back into his passion-filled eyes.

She was breathless in anticipation of every corte dance move. Each time the firm hand against her shoulder blade guided her toward him upon his lunge backward, she found her body tightly held to his. His arousal pressed against her through the thin dress, and much to her shame and embarrassment, her imagination went wild. Feeling her cheeks blush, she was sure that he noticed the effect he had upon her. She certainly noticed the effect she had upon *him.*

Over the remainder of their eight-minute dance, they didn't speak to each other. However, never once did they relinquish eye contact. Things were expressed between them without words, both understanding completely what was transpiring. Lizzy no longer felt he was watching her with derision, rather quite the opposite. Neither could deny how they made each other feel in their arms. In a word: inferno.

The dance ended, and they were supposed to separate from each other. The look upon the mysterious man's face when their bodies slightly parted caused Lizzy to wonder what was going through his mind at that moment. He seemed not to want to relinquish his hold upon her. It was okay; she felt the same way. After the music stopped, long seconds passed, which seemed to halt time. She breathed in deeply once, holding her breath while caught up in the moment.

The other students, including Bill, noticed the couple's unwillingness to part.

Darcy broke the hypnotic gaze between him and Lakmé. He cleared his throat and finally released her from his hold—a hold that went way beyond the physicality of the dance or his dance frame—and it frightened the crap out of him.

His deep, sexy voice washed over her. "Thank you for the dance, Liz."

Strangely, she felt bereft and would have been quite surprised to know that he felt so much more than the loss of her physical nearness when he left the dance floor.

Iceman's face was set like well-controlled stone when he turned his back to the gaping onlookers and strode toward the office. He grabbed his leather jacket from the chair and, with formidable steps across the studio, exited the building.

Rick was going to have to wait. Darcy needed a cold shower and the remainder of that Jack Daniels bottle.

Some of the students watched his retreating back in shock and awe; others practiced their new tango steps in the silence. No one noticed Caroline's mouth tightly set in jealousy, Charlie's laughing countenance, Jane's knowing nod, Jared's intent stare at the most perfect ass he had ever seen, or Bill's curiosity at the whole exchange. Most of all, no one noticed Lizzy's reddened face and sparkling eyes as she watched the biker's exit, and certainly, no one could feel the pounding of her exhilarated heart.

The last image she saw after hearing the pleasant jingle of the bell above the door was him kick-starting his Harley before driving away into the night. *How did he know my name?*

~♠~

7
Facing Fears

Darcy never made it back to the safe house where a cold shower and a glass of whiskey awaited him. Instead, he found himself riding full tilt, heading north on Route 7 out of DC. He wasn't sure why he decided to go or what he planned to do once he arrived, but he was headed home to Pemberley and its horse pastures in Leesburg, Virginia.

It didn't matter that it was close to ten o'clock at night and that he hadn't been back home in five years. No one was there anyway. Just haunting memories remained, memories he ran away from a long, long time ago.

Tonight's dance with Liz opened the door to something he couldn't turn his back on now. She *saw* him. She looked inside him and *saw* his raw essence, the real man below the tough persona he had donned the day he signed up for the Navy. Liz didn't say or do anything that led him to believe she understood who Fitzwilliam Darcy was, and shit, it was only eight minutes of dancing, but he felt something different in the way her body responded to him. Moreover, he felt it in the way *he* responded in reply. He was being reborn, and that alone made him uneasy. No, more than uneasy—scared to death.

His thoughts were everywhere. One minute up and another down. He hoped the one place to find the answers was at Pemberley.

The paved road at the property's entrance loomed pitch black when motorcycle and rider arrived. Darcy stopped and placed both feet on the blacktop pavement. *Five years…and even then, I only stayed for thirty minutes.* He involuntarily shuddered and refocused his thoughts. The recollection of a particular movement of Liz's hair shook the weight of horror from his memory.

Setting the kickstand, he got off the bike, pulled out his keys, and opened one side of the massive wrought iron gates. A menacing looking *P* centered in the decorative metalwork stared back at him as though in taunt. He pushed the Harley through and locked the gate behind him.

Through his helmet's open face shield, he hardly made out the cherry blossom trees arching together above the drive from both sides. Beyond the beam of light from his bike's headlight, he could see nothing past thirty or forty feet ahead. To another, it would feel portentous and mysterious, as if one had arrived in an Edgar Allen Poe novel. He expected it though given the death and misery that infused these grounds he once called home.

Remounting his motorcycle, Darcy tuned the music within his helmet to play a Metallica song and fully gassed the throttle, ready to push both the Harley and himself to the limit. He was freeing himself to laugh death in its face. The one thing he cared about in that moment was balls-out speed and the fuel of adrenaline.

It was a long, straight two-mile run to Pemberley. Most likely, there weren't obstacles ahead. Hell, he paid enough money to assume the road's surface would be cared for and kept clear of falling debris. He shrugged, uncaring either way as the bike barreled into the black of night toward the mansion.

One hundred miles per hour hardly seemed to faze him. So he pushed the bike to 120 mph, yet the high of reckless speed and the danger of pure darkness didn't spur his adrenaline. There was no rush, no power trip. He didn't feel invincible. His ultimate thrill was no longer going to be found defying death or even in doling it out so deservedly. The thrill that put them both to shame was the one he had felt while holding Liz in his arms. That thrill had a signature song all of its own making, and it was the only one that would ever play if he had the chance to hold her again. It would be the sound of his heartbeat echoing in his ears from the sublime feel of her skin against the palm of his hand. No, he knew he'd never see her again. Operation Virginia Reel was over, and he was going back to North Carolina to stay.

In less than two minutes, he had arrived at the circular drive of the massive house. Two storeys of eerie cold stone surrounded by one hundred acres of blackness stood before him. Beyond the structure stood the stables, which he thankfully could not see. It would be there where he would face his demons and attempt to exorcise the metaphoric haunting that kept him away these many years. It was the place where his father shot his mother then himself and the place where he had witnessed it all.

The dark sky was cloudless and filled with thousands of glittering stars made all the more brilliant since there was no moon. He parked the Harley, removed his helmet, and took a deep breath of the sweet country air and the night jasmine blossoming around the sides of Pemberley. His mother loved those jasmine plants, and his father swore up and down they would never survive a Virginia winter. Yet, here they were still blossoming some twenty years later to tell the tale of love gone awry. A love despoiled by infidelity and betrayal.

His Bluetooth beeped in his ear, and Darcy tapped the side. It seemed odd to speak on his cell phone at that place and in that somber moment, but he did. He owed people answers about his actions earlier in the evening and needed to tell someone where he was in the event of an emergency.

In the silence and stillness of the inky darkness, he answered the call. "Yeah?"

"What the hell happened?" It was Rick, and he was worried.

"I'm sure Caroline filled you in over dinner."

"What...Why would I have dinner with—?"

"Caroline...the girl you've been screwing these past twelve months? Didn't she tell you what happened at the dance studio while I was waiting for your sorry ass to arrive?"

"You know about me and Caroline?"

"What do you think I am? A fed? Of course I know. You don't pay me two mil a hit not to observe everything that goes on around me."

"You...you don't sound very upset about it."

"Why should I be? Caroline's a typical woman, jumping from one bed to the next. It's in her chemical makeup. Besides, there was nothing beyond the physical between her and me. If you're happy, then I'm happy, but you should have told me. I can't help but be disappointed by that, but I'll get over it. Hell, I've grown accustomed to disappointment by those I care about. Look, Rick, as much as I'd love to get into this with you, I'm kind of preoccupied right now."

"Sorry about the deceit. I really was just trying to protect you."

Darcy could almost hear his cousin's regret in the awkward silence that followed until Rick changed the subject.

"Where are you?"

"Pemberley. I had to get out of DC. I'm sorry I didn't wait for you at the studio, but she was there. The girl I told you about…from Bennet's. We danced."

"You…you…danced?"

"Yeah. Look, I got shit to deal with. I'll call you in a few days."

"Man, you're at Pemberley. I can't believe it. Do you need anything? I mean, can I do anything? Do you want me to drive up? I don't know if it's a good thing you being up there by yourself."

"No, I gotta do this alone. Then I'm going back to Asheville to spend some time with Georgiana. I'll be in touch. I just have to make some decisions that I've ignored making for a very long time."

"This girl, what was it about tonight that made you flee back to Pemberley?"

"I saw myself in her eyes…in her soul, and I knew I had lost my way. Anyway, she's getting married. You were right; it's an irrational obsession, and I'll never see her again, but I can't run from my conscience any longer."

Darcy looked up at the stars, taking in all their beauty. "Look, I'll call you. Please apologize to your girlfriend if I screwed up her tango class tonight. It was really unexpected."

"Sure, Darce. She didn't seem to be as put out as you or I would expect, but I'm sure she'll appreciate the gesture. Be careful up there. Be careful as you unpack your memories. You don't have to let them take you where you don't want to go. Remember that."

"I remember that every day, Cousin. Why do you think I've been on the run the last thirteen years?"

Both men clicked off their phones, one in worry and amazement and the other filled with fear and trepidation for the journey he was about to make. As tough as leather as he was, the ex-Navy SEAL was knowingly making a journey into hell.

Darcy pulled two items from the leather saddle bag hanging from the side of his motorcycle. The first was an old set of keys, and the second was Liz's sketchbook. He didn't know why he was bringing it to his childhood home with him, but in some small measure, it gave him a sense of peace. He had come to know her through her drawings. He shoved the book into his jeans' back pocket.

The key still fit in the lock, and he pushed the door open with a hard shove. The hinge joints were rusty and stiff after years of inclement weather and neglect. Entering into the massive marble foyer, he smelled the mustiness and stale air permeating the old, uninhabited building.

His powerful tactical flashlight shined over the interior of the house, and he noted how everything was just how he left it: covered with white linens and dust. Cobwebs probably existed, but he didn't notice until he walked into a spider's personal zip line that spanned the width of the hallway. The wood floor creaked below his heavy boots as he made his way within the beam of light to the main electrical circuit breaker in the kitchen.

Covered paintings and photographs still hung on the walls leading toward the kitchen. He pulled a white sheet from one, letting it float to the dusty floor. Below was the shadow box with his polo medals and the portrait of when his team won the USPA Intercollegiate Polo Competition his first year at the University of Virginia.

Walking down the hallway, he pulled off the next sheet. It revealed a photograph of Georgiana and him at the same event. She was six, and he was eighteen. He tugged at the next sheet, revealing his parents' formal portrait at the country club on their tenth wedding anniversary. His posture grew rigid as he took in the photo before him until he finally moved the light closer, examining his parents' smiles. They looked genuinely happy and in love, and he resisted the childlike urge to stick his tongue out at his mother, or worse, flip her the bird. He fought back the words he wanted to say but instead, he moved to the next photo, his hand freezing before pulling at the sheet. No, he knew what that photo depicted, and he didn't want to see it. One day, he would burn that covered photograph of Wickham and him in their orange UVA polo uniforms. He just never had the time before. It seemed easier to cover the picture and conceal the hurtful memories that the image evoked.

The door to the kitchen creaked open, and he panned his flashlight over the countertops, windows, ceilings, and floor before he entered, making sure that everything was as he had left it. He had always wondered if the building was penetrable by squatters. Although he paid a groundskeeper to take care of the pastures and driveways as well as maintain the exterior of the estate's buildings, he couldn't be sure of the status of the interior. One thing was sure though, Aunt Catherine faithfully drove by the estate to check on it. She had been chomping at the bit to purchase Pemberley these many years. Not even Darcy's consistent "not for sale" would deter her. Maybe now was the time. That was why he was there, wasn't it? Get rid of the estate, get rid of the memories, and begin the next chapter of his life, whatever *that* was.

From the main breaker in the empty pantry, he illuminated the entire house with the flip of one switch. It was like a beacon of light shining out into the blackness of the surrounding pastures.

He walked from room to room, leaving everything undisturbed until he found his way to his old bedroom at the top of the stairs. It was the only room he had avoided on his last visit to Pemberley. Not since he was a twenty-one-year-old, naïve rich boy who had just lost everything he loved had he been in that room. Now, he was thirty-four, experienced and hardened to the world around him, and he still had nothing. Nothing except useless money, his sister, and the recollections of that fateful day.

This room had escaped the veiling of memories. There were no white linens, and everything was covered in dust. Polo medals, photographs, and posters hung from the walls. Blue, red, and yellow rosette ribbons and sashes covered one whole wall, paying tribute to two of his favorite polo ponies: Perseus and Shiloh. He remembered the sad day after their sale when a teammate drove them away to their new home.

Other cherished childhood memories tugged at his heart. The solar system that he and his father made together for a science project still hung from the corner of the room. Books—many first editions—filled the case beside the window, which looked out to the Olympic-size pool below, now drained and lifeless like the rest of Pemberley.

After removing his leather jacket and riding gloves, he sat at his desk chair and looked around the room. It was somewhat comforting. Twenty-one years of happy recollections were preserved in that room, memories of the young man he once was. A dusty invitation to Emma Woodhouse's university graduation party lay beside his tattooed forearm. Yeah, she was a viper, too, but beautiful, refined, and high spirited. In the end, she was too spoiled and too conceited for him. He never did go to the party; his parent's funeral took precedence.

Darcy leaned back in the swivel chair and stretched out his legs before him. Looking up at the solar system, he thought of the argument he'd eavesdropped on between his parents the night before their deaths.

He vividly recalled their turbulent words from that long-ago night as he sat there, a big man in a boy's room. It was so clear, so loud. It was as though the house was haunted by that argument.

His father, George, had overheard his mother, Anne, talking on the telephone to someone with whom she was arranging a rendezvous. Darcy could feel his father's heart break with each accusation countered by her fervent denial. Then George told her he'd hired a private investigator who was bringing by photographs in the morning, proof that she had been sleeping around for months with the same young—very young—man.

Anne's son hated her that night, hating what she had done to his honorable, kind father who was a good man in every way. Darcy hated that a woman could betray not only her vows but also her family for her own selfish desires. Every lie and retaliation that came from her lips began the deconstruction of everything he had believed a lover, mother, and wife would be, and he began to see most women as having the potential to wound and destroy that which he viewed as sacred. He shut off his heart from getting too close lest, like he advised Charlie, a woman would knowingly castrate him.

He looked at the photograph staring back at him from the side of his desk. *How did I miss throwing that away?* There he stood with his best friend through childhood, the groundskeeper's son, who was raised as if a Darcy family member: George Wickham, his mother's lover.

After flipping the photograph face down on the desk, Darcy rose, walked to his small bed, tossed the dusty pillow onto the floor, pulled the filthy blankets back to the foot of the bed, and lay down. He removed the sketch pad from his pocket and began to examine each drawing until he finally fell into a deep sleep. At daybreak, he would look for peace.

~ ♠ ~

Darcy awoke to a beautiful day. There was a vibrant red cardinal and his mate sitting upon the window ledge chirping their distinct call. Stretching flat across the small bed, he reflected upon how he had a sound night's sleep. For a brief moment, he forgot exactly where he was, and then the reality of Pemberley came rushing back. Yes, that's right. He was there to face his past head on and deal with the horrors locked away in the dungeon of his mind. In the light of day, and what a glorious day it appeared, it should be a walk in the park.

He rolled over to his side and onto the sketchbook and pulled it out from under his hip. Through the drawings, he was coming to know the spirit and thoughts of the woman he'd held briefly in his arms. The images of a pond with a child swinging from a tire, a row boat tied to the shore of the Potomac, and two girls flying a kite in a field came rushing back to him from the night before.

Those were *her* memories, things Liz felt and held dear. Obviously, sketching them kept those happy moments fresh and alive, even after the events were long over. He had done the exact opposite. He buried his happy recollections in the same emotional lockbox alongside the *horrific* events he sought to forget.

Rising, Darcy walked to the window and looked down at the empty swimming pool and the luscious green fields beyond. In his mind's eye, he saw himself on Pegasus galloping toward the stables. *Today's the day, Fitzwilliam.*

He didn't know just how long he would remain at the mansion. There was no great plan. Hell, he didn't even expect to be there. Walking to Georgiana's room, he sought only one item to take back to North Carolina with him: the teddy bear their father had given her on her fifth birthday. At twenty-two, she would be so happy to have that beloved friend as a memento of happy times.

Pemberley was quiet and still in the morning light. It was an entirely different house than the night before. The sun's fullness, rising over the eastern field and shining through the hazy windows of the dusty library, spoke of renewable life. God, how he missed this house. At one time, it was his favorite place on earth. Every room on every floor had once been light, bright, and welcoming. Now it was a mausoleum.

His cell phone beeped signaling an incoming call, but he ignored it and promptly headed out the kitchen door toward the stables. He wasn't going to waste any time. It wasn't in his makeup. Procrastination was different from avoidance, and today, neither were welcome.

The sun's reflection caught the tall weather vane situated at the top of the red and black ten-stall stable. His long legs climbed over the white split-timber fence that enclosed one of the verdant horse pastures, and his heart rate sped up. He diverted his thoughts and growing fears by noting how the green field of early summer was perfect for horse turn-out. Pegasus had loved his early mornings grazing and playing here with Anne's mare, Kismet.

The normally ice-cold, unfeeling man felt the enormity of what lay before him with each step across the field. Thick morning dew on the grass below his feet left water droplets and hay clinging to his heavy black boots. He stopped before the locked barn door, and with key in hand, he closed his eyes, deliberately breathing in the last vestiges of beauty and sweetness that lingered in the morning air. He attempted to cling to the splendor and joy of all that was good and untainted at Pemberley.

Surprisingly, Darcy readied his heart with thoughts of Liz's sketch, the freedom of the kite with the word *volat* written in cursive beside it. He had become a kite. Could she be the one to hold him tethered to the ground? Hold the string to his frozen heart? Keep him in one place long enough to commit to something good and pure and keep him from flying away when the winds of anger and denial sought to blow him to the four corners of the earth? Since she was marrying another, he was sure he would never know, and sadly, he acknowledged that she would have probably come to lie and disappoint him in time anyway. Such a strange internal monologue he was having. He didn't even know her, yet he did. In that one silent night of dancing and through the pages of her sketchbook, he had come to know Liz intimately.

With shaking hands, he opened the padlock and pulled the thick chain from the barn door handles.

It began almost immediately. A rush of raised voices assaulted his ears the minute he looked upon the remains of hay scattered on the near-bare ground in the center aisle of the stable. Darcy stood ramrod straight beside the tack room at the end of the structure, remembering that fateful day. After having ridden Pegasus after practice one day, both were just outside the barn doors, hidden from his parents' view.

"He's your lover, Anne! My God, all this time under my roof you both have

been betraying me." George wept and threw the photographs at his wife's feet.

Fitzwilliam peeked around the wall to see the 8 x 10 glossy photograph images that lay scattered.

"That's not as it appears!"

"Don't lie to me! It is exactly how it appears!"

"Fine! If you must know, I have no regrets! He makes me feel alive! With him, I escape the drudgery that has become my life with you!"

"Why, Anne, why? I loved you. We raised a family together and have shared our lives for twenty-three years! Of all people, of all the men who come in and out of our lives, you cheat on me with a boy: your son's best friend, who I brought into my home as a child when his father died! What will I tell Fitzwilliam?"

"Nothing, George, Fitzwilliam is never to know. It would destroy him."

His father's anger truly surfaced when he screamed, "You should have thought about that six months ago before you entered into an affair with Wickham! What did you hope to gain by that? Was it meant to wound me, or was it in retaliation for my changing my will? Or did you just care about the sex and virility of a younger man?"

"All of that! To have written George, who has been like a second son to you, out of your will after all these years, was another abominable display of that haughty Darcy pride and arrogance! Because he is not your blood, you left him nothing. How could you do that to him?"

"George Wickham was my ward! He could never be my son. That distinction belongs to Fitzwilliam alone! The Darcy fortune belongs to my heirs, not a young degenerate who has used us to feed his sick competition with Fitzwilliam, both on and off the polo field."

"That competition has pushed our son into being the exceptional player he is! As for George's virility…he is attentive and makes me feel young and beautiful, which you stopped doing a long time ago. I would rather choose a future with him than remain by your side."

Darcy couldn't see how George's hand went to his heart as if shielding it from the stabbing jagged knife her hurtful words became.

Silence ensued, and he knew his father was deeply, deeply wounded. The son's disgust for his mother rose like bile in his throat.

He was afraid to reveal himself to them. When he heard his father's next words, it was already too late to react.

"Well, my deceitful, callous wife, then you will have nothing: not your *young lover, not me, and certainly not any of the Darcy fortune."*

The gunshot to Anne's chest was fast, and Fitzwilliam rushed inside the stable as the blast still echoed. His father turned to look at him with sorrow when he mouthed the words, "I'm sorry," before putting the pistol to his own heart and pulling the trigger.

The polo mallet fell from Fitzwilliam's hand to the floor, and then so did he, dropping to his knees with wracking sobs and wails that would have summoned help had the gunshot not already done so.

Mrs. Reynolds and her husband, the stable master, came running in response, only to find Fitzwilliam holding his father's blood-soaked body in his arms. The young man's cheek and hands were smeared with blood, his tan riding pants saturated from the seeping hole in his father's chest.

Within a week of the murder/suicide, the once best friends became sworn enemies. Within a month, George Darcy's will had been read. Wickham, unhappy that he was left nothing, in an act of revenge and desperation for money, kidnapped nine-year-old Georgiana Darcy and held her for ransom. Almost immediately upon Georgiana's safe return to Pemberley, Darcy's aunt Catherine petitioned the courts and won guardianship and custody of the young girl. Too immature and emotionally scarred by the trauma of the months preceding the verdict, Darcy was too tired to fight the decision. So he put his hands up in defeat. The moment Georgiana left Pemberley for Rosings, he sealed the house, paid the Reynolds a handsome retirement living, and joined the Navy. At that point, he had become cold and indifferent and stripped himself of any acknowledgment of emotional expression.

Until this very moment, he had never looked back on the events of that horrible summer of his twenty-first year although they were never far behind him, nipping and gnawing away at him.

Thirteen years later, as he walked down the stable's center aisle to the spot where he had cradled his father's body, his heart hurt as much as it had that day. There was no amount of time or distance, no number of cold-hearted CIA assignments, or amount of careless living that could heal the wounds of betrayal and loss permanently inflicted upon his heart.

Alone, beneath the barren rafters and the abandoned stalls, Iceman allowed himself to weep unabashedly until every tear was shed.

When the tears finally abated, he wiped his cheeks, gathered his spent emotions, and walked purposely from the stable. After re-locking the doors, he stormed to the house and grabbed his things, making sure to lock Pemberley securely for what he assumed would be the last time.

The only thing his visit accomplished was the opening of his private Pandora's Box. He was as broken a man as when he arrived.

Darcy kicked the Harley to life, then headed home toward Asheville and the peaceful sanctuary of his dwelling in the mountains along the Blue Ridge Parkway.

~ ♠ ~

8
Confrontations

Lizzy stood on the platform in the center of three huge mirrors, looking at her reflection. It was wedding dress shopping day, and after the night before at the dance studio, it was a welcome reminder to stay the course, do her duty, and remember that Longbourn and her father's mental health lay at stake.

"I love it!" Jane exclaimed in regard to the overly froufrou Cinderella gown she had picked off the rack at David's Bridal for her sister to try.

"Yuck. You really love this? All this meringue and tulle makes me look like I should be standing on top of a cake. In fact, I look like I *am* the cake."

"It's romantic, Lizzy. Your wedding will only happen once. At least get a dress you'll remember even if you wish the groom were someone else, specifically someone tall, dark, and gorgeous, who straddles a Harley with thighs built for riding."

"Oh, I'll remember this dress alright, for all my eternity in *hell,* and I don't wish the groom were someone else, even if you do. Look, this preoccupation you have with that guy's thighs is a bit extreme, you know."

"Just sayin.'"

Stepping down from the platform, Lizzy lifted the gown's train so as not to get it caught in her spike heel. Her mind traveled to Jane's comment. It was all they had talked about on the telephone once both arrived at their respective homes following the dance lesson. Well, that and Jane's new infatuation with Charlie and their arranged hookup for drinks later in the week.

Trudging back to the fitting room to remove the ridiculous gown, she assumed Jane never detected her preoccupation with the tattooed biker. Thinking she'd concealed her discombobulation well, now after Jane's comment, she wasn't so certain.

And what an unexpected, unnerving turmoil it was. Last night, she hadn't slept a wink, replaying their eight minutes of dancing over and over in her mind. She saw something in that man who heated her to the core. His stare upon her consumed her like molten lava. A myriad of emotions and secrets, denials and fear, hid behind those dark eyes of his. A man so wholly unknown to her was someone with whom she felt a strange kinship. That tango had been the most profound, erotic moment of her life. However, it was now long over, and she knew she would never see him again. That was for sure. *I'll never see him again! Thank God! A man like that would only bring trouble with him.*

"I'm trying on the short one. Help me out of this mess," Lizzy stated.

"Please try on the fitted one with the flare or the halter with the high slit next."

Lizzy looked aghast. "Ahh, no. This is an outdoor wedding under Bennet Oak, not a rap music video. No one wants to see me in a dress that you would wear, and I don't need to impress anyone."

"But you do impress—all the time! You're deliberately deluding yourself, Sissy dear. That biker-guy last night wanted you. It was written not only all over his face but in the way he held you and didn't want to let go, not to mention the fact that you were clinging to him just as tightly. It was as plain as the nose on your face. You were highly aroused by him."

"That is so not true!"

"Ah, hello…that sheer strapless bandeau bra thing you wear did nothing to cover up your arousal."

"Oh my God! Why didn't you say anything! That must be why that slimy guy with the sweaty palms I danced with afterward couldn't stop staring at my boobs."

Jane laughed. "You thought you could conceal your emotions from me, but your tits gave you away, not to mention all that crap you fed me last night on the phone. You said way too many things very softly. Simply put, you lacked conviction. Why the hell are you going through with this sham of a wedding?"

"Neither my tone nor my boobs gave anything away. It was…it was cold in there! I'm officially ignoring you now, Jane."

In the fitting room, Jane placed both hands on her sister's bare shoulders, turning her to face her. Her hot pink fingernails completely contrasted with the serious mien she assumed.

"Since you are forcing me to go there, I am only going to say this once, so you better listen to your big sister. Because I love you, I only have your best interests at heart. While I'm not gunning specifically for Mr. Adonis, who can tango like Don Juan himself, I *am* gunning for you *not* to marry Bill. Read my lips, Lizzy. Bill. Is. Gay."

Lizzy's hazel eyes widened, and her long lashes fluttered several times. She was exasperated by the levels to which Jane would stoop in order to put an end to the engagement. She took a deep breath, placing her hands on her hips. "Well then, that takes care of your previous concern about my having sex with my husband, doesn't it?"

She snorted. "He's not gay, Jane. I think I would know if my fiancé was gay. Besides, gay men don't marry straight women."

"Sissy dear, haven't you ever heard of a beard? For God's sake, he chose a wedding invitation with a rainbow on it!"

"Of course it has a rainbow. Bill is a religious man. He explained that it is symbolic and the design should incorporate Bennet Oak with the colors."

Jane threw up her arms. It was futile. She removed the short vintage-style wedding dress from its hanger and handed it to her sister. "Here, this is for the Lizzy who is sensible and practical in addition to her deliberate blindness. This dress is perfectly suited for the young woman who is afraid to take chances, to push the envelope a little, or to attempt to follow her sense of adventure and heart's desires."

"I'm so happy you finally understand me after all these years." Lizzy smiled fast and false. Jane gave her the same feigned smile. Giving a mock sort of smile to make their point was a game the two often played.

Once Jane zipped the back of the dress, try as she might, she couldn't help but shed tears. It was perfect for her sister—elegantly beautiful as if she were Audrey Hepburn. The Oleg Cassini dress, paid for by Bill, had graceful lines with just the right amount of lace on the fitted bodice. The delicate illusion-netted neck and cap sleeves were demure and classic.

Lizzy conveyed the epitome of femininity and grace.

Standing behind her sister, Jane looked over her shoulder at their reflections. "You're right; this is the dress. You're stunning. You make a beautiful bride." A tear rolled down her cheek, and she became choked up. "Thank you for this…for sacrificing and doing what I never could for the sake of our family and that miserable house."

Lizzy turned, and the two sisters hugged, both shedding tears before Jane pulled away. Wiping her tears, she smiled brightly, letting her sister know it was time to move on from sentimentality. "I know you said you didn't want a bridal shower, but I just got you something…small." Grabbing her huge purse, the one Lizzy often joked could hold the kitchen sink, Jane removed two items wrapped with Wonder Woman comic paper. The paper was in direct, colorful contrast to the sophisticated white bridal dress.

"I'm almost afraid to find out what you have in those."

"It's good. You could use them since your wardrobe seems to be a little…shall we say 'puritan' these days."

Tearing open the first package like a child, Lizzy lifted a tiny, red lace panty with string ties and laughed. "These are so you, Jane, and they are definitely…small."

"I know. I have ones just like them in aqua."

Lizzy tore open the next gift. "You're giving me blue jeans?"

"Since you don't have a pair, I thought it was about time. You never know when they may come in handy, particularly the panties."

"Thank you. Although, I don't see myself putting either to good use." She kissed her sister.

"We'll see. I have hope for you yet. You just may wake up and say, 'Fuck it' and put on your sexy red underwear and jeans, get in your Jeep, and we'll never see you again."

"Not likely. I'm not Mom. When I make a vow, it's for a lifetime. You know that."

~♠~

Thomas sat at the picnic table reserved for Pentagon employees during their lunch and cigarette breaks. In the distance, the large fountain in the pond splashed and sent its peaceful cadence through the air. He unwrapped the sandwich Lizzy had made for him that morning. Peanut butter and jelly wasn't really his favorite, but it was all he could afford right now.

He was thankful she was home from teaching for the summer so she could take care of him. He smiled thinking what a good girl with a noble sense of duty and honor she was. She was so unlike Jane, whom he remained annoyed with for leaving after Patricia divorced him. Lizzy was the son he never had, and he was darned proud of her commitment to maintaining the Bennet family legacy. After all, he was the last of the male Bennets, and someone had to continue his heritage.

It came as quite a surprise to him when he awoke two days ago feeling refreshed and optimistic about the future of Longbourn. Suddenly, with Lizzy's impending marriage to Bill, the plantation's restoration would be possible without his treasonous act. It was in that joyful realization that he decided not to complete the source code. There would be no sale; he'd back out of it. His conscience prevailed, and he was darn happy to have read *Crime and Punishment* to help him realize that. Thomas allowed the words from chapter five to confirm his decision.

"Good God!" he cried, "Can it be, can it be, that I shall really take an axe, that I shall strike her on the head, split her skull open...that I shall tread in the sticky warm blood, blood...with the axe...Good God, can it be?"

Selling that code to enemies of America in desperation—for self-profit—was the most despicable act of betrayal he could imagine, yet he had stooped that low. He would let Crawford know when he joined him for lunch. He wanted out.

A slap to his shoulder alerted Thomas the moment arrived.

"Tom, how's it going?"

"Great, great. Have a seat. Let me tell you all about Lizzy's upcoming wedding on the third at the plantation. We have some exciting things happening at Longbourn. We're turning a corner."

Crawford smiled falsely. He was good at that. Disliking Thomas Bennet immensely, he was glad his sucking up to him and this assignment was coming to an end. He had put a lot of plans on hold in order to go inside the Pentagon for the sole purpose of turning the EMP programmer. If he couldn't succeed with ideology or with money, he would resort to a threat of death to either Bennet or his daughter, but Crawford hadn't the need of that...*yet.*

Certainly, money had been the easiest enticement. Crawford was never successful at preaching a religious ideology he didn't believe in. Of course, the man he worked for only pretended to be a religious extremist. Al-Hanash wasn't really what it—or rather, he—appeared to be. No, they weren't religious at all, and they weren't even entirely Middle Eastern. They were just your run-of-the-mill, evil men who wanted to rule the world, and he wasn't involved with Al-Hanash because he personally believed in their real purpose either. Plain and simple: it was for the money. In that regard, he wasn't too dissimilar from Bennet. He knew well the reasons the man caved as easily as he did: it was that dump he was trying to save. *Sucker.*

"So your Lizzy is getting married? I could have made her very happy, Tom, if only she had given me a chance. She's quite a beauty and very personable."

"That's my girl, all right. All that is good, honest, and reliable in the world. As much as I like you, Henry, she's made a fine match for herself. Bill is well-off and just the sort of man Longbourn needs."

Crawford raised an eyebrow. "What are you implying?"

"No offense meant to you or your employer, but I've had a change of heart. Bill has agreed to pay for the renovations in return for Lizzy's hand, and she has willingly consented. So there is no need for the additional funds that our verbal agreement would have provided."

Crawford's face grew dark, dark enough for Thomas to lean back a bit in fear.

"I'm not sure you understand, Tom, but my employer is expecting delivery, at the very latest, on the first of July. If you renege on this deal, it could have dire consequences."

"Consequences?" the diminutive man swallowed hard, and Crawford noticed. He had seen that sort of fear in a man before. Like the time he held the pruning shears to the fingers of the MI6 agent in Istanbul.

"Yes, consequences. They don't take kindly to a man listening to his conscience. Better for you if you continue to deny its existence."

"Henry, I don't understand. I thought you and I were friends. I opened my home to you. I fed you at my table. We broke bread together. Certainly, you can see and understand my reasons for not selling the finished product? This isn't the legacy I want to leave my children. I don't want the last of the Bennet men to be known as a traitor. I can't do it. No, I refuse to do it."

Crawford rose from the picnic table, walked around it, and stood right beside the frightened man. He rested his hand on Bennet's shoulder and looked down at him. His face remained pleasant and understanding, but his blue eyes spoke something entirely different. "Thomas, *I* understand. I *really* do, and we *are* friends. I will try my hardest to see what we can do to release you from your promise. After all, they will view this as a betrayal of the worst sort, but I will try to help them see reason."

"Thank you, Henry. Thank you."

The terrorist left the fool sitting with his conscience and his sandwich. *Bad move, Bennet. You're as good as dead, and if not you, then your daughter unless of course I can personally save* her *from what's bound to come.*

~ ♠ ~

The next day, the greenhouse was a hive of activity. Actually, a tornado was blowing through it: Lizzy.

Potting material, baskets, and gardening tools were turned over, pushed into the aisles, and knocked down, all in search of her sketch-book, which she hadn't noticed was missing until that very morning. She was counting on that little piece of her private life to be right where she left it. She desperately needed it.

The sketchbook had become her lifeline, her escape hatch if you will. Not only were there drawings of happy memories but also of her dreams and yearnings. Sketches that set her spirit free while she lived in a prison of self-sacrifice and duty. Words that only she knew the meaning of were written in the pages alongside the images. Latin words that she chose from her dictionary: *liberatas, animus, cupido.* She literally poured herself onto those pages with her pencils. The book's misplacement—or theft—was extremely vexing, and she considered it a violation of her privacy in every sense.

Down on all fours with her head and upper torso concealed by the plant bench above her, Lizzy spoke to herself, lost in her frustration and unaware she had an observer.

"Where the heck is it? I distinctly remember leaving it on the bench beside the *Phalaenopsis tetraspis.*"

As much as the observer hated to disrupt the provocative vision of her perfect ass rocking back and forth, the man behind her cleared his throat, startling her and causing her to bang her head.

"Ow!" Lizzy looked over her shoulder to see Henry Crawford leaning against a bench, grinning.

"Hi, Liz. Don't get up on my account."

No, Liz is not allowed by you! She rose, trying to conceal her assets from him. "Oh, hi, Henry. Here to see my father?"

He bent and sniffed a non-fragrant orchid. "No. Actually, I'm here to see you."

Pretending to look busy for the sake of avoidance wasn't usually her thing because she never needed to pretend. There was always work to be done. She continued her search and subsequent cleanup as though unaffected by his presence. "Here to see me? Whatever for?"

"To give you a couple of chances. One, I'm giving you an out before you make the biggest mistake of your life by marrying Collins, and the other, to help your father. Actually, they are one in the same."

"How could you possibly convince me to do either? I'm sorry, Henry, but your influence over me and my decisions is nil. While I respect that you're my father's good friend, I must, once again, reiterate that you are not mine. An acquaintance by association, yes, but certainly not a friend. And in regard to the matter of which you speak, my own beloved sister has not had any influence, so why should you?"

He changed his tactic by approaching her. Standing beside her, he drew his index finger down her arm. Touching her soft skin drove him mad with desire, and his heart rate sped up. "What were you looking for under the table? Have you lost something?"

To Lizzy, that was as good as an admission. "The sketchbook you stole from my plant bench."

His smarmy fake façade oozed, and she felt repulsed when he said, "Had I known that you drew, I certainly might have taken your sketchbook, but I didn't know. What a delightful hobby. I imagine you're very good." He took her dirty hand in his. "You have beautiful hands, soft and eager."

Turning to face him, she quickly removed her hand from his grasp. He truly gave her the creeps with his clearly dyed blond, slicked-back hair and that pockmark between his eyes.

"So tell me, Henry. Get to your point. How can my not marrying *the love of my life* help my father?"

This time, he moved even closer, causing her to press her back against the glass wall behind her. Bearing down on her, his heat was entirely different from the biker at the dance studio, and it caused an altogether different heat in her, certainly not the heat of passion or desire. Instead, it was borne from infuriated anger at his presumption and his physical violation.

Crawford brushed her long hair from her shoulder and smiled that crooked smile of his, clearly admiring the sight before him. "Because if you agree to leave with me for Monte Carlo on the third, then certain *events* may be avoided. Ours could be a whirlwind romance to exotic locales like Monaco and Spain. Our trip would be filled with steamy nights of passion under Moroccan skies."

"Events? Monte Carlo? Morocco? I don't think so."

"Yes, events. Yes, Monte Carlo and Morocco. You may decide otherwise if you knew the places I could take you, places you've only dreamed about, Liz."

"It's 'Lizzy,' not 'Liz.'" She was not only repulsed but also a hair's breadth away from stomping on his foot. "The only event that will take place on the third is my wedding on the front lawn. That's about as exotic and romantic an *event* as I desire. I'm sorry, really, and I don't wish to be rude, but please leave the greenhouse so I can continue cleaning up."

Crawford backed away when he saw a flash in her eye that he had failed to recognize whenever he challenged and pushed her buttons before. Perhaps it had always been there and he just never noticed it, but it was there alright, and he knew that she would not be acquiescing. In fact, her response to him had changed considerably. While she was cordial and polite, he sensed a real defiance and challenge in her voice. This was new, but he liked it, intrigued that perhaps there was something more to the virginal object of his desire.

He smirked at her bravado and wondered if she saw through his lies. She had no way of knowing the trouble her father was in, and, in truth, there was no way to protect Bennet from the repercussions of his decision, and certainly, there was nothing she could do about it. Al Hanash had already made his decision, but hell, leaving the country with Lizzy would have benefited *him* greatly.

Walking to the door, Crawford turned back to see her continuing the busy work of tidying the greenhouse. He noticed that her hands slightly shook as she stacked the orchids' empty wood-slat boxes one upon the other. With a sly smile, he laid it on thickly with as much obsequiousness as he could muster. "I'm sorry it has to be this way, *Lizzy*. It's not likely I'll see you again since I will be leaving as planned on your wedding day, but I wish you every happiness with your gay husband."

Gay? Why does everyone think Bill is gay? "Thank you for your concern, but it is not necessary. I will be very happy with my *straight* husband."

The moment Crawford left the greenhouse, she sighed in relief and sat down upon the tall stool before three of her favorite fragrant orchids. She hit the play button on her cassette boom box. The sounds of Chopin's "Andante Spianato" filled the glass room as she deeply breathed the orchids' aroma, closing her eyes to find her peaceful center amidst the sounds of the piano.

Long minutes later, she emerged from her meditative state and reached into her back pocket, pulling out a letter her aunt Elinor Gardiner had written. She and Uncle Edward were the Bennet girls' only connection to their mother's family, and as far as Lizzy was concerned, Aunt Elinor was the mother figure she so desperately needed. She was her rock, not only with keen insight but also a persuasive perspective on all things. Her aunt's common-sense approach to issues on life and of the heart had supported her the last couple of years in staying the course when her irrational emotions and inner urgings spoke otherwise.

My Dearest Lizzy,

Your uncle and I miss you and Jane so terribly and regret wholeheartedly that we cannot make the long journey to be in attendance for your wedding. Please accept the enclosed check as our wedding gift to you and Bill. Please don't baulk at the amount. You are very dear to your uncle and me, and we are so proud of you. It is the least we can do to offset the discomfort that I know you are experiencing.

Lizzy dear, I know that at times you must be confused by the rapidity of your decision as well as the soundness of it. Entering into a marriage where you do not feel the deep abiding love that your uncle and I do or others in your circle, can oftentimes be disconcerting, perhaps even feel like a betrayal of your own heart, which has most likely waited for Prince Charming and all that would come with him. But rest assured; you are doing the right thing, the logical and prudent thing. Not everyone is destined to have a marriage filled with passion and desire let alone a oneness of heart, mind, and soul. It is a rare thing, to be sure. Some wait and waste their whole life in anticipation of something that may never come. Women like Jane hold romance and desire as the be all and end all. Bless her heart. While you are all sense, she is all sensibility. Just like me and my sister, Marianne. Thankfully, Marianne had the sense along with her sensibility to marry Christopher Brandon.

I am overjoyed at your decision to enter into an amiable marriage that, if nothing else, is one of respect and mutual understanding, two things that are often lacking in the tumultuous romances of today, filled with only sex and physical attraction. No, your marriage to Bill will be a predictable one because neither of you are consumed by the need for the type of marital relationship that most of the world desires these days. You are not getting any younger, you know, so your decision to marry Bill is wise.

My dear niece, you are constant and true and as honest with yourself as you are with others. I am proud that you have taken up the role as the mistress of Longbourn, which was foolishly vacated by my sister-in-law, and we wish you much felicity in that role as well as your future role as Mrs. Bill Collins.

Do not waiver, Lizzy. This is the best decision for everyone, and in the long run, it is one you will be very glad you made.

All our love,
Aunt Elinor and Uncle Edward

Although feeling better, she wished next week was all ready upon her. She wanted it over before she had a chance to change her mind. Longbourn and her father needed this marriage to take place.

What could be said of Bertram that hadn't already been said? Well, if Rick had to say one more word on that subject it would be "jackass."

The crowded coffee shop on 18th Street NW in downtown DC was filled with young and old professionals with their computers or their colleagues or both. Tryst was the place to sit back, relax, and enjoy a drink, whatever your poison: coffee, tea, or scotch. Bertram had insisted this was where he and Rick should meet to discuss the failed Operation Virginia Reel.

Sure, expose us to the public, jackass.

Rick sat waiting at the tall counter on a stool, facing the busy street. It was eleven in the morning, and even the tattoo parlor the Ink Spot was crowded. He shuddered. There was no way in hell he would ever ink himself. His cousin was insane to have begun that obsession. Before long, he would most likely have more on his calves or across his shoulder blades. What was next, piercings? He shuddered again when a young woman with a large flowery tat covering her entire left arm exited the ink shop. *Carrie wouldn't be caught dead!*

Bertram passed by the window and overtly waved to Rick. *That's it, call attention to us, jackass,* Rick sarcastically thought.

Ordering his coffee and taking his seat beside Obsidian's director, Bertram opened six sugar packets at once, scattering granules all over the counter. He tossed the empty paper packs onto the counter.

"So your man blew it. I knew he would. You military types are all the same. You assured me, Fitzwilliam. In fact, you were so indignant that you wouldn't fuck this up that now you've made yourself look like quite the jackass."

"As usual, I think you have this all wrong, Bertram. He did *not* blow it. He couldn't get it cleanly accomplished that is all. There were unexpected guests at the location. It would have been messy, made the press, caused scrutiny and then connections would have been exposed, not to mention the CIA's hidden agenda. If you ask me, we saved not only *your* jackass from scandal but also the administration's."

"Word from my source is that your man went off the grid. Is that correct?"

"Your source?" Before taking a drink of his double espresso, Rick shrugged, acting all unaffected by that slip of Bertram's tongue. *Does he mean mole?* "Small vacation, destination unknown."

"Yeah, well, don't worry about bringing him back. Rushworth is going to handle Virginia Reel from here on out. At least he knows what he's doing."

Rick laughed boldly. "Sure, if we replaced high-velocity rifles with slide rules and thesauruses. The guy is a disgrace to your organization. He should go back to teaching third grade instead of mixing with the big boys in international espionage and foreign affairs."

"Very funny, Fitzwilliam. If I didn't dislike you and Obsidian so much, I might actually laugh at your attempt at humor. Oh, by the way, we want our two million back."

"Sorry, non-negotiable. It's in our contract. We are willing to complete our end of the deal, so the fee is non-refundable. It is not our fault if you are choosing to use one of your own greenhorns. Shit, that fat ass Rushworth couldn't hit the broadside of a barn. We shall see who screws up what." *Jackass.*

Bertram's beady brown eyes bore into Rick's brilliant blue ones. "Be that as it may, our cleanup of *your* mess is scheduled on the third, and we expect the return of our money by the fifth."

Rick didn't like this one bit. The CIA was going ahead with the hit on their own. All of Darcy's intuition and principles were for naught. But even Rick had to admit that politics or not, the fate of the United States hinged on stopping that code from entering the hands of Al-Hanash or any other terrorist. Besides, Darcy admitted that his obsessive fascination with the girl was over, and Rick knew that as far as his cousin was concerned Operation Virginia Reel was a closed case. There was no need to tell him, Charlie, or Caroline that Bennet was as good as dead come next week. There wasn't a damn thing any of them could do about it anyway.

~ ♠ ~

9
Recalculating

Darcy's vintage hog rode into Alexandria for no particular purpose. Ten days had passed since that fateful night when he danced with Liz at the studio, and for some strange reason, he found himself needing to see her just one more time before leaving for Hilton Head, South Carolina to execute Operation Shag.

After his disastrous visit to Pemberley followed by a much welcome and heartfelt stay with Georgiana in Asheville, he acknowledged that he wouldn't be leaving Obsidian any time soon. The mold had already been cast. No longer *that* Fitzwilliam Darcy of Pemberley, he was reconciled to the fact that he would remain the Iceman for the rest of his life. There was no going back. End of story.

The only semblance of his former self emerged when he and Georgiana attended the symphony together. It was something he had promised to do with her the following month but knew he wouldn't be able to commit to the future, so they had taken advantage of the time together they had now.

He had made his decision to head back north, back to the grind and the distraction of killing low-life scum. Before checking in at the dance studio for intel and recon on his next hit, Darcy found himself riding south on Route 1, heading straight for Longbourn. He didn't explore the impetus to see Liz again, but when the motorcycle turned down the picturesque tree-lined dirt road, something felt right.

In the distance, he could make out a large party tent on the front field where white fabric billowed in the air at the four openings of the tent. Flowers and green vines were wrapped around the vertical tent poles of the two peaked structure. Under the tent, elegantly covered tables welcomed guests with towering white and green orchid centerpieces. Crystal and china place settings caught random sunrays streaming through the southern side of the tent.

As Darcy rode closer, he noticed a small gazebo—the type people rent for show—under the towering knobby oak tree in front of the house. The Iceman's frozen heart lurched in his chest and began to thaw. *Today must be her wedding day.*

In stark contrast to his black leather apparel, his heavy biker boots, and the ominous black Harley Davidson, everything was white and innocently elegant. To the observant eye, he looked like one of hell's angels arriving to exact destruction upon the Garden of Eden. Nothing could be further from the truth.

After steering the motorcycle behind the forest's tree line edging of the estate's property, he cut the engine, removed his leather gloves, and walked through the lush green trees, carefully remaining hidden from view. *Just one glimpse. Just one look at her as a bride will be enough to sustain me for a lifetime.* To covet another man's woman, on his wedding day no less, was entirely wrong, and it got under Darcy's skin. However, the groom was a man who harbored his own betrayals. No, that guy didn't deserve such an incredible woman or the respect Darcy found himself unwilling to give him. That man knew full well he was deceiving his bride-to-be.

It was early, and no one had arrived for the wedding yet, so Darcy waited. After all, it was what he did best. Today of all days, he would be patient. His target was one that his heart sought, not his bullet. Leaning his back against a tree, he let the sun hit his face as it streamed through the canopy above. It was a beautiful day with a cool breeze off the river. No clouds would hinder Lizzy's wedding day; he wished that for her. Yet, in his heart, he knew it wouldn't be enough to make her happy that day or any other. The night at the studio, she seemed entirely ambivalent about marrying this man. Darcy had seen that and had come to know her well through her drawings. He couldn't help but wonder if she was being coerced in to this marriage. Why else would she agree to it?

Across the field, within the opposite tree line, his eyes caught a bright yellow movement within the darkened forest of pines. Pulling out mini, high-powered binoculars, he scanned the trees until spotting the interloper. His eyes widened with surprise and dismay at seeing CIA agent Rushworth. Darcy would know that jackass fuck-up anywhere and felt disconcerted in the knowledge that Rushworth's presence meant only one thing: disaster. He went into hyper alert at all the things that could go wrong on Lakmé s wedding day.

Once again, he became the observer, blending in to the trees, clinging to the bark as though a tall pine himself. His eyes grew darker in the presence of possible danger. *What was the CIA here for? Are they watching Bennet or worse, about to execute the hit?* He changed his focus. No longer attentively watching the arrival of each guest, he kept one eye trained on Rushworth at all times. That didn't mean he didn't note the color and model of each car.

He hadn't heard from Rick since that night at Pemberley. His cousin hadn't been around or free to take his calls, so the state of Virginia Reel was unknown, and that concerned him considerably. Could Rick have deliberately avoided his calls? Was he concealing something, given he was well aware of Darcy's attraction to the Bennet woman? It was possible—and likely. Was everyone he trusted destined to be deceitful?

~♠~

Inside Longbourn, Lizzy stood looking at her reflection in her grandmother's floor-length oval mirror. She smoothed the wedding dress and smiled half heartedly at the image looking back.

Walking by the open bedroom door, Thomas noticed her sad countenance and stepped in. He hardly noticed her beauty and therefore said nothing of how lovely she looked or how it was his joy to walk her down the aisle. He was entirely distracted and somewhat inpatient to get on with the proceedings.

Of course Lizzy noticed his preoccupation. She always noticed. With each passing day, as though the veil was being slowly pulled back, it became clearer and clearer that her father was a very selfish and self-absorbed man.

"Ready, Lizzy?"

"Of course!" She feigned a bright smile. "Yes! Of course I'm ready. Well, with the exception of not having anything borrowed I am. Other than that, I am ready."

"Why would you need to borrow anything? Bill will buy you everything *new*. Do you have any concept of what he is worth? You're in good hands, Lizzy Bear. He has promised to spoil you like you deserve."

Lizzy's fingertips bounced on the side of her thigh, and her thoughts drifted off. *Run! Run!*

Her father came to the mirror and rested both hands on her shoulders, his eyes welling with tears. "I'm proud of you. I've never been so proud of you in all my life. You're the best daughter a man could have, and I could not have parted with you for anyone less worthy than Bill Collins."

"Thank you, Daddy. Bill is a good man and will be a good husband. I'm sure I'll be happy."

He kissed her forehead. "I love you, kitten."

"Love you, too. Well, shall we get Jane and go downstairs now?"

Truly feeling as though she would be ill, Lizzy's heart clenched and stomach rolled, but she buoyed herself, remembering Aunt Elinor's words and her father's happiness. She held on tightly to his arm as he escorted her through the bedroom door and down the stairs, resolving that her sacrifice was nothing when faced with the loss of the Bennet legacy.

An hour had passed when Darcy noted Rushworth edging his way through the trees, closer toward the gazebo. He did the same on the opposite side of the field, but the gazebo loomed closer to Rushworth's position.

By now, the guests had assembled. The air was filled with the freshness and newness of happy beginnings. Kisses and smiles of acquaintances new and old were taking place below the mighty oak. Smartly dressed women in beautiful hats took their seats on white folding chairs draped with fabric and flowers.

Darcy smiled slightly at the scene. It was the first smile he made since leaving Georgiana's company two days earlier. This was just the kind of wedding he always thought *he* would have. Acknowledging that it was a strange thought for a guy, he remembered that he had once been a romantic at heart. Just ask Emma Woodhouse.

Cars lined the dirt road leading into the estate. Some drove upon the newly-mowed flat, grassy field. It was no longer the vast weedy, over-grown pasture where he had lain in wait for his kill shot.

Standing as close to the oak as he could get without being noticed, he had a clear view of the little gazebo where the groom stood fixing the best man's bow tie. The white, plastic runner that led the way to the gazebo from Longbourn's front door moved slightly in the breeze. With one eye fixed upon Rushworth, Darcy held his breath in anticipation for the door to open.

The cellist's bow upon his instrument executed the first of eight rep-etitious notes. The baby string quartet grouped beside the gazebo began Pachelbel's "Canon in D" when the door to the house opened.

Jane came through the door first, holding a pink and white nosegay of orchids. Darcy hardly spared at glance at her stunning rose-colored sheath dress and spike heels. He was too busy looking behind her at the vision standing in the open doorway.

Liz stood at the threshold, looking radiant on her father's arm. Time stood still, and Rushworth was all but forgotten. The gay groom was a figment of Darcy's imagination. Instead, it was *he* in his mind's eye, standing in the small gazebo in stunned awe of her elegance and beauty, waiting for her to join *him* in matrimony. He shook his head to clear his mind of such crazy thoughts and reminded himself, *She is probably no different than any other viper.*

She began to walk slowly and resolutely in time to the heavenly cadence of music as it floated in the air. She held a small nosegay of white japhet orchids at her waist. Darcy knew those delicate blooms well. Her hair was coiled and rolled up, displaying the long neck he had so wanted to kiss in the dance studio. Within her chestnut locks, tiny seed pearls and three small white japhet orchids adorned within the weave of her hair behind her ear. The wedding dress was pure femininity and grace, and his heart swelled. Darcy was unsure of everything he felt, but he knew he was experiencing a tenderness he had never before experienced.

He didn't notice the smiles on the faces of the guests as his eyes took in every curve of Lakmé's face, noting that she wore just a small amount of makeup. Or was that her natural blush? She glowed, and her eyes sparkled with effervescence while her smiling lips taunted him. *Fitzwil-liam Darcy, you may kiss the bride, your bride, Elizabeth.*

The summer breeze blew gently, slightly moving the loose tendril at her temple. That small kiss of air upon her porcelain skin was his undoing. His heart rate soared exponentially, and the melody played by the quartet reeled him in. Suddenly, Virginia Reel took on a whole new meaning.

Tearing his eyes from the angelic face that had haunted his dreams, he looked to the groom in the gazebo, a man who looked scared and unsure of his decision. Perhaps, mused Darcy, it was his conscience. He knew personally how difficult it was to deny its existence. The promptings of one's inner voice that spoke of truth and honesty were persistent no matter what. The denial of one's conscience could only be avoided for so long.

In that moment, he hated that man in his grey tuxedo, awaiting a woman who should be another man's wife. Deceit of every kind was Darcy's abhorrence, except of course, when it was his own, and even then, it was in service to his country. In truth, he was a principled man.

Her walk was slow and, in his keen observation, it appeared an unhurried mercy toward her destination. He couldn't help but to wonder if she was about to bolt.

Darcy moved closer to the edge of the tree line in the hope that he could hear her voice when she arrived beside her groom.

In attentive fascination with the bride's beauty and grace, his excellent skills of observation remained focused and captivated on only one thing: the wrong thing. That was how much she spellbound him. At that moment, all the things that made him unparalleled in his career abandoned him. He failed to notice the two most important things taking place around him.

One, Rushworth was screwing the silencer onto his pistol, readying to take out his target, and two, a white van with tinted windows sped down the dirt road toward the house, creating a cloud of dust and debris.

What happened next came without warning, and by the time Darcy reacted accordingly, the nightmare had already advanced, unfolding to the beautiful sound of Pachelbel's canon.

Before Lizzy and her father reached the gazebo, the white van left the dirt road, barreling through the field directly toward them. Its side sliding door was open for easy extraction of their target and, if necessary, gunfire.

Darcy's peripheral vision caught the white movement too late. Within split seconds, the van drove beside bride and father. It abruptly stopped.

Two masked gunmen wearing dark coveralls squatted at the open door.

The screams of the guests filled the air like a murder of crows, and many dropped to the ground in fear. The bride held onto her father tightly. His expression was terrified confusion.

In that same moment, the two agents on opposite sides of the field reacted differently.

Darcy bolted toward Lizzy and her father as Rushworth began to fire at the van. His first shot hit the cellist's instrument. His second shot landed in the wood structure of the gazebo nearly hitting the justice of the peace in the shoulder.

One of the terrorists jumped out of the van and quickly covered Bennet's head with a black hood, grabbed him, and pulled him backward. Lizzy tugged his arm forward, attempting to maintain her hold on him. It was a tug of war for Bennet, and her shouts went unheeded by the abductors, who only had one thing in mind: terror.

Gunfire continued between Rushworth and the second masked man in the van as Bennet was dragged into the vehicle. Screams mixed with gunshots in a hail of bullets flew over and around Lizzy, who was on the verge of being shot within the melee of bullets where she stood unprotected and frozen in fear.

With everything Darcy had in him, in a running leap, he hurled himself upon her. From the impact of his massive frame and their landing upon hard ground, the wind was knocked out of Lizzy, rendering her momentarily unconscious.

He covered her with his body as the shootout continued above their prone figures in the grass until one of the two shooters fired a final unanswered shot.

Rushworth lay dead.

The van door slid closed with Bennet hooded, gagged, and captive within. Tires spun, kicking up grass and dirt, and the terrorists took off as quickly as they had come.

Random gunshots continued to fire from the passenger-side window of the van to keep the wedding guests cowering until the vehicle had made a safe getaway toward an unknown destination.

With Lizzy still below him, Darcy tapped the side of his Bluetooth. Charlie answered.

"Charlie, I need an immediate satellite fix on a white, Dodge panel van, late model, possibly heading north on Route 1 out of Alexandria. Virginia plate number XJ2978."

"Right. Working on it." Charlie sat at his laptop in the dance studio's office, typing in coordinates and information. "What's happened?"

"Virginia Reel. The target, Bennet, has been kidnapped." Darcy looked over his shoulder to see people getting up while the cries continued. "I think Rushworth is dead. Call the authorities. I've got to get the Bennet daughters out of here to a safe zone."

"Bennet daughters? As in Jane and Lizzy Bennet, my students? Jane is the target's daughter?"

"That about sums it up."

"Did you know this at the studio that night?"

"Listen, we can hash this out later. Right now we need to focus on their safety and tracking that van."

Feeling the weight of his body upon her, Lizzy started to come to.

"Later," Darcy said, ending the call to Charlie.

She cried out and pushed against his chest. "What the...Oh God! Daddy? Oh God, they took my father!" Her wedding dress was torn and stained. Long dark tendrils of hair had fallen with orchids askew, and mascara had slightly run from her tears. "Jane! Jane! Where's my sister?"

"Are you hurt?" Darcy worriedly asked, rolling and turning her from side to side as he checked her arms and body for gunshot wounds. In that moment, he really could care less about Bennet and Jane. All he could focus on was Liz.

"No, no...stop...get me up. Please. My father!"

He helped her sit up and then to stand.

She gazed into his dark eyes, suddenly taken aback. "You? You're that guy from the dance school."

He slightly smiled. "Yes." His soul delighted that she remembered him.

She looked to the gazebo to see Jane running toward her, a spike heel slipping sideways in her haste, obviously struggling to keep her footing and get to her sister. Lizzy also noticed how Bill and Jared crouched in the gazebo hugging and holding each other in fear. "He *is* gay," she quietly said in defeat.

"Yes," Darcy solemnly confirmed.

Jane ran to her, and the two embraced and cried, both smoothing the hair surrounding their tear-stained faces. "I'm okay. Are you okay, Sissy?"

Lizzy nodded and looked to the gorgeous guy in leather pacing beside them, listening to someone on the other end of his cell phone. He spoke random words "Safe house...meet you...thirty minutes...sister with us."

Lizzy lifted her chin in his direction. "He saved my life."

"Isn't that the tango biker guy?"

Lizzy nodded, again.

Darcy came to stand before the sisters. "You two have to get to safety. I need to get you both out of here for your own protection. Those men who took your father may well come back for you, or worse. Do you understand what I'm saying? We need to do this before the police arrive and the questions begin."

Jane stood open mouthed as though he was talking Greek. After all, he was a god.

With a hand on her hip and eyes of fire and tears Lizzy asked petulantly, "And who are you to know this? You're just a dance instructor."

Already, he loved her sharp tongue and released spirit. "I'm not a dance instructor, and right now, I'm your only hope for securing your safety and finding your father alive before they kill him. *That's* who I am."

"But it's my wedding day...these people...I have a responsibility."

He bent, locking his eyes with hers as he put his hands on her shoulders. Lakmé's tear-stained face nearly broke his now-melting heart. "Liz, listen to me. Your only responsibility right now is to survive and help me get your father back. Please trust me. I'll protect you."

She looked for direction from Jane, who quickly said, "We trust you."

"Good. Jane, do you have a car?"

Without realizing what he had done, Darcy slid his hand down Lizzy's arm and clasped her trembling hand within his. Neither even noticed that their hands fit perfectly as though meant for each other.

"Yes. My car is around back."

"We'll meet you at the edge of the estate by the mailbox. You'll follow us to someplace safe on U Street. Go! Quickly!"

~♠~

Lizzy turned away from the guests and her fiancé, who was apparently unconcerned for *her* well being and not upset by her father's kidnapping, but instead, almost hysterically focused on his mother and the best man. She looked up at the man holding her hand and instantly realized his determination to protect her and Jane. In that one act of his throwing his body onto hers, he became her knight in shining armor.

With long, fast, purposeful strides and hands still clasped, Darcy led Lizzy through the grassy field into the trees toward his Harley. Behind them, they heard Bill's mother's shrill lament over his bride leaving their wedding with another man. Words such as "foolish" and "headstrong" pierced the chaos. The groom called after her but did not run from his position.

It was crystal clear to Darcy that she had no intention of looking back – either at her life or at her ex-fiancé.

Lizzy ignored Bill's pleas, though the reality of the mistake she had narrowly escaped making had yet to sink in. She was overwhelmed by both the sudden abduction of her father from her grasp as well as the appearance of the tall, dark, and handsome stranger.

With each step, she trailed behind her savior by a pace, bombarding him with questions to which he gave her no answers.

"Who were those men? Why did they take my father? How do you know about this? Who are you? Were you spying on us? Where are you taking us?" Question after question came until they stood before a black motorcycle.

He finally spoke. "Have you ever ridden on the back of a motorcycle before, Liz?"

She shook her head in fear. For all her adventurous inner yearnings, she was fearful when it came to the actual execution. Living balls to the wall was only a temptation, not something she actually had the guts to do. In her fear, she lost her voice and her bravado. The horror of what had just happened cut off her reason and logic.

Finally releasing her hand from his, he placed his helmet on her head. "Hold tight around my waist; put your feet on the foot pegs, and watch out for the exhaust pipe."

He bent down and, through the open shield of the helmet, locked eyes with her again. She had fear written all over her face. His eyes communicated with her soul. He said evenly and calmly, "Don't be scared. If

I turn right, just look over my right shoulder and the same for the left. Your weight will transfer accordingly. Don't lean if we aren't turning. Liz, you can do this."

She nodded, trying to make sense of what he said. Her mind was terribly scrambled and all she could say was, "What…what is your name?"

"Darcy."

"And how do you know mine?"

"I just do," he replied as he straddled the Harley and kick started it. The hog's distinctive, powerful engine and the roar of the exhaust brought the forest to life, sending birds into flight.

Lizzy slightly hiked up her wedding dress to climb on the back of the motorcycle behind him, pressing her body close to his. Hard-core black leather and feminine white lace innocence intertwined.

The moment her arms circled his waist and Darcy noted her stocking-clad knee resting beside him, he felt himself waking up inside. His hand, now gloved, moved to cover her left one resting upon his abdomen. Ignoring the tiny engagement ring, he reassuringly squeezed her fingers and asked calmly, "Ready?"

"Ready."

~♠~

10
Interiors

A Cessna Citation stood at the end of the runway at one of Dulles Airport's four FBOs where private aircrafts and charters left for domestic and international flight destinations.

Inside another van, a grey one, Thomas waited alone. His ears remained attentive, even if his other senses were temporarily restrained. Very rarely, he would hear English spoken, and if he did, it was an engineer or serviceman refueling. Mostly, he heard French and an unusual Arabic language. His linguistic skills were restricted to computer code, so he was at a loss in deciphering origin.

He assumed they were at an airport as loud roars of takeoff were all around him. Yes, they were clearly taking him far away, and he knew why. Hadn't Crawford warned him just last week? Wasn't it obvious what they wanted with and from him? Shuddering, he thought of what may have happened to his daughters once the gunfire commenced at Longbourn. His traitorous act brought this on, and he acknowledge within his heart that it was entirely his fault. The words from *Crime and Punishment* taunted him.

"Surely it isn't beginning already! Surely it isn't my punishment coming upon me? It is!"

He was afraid, very afraid, and with his mouth secured with duct tape, his wrists bound with zip ties behind his back, and his ankles tied as well, the metal floor of the van absorbed his trembling. He knew he would do whatever they asked of him—*anything* to save his life and his girls...if they were still alive.

On the tarmac outside the airplane were the four men who abducted Bennet. Each had discarded their black coveralls in favor of business suits and ties. They worked for one man and one man only, and that man sat drinking champagne aboard the Cessna while awaiting final clearance. He was and embodied Al-Hanash. Translation: the snake.

His classic blue pinstripe Yves Saint Laurent suit, at a cost over 2000 Euros, spoke of style and sophistication, and his manicured fingernails conveyed the meticulous attention he paid to everything in his life.

Suave, fit, and exotically handsome, Devlin Renaud had more money than anyone he knew, and he dallied in business with everyone. As a result, he was untouchable. He wielded power and threats over his rivals for the sole purpose of the game and his own humor. Never a player in politics, which was a fool's folly in his opinion, he only participated to the extent necessary to obtain what he wanted. In a word: everything.

Renaud, whose father was a French diplomat and whose mother was a Moroccan prostitute, made his money the easy way. He began as a simple gun runner. In time, he became the internationally known and feared arms dealer that he was today. Sympathetic to no man, country, or plight, he only used political or religious ideologies as his front. Those who knew him understood he was ruthless in both his business dealings and in dealing out death. Compunction on those two fronts wasn't a word he recognized or respected. He brought both danger and fear into every boardroom or arms deal. There was no terrorist faction or rebel army that could stand against him. He was a cold, calculating, and intelligent king cobra, and death from his venom was feared by all who entered into business dealings with Al-Hanash.

His trusted adviser, Omar, passed through the luxurious fuselage. He carefully straightened his tie then adjusted the ornate ring on his finger, preparing to enter the private study at the back of the plane. It was a ring only Al-Hanash's most loyal servants wore while his underlings wore the distinct cobra on a crescent moon in tattoo form.

"Sir, we are about to load the cargo. A room in the baggage hold has been prepared. Is there anything else you would like me to attend to before our departure?"

Renaud swiveled his Italian leather chair around to face the only man in the world whose opinion he valued *almost* as much as his own. His dark eyes, framed by long black lashes, maintained their usual intensity in all things, yet his laid-back demeanor conveyed something entirely different.

"No. See to it that he is unharmed and cared for. It is a long flight home, and I need him to complete the program upon arrival. Jet lag shouldn't come between him and completion of the code."

Raising a champagne flute, his cobra diamond pinky ring twinkled in the ambient light of the cabin. He drank deeply, savoring the Pernod-Ricard Perrier-Jouet.

"Yes, sir. I will look after him personally."

Renaud sighed and lowered his glass. "I resent traveling across the globe to complete an assignment that sycophant Crawford promised would be accomplished without difficulty. My wife's pregnancy has been very difficult, and to be away causes her a great deal of stress. Crawford will be sorry for his failure."

"And Bennet?"

"He will be sorry for his betrayal. You will kill them both when we have sold the successfully completed virus to the highest-bidding nation."

"I wonder, Mr. Renaud, if Crawford will remain here in the United States? Surely, he will not be too eager to account to you for his failure."

Renaud swirled the last of the champagne in the crystal flute, watching the remaining bubbles float to the top. "I venture he is not, but do not most dogs eventually find their way home with their tails between their legs? We will wait. I am a patient man. It would please me greatly to witness his execution."

"There is something you should know, sir. There was an unexpected shooter present. He was in the trees when he opened fire upon us. Of course, we fired back. Other than the shooter, there were no casualties to my eye, but I was driving. I cannot be sure."

"Most likely CIA or America's redundant, ineffectual Homeland Security. I am sure they have been on to Crawford for some time. No worries; we will be ready. Tighten security around the island when we get back. You are sure the Bennet daughter wasn't killed in the crossfire?"

"Of that I'm positive. Someone came to her aid."

"Good, we may need her as leverage at some point if we can't get

Bennet to cooperate. Thank you, Omar. Excellent work as usual."

The pilot, another one of Renaud's most trusted men, spoke through a small intercom atop the desk formed from solid black onyx. "Mr. Renaud, we have clearance for departure and should arrive in Marrakech in nine hours."

~♠~

The alley behind the safe house on U Street was empty, given that lunchtime had long passed and the dinner hour hadn't yet begun. Besides, it was the Fourth of July weekend, and most people had cleared out of DC to head for the Maryland shore, seeking out sun and surf.

The motorcycle, followed by Jane's restored Camaro, pulled behind the fake store front disguising the first floor of the safe house. Darcy waved Jane to follow him. With the press of a button, a garage door opened, allowing both vehicles entrance. Charlie's Hummer had already arrived.

Lizzy had not had a lot of time to think about the events of the prior ninety minutes. Sitting on the back of that Harley with her arms wrapped around Darcy and the feel of his hard body beneath her hands was overload with what she was already feeling, worrying about her father, the gunfire, and all those guests whom she left on the front lawn. Not to mention, as much as she tried to sequester the feelings of exhilaration she felt while riding fast and furious up the expressway, she couldn't. It was all new and exciting, and she could almost taste her desire for more.

Darcy pulled the bike beside his other Harley and cut the engine, removed his Ray Bans, and turned in his seat to help Lizzy. Lifting the helmet from her, he suppressed a smile at the delightful disarray of her hair. Very gently, without her even realizing what he was about, he plucked the flowers and a couple of pins from her hair, causing it to cascade in waves down her shoulders. In response, she shook out her locks as though feeling free. In doing so, she didn't notice him smell the solitary japhet orchid clutching in his hand.

"Are you okay?" He asked.

She nodded. It seemed to be the only thing she could do around him. His tender attention to her was in direct contrast to his visual persona, and it confused her.

That tenderness was deliberately smothered when his next words came across as stern and almost demanding. "Be careful of the exhaust pipe when you climb off the bike."

Her "okay" was filled with nervous anxiety, and her dismount from the motorcycle caused her legs to become shaky.

Darcy saw and quickly grabbed her hand in support. He couldn't help himself. Disengaging his attraction and emotional pull for her was going to be harder than he thought, but he was damned determined to do so. He had to. It was the only way to protect them both.

Jane stood beside her car, watching the exchange. *Yes, this is exactly what she needs.* "Lizzy, are you okay?"

"I am. And you?"

Jane walked to her sister. "Damn confused by what went down at Longbourn. Who knew that prim and proper Lizzy Bennet's wedding would be so exciting? A real shootout at the Alamo."

"Not funny. Someone *shot* at us and kidnapped Daddy. All those people were terrified and in tears. The least you could do is act worried."

"I *am* worried. I'm just trying to bring a little levity to the situation. Lighten up."

Lizzy bounced her fingers upon her thigh and turned to watch Darcy fiddling in the Harley's saddlebag.

"Who would have ever thought to see you on the back of a Harley Davidson? Did you like it?" Jane inquired.

How could Lizzy tell her sister that she felt simultaneously fearful yet alive? How could she share that Darcy's curls at the collar of his leather jacket drove her mad with desire and that the thrill of pressing herself against him and holding on for dear life was like coming home to a place so seemingly foreign *and* fantastic that it unsettled her immensely yet caused her to rejoice? It was as if the cravings of her long-denied conscience were slowly being fed the very nutrition it required.

She apathetically shrugged her shoulder. "It was alright, too reckless for my blood."

With the slap of Charlie's flip-flop footsteps coming down the staircase toward the garage, the detached Iceman in Darcy took over when he approached the sisters.

"Hate to break up this little reunion, but we have to get you both upstairs."

Charlie flung the stairwell door open and noticed Jane standing tall and pink and looking like a goddess. "Jane!"

"Charlie! What are you doing here?"

"Darcy called me in to assist you." He looked to his friend. "Apparently, he has assigned me to be your bodyguard. What a small world."

Jane looked at him quizzically. *What was so small about it? You both work at the dance school.*

Charlie acting as her bodyguard was altogether intriguing and highly inviting. After their one night stand three days ago, the only person she needed protection from was Charlie himself. The guy was a madman in the sack, empowered like the Energizer Bunny. To date, he was the only one who could give that Tulsa lover a run for his money. She licked her lips in remembrance of what he could do with that magic tongue.

Charlie took Jane's hand and led her toward the stairs.

Darcy frowned, back to being stone-cold and all business. He was Obsidian's most serious agent, and he was back on the op and would not—no he definitely would *not*—be mixing with a woman during the salvaging of Operation Virginia Reel. Too much was at stake here, and the weight of responsibility he felt was overwhelming. It was because of *him* and his blasted conscience that this had occurred. Had he just taken the shot that night, then they never would have found themselves at this juncture. He would make this right and didn't need any outside influence or viper distraction, no matter how she made the blood rush through his veins.

Looking up at Darcy and the severe mien upon his handsome face, Lizzy asked, "Why are you helping us?"

He ignored her, and she was surprised by the disappointment she felt. He was ominous, and she internally chastised herself for wanting to talk to him.

Before ascending the steps behind Jane and Charlie, she put her hand on Darcy's muscular bicep to stop their progress. "Darcy, I…um…thank you. Thank you for protecting me and my sister."

What he wanted to reply was, "No thanks necessary. It's because I feel something for you—because I've come to know you and am falling for you in every possible way." Instead, he tonelessly replied, "Nothing I wouldn't have done for any woman in trouble."

His clipped, hurtful words unexpectedly wounded and mortified her pride. "Any woman? Surely...that can't be true?"

"It is. You needed help. I was there. Nothing more." He hated to say the next words, but he did anyway, not only for her benefit but for his as well. "Look, don't romanticize this, Liz. There is *no* other reason why I came to your aid today. Let's not read things into it or make it into something it definitely isn't. I'm not some altruistic knight in shining armor rescuing a jilted damsel in distress."

She stormed passed him in an indignant huff, promptly taking the steps before him. "Well, it's a darn good thing that I'm not a romantic, Darcy. Contrary to what your ego may believe, I was simply thanking you, not expecting a marriage proposal. Jane and I will try not to overstay our welcome."

Her initial wounded expression gripped his heart. Brought on by his insult, her expression stabbed him as though his heart had been pierced below her spiky high heel.

She turned her back to him and ascended the stairs. Unfortunately for Darcy, his abrupt, hurtful words and his reason for voicing them did nothing to stem the tide of regret for deliberately hurting her feelings. Nor did they convince his body's natural reaction when the curves of her waist and backside before him tempted his hands to caress her. He was besotted, and it would take every bit of his strength to remain impassive.

In Lizzy's opinion, the apartment she entered was a masculine space filled with cold stainless steel, blacks, and grays touched by red accents A state-of-the-art flat screen, wall-mounted TV, black leather seating, and fully stocked bar were every modern guy's wet dream, and strangely, it appealed to her. It was a direct contrast to her home and life at Longbourn. There wasn't a musty old antique within sight, not one faded photograph or a dried flower arrangement decaying beneath a dusty glass dome, and thankfully, no furniture stuck in the time warp of the seventies. The apartment looked new and clean and modern. She unconsciously ran her index finger over the smoky-glass console table situated in the hallway below a hard edge abstract painting. That, too, felt cool and menacing. In her presumption, she understood why this was Darcy's apartment.

"You ladies will want to freshen up, I imagine. You've had quite a morning," said Charlie, looking at Lizzy's torn wedding dress. "This room here is comfortable, and there is a bathroom for your privacy. You may be here for a while until we sort all this out, so please, make yourselves at home."

Walking into an ivory and russet colored room, it was clear it was a woman's bedroom. Charlie opened a dresser drawer and the closet door in invitation. "This is my sister Caroline's room. You met her at the dance studio. Feel free to make use of anything in here: her clothes, cosmetics, whatever you need. She won't mind in the least."

"Thank you, Charlie," said Jane, elbowing Lizzy out of her distracted stupor.

"Yes, thank you. We really appreciate your kindness."

The moment he closed the door separating the men from the women, two conversations immediately commenced.

"This is creepy, Jane."

"What are you talking about, creepy? Charlie is not creepy, and I trust him implicitly. We had sex, you know. Mind-blowing sex."

Lizzy rolled her eyes. "Gee, there's a surprise. See, conversations always come back to your overactive sex life."

"I'm only telling you so you understand how much I trust him."

"Not every guy you have sex with is trustworthy. What I meant was, what was that Darcy guy doing at my wedding? Didn't that strike you as weird? Or were you just focused on his thighs when he threw himself on top of me?"

"I think you're over thinking this. The question in your mind should be who took Dad and why."

Jane began to rifle through the dresser drawers, removing two pairs of jeans and two T-shirts. "I'm not about to look a gift horse in the mouth. If Charlie, or Darcy for that matter, thinks we are in trouble, then I would rather have two men like them protecting us than you and I attempting to go it alone. Just because I work in the spy museum doesn't mean I know the first thing about this sort of thing."

"And they do? They're just a couple of guys who work at a dance school. Heck, we don't even know *why* we need protection or from whom." Lizzy bowed her head and looked down at her clasped hands. In a small voice filled with shame and embarrassment, she admitted, "You were right, you know."

Jane smiled, nodding knowingly. "About Darcy's thighs and his attraction to you?"

"No! Not Darcy's thighs and especially not his non-existent attraction.

He made that clear enough in the garage. I meant that you were right about Bill being gay."

"Here, put these on." Jane tossed a pair of Lucky blue jeans and a peach colored T-shirt onto the bed. She turned Lizzy and unzipped the wedding dress to help lift it over her head.

"Of course I was right. If there's one thing I know, I know sex, and I knew he wasn't going to be having it with you. I thought you would eventually figure it out. Of course, I figured it would be on your wedding *night*, certainly not in the midst of a shootout and kidnapping on your wedding day."

"Am I so pitiful that only a gay man would want me as his...what did you call it? His mustache?"

Jane laughed. "Beard, Lizzy. You would have been his beard."

"Whatever! He deceived me in every way. Why would he be so selfish and lie about something like that—to pretend to love me and let me commit my life to him as his wife?"

"Why? Because he is probably afraid to come out of the closet. Maybe he sensed your willingness for a marriage of convenience and thought it wasn't so much of a deception. I don't know why you feel so affronted. I thought you were practical, dear sister? I thought you weren't a romantic?" Jane raised a questioning eyebrow.

Yeah, good questions. I thought so, too.

"As for you being pitiful, you're hardly that. Just ask Darcy out there, particularly after he sees you in those jeans."

"He probably has already seen these jeans on the real owner. I'm sure this is his apartment and he lives here with the owner of the dance studio. For all your protestations about his wanting me, perhaps you can explain why he lives with another woman."

"You're jumping to conclusions, Lizzy. We don't even know these people. Maybe they're just roommates. Anyway, I thought you weren't interested?"

Lizzy snorted a laugh, looking into the mirror. "I'm *not* interested, and you're right, we *don't* know these people." She turned this way and that, looking at her reflection and how the jeans fit. "They feel weird."

"I'm sure they do. You're not used to wearing anything other than your underwear on your hips. They fit you nicely."

Lizzy couldn't help but wonder at Darcy's reaction. Strangely, she wanted to make him eat his insulting words and ram his cold-hearted attitude down his throat with a Lucky fist.

While Jane changed her clothes and Lizzy used the bathroom, Darcy and Charlie hid behind closed doors in the office at the other end of the apartment.

Wearing tan cargo pants and a vintage Grateful Dead concert T-shirt, Charlie stood drinking a Yoo-Hoo chocolate drink, gaping at his friend. "Darcy, this is unbelievable. I still can't get over the fact those two women are the daughters of Virginia Reel."

"I couldn't believe it myself when Liz walked into the studio."

"So you saw her at the house then?"

Darcy slammed back the small amount of Jack Daniels at the bottom of the glass tumbler. "Yeah."

"She's the reason you didn't take the shot, isn't she?"

"Yeah."

"If you knew she was getting married and that she was the daughter of Virginia Reel, then what were you doing at Longbourn today?"

"Putting to bed more demons. It didn't quite work out as I planned. Damn! I screwed this whole thing up. I knew it, Charlie. I knew the minute I was laying in that field that this op was bad luck. Every fucking time a woman is involved in anything in my life, it comes to no good."

"If you want to keep telling yourself that, go ahead, but if you ask me, this is fate."

With a skeptical look on his face, Darcy eyeballed his friend. "How do you figure that? I got Bennet kidnapped, and I put the nation in the worst security risk ever. Because of that, his daughters will most likely become targets should Bennet grow a conscience and not cooperate...all because I didn't take the shot! If I had just taken that shot..."

"Either way, Bennet's fate was going to hurt his family. The way I see it is you have become infatuated with that girl, and she just may be your ticket out of that personal prison you have trapped yourself in since Steele's betrayal."

The look on Darcy's face confirmed Charlie's suspicion: Iceman had fallen hard and fast.

"What do you want to do, Darcy?"

"I need for you to watch over the women when I go after their father. Perhaps Rick will have some intel that could point me in the direction of Al-Hanash. He's been itching for a way to stick it up Bertram's ass since Bertram began trying to find ways to stick it up Obsidian's. Finding

Bennet means finding Al-Hanash without the agency's involvement. If my hit can take out the terrorists' leader on his turf, then Bertram will never mess with us again."

"I hope you know what you are doing. Are you sure that you don't want me along?"

"No, you're the only one I trust to protect them effectively. Caroline would let her jealousy get in the way of safeguarding Liz. You saw her that night at the dance studio. She was ready to strike and kill, and Rick's mind and body is so wrapped up with Caroline, I fear he might lose his objectivity. I know my cousin; he's loyal to his woman to a fault."

"You might need to call in some favors from your SEAL days, especially if you are headed to the Middle East rogue and alone."

Darcy ran his hand over his chin in deep concentration as he paced the office. "I think I need to speak with Liz first and see if she knows anything that may point us in the right direction. Rick and the SEALs are my last resort."

"What are you going to tell them—the girls? For Christ's sake, they probably think you are a dance teacher. Are you going to tell them the truth—the truth about Obsidian?"

"We're professional assassins, Charlie. We lie for a living. I'm certainly not going to start telling the truth now, especially since I was hired to kill their father. You may feel compunction to do so, but I certainly don't. The less Liz and her sister know about what you and I really do for a living, the better. I'll make up something believable."

"And what about what you feel for Liz?"

"I haven't admitted to feeling anything. Even if I did, it is negligible. I can't allow myself ever to become involved again. It's just not going to happen."

"Then just take her to bed, and release this tension you have, and just give in to the fun of the moment."

Darcy looked aghast. "As tempting as she is, Charlie, I would never use Liz like that. A woman like her deserves more than anything I could ever offer. Then again, her tongue is so razor sharp when she's intimidated that she's probably as venomous as your sister. All the more reason to stay away. You know my dislike of vipers."

~♠~

11
Breaking News

The office door opened to reveal Lizzy and Jane standing in the middle of the living room. One sister held the TV's remote control, and the other one rested her hand on her curvy, tightly jean-clad hip. Darcy's mouth went slack, and he stopped dead in his tracks at the sight of Lizzy's pear-shaped ass staring back at him. Caroline's T-shirt was just a bit too small for her, inching up in the back, exposing the indentations of her body to his lustful, hell-bent-on-denying eyes.

Charlie looked to him and snickered. *Negligible my ass.*

The news blared on the TV, and Longbourn was the subject. Police, firemen, ambulances, and emergency crews were spread out on the great field. A news crawl traveled across the bottom of the huge flat screen TV. Ticking by, it read: Breaking News—Massive shooting at Longbourn Plantation House in Mount Vernon during wedding—Bride and father kidnapped; Two guests wounded, one dead.

Lizzy's other hand covered her mouth in shock and dismay while she watched the flashing red emergency lights of the police vehicles circle in the background. The on-scene female news reporter stood on the bottom step of the gazebo under Bennet Oak interviewing Bill. Alternating her microphone back and forth the interview filled the flat screen.

"Is it true that today was your wedding day?" asked the reporter.

"Yes, this is just terrible, just terrible. I don't know what happened.

One minute Elizabeth was walking toward Jared and me, and the next minute, her father was grabbed and thrown into the back of a filthy white van."

"Was the Bennet family involved in anything criminal to have brought this on?"

"No. The condition of the estate might have angered many of the locals, but the Bennets are good people. I certainly would not have married into a family that would bring shame and scandal upon my future enterprise."

The reporter chuckled. "Enterprise? Do you consider your nuptials an enterprise?"

"Of course not! I mean the Longbourn Country Inn that will be opening in six months. With the restoration of the plantation, Jared, Elizabeth, and I will be opening a bed and breakfast. Until she is returned with Mr. Bennet, I will remain here at the estate and begin our dream. The first thing we plan on doing is to install shelves within these old closets."

"Elizabeth is a school teacher in the area isn't she? Would you consider this a school-related shooting? Perhaps one of her students went crazy?"

"No, no...Elizabeth teaches kindergarten. All her students love her. She would make a wonderful mother, although we don't plan on having any children."

Darcy and Charlie came to stand beside the women as Lizzy pulled the remote from her sister's hand.

"I've heard enough of this sh—stuff." She shut off the television.

Jane furrowed her brow. "Lizzy? Is it true that you were going to turn Longbourn into a bed and breakfast?"

"Of course not!" Lizzy sat down on the black leather sofa, propped her elbows on her knees, and cradled her head in her hands. "Could this day get any worse? Now my gay ex-fiancé is going to live in my house and turn it into a B&B while I'm hiding in some Hell's Angel's apartment in the gay part of town."

Darcy sat in the club chair beside her, and Charlie headed to the kitchen to prepare something for everyone to eat. He was considerate like that, knowing the women were most likely hungry and thirsty from their long day and this ordeal. He had spent enough time with the opposite sex to understand them acutely, unlike Darcy, who forged right ahead with his questioning, seemingly oblivious to the tumult of emotions Lizzy was experiencing.

"Liz, I know you are trying to digest what transpired today, but I need to ask you a couple of questions so that Charlie and I can help you."

Gone was the amiable Lizzy of old. Her repressed snarky alter-ego, the side she now thought of as Liz, emerged. "Really? And how can two *dance instructors* help us with the apparently orchestrated theft of our home, the fact that I found out the man I was seconds away from marrying was not only gay but never had any intention of giving me children, not to mention the horrific kidnapping of my father in a hail of bullets under the Bennet oak tree? We should be talking to the FBI not the BDS. How the heck are you going to help us? What, you're going to teach us to waltz?"

Darcy tried to suppress a smile at her courage and the clever acronym for Bingley Dance Studio, but he couldn't. "Funny...BDS...clever and funny, and I don't waltz. Tango, fox trot, and rumba, but I hate the waltz."

She gave him one of those mockingly fast, fake smiles she usually gave Jane whenever they bantered.

"I'm not a dance instructor. I'm actually...um...CIA, and so is Charlie."

Liz sobered, immediately straightening her posture at his proclamation.

Her eyes traveled to the tattoo wrapping around his muscular, bronzed bicep at the same time as Jane's eyes raked up, down, and over Charlie's bent body looking into the refrigerator.

CIA? Now, that was new, Jane mused. She'd slept with firemen, computer programmers, translators, politicians, race car drivers, and a myriad of other interesting professions but never a spy! She subconsciously licked her lips at the sight of the sway of his hips when he dug deeper into the lower recesses of the refrigerator.

"CIA?" Liz asked slowly.

Darcy could tell from her expressive eyes that she believed him. He wondered if it was the serious tone in his voice or if it was that Charlie didn't contradict him?

"Yes." He cleared his throat. "We've been investigating some suspicious events that have been going on within the Department of Defense computer lab and the possible sale of software to an enemy of the United States."

"Wait. Are you implying that Daddy may be a traitor? My father? Impossible."

Jane spoke in Darcy's defense. "He's not implying anything. Clearly, Dad was taken for a reason, Lizzy. Let's just listen to what he has to say."

Liz challenged, "An investigation? Is that why you were at my wedding today and why you were at the dance school? Was that a coincidence, or were you spying on me there as well?"

Charlie sheepishly looked away, and Darcy held her stare and replied calmly. "The dance school was a coincidence."

That was true, but because he was a skilled liar, she was none the wiser when he added, "As for your wedding, yes, I was there as part of the investigation. One of our agents was shot during the stakeout. We were trying to identify anyone who may be involved in the theft. Do you know if your father was working on anything or with anyone outside of the Pentagon?"

"Of course. He is always freelancing with different computer jobs so he can make some extra money to restore Longbourn, but he was working on one particular project with a co-worker of his for a deadline last week. Surely, you can't be implying—"

"Yes, I'm implying just that," Darcy replied stone-faced before she could finish her sentence.

Charlie placed a large platter of cheeses, salami, hummus, and pita before them on the coffee table. "Do you know the co-worker's name?"

"Henry, Henry Crawford."

Darcy rubbed his forehead. Yes, he had heard that name before from Rick two weeks ago. He was Al-Hanash's inside man.

"You look as if you know that name."

"I do. He may be our link to finding your father."

"I never liked him. We won't find Daddy through him though. He left the country this morning. He tried to get me to go with him to Monte Carlo." Liz snorted. "As if I'd go anywhere with that creep."

Darcy wondered what in her estimation constituted a "creep." *Does she think I'm one as well?*

His eyes couldn't help but travel over the tight peach T-shirt and the body below it. He secretly wished she would go every place and any place with him. For days now, he had imagined her fire and what her flame was like. He wondered about the spirit that battled below her proper exterior and the sketches within her book. However, in person, Liz's courageous challenges and her refusal to reconcile her curiosity easily with his curt responses did something to him. She was more than a beautiful face with a gorgeous body, and she was more than a woman who held her secrets and yearnings concealed. He had met his match; she was his equal. She was the elusive rare serpentine, and his warning bells continued to ring loudly.

He couldn't help but ask, "And why is that? Why wouldn't you go anywhere with him?" It wasn't a question that he asked in order to glean intel. It was a question for his own edification. *What the hell are you doing, Darcy? Stop this. Back. A. Way.*

Liz's hazel eyes locked with his like they had on the dance floor. Charlie and Jane ceased to exist in the room. Her heart rate sped up. She was no dummy. She perfectly understood the undertone of his question. Apparently, he wasn't so immune to her after all, and truthfully, she delighted in it.

"I wouldn't go with him because his intentions were to use me, and I won't be used by *any* man. I don't sleep around and would only sleep with a man if my heart was engaged."

"Yet you allowed yourself to be used by your fiancé."

Jane and Charlie watched the interaction as if silently watching a tennis match, with heads switching from one opponent to the other. Of course, Jane saw right through Liz's lie. She had allowed her father to use her for years. Finally, Charlie took Jane's hand and led her from the room. Yeah, that was fine by her. She knew where her sister and Darcy would eventually end up: in bed.

Darcy leaned forward in his chair, eagerly awaiting Liz's reply, hiding his smirk behind an impassive face. He deliberately pushed her buttons, hoping to see more of that fiery passion.

Taking the bait, she stammered her defense. "I...I was blinded by... practicality and persuasion. I misunderstood his true intentions!"

"Willfully misunderstood, if you ask me. You clearly ignored your own common sense."

The smirk on his face and the mockery in his tone might just as well be directed toward himself. She hadn't a clue that he did the same on a daily basis. His natural instinct to act the romantic and express sensitive emotions were things he long denied himself until her.

She stood before him, her hands gripping her hips. The flash in her eyes delighted him, and he was completely turned on by her anger, having deliberately provoked her. Her courage had certainly risen to the occasion.

"I didn't willfully misunderstand anything! I knew exactly *why* I was marrying, just maybe not *whom*. Longbourn and my father needed me, and I was tired of waiting!"

Darcy couldn't help himself. He stood inches from her, staring down at her luscious lips and eyes of fire, even as the alarm within him warned: *Danger! Danger! Danger!* He did the unthinkable, bending to her ear and speaking seductively, "Waiting for what?"

How could she say what her soul was screaming out? How could she possibly express to this magnetic, tattooed stranger that he did things to her in places that had never come alive before? How on earth could she possibly speak the words that were on the tip of her tongue? *Waiting to feel like you make me feel.*

She tilted her head upward, their lips now only inches apart as their eyes locked, reading each other's unspoken words, desires, and needs.

Darcy's lips seemed to move a tiny bit closer to hers, and she thought he would kiss her. Liz didn't flinch but strained her chin toward him just slightly in tentative reply. She wanted him to kiss her more than anything. The feeling was too strong, and she couldn't deny it, wanting to ignite the passion and electricity humming between them.

A second before the desiring yet hesitant touch, Darcy suddenly broke away from her before their crashing, needing hearts met.

He left her standing in the living room, flushed and feeling as if she melted into a puddle. All she heard of his retreat was the slamming of the office door and the rhythmic beat of the slamming heart within her breast. Both sounded remarkably similar to the reverberation of his Harley's exhaust that night at the dance studio when he drove away.

~♠~

Outside of Ocean City, Maryland, an hour away from U Street, Rick stood in his gourmet kitchen, wearing a pristine white chef's apron. The sound of crashing waves beyond the deck of his beach house was drowned out by the events broadcast on the television within.

The large TV above his fireplace in the connecting great room stole all his attention from the chicken cacciatore he was preparing. Caroline sat at the counter with a glass of pinot grigio, focused on the news as well. Rick stood immobilized, grasping the TV remote in one hand and a pepper mill in the other as both watched the news reporter with mouths agape.

"That's...that's..."

"Darcy," finished Rick, raising the volume.

The reporter continued with her narration. "Witnesses and this home video confirm that suddenly out of nowhere this man threw himself onto the bride, protecting her from the storm of gunfire around her."

"What the heck was he doing at Longbourn with that Bennet woman anyway? Operation Virginia Reel was supposed to be completed almost two weeks ago." asked Caroline.

"I have no fu—stinking idea what he was doing there, but I'm damned sure going to find out." Rick was madder than blazes watching the news as they repeatedly looped the newly released home video taken by a wedding guest. There, captured on film, in all its fresh innocence and set to the romantic notes of Pachelbel's canon, the beautiful bride held onto the arm of the unknowing target as they walked along the white runner toward the gazebo. Suddenly, the target was seized, gunfire ensued, and the subsequently newly nicknamed "Hero of the Bride" tackled the target's daughter to protect her from getting shot.

Over and over, the special news bulletin showed Darcy leaping into the air like Superman and crashing into the bride, covering her with his full body, making sure not an inch of her was vulnerable to gunshot.

Rick slammed the pepper mill onto the marble counter and reached for his cell phone.

Behind the closed door of the study, Darcy recognized his cousin's distinct ring tone: ZZ Top's "Sharp Dressed Man."

He rolled his eyes. "Great, *this* is all I need right now."

Picking up the phone, he deadpanned it. "Yes?"

In a mock Ricky Ricardo Cuban accent, Rick said, "Darcyyy, you've got some 'splainin' to do."

"About?"

With shouts that could be heard in Cuba, Rick let loose, causing

Darcy to hold the phone away from his ear.

"About what, you ask! About your face being plastered all over the news, that's what! About you showing up at Virginia Reel when I distinctly told you to lay low! About you interfering in the CIA's scheduled hit! About you getting involved with that girl who you swore to me was nothing more than an infatuation you would never see again! And there you are all over the news playing superhero for the camera! Do you have any idea what kind of heat I am going to get from Bertram on this? Do you? Do you Darcy! He is hell bent on destroying Obsidian, and you gave him the perfect justification."

"First off, you never told me to lay low, and if you had answered any of my phone calls, I would have told you where I was headed. Secondly, it is *you* who failed to tell *me* that the agency was proceeding with the hit on Bennet using none other than that jackass Rushworth. While I concede I may have put the events of today in motion by failing to do the job in the first place, you cannot make me the fall guy for this fuckup, Rick."

"No, I'm not going to, but Bertram will. His agent is dead for God's sake."

"Yeah, because he was a poor shot, not because I protected Liz from getting killed on her wedding day, Cousin. The damn CIA intended to kill her father on her wedding day right before her eyes!"

"Be that as it may, you absconded with a material witness to the kidnapping, and now everyone most likely thinks you are the kidnapper. They have you on film holding her hand and escorting her from the scene of the crime. Now I have to face Bertram and ask him to stop his attack dogs from hunting you down. Didn't you think, Darcy?"

"No! I didn't think! I reacted. I reacted to her needing protection that only I can give her. You would have done the same if it were Caroline."

Rick hung his head and breathed deeply. It was clear Darcy felt something for this Miss Bennet. "Where is she now?"

"Here at the safe house with her sister and Charlie."

"The safe house? Oh, c'mon, you're killin' me, Darce."

"There's more. She's confirmed the connection between Crawford and Bennet. Crawford has left the country for Monte Carlo. I'm going after him. He'll lead me to Bennet and ultimately, Al-Hanash."

Darcy didn't expect to hear it, and certainly, Rick didn't plan to do it, but he reacted, too. The pepper mill smashed against the sliding glass doors of the kitchen with such force that it cracked the thick tempered glass straight across the center. "No!"

Caroline jumped off the counter chair in fright. She had never witnessed calm, cool Rick so angry before, but hell, she was angry, too. Darcy had just thrown his body onto another woman.

"Yes, I'm going! And when you get in touch with Bertram, I want him to e-mail me the encrypted file of whatever intel and photographs he has of Crawford, and I want everything the CIA has on Al-Hanash. This is one operation that I *will* take full responsibility for."

Rick sighed. "Why are you doing this? Leave this to the CIA. You're not a spy. You're an assassin."

"Because this is *my* responsibility, and my killing Al-Hanash and returning Bennet to face true justice in the legal system is the only way to get Bertram off Obsidian's back."

"Bullshit, you're doing this for the girl."

Surprisingly, it felt good for Darcy to say it, "Yes, I am. I'm doing it for the girl. As you and Charlie so astutely pointed out, I'm head over heels infatuated with her."

After an hour spent tracking Crawford's flight plan using the FAA's database and booking his own first class flight to Nice, France, Darcy made hotel and car arrangements through one of his many international contacts. He continued to hide from Liz, sequestered in the office until cooling down from both the heat of his cousin's phone call and the heat of Liz's nearness. Finally, he exited the office and went in search of her.

With the exception of the click, click, click of the fast-rotating ceiling fan above the sofa, the only other thing his acute hearing detected was Jane and Charlie's moans of passion coupled with the slamming of the headboard in the bedroom designated for the men of Obsidian. Darcy rolled his eyes. *Bad idea calling Charlie in on this.*

"Liz?" He called out.

No answer.

He walked down the hallway. "Miss Bennet?"

Nothing.

He entered Caroline's bedroom. "Liz, are you in here?"

Nada. Not even her wedding dress remained.

She was gone.

Bolting down the garage steps, he barreled through the door only to find that Jane's Camaro was missing and the garage door left open.

"Damn!" He pressed the door button to shut it and raced back up the stairs two at a time.

With a loud, tight fist Darcy pounded on Charlie's door. "Enough, lover boy! Liz is gone!"

Charlie opened the door, attempting to tie his robe around his body. His blond locks were in disarray, and his lips swollen and red. Jane sat in the middle of the bed with the covers pulled up over her chest. Her lips and hair looked very similar to her lover's.

"What happened? You were supposed to be watching her, Darce. I'm watching Jane, and you're watching Liz, right?"

Jane called from behind Charlie, "If she's left, there is only one place where she went. You'll want to get there before she decides to confront Bill. She's been a ticking time bomb for about two years now, and I imagine she's reached her Miss Congeniality threshold."

Darcy knew where she was. Hell, didn't he do the same thing by running to Pemberley? "Is she at the greenhouse?"

"Yeah. How do you know about her greenhouse?"

He didn't answer but noted how Jane wasn't in any rush to run after her sister. "Don't you want to go with Charlie to get her? I've got an international flight to make in three hours."

She gave a half smile. "No, I think my sister would actually respond better to you."

"Sure, if you mean that she'll most likely run in the opposite direction."

Jane chuckled softly, closed her eyes, and lay back on the bed. She pulled the blankets over her head. "Charlie, come back to bed."

Charlie smiled wickedly and slammed the bedroom door in Darcy's face.

"Great. Fantastic." He grabbed the keys to his new Harley V-Rod Destroyer, figuring it was as good an opportunity as any to open it up on the highway and push it to its limits. He had to get to Liz before either the press, police, or terrorists got a hold of her on Longbourn's property. Thankfully, it was growing dark, and many of the curiosity seekers and photographers would be gone.

Liz parked Jane's Camaro at the end of the dirt road that ran beside a neighboring plantation. Driving by the estate's unpaved entrance, she had noticed a myriad of police still investigating as well as some remaining news vans with their satellite antennae raised for round-the-clock reporting on the big event of the day. Never mind the early Independence Day fireworks along the Chesapeake Bay deserving the coverage, the Longbourn Mount Vernon kidnapping was the top news headline story.

Walking through the woods along the shoreline of the river, Liz saw the plantation house come into view through the trees. Every light was switched on. Clearly, Bill—her lying, gay ex-fiancé—had already become a squatter.

The house would be Liz's second destination, where she was going to wholeheartedly kick his sorry, closeted ass into the hedgerow below the first floor window. Her first stop was the greenhouse. The sun had just set, and the shades were still drawn inside the hothouse. She didn't turn on the small grow lamp resting beside her drawing pencils and the cassette radio. It was dark and comforting and the only place where she felt the peace needed after the distressing day she'd had. All she wanted to do was crawl into a ball in the corner of her sanctuary and go to sleep. Maybe in the light of day, she would realize it was all a dream. Of course, she didn't want *all* of the memories of the day to disappear, but certainly most of them.

Her footsteps were slow and deliberate upon the concrete floor so as not to be seen from the outside.

Suddenly, without warning, a large hand appeared from behind and covered her mouth. Liz's eyes went wide with fear.

She hadn't noticed the news reporter surveying the property beside the west wall, looking for his next big scoop, but the tall man inside the greenhouse behind her had immediately noticed.

"Don't move or scream." Darcy whispered into her ear. "We're not alone."

She turned her head slightly and looked over her shoulder into his dark eyes and then closed hers in defeat. *Damn!*

He loosened his grip and spoke low again. "Surely you knew I'd come after you. It's not safe here."

Jerking herself from his grasp once the reporter moved toward the tree line, she ground out through clenched teeth, "How did you know about my greenhouse?"

"Jane told me. C'mon. We have to go back to DC where it's safe."

"No. This is my house, and I'll be darned if he's going to take it over."

"You're not listening to me. The people who took your father will come for you. *Here*. Do you understand that? You need to be hidden and protected by Charlie."

"Not you?"

"No, I'm leaving on a flight to Nice in two hours. I'm going to get your father."

"Then…then…I'm coming with you!"

"No…you're staying out of harm's way in the safe house with your sister."

"You said *you* would protect me."

"I did, and Charlie will do just that. What did you think? One ride on a Harley makes you tough enough to become a CIA agent? I don't think so; I'm sorry, but you're staying right here."

"No…*I'm* sorry, Darcy, but you said that *you* would protect me, not Charlie, who apparently will have his hands full with my sister."

"Stop this. I can't travel across the globe, save your father, and safeguard you from harm if you are there next to me. It's dangerous." *You're dangerous.*

Liz wasn't entirely sure why she did it, most likely denying the real reason, but when she placed her hand on his chest with the intent of manipulating what she thought could be his attraction to her, she nearly came undone herself.

Flirtatiously, she asked, "Why? Don't you want me next to you? Is it because of your girlfriend, Caroline?"

Darcy was slightly amused, thinking her jealous. "No. She's not my girlfriend. She's also an agent."

Her palm smoothed over his hardened nipple, and he stammered in response, "I…I…don't want anything to happen to you. Coming with me is *not* an option."

In the dark, she moved closer to him, pressing her body flush against his. Her pale, scanty T-shirt did nothing to hide her arousal, particularly when she pressed her breasts against his hard chest. Her hand slid up his pectoral, her fingers threading into the curls at the back of his neck, playfully fingering them with delight.

Liz felt his arousal come alive at her hip when his arm wrapped around her waist, sliding down her backside to pull her further onto him. God, he felt and smelled so good. She didn't want to stop the feeling of intense excitement that contact with him elicited in her, but that was not the purpose of this teasing demonstration of hers.

Standing on her tiptoe, she seductively whispered into his ear, "I'm *coming*. I want to come *with* you. You can protect me best if you and I are joined at the hip."

Darcy smirked. Oh, she was good. *Very* good. The *perfect* viper. *Should I kiss her now or play her game?* Truth was, he was about three seconds away from ripping off her clothes and making love to her on the damn plant bench. It was a good thing for them both when she pulled away suddenly and smiled demurely, only after the palm of her hand "accidentally" slid slowly down his very large, thick arousal. Yes, he thought he would die when she did that.

And so did she.

His eyes bore into hers, and he saw exactly what he hoped to see. Her hazel greens were dilated and dark, filled with passion and desire. They sparkled with life and electricity. He was galvanized, and it was his final ruination when she gently bit her bottom lip and artfully played coy. Then, she raised *that* eyebrow.

"Fine, Liz. You can come with me."

~ ♠ ~

12
Accommodations

The overnight Swiss Air flight to Nice was packed solid, but that didn't affect Darcy. Up in first class, after a gourmet meal, he stretched out in his private armchair cabin.

The stewardess was particularly attentive to the handsome man traveling alone. Her eyes repeatedly raked over him. That snake tattoo on his forearm, visible below his rolled up sleeve, held her rapt attention. If he so much as moved, she came rushing to his every need. "What can I get you, Mr. Darcy? Would you care for another whiskey, Mr. Darcy? Another pillow? Is your internet connection sufficient?"

He would smile politely and answer in his usual monosyllabic manner. On this trip in particular, he was in no mood for the sycophantic behavior of a horny flight attendant.

Before sleep and with eight hours remaining on the ten-hour flight, Darcy needed to get to work. His mind hummed with adrenaline at what lay ahead. Operation Cancan, the stupid name coined by Caroline, had begun. Only this time, taking lives coincided with saving lives. The weight of responsibility was nearly suffocating. He hit the Bluetooth, which housed his travel music, and found the song that best reflected his mood. No, tonight was not rock or heavy metal. Tonight was opera. Surprisingly, opera had somehow re-entered his playlist.

As the voice of Maria Callas singing Puccini's aria "O mio babbino caro" filled his head, Darcy slid the window shade up to peer out at the black sky. The only thing he could discern was his own thoughtful expression gazing back at him from the vague reflection in the weathered Plexiglas. He was thinking of Liz. *I bet she likes this aria*. He smiled slightly to himself and thought of her insistence on entering Longbourn after their near kiss in the greenhouse.

The way she had stealthily maneuvered to the backdoor of the house from the orchid hothouse was certifiably expert. She had skills. The way she had confronted Bill and Jared all on her own as he held back to look for clues within her father's study was audacious. She had spirit. Her authoritative style was uncannily similar to his own when she ordered both men from the dwelling post haste. She had command. Yes, Liz Bennet was no longer "Lizzy." It was clear to him that she was taking back part of her life.

Her visit back at the safe house while he gathered his gear and luggage was brief and unemotional. Jane seemed to understand exactly what was going on. Apparently, she thought Liz's leaving with him was the cataclysmic event she had prophesied: Liz was running away.

Darcy was stunned and impressed by Liz's matter of fact, disconnected proclamation of "I'm going to France with Darcy. I'll call you when we arrive in Monte Carlo." She was beginning to think like an operative, and for a split second, he thought that bringing her along could be a good thing. After all, she knew Crawford, and Crawford was infatuated with her. *Seems as though everyone is.*

He actually thought that maybe Liz could be an asset to the mission. There, staring out of the airplane's small window, he wondered if he was rationalizing his rash decision to bring her, not just to protect her, but more because his awakening heart yearned to be near this woman.

He slid the privacy wall up to decode and review the encrypted intel that Rick had begrudgingly—not to mention angrily—sent him. Just as he finished with the covert data and lowered the wall, the flight attendant returned. She bent low to his ear, and Darcy caught the trace of Chanel No. 5 below her tied neck scarf.

The stewardess whispered with an air of disdain, "There is a woman in *economy* asking for you."

He faintly smiled. Liz was asking for him.

"Should I tell her that you are sleeping, Mr. Darcy?"

"No, Cynthia. I'll take care of it myself. Thank you."

When he stood, his presence filled the first class cabin. For the first time in well over a year, he had chosen to wear a stylish pair of Hugo Boss charcoal trousers and a deep-grey dress shirt. His black Magnanni oxford shoes showed off his size twelve foot beautifully. He couldn't explain the reason behind his choice of apparel. Gone was the dark, brooding, biker image, and gone were the heavy motorcycle boots, the black jeans, and leather. In their place stood a wealthy, sophisticated, and fashionable Adonis.

Cynthia's mouth watered at the view when he arched his back in a stretch.

Walking through business class and finally arriving at the curtain into economy, Darcy's eyes immediately found Liz curled into a ball, hugging the wall of the airplane. The man beside her overflowed from his seat into hers, not because he was overweight, but more because he wanted to. The armrest between the two seats had been lifted.

Darcy leaned over and across the man, giving him an ominous look in the process as he lightly tapped on Liz's foot. "Liz, are you okay?"

She held out the sick bag without looking up.

"Is this your first time on an airplane?"

She nodded and glanced over her shoulder at him. Even in her travel sickness, she couldn't help noticing how devastatingly handsome he looked. He was dangerously sexy in black, but he was a sophisticated god in grey, and here she was sick as a dog and looking like shit.

Taking in her peaked complexion and pale lips, Darcy's heart broke, and he held out his hand. "Come with me."

Much to the dismay of the man beside her, Liz didn't attempt to climb over his reclining body. Instead, she gave him a scathing look to match Darcy's ominous one. When the man reluctantly stood, he was outwardly intimidated by the expression on Darcy's face when he looked down at him with a stare that brooked no opposition.

He clasped his hand tightly to hers, entwining their fingers to support her exit from the row. Saying nothing, he led her down the aisle, trailing behind him through the length of the airplane toward the eight-seat first-class section. Finally, they stood before his seat.

He motioned to the luxury cabin. "Get in."

"Where will you sit?"

"Never mind that. You didn't tell me you've never flown before. What else didn't you tell me?"

"Nothing. I didn't think it was important to tell you."

Darcy tapped her collar bone, and she reluctantly sat.

"Let me see if I understand this correctly. You had a passport, but you have never flown before?"

She shrugged one shoulder. "What can I say? I dream big."

He looked up at the ceiling as if praying for deliverance. "I knew this was a mistake." *I knew you were bad luck.*

Indignant, Liz tried to get up from the comfortable accommodation, but he blocked her passage. "Sit back down. You're not going anywhere." The press of a button sent the seat and Liz backward onto an eighty-inch bed.

Darcy reached over her and flipped open the wood console to withdraw a water bottle. She breathed deeply, inhaling the masculine scent now identified as distinct to him alone. His neck was so close to her lips, and she just wanted to tuck her head there, nuzzling and cuddling up to him for the rest of the night.

"Drink. It's important to stay hydrated."

He motioned to Cynthia. "I want you to give Miss Bennet every attention and amenity that you would give to me. This is her seat now, so please treat her with the utmost respect and the courtesy Swiss Air is known for. I'd like you to bring her something for her airsickness, and please bring her some pajamas to change into. Don't forget linens for the bed."

"Yes, of course, Mr. Darcy. Will you be remaining with her?"

He raised an eyebrow. "I hardly think this could accommodate both of us."

He leaned over to Liz and rested the palm of his hand on her forehead. She felt cool and clammy, and he wished he could stay and hold her, but her solitude in first class was better. It was what she really needed, not him. Just because he had held her in the greenhouse, didn't mean that was what she wanted. Like most women, he was sure she had used the situation and the skill of her hand to get what she really desired: a trip to France and an adventure of a lifetime.

"Try to get some sleep, Liz. We hit the ground running when we arrive in Nice. If you need me, I'll be back in economy."

Before he departed, she grabbed his hand. "If you keep coming to my rescue, I might *have* to consider you my knight—maybe even romanticize this."

Unconsciously, Darcy ran his index finger down her cheek and, in an unprecedented occurrence, smiled from his heart. He wasn't quite sure what to say, only managing, "Get some sleep," before turning on his heel and departing toward Liz's seat and a very, very long, uncomfortable night with the armrest firmly in place.

Three hours later, in the darkened fuselage where only the emergency floor lights and random reading lights shone down on insomniacs and those who fought sleep, Liz pulled back the curtain to economy. In her now favorite, black pajamas and soft, cushiony slippers, she padded toward a sleeping Darcy.

His tall, massive body was squished uncomfortably beside the man whose leg had kept "accidentally" rubbing against hers until she vomited in the little white bag. Darcy's arms lay crossed against his chest, and his head awkwardly craned against the window on a small pillow. His ear buds were precariously dangling as though about to fall out.

As if instinct awoke him or perhaps he always slept with one eye somewhat open anyway, a necessity in his line of work, his dark eyes snapped open at her arrival and immediately locked with hers.

She smiled and he smiled back. Her heart beat faster when she first noticed that he had the most adorable laugh line. *Oh God!*

To Darcy, Liz was a dream come alive. It was dim in the large cabin, and there she stood silhouetted by the few reading lights behind her. She looked absolutely adorable wearing pajamas that were too big for her, having been meant for him. He imagined, in that split second of seeing her, wearing *only* the top after he had made love to her. *His* pajama top, not that he actually wore one, but he imagined one just the same. Her hair was tousled as it would be the morning after being loved repeatedly, and he imagined what that morning after would be like. Steaming coffee on the deck overlooking the valley with her sitting on his lap and arms wrapped around him as she seductively said, "I love you, Fitzwilliam."

Darcy's daydream ended quickly when she handed him a large water bottle and one of her blankets. He pulled the ear buds down and whispered, "Do you feel better?"

She nodded and replied shyly, "Yes, thank you. Do you want your seat back?"

"No, I'd rather you get a good night's sleep. Thanks for the blanket and water."

What she wanted to say was, "Come back with me. I'll make room for both of us. Hold me. I'm kind of scared about this adventure, this flight, my father...my confusing feelings for you." Instead, she simply said, "See you when we land."

~ ♠ ~

Crawford's British Airways flight had arrived on time in Monaco, which was exactly nine hours before the Swiss Air arrival of Liz and Darcy.

Plain and simple, he was avoiding his looming punishment, and his day of reckoning was closing in fast. His employer, Devlin Renaud, didn't like when a well-planned and heavily-financed deal went south, and he liked it even less when one of his own men didn't see it coming or worse yet, caused it.

The fact of the matter was that Crawford always knew that Bennet was weak. Therefore, he had been quite surprised that Bennet had the guts to turn traitor in the first place. But there you have it. In a fit of conscience, Bennet had reverted to his true self—a downright weakling—and had changed his mind. *Weak and foolish.*

Now Crawford was left holding the bag, and Renaud was en route to pick up the goods himself. The last thing Al-Hanash wanted to do was leave the solitude and security of his island compound on Ile de Mogador in order to salvage the deal.

Crawford shuddered. It was just a matter of time until Renaud found him, too. He mused that maybe he would be shown leniency if he prostrated at his feet after a period of absence. In time, after the software was sold, he hoped to return to the compound, seeking forgiveness and the money due him.

With newly styled, dyed black hair, a week-old mustache, and small goatee and wearing a Dolce & Gabbana, silver sharkskin suit, he thought himself dressed to kill. He stood below the stained glass dome and chandelier in the lobby of the famous Hotel de Paris in Monte Carlo. Straightening his posture and his tie, he admired his reflection in the mirrored wall. At six hundred dollars a night and with an uncertainty of life ahead, he was going to enjoy every moment of living beyond his means, social circle, and hopefully, his possible life expectancy.

For a man like Crawford, who was very good at pretending he was someone other than who he really was, mixing with wealthy international players on the baccarat and roulette tables as well as infiltrating their society on the beaches and grand prix circuit, was easy and exciting. Monte Carlo was the paradise of the über rich, a playground for the famous where anything and everything—or anyone—could be had at any given moment for the right amount of money.

But he had only one regret: *she* was not with him.

The exotic-looking concierge watching him smiled, and he smirked, feeling overly confident that the beauty with ebony hair could be his. *She certainly could be had.* He couldn't even imagine that she didn't want *him*.

That was his way, always biting off more than he could chew and always wanting what was out of reach. He never realized that pretty much everything he ever touched turned to crap or would willingly reject him. Liz was a case in point.

For six months, he had lusted after her, and for six months, she rebuffed him. He'd watched her when she wasn't aware, stalked her when she thought she was alone. He knew every part of every curve of her supple, sexy, big-breasted body, and had long wished he could be the claw-foot bathtub she bathed in. She never knew.

Bennet was not only a desperate man, but he was also unobservant and self-absorbed. He, too, never noticed when his "friend" disappeared frequently for long periods of time whenever he came to Longbourn. The man had been too engrossed in his programming, and time just slipped away.

Crawford had never wanted anything more than to fuck Liz Bennet. Convinced she was a virgin, he wanted it so badly that his balls hurt. Hell, with all that purity and innocence, he was positive she was untainted by another, and that made him want her all the more. She was his obsession, and most likely, the last American virgin. He had expected to wear her down and that she would be all his, but to his great regret, it never came to fruition. His balls still ached just thinking about her.

Beside the concierge desk, he folded two hundred-dollar bills inside a handwritten note as a tip and handed it to a diminutive man on the other side of the marble counter. Without a doubt, he needed to alleviate the ball-clenching need, and Monte Carlo had some of the finest, classiest VIP women willing to do so.

With a quick read and even quicker nod by the concierge in understanding of the client's requirements, it would be only two hours or so before Crawford could imagine it was Liz sitting on top of him rather than the leggy, French brunette who showed up for the small price of one thousand Euros.

His specifications had been exact: long legs, curves, porcelain skin, large breasts, hazel eyes, and long brown hair. He didn't need nor desire an escort with conversational skills, manners, or impeccable dress. What he needed was Liz, and a visual likeness of her is what he would get. After all, he had some money. Monte Carlo had the best, and he had a more than willing cock ready to screw her to his heart's content.

By the time both Crawford and his escort, Angelique, were engaged in round two, after having finished their third bottle of champagne, the Swiss Air flight from Dulles International Airport touched down in Nice, fourteen miles away.

Darcy and Liz had arrived and were headed to the same hotel.

At the baggage claim, Liz stood watching the luggage slowly launch haphazardly from the central chute while she waited to greet a late-coming Darcy.

As he descended the escalator toward her, he noticed her waiting, oblivious to the looks of approval she received from male passersby. He observed how her left hand lingered upon her thigh, alternately smoothing the form-fitting fabric or tapping in nervous anxiety.

She had changed her clothing, wearing a different pair of blue jeans, not Caroline's, and certainly not ones he had seen her in before. Gold stilettos accented her slender legs, making her appearance savvy and totally stylish, and he approved—boy did he approve.

Approaching her, he uncharacteristically smiled, noting how she had already collected both of their small suitcases from the conveyer belt. For the first time in his life, he felt afraid of something other than his demons. He was absolutely petrified because he acknowledged that he had fallen for Liz in every possible way. Further, he was positive that when it came time for her to sever his balls, like every woman eventually did, he might not survive.

"How do you feel?" He knit his brow with concern, causing little wrinkles on his forehead.

"Better, much better. Thank you for switching seats with me. I feel bad that you got stuck at the back of the plane."

"Ah...the benefit of flying preferred first class: early disembarkation."

"Well, I'll remember that the next time I fly."

Darcy raised an eyebrow. "Next time?"

"Sure, you're not going to leave me here, are you?" She looked away unable to meet his gaze. "We're a team now, you and I."

Yeah, you and I. As appealing as that was, he remembered the last time he was teamed with a woman. Lucy Steele's deception had cut him to the quick. No, he wasn't really looking forward to going back to a two-man op, even if the second "man" was Liz.

Liz didn't notice the attractive bald man standing behind them, leaning against the wall with his arms crossed at his chest, but Darcy had spotted him the second the escalator proceeded downward.

He also didn't fail to notice how, even concealed by reflective Foster Grant sunglasses, the man couldn't tear his eyes from Liz's backside. Neither could he for that matter.

Taking hold of both their suitcases, he guided Liz toward the silent observer.

Darcy kicked the man's foot, causing him to lose balance. "Wakey, wakey, Knightley."

Liz couldn't help smiling at the playful side of Darcy, a side she'd not witnessed before. Heck, she had barely witnessed any side of him. She didn't know a single darned thing about him, but one thing was for sure: the smile he gave this Knightley guy indicated that his severe mien and wordless staring perhaps were selectively employed.

Knightley seemingly woke up, and the two men hugged.

Did I just see Darcy hug a man? Yes, I did, and they are laughing, too, like old friends who hadn't seen each other in years.

"Hey, old man. You're looking as decrepit as ever."

"At least I still have my hair, chrome dome. John, this is Liz. Liz, this is my good friend John Knightley. We were SEALs together."

Did he just say SEALs? As in Navy SEALs? Oh. My. God.

"You're a brave girl, Liz, to get involved with the Iceman. Whether you're here on business or pleasure, you'd better eat your Wheaties. There are no limits to his insanity or daredevil stunts. Hope you have a good life insurance policy."

Iceman? Knightley's comment scared the bejeebers out of her. She truly had no idea what she had gotten herself into. Heck, this whole trip embarked as a leap of faith. Never in a million years did she imagine that she would actually have the guts to leave Longbourn, let alone go in search of her father, not to mention with a man wholly unknown to her. *His nickname is Iceman?*

Darcy looked down at Liz when he spoke. "She's tougher than she looks. She's...um...tagging along for...business. She can handle it." What could he say, really? She *was* tagging along; only, he didn't know exactly in what capacity. Although, the way he felt about seeing her in those jeans, his fantasies ran pretty close to her fulfilling the role of lover, forever.

"Nice to meet you, John." Liz held out her hand, and Knightley, after removing his sunglasses, bent to kiss it, dazzling her with a seductive smile and his piercing blue eyes. He was another gorgeous, hard-bodied god.

As he bent to kiss her hand, she stammered, "Yes, business. I'm here with him on business...not pleasure." She shook her head vehemently; the chandelier earrings she bought at the airport kiosk banged her jawbone in the process. In truth though, her mind and heart weren't entirely sure, let alone in sync with each other about whether it was business, pleasure, or the supposedly official reason she came: to save her father.

Knightley continued to hold her hand after his kiss. She didn't notice the look on Darcy's face that said, "Get your bloody hands off her, or I'll pound your head into the concrete," but Knightley, who was in the same observation business as Darcy, saw the scowl. He chuckled. *Business my ass.* "Well, business it is then. Follow me, and I'll lead you to your wheels. It's all yours until you leave Monte Carlo."

"Did you arrange for the other items I requested? Were you able to get the surveillance photos?"

"Some of the items are in the boot: Beretta 9mm, listening device and body wire, tuxedo. As for the photographs, your man Crawford doesn't exist in Monte Carlo yet, and no one has registered under that name in any of the hotels. So I have nothing for you on that account. My suggestion would be to hit the Casino de Monte Carlo tonight. Anyone and everyone who wants to be seen will be there. It's a Mecca for the who's who and the wannabes, particularly tonight because there is a special opera performance for the prince by some Russian."

"The opera house is in the Casino de Monte Carlo, no?" Darcy asked.

"Yes, your friend at the hotel has the ticket I left for you. Had I known you were bringing company, I would have arranged for two tickets."

"It's better this way." Darcy looked over his shoulder to where Liz stood fixing the strap on her shoe. "She's not really here on business. I don't want her in the way. I need to keep her safe. Besides, she loves the opera."

"So it *is* pleasure. You hound dog, you."

"Hardly that, either."

Parked at the curb outside the glass-domed airport, sat a radiant, red Ferrari 458 Italia. Knightley dug into his pocket and hit the unlock button on the key. "All yours, compliments of my employer."

"Who is?"

"Never you mind. I'd tell ya,' but I'd have to kill ya.'"

Darcy smirked. "Like to see you try."

"Listen. Anything you want or need, Darce, I am at your disposal. You know how to reach me, so don't hesitate to ask. You've done enough solids for me over the years. So any way I can help you get these rat bastards, just ask."

They shook hands tightly, and Darcy gave his friend a stern, quick nod, remembering several of those solids he had done back in the day. Sobering stuff. And as quickly as it had arrived, gone was the affability he had displayed for the last ten minutes.

Liz noticed the change in his countenance when Knightley bid her good-bye and opened the passenger door for her.

"It was a pleasure to meet you, Liz. Take care of yourself, and"—He looked at Darcy, who stood at the boot loading their suitcases—"take care of him. I haven't seen him out of black in years. Perhaps that's your doing?"

She shrugged and strangely thought of her Lucky blue jeans.

~ ♠ ~

13
Shifting Gears

Darcy surreptitiously watched Liz settle into the soft leather seat of the Ferrari, diligently fastening her safety belt. He depressed the ignition button embedded into the steering wheel and pressed down on the gas pedal.

The sports car's distinct starting purr roared like a growling tiger, and he thought, *God, it feels amazingly good to be once again behind the wheel of a powerfully assembled machine such as this.* Not since his junior year at UVA had he driven one of Italy's finest super cars. His heart raced like the car below him, especially when he looked over at Liz. *Can it get any better than this? Her, this car, this feeling?* Yeah, it could. He could save her father, win her heart, and make love to her 24/7. Yeah, life could get a whole lot better, but that was never going to happen. Her father was a viper, Crawford was a viper, Al-Hanash was a viper, and most likely, she was, too. Unfortunately, experience had taught him that he most likely was going to end up face down in some ditch, done in by one, if not all of them.

Liz looked both frightened and excited. Her hand pressed up against the car's ceiling as though bracing herself for the ride of her life. Yeah, he was going to give her that. Before clicking his own seatbelt, Darcy leaned over to her and gently removed her hand from the Ferrari's smooth ceiling. His hand lingered for just a small moment upon her soft fingers. The right side of his body pressed against her when he spoke calmly, placing her hand on her lap. "Don't be afraid. Enjoy this, Liz. Let yourself *feel* the ride, not in fear but in excitement. Sure, danger is real, but if you allow the fear, then you'll never enjoy the thrill of the experience."

Her mind screamed in reply, *Oh. My. God. Kiss me. Please, kiss me. I want to experience the thrill of your lips on mine.* She nodded in quick, successive movements but said nothing.

Darcy paused a moment. "I won't ever let anything happen to you. Trust me." Then he did it again; he brushed his index finger down the side of her cheek before abruptly moving away from her. He smiled mischievously while engaging the control button to retract the convertible top, deliberately removing her safety net.

In two quick movements, he slid his mirrored sunglasses on then threw the Ferrari into gear. They sped from the airport with the super-car's three exhausts and 570 hp burning rubber.

The route from Nice to Monte Carlo was roughly fourteen miles of intense, winding, two-laned roads and breathtaking vistas. Coupled with the speed of the Ferrari, tracking the rocky cliffs and ascending the hills, Darcy was in his element, feeling the thrill of the ride. He reached into the small satchel stashed in the console hold, retrieved his iPod, and docked it into the sound system. Jefferson Starship's lead guitarist ushered in five minutes of "Ride the Tiger" at maximum-overdrive sound as the sports car whipped around curves and narrow turns.

He quickly chanced a glance at Liz, who seemed to be holding onto her open window frame for dear life, but she was smiling like he had never seen her smile before. She was either looking at him or looking at the hillside beside him. Then for long periods of silence, she would face out to the right, taking in the spectacular view, the deep aqua Mediterranean, and clear blue sky that joined below the roadway. He was elated that this intoxicating woman trusted him enough to let go of her fear, and that meant the world to him.

He found himself never wanting to disappoint her and always wanting to give her adventures beyond her wildest dreams. Anything—he'd give her anything she wanted, even his heart if she asked for it. He'd risk castration again, if only to share a few moments of his life with her like this.

"Faster!" she shouted above the guitar solo with her hair whipping all around her.

Darcy's breath caught. She was the filly running in her sketch.

"What?" He laughed in reply to her demand. He'd heard her the first time but wanted to hear her excitement again.

"Go faster!"

Flipping the shift lever mounted on the steering wheel, the dual-clutch of the Ferrari seamlessly moved into fifth gear. The growl of the super-car roared louder when 3,400 pounds of mechanical perfection made sweet love to the road with symbiotic grace. Turns became hairpin, and Darcy didn't even need concentration to maintain control. The sleek red machine did it for him. Man, he loved horsepower. His blood coursed through his veins. It was the thrill of the zip line escaping the Amazon basin all over again, only Liz was hanging onto him as they soared.

Ahead was a scenic lookout, and without warning or preamble, the Ferrari came to a screeching halt. Lakmé's face was flushed, and her eyes were on fire. To Darcy, she looked as though she had been consumed by rapture, a kind of rapture that he alone could bring to her.

"Why...why did you stop?"

He pointed out toward the Mediterranean with a smile. "Look."

Removing his sunglasses, he got out of the car. Casually, he walked to her side and opened the door, offering a gentlemanly hand of assistance, but he didn't expect her shakiness from the intense drive. Her legs gave way when she stood, trembling from the excitement of all that danger.

Liz fell into his open arms, crashing against his body when he caught her. She struggled to right herself, clearly embarrassed and nervous, but Darcy didn't let go of her until she had found solid footing. In fact, he wasn't really too eager to let go of her at all. As much as she was affected by the drive, he was affected by the feel of her narrow waist below the palms of his hands.

"I'm okay. I'm such a klutz." She moved away and looked to the sea spanning out before them with all its inherent splendor. "Is that Monte Carlo down there?"

"Yes, Monaco is the second smallest nation in the world. It's about the size of Central Park in New York City."

"I've never been to New York City," she replied dreamily. "Or any-where else for that matter."

She grew silent, taking in the spectacular view in awe.

He looked at Liz's perfect profile, admiring her pert nose, full lips, and long lashes. Her elegant bone structure and long neck captivated him. "Beautiful isn't it?"

"Yes...beautiful."

Yes, beautiful, indeed. Looking at her, he was in awe, too.

"Never in my life did I expect to see anything remotely like it." Liz snorted. "Heck, I never expected to leave Virginia. Dreamt about it, but I never thought I'd actually do it. Yet, here I am." She looked down at her Lucky blue jeans and metallic high heels. "Shoot, I never thought I'd be wearing jeans either. In one day, I've done more than I have in the last eight years combined."

"Eight years? Why eight? What held you back?"

"Eight years ago, my Mom left us, and then Jane left right after. My... my father and Longbourn needed me."

Darcy said nothing but gleaned so much. *Two sides of the same coin. We were both children disappointed by our mothers.*

It was a small thing Liz had shared about herself, but it didn't come as a surprise when she asked him to share something of himself in return. It was such a perfect day; he would answer her anything. For the first time in his life, he found himself wanting to talk about his past.

"So you were a Navy SEAL. For how long?"

Leaning against the Ferrari, Darcy folded his arms across his chest. "I was in the Navy for nine years. After five years, I became a SEAL. I left the military four years ago."

"And that was when you joined the CIA?"

It killed him to lie to her, but he had been trained to deceive, and his experience had taught him that lying was always the best policy. "Yes."

Liz walked toward him, stopping directly in front of him. "Have you been to Monte Carlo before?"

"Yes, quite a few times. I don't think we will have trouble finding Crawford. Now, that's two questions to my one. It's my turn for another question. Why did you come with me, Liz? Did you really come to get your father, or was there another reason?" *Say it. God, say it, Liz, and I'll never stop kissing you.*

She looked away from his dark gaze. The heat was too intense for her. "What other reason could there possibly be? I know Crawford. I can help you."

"Is that the only reason?"

Darcy rose from the car and stood toe to toe with her gold spike heels, forcing Liz to look up at his lips so near to hers. Both of his hands grabbed onto her shoulders as if demanding a *specific* answer. "You came because of Crawford?"

How did it get that hot that fast on an open vista where the crisp breeze blew and the occasional car drove past unheeded? Would it always be like this between them? Challenge and intensity, danger and desire whenever they came together? God, she hoped so. Darcy had the power to push every latent button within her, and it drove her wild. She wanted more, more, more.

Liz wanted to scream at the top of her lungs, "I came because of you!" Instead, she did something unthinkable, so un-Lizzy like.

With her newfound seductive skill and a large measure of teasing, she brushed her thumb over his lips in one long, smooth stroke, reveling in the feel of their kissable softness.

She said, "I wanted to come to Monte Carlo. I heard it was an exciting city."

Darcy released her shoulders from his grasp. It wasn't the answer he wanted to hear. To his ears and his already-wounded mind and heart, she had confirmed what he suspected: she *was* using him.

"We better go. My contact at the hotel is expecting us." His expression turned dark and impassive. The Iceman was back in place once again, and she wasn't sure what had set him off. She had grown accustomed to his changing moods. Their reason for change, she had yet come to understand.

The rest of the drive toward Monte Carlo was deliberate and silent, reflecting a controlled moderation of the tethered Ferrari as well as the couple it contained.

Pierre, who wasn't really Pierre, but Peter Andrews of Schenectady, New York, stood behind the concierge counter of the Hotel de Paris. His very good fake French accent greeted incoming and outgoing guests with amiability and competence. He, too, was in the observation and deception business, had been for years, and that was how Darcy had come to know him during Operation Fandango down in Portugal.

Pierre, like Knightley, worked for a well-connected private entity who was one of the richest men in Europe. Both of Darcy's friends were paid handsomely to be the eyes, ears, muscle, and gun—if necessary—for anything or anyone not in their employer's best interest around the French Riviera.

When Liz and Darcy entered the gorgeous lobby of one of the finest hotels in the world, she noticed immediately that the concierge's face lit up with recognition and genuine welcome at seeing her traveling companion. In a greeting similar to Knightley's, Darcy's countenance changed again. *Was he ever changing? Why so inconsistent when it comes to me?*

"Mr. Darcy! Welcome back to the Hotel de Paris."

The men shook hands over the antique marble counter. "Pierre. It's great to be back. Good to see you, old friend."

"We have your room all prepared, and several different event tickets have been set aside especially for you. Just in case you are interested, the baritone Dmitri Hvorostovsky is singing in the Salle Garnier tonight. It is a special concert of Arias and Russian songs."

Liz's eyes widened. *Opera—he likes opera?*

"Thank you. I've never been one for baritones, particularly Hvorostovsky, but perhaps my guest might enjoy seeing him."

Liz's thoughts immediately went to, *Me? How does he know I enjoy opera?*

"Pierre, I'm afraid we will need two rooms on this visit. Is there any way you can accommodate us? The additional room will need to be beside or across from mine."

"Yes, of course. For you, Mr. Darcy, I can do anything necessary, even in the height of the season."

Liz stood amazed at the interplay. Her image of Darcy, up to this point, had been one determined by classic provincial prejudices. She thought him one of Hell's Angels: a reckless, bad-boy, tattooed motorcycle god who listened to and lived in a hard rock, heavy metal world. His abrupt words, brooding, temperamental silence, and stares were as selective as his smiles. The danger that rolled off him at just about every moment lived in tandem within a man who, on occasion, had shown her great tenderness and protection. Inside that tough exterior lived a man who tangoed, enjoyed opera, made love to expensive exotic cars, flew first class, and was well known and liked by the international jet set of the wealthy and elite. He had frequented Monte Carlo as well as this luxurious hotel where money seemed to be no object, even on what must be a meager CIA salary. Darcy was a complete enigma.

Pierre looked to her. "Welcome to the Hotel de Paris, Miss…"

"Bennet. Liz Bennet."

He slid the key to her resting unpolished fingers. "I hope you enjoy your stay, mademoiselle."

"Thank you, I am sure I will."

"Pierre, did you receive my e-mail?" asked Darcy.

"Yes. No one by that name is registered at the Hotel de Paris or any of the Spélugues's finer accommodations. However, we have had a recent arrival who has a certain similarity to the photographs you provided. He has enjoyed the services of Monte Carlo's finest escort service and has secured entrance into the Salon Privé at the casino this evening. Perhaps he is the gentleman you are seeking. A Mr. John Thorpe."

Darcy looked to Liz, who shrugged her shoulders. "I don't know that name."

Pierre studied her face. "In fact, Mr. Thorpe's requirements were very specific, Mr. Darcy. Does Miss Bennet know the person you are seeking?"

"Yes, why?"

"Because Angelique, the woman we sent to him, could be Miss Bennet's spitting image. Of course, it could be just a coincidence."

No, Darcy didn't think it was just a coincidence.

Just as Liz predicted, Darcy's mood once again changed to dark and ominous. Gone were the charismatic smile and affability, and in his place was a man she hadn't imagined existed, one who was jealous and concerned about another man's obsession with her.

There was no doubt in his mind that Crawford was here. "Can you get us two tickets into the Salon Privé tonight? I have an itch to play some baccarat."

Holy moly! Baccarat? He is James friggin' Bond!

~ ♠ ~

Liz settled into the elegant blue and yellow, superior exclusive room over-looking the sea. She stood at the open window behind the black railing while looking out at the harbor and all the luxury yachts and sailboats. She could almost make out the myriad of topless sunbathers at the sandy, white beach. Liz literally pinched herself, checking to see if she was truly here. Much to her shame, she wanted to squeal with delight. It was then that the guilt rushed in.

She was on the adventure of a lifetime, all in the hope of finding her father, or was there another reason for her rash decision to go with Darcy? Really, what could she possibly contribute to his CIA operation? Nothing. She knew that. Absolutely nothing. She wondered if she was so insensitive to her father's plight. During the last twenty-four hours in Darcy's presence, she had never once even asked him about the CIA's investigation into her father or why he was kidnapped. Was it that she didn't care? No, that couldn't be it. She rationalized that she would have asked if Darcy hadn't been so darned taciturn or she was it because she had been so tongue-tied in his presence? Whatever it was, she decided it was going to change. As soon as he came back from his errands, she would go across the hall, confront him, and demand answers about her father.

A knock sounded at the door.

Pierre stood at the threshold, smiling and holding a long blue and green leopard print Versace garment bag. In his left hand hung two other shopping bags. One from Lalique and the other from Christian Dior.

"Compliments of Mr. Darcy, Miss Bennet. He requests that you are ready to escort him to the Salon Privé at precisely ten o'clock this evening. He chose these especially for you to wear tonight."

"For me? To keep?"

Pierre chuckled. "Yes, to keep."

She reached to take the shopping bags from him and noted her un-manicured fingernails, then promptly looked down at her toenails. Cringing, she hesitated and then asked, "Pierre, can you make me a salon appointment? It's not too late, is it? I'll gladly...um...pay for it myself if I need to."

Pierre chuckled again. "It has already been taken care of by Mr. Darcy. You have an appointment in the spa in one hour. Everything is to be charged to his account. I have explicit instructions to tell you that you are to spare no expense. Relax, enjoy yourself, but do not leave the hotel for any reason."

"Why ever not?"

He leaned into her. "I think because he worries about you."

"You seem to know him well. What can you tell me about Darcy? He's somewhat of a mystery to me."

"The only thing you need to know about him is that he is fiercely loyal, generous, and protective of those he cares about. You appear to be one of those people. Cross him though, and you'll wish you never had."

Liz couldn't help the chill that ran down her spine. She could tell that about him but wondered if Pierre's assessment of Darcy's caring about her was just speculation, poor observation, or truthfully accurate.

Pierre's career was the business of observation and had been for a very, very long time. Hotel concierge was only his day cover in order to keep his finger on the pulse of Monte Carlo for his employer. He had seen firsthand what Darcy did during Operation Fandango three years ago and knew Darcy could be lethal with his bare hands if need be.

~ ♠ ~

14
Encounters

Darcy stood with his hand poised to knock on Liz's closed hotel room door. He hesitated, lowered his hand and fixed his black bow tie nervously. He then unconsciously tucked a non-existent piece of long hair behind his ear, forgetting that his hair had been cut and styled that afternoon and the wayward lock was long gone.

On the other side of the door, Liz stood at the open window overlooking the city lit up and glittering in the moonlight. It was a spectacular night, but she was an anxious wreck. Her hands shook terribly as she waited for Darcy. It was two minutes to ten, and she nervously strummed her fingers against her thigh.

He knocked before sliding his spare key into the door.

She had not the time to bid him entry and was unaware that he possessed a key to her room, but her immediate response to object or to challenge his officious entry relented the moment she turned to greet him.

In tandem, they froze, standing motionless and breathless before the other.

Darcy was the most beautiful man she had ever seen. The black, single button tuxedo fit effortlessly, as though his body had been designed to model its elegance. The jet-black of his silk bow tie matched the depth and passion in his eyes. His newly trimmed hair was fashionably styled, yet the curls at the back of his collar were still there to tempt her. Ebony patent leather shoes were the formal masculine match to the ones he had sent to her, only hers were peep-toed with almost four inches of heel. She was now his height, his equal. Gone was the bad-boy, Harley rocker and standing in his place was a smooth and suave James Bond. Liz was shaken *and* stirred.

"Hi," she finally managed to say.

Darcy said nothing. He stood spellbound with his heart fluttering.

The midnight Versace gown he chose for her was spectacular in its own right, but *on* Liz, it was mind blowing. The deep V front neckline left nothing to his imagination, displaying her ample cleavage, full and tempting. She was clearly aroused by his presence, her nipples straining against the thin fabric. It was obvious to him that she wasn't wearing much of anything beneath the gown. How could she? The dramatic, back V plunged dangerously low, extending all the way to reveal her dimples of Venus. The enticing front slit of the gown ran high, and when Liz shifted her weight, her long shapely leg called to him like a siren.

Held upward by two onyx, lacquered hair sticks, her brunette locks were coiled and woven in a sophisticated style.

Darcy instantly became aroused by the sight of the goddess standing before him. His eyes traveled to her long, slender neck.

There, resting above her tempting breasts was the one gift that had special meaning: the necklace; white gold, 812 diamonds, 17.9 carats formed a serpent with red ruby eyes. He wore the matching cuff links. It was his way of trying to get over his aversion to snakes.

Everything about Liz yelled, "Danger, danger, danger." Red painted toes, fingers and lips, deep, cat's-eye black eyeliner above long, thick lashes caused his arousal to twitch with need. She made him feel things that he hadn't ever, *ever* felt before, and it scared the shit out of him. Sure, he feared no man, but he feared the captivating woman standing before him, feared how she made him need and want her beyond reason.

"Hi, yourself," he finally managed. "You look gorgeous, Liz."

"Thank you. Thank you for everything. You have excellent taste in evening wear."

Darcy's voice dropped an octave. "It's not the evening wear I have excellent taste in."

Liz blushed, fully understanding his compliment. She wondered if he was feeling the same things as she. There was no doubt in her mind that her heart and body came alive and engaged by all the many moods and dimensions of this enigmatic man. If he asked, if he wanted her, she would give herself to him completely.

He walked toward her, his gaze locked with hers, resisting the pull downward toward the exposed curves of her breasts. "Before we go to the casino, there are a couple of things I need to go over with you. Most importantly, are you ready for this, ready for the slim chance that we may run into this creep?"

"I am. As much as he repulses me, I'm ready to do whatever I need to do to lead us to my father."

He smirked. "Within reason."

Reaching into his tuxedo's inside pocket, Darcy removed two very small devices. "This is a microphone and radio transmitter—a wire, if you will. If for any reason we get separated and you run into Crawford anywhere, I will hear everything through the small earpiece I am wearing. I will be there in a flash."

What he did with that transmitter surprised Liz, but she didn't question him or object. It turned her on immensely.

His right fingers slowly traced the gown's edge at the V along the side curve of her breast. He stopped its descent just below her breast where he secured the listening device within the fold of the fabric.

Under the fabric of her gown, his unexpected and obviously deliberate brush along the bottom curve of her fullness with the tip of his index finger was salacious. Liz closed her eyes, her breath hitching at the exquisite sensation of his touch as she imagined so much more: his palm, his lips, his tongue stroking and gliding upon her.

Darcy noticed her expression and brazenly raised his finger to stroke very slowly over her erect nipple.

She dropped her head back slightly, clearly enjoying his tease.

He boldly brushed over her a second time, feeling her nipple raise and harden further under his attention. His lips grew hungry, wanting to feel her peak in his mouth. His tongue grew needy, wanting to lave her supple skin and taste the sweetness of her succulent berries.

Liz felt the moisture grow between her legs. It was the first time sparks had shot straight to her apex so fast and with such intensity, just from the slow movement of his finger - once, twice, then a third exquisite time.

She thought for sure her legs would buckle below her, and she clenched her womanhood in response to the building need in her. His caress was a sweet, erotic torment.

Darcy smiled wickedly, removed his hand, then reached up to her ear. He placed the other small device within and leaned into her, speaking softly. His warm breath almost knocked her off-kilter. "This is so you can hear me tell you all night long how beautiful, sexy, and intoxicating you are."

"Do you...do you really think so?"

"Liz, you're the most beautiful woman of my acquaintance."

She never expected Darcy's tongue to trace the curve of her ear, but it did, just as his finger ran down the open V at her back, straight down her spine to just above her backside where the palm of his hand settled, tucking below the fabric to feel the unclad curve of her bottom.

Her hand instinctively sought the hair at the back of his collar, entwining in his soft curls as she pressed herself against every inch of his rock-hard body.

In erotic tandem with his tongue upon her ear and his left finger tracing her gluteal cleft, Darcy's right thumb brushed over her taut nipple through the thin fabric. She was lost in rapture with each delicious stroke until his firm pinch to her fully hardened tip ushered in a rush of exquisite ecstasy and explosive electricity. Liz couldn't help the orgasm erupting throughout her body. She fought to hold back the tide of shattering tremors when his tongue and lips continued to suckle her ear gently while his traveling fingers continued their pleasurable assault.

Her fingers clasped onto his lapel when lightning sparked and white flames erupted within her. She attempted to maintain composure, never once letting on that she was experiencing rapture from the skill of his mouth and fingers. Biting her lip, she kept from crying out when the earth-shattering explosions kept coming one after the other with each swirl of his tongue and boldness of his touch. All hope seemed lost when Darcy kissed below her ear.

Her breath was labored when she finally found the strength to push herself gently away from his scorching lips and the powerful hold of her senses he had gained.

Darcy felt bereft when her heated, flushed body separated from his. The words he was about to speak died upon his lips. *I want to make love to you.*

"Stop, please stop." She felt mortified, but thankfully, she believed he had no idea what he had brought about in her.

Oh, but he knew alright because it was evident all over her glowing face and dilated pupils, not to mention the way she had clung to him. One thing he couldn't deny was that he delighted in the knowledge of bringing her—and almost himself—to climax without even taking her to bed.

However, in true Darcy form, he was upset with himself for having crossed the Iceman line, but she did that to him. He couldn't help himself. Damn if he wasn't so head over heels with this woman that she caused him to lose both reason and himself in her. He had never wanted anyone more than he wanted Liz Bennet.

"I'm sorry...I...that was very ungentlemanly of me. I'm sorry."

"I...I just need to freshen up." Liz placed her hand on his chest. "Don't...go away. I'll be right back." Walking unsteadily in her four inch heels into the bathroom, she was mortified to see in the mirror the afterglow of love-making upon her face, and she hadn't even had sex with him per se. *Damn!*

Liz's subsequent exit from the bathroom and their companionable walk toward the elevator was accomplished in awkward silence until she found her nerve to speak. Now composed, she innocently asked, "Am I not going to the concert then?"

"No, I would rather keep you within range of my eyes and ears. If Crawford is here, I don't want you too far from me. It would be a risk to send you to the opera without my protection. Besides, you'll be able to point him out to me if I fail to make the connection between his photograph and new identity. As soon as we identify him, you'll be headed back to your room. He can't see you, or he'll know we are tracking him to find your father. Dressed as you are tonight, it's unlikely he'll recognize you."

"But it's okay if he sees me. You should use me for that purpose. He has already invited me here. I could say that I changed my mind and followed him, and then he could lead us both straight to Daddy."

"No. I'll never use you."

The elevator dinged, and they entered the empty car for the ride down to the lobby.

She looked straight ahead at the closing doors. "Yes, use me."

Darcy wondered for a split second if they were talking about Crawford or something more intimate.

"I said no, Liz."

"We'll see." She jutted her chin ever so slightly, and he knew what that meant.

"Liz, I'm not fooling. Don't underestimate these people. You're ill-equipped to pull off something like that. Very few women possess that skill. I know of only two or three vipers who can manipulate a man with that amount of cunning."

Liz fingered her new necklace. "Viper?"

"Yeah, viper."

She gave Darcy a satisfied smirk. "You're jealous, aren't you?"

"Jealous? No. I'm not jealous."

"Bull dinky."

"Bull…what?"

"You heard me, bull dinky. You're jealous. After what just happened between us upstairs, I think you're jealous of me being in the presence of another man who also desires me."

"What happened between us upstairs?"

Liz sighed in mock annoyance. "Nothing, Darcy. Nothing at all happened upstairs. I suppose the *Carinatus* in your pants was neither an indication of how you felt or what you think."

"What do you *presume* to know about either my feelings or my thoughts?"

As the elevator neared the casino floor, she turned to him. "I don't presume to understand you at all. I am having a difficult time sketching your character because you perplex me exceedingly. You vacillate with such frequency. Therefore, I have no true understanding of either your feelings or thoughts. I can't even begin to comprehend who you really are, particularly because you are a man who insists on only going by one name."

He smirked and continued to look straight ahead at their reflection in the elevator's gold-toned doors. "Well, I hope to offer you greater clarity then."

"Well then, what is it?"

"What is what?"

"Your full name, darn it!"

Darcy smiled at her aggravated expression. Yeah, he was pretty sure at that moment he was damn-near, if not already, in love with her. *Damn!*

"Fitzwilliam."

"Fitz...what?"

"You heard me. Fitzwilliam. Fitzwilliam Darcy."

With a ding, the elevator doors opened to one of the most incredible and dangerous nights of Liz's life, yet she couldn't stop her knee jerk reaction to laugh at his ridiculous name.

~ ♠ ~

Liz was silent with awe when they entered the Casino de Monte Carlo. The stately building alone was intimidating, causing her to feel as though she entered a museum or a palace for a gala event. Everyone heading toward the gaming tables, Salon Privé, or Super Privé rooms was dressed to the nines. Mindful of each exacting step she took, so as not to fall and embarrass them, she held onto the crook of Darcy's arm.

Thirty-two hours ago, she was walking down a plastic white runner toward a rented gazebo situated over Snowflake the cat's grave, and now she wore Versace, mixing with the elite. Boy, she had come a long way since nearly making the mistake of a lifetime. She hated to admit it, but her father's kidnapping had certainly changed her life. That little voice way deep down inside her had finally shut up, having gotten its wish. Freedom!

Liz tapped her left hand on her thigh, and Darcy looked down, noticing the familiar nervous tick of hers. He leaned to her ear and whispered, "Stop fidgeting. You look beautiful."

"Thank you, *Fitzwilliam*."

"You call me that again in that tone, and I'll take back that three-hundred-thousand-dollar necklace wrapped around your gorgeous neck."

Her eyes grew wide in shock, and Darcy chuckled.

"Stay focused, Liz. Let me know if you see him. As much as I'd love to be here for pleasure, we're here for one purpose only. Well, two actually."

"What's the second?"

"To see you wearing that gown."

Yeah, sure, nothing happened between us in my room. "You never said what you were going to do with Crawford once we found him."

Darcy smiled wickedly, whispering in her ear again, "Torture him."

"No! Really?"

"No, Liz. I'm going to invite him for a cup of tea, maybe have him over to the hotel for a cozy nightcap so we can listen to *La Bohème* all night from the veranda."

"Stop joking with me. I'm nervous enough as it is."

Unsure if he was truly joking, she decided it would be best to change the subject. "Do you really like opera, Darcy?" *Because I'm shocked by that!*

"I used to…I still do. My favorite is *Lakmé*." He lied; his favorite was *Turandot*.

"The 'Flower Duet'!"

"Yes, Princess Lakmé. I love the 'Flower Duet.'"

"You're not going to abandon me out of duty and responsibility like her soldier did, are you?"

Darcy stopped walking, turning to gaze deeply into her hazel eyes with a curious expression. He knit his brows thoughtfully. "I haven't yet, and it's not likely I ever will, princess."

A security guard, wearing the standard green uniform jacket, stood before the doorway of the Salon Super Privé Cabaret, and Darcy presented their tickets and names for exclusive entry.

Vaulted frescoed ceilings spanned around glittering crystal chandeliers greeting the couple as they entered the prestigious energy of high-class roulette, punta banco, and blackjack. The sky was the limit, as there were no limits on these tables. Everything was high stake, and to those with money, the stakes were negligible. To those without, the stakes were higher.

Within seconds of their entrance, Darcy handed Liz a crystal champagne flute, which he procured from the silver serving tray of a passing waiter.

Inside his jacket pocket, he turned on the radio transmitter and, raising his champagne glass, spoke into his snake cufflink. "Can you hear me, Liz?"

His deep, sexy voice inside her ear canal sent shock waves through her. It seemed too intimate, so private, as though he was inside of her. She couldn't deny that she liked it and nodded to his question.

He spoke again into his cufflink, "Say something."

"Your fly is open."

Darcy nearly sprayed the champagne from his mouth. He certainly didn't expect her to come back with something playful and teasing.

She had more to say, and her words traveled deep into his inner ear. "Is that a snake in there?" Clearly, she was beginning to feel relaxed in this setting so foreign to her, and he was thankful, not to mention overjoyed.

He chuckled and took Liz's free hand, entwining his fingers with hers to escort her to the European roulette table.

She watched how his vision traveled everywhere. He didn't miss a single thing, noting every movement made by the dealers and the roulette's croupier and every bet made by each player. She could almost see the wheels of observation, similar to the wheel of the roulette, turning in his mind. It appeared to her own keen eye that Darcy was burning mental images upon his brain for later reference, perhaps to recall faces and make connections. She copied him, scanning the crowd of elegant guests in the Salon Privé, all the while looking for one man and one man only: Crawford.

Darcy slipped six one-thousand-euro chips into her hand. "Play, enjoy yourself. Do *not* leave this table because I need to keep you in my line of vision at all times, but I will be back." He smoothed his finger down her cheek and smiled. "Stay focused. If you see him, just say something to the effect of…how much you like my *Carinatus*." He flashed a brilliant smile. "You know that I'll be beside you in a heartbeat."

Her heart thundered so loud that she was sure he heard it above the intoxicating din within the salon. "I promise, and yes…I do like snakes."

She asked his retreating back, "Do you have a favorite number?"

"Number three and black." It was his polo position on the field and the color of Pegasus.

Just like that, Iceman was gone, having blended into the crowd of black ties and evening gowns.

When Liz sat beside an Arab sheik, she concentrated on the metal ball circling in the opposite direction to the fast-spinning wheel. It was exhilarating, and she felt like one of the affluent gamblers seated around the table. After the croupier gathered all the losing chips with the rake, she excitedly placed one chip on number three and waited.

She didn't see Crawford enter the salon. With her back to the entrance, her eyes remained transfixed upon the wheel and the swish and clicks of the ball finding its home in the pocket. Even if she could see him enter the salon, the man looked so different from the Henry Crawford she had known. He wore jet black hair, a Spanish-style mustache and goatee, and an expensive-looking tuxedo, and he escorted a tall, elegant brunette on his arm.

Crawford stood at the roulette table, watching the wheel and the amount of money being bet. Stakes were high. Several men won consecutively, and he felt lucky as a result.

An alluring female French accent above Liz caught her attention. "Jacques, will you place a bet on my lucky number seventeen?" Liz could smell the woman's overpowering perfume. She didn't know what scent it was, though she assumed it was expensive. Even expensive perfume could smell like manure when overly applied.

Crawford looked down at the woman seated before him, admiring her elegant, long neck, the diamond snake around it, and the exposed bare curves of her breasts displayed in the deep V of the black gown. There was something familiar about her bone structure.

"Sure, angel," he replied to his escort.

Liz knew that voice and knew that small hand as it reached around from behind her, placing his chips on the soft felt table. She breathed in deeply and quickly glanced to her left, away from him, looking frantically for Darcy. Neglecting their code word—because it seemed awkward to voice at that moment—in a rash decision, she took matters into her own hands. Defying Darcy, she chose to play the viper.

She, too, placed her chips on the table before her. Her hand deliberately smoothed and brushed against Crawford's, hoping he would turn to see her.

Liz's thoughts fired fast and furious, and she blatantly ignored the screaming of her conscience replaying Darcy's warning over and over in her mind, but it was too late, the decision had been boldly—albeit foolishly—made.

Iceman stood at the blackjack table, which had an excellent view of the entire salon, not to mention Liz. He felt she was safe so long as she remained occupied by the fast movement and excitement of the roulette. Besides, from this view, he could gaze at her gorgeous profile from time to time. He blended into the sea of black tuxedos, becoming just another affluent man seeking the diversion of the tables. Lost in his observation and silent stalking, he was jarred from his private world when he heard deep in his ear canal, "Lizzy, is that you?"

Fuck!

As Darcy attempted to casually traverse the salon to get to her, the conversation unfolded in his ear. He nonchalantly attempted to talk into his cufflink while hurriedly making his way through the crowd, feeling powerless until he could get to Liz. He cursed himself for leaving her alone so he could get another view of the salon.

"There you are!" Liz replied happily to Crawford.

"What are you doing, Liz?" *Oh God. No!* Darcy panicked, speaking to her within her ear canal.

"What...what are you doing in Monte Carlo, Lizzy?" Crawford asked.

"You invited me, didn't you?"

"No! No, no! I told you, no!" Darcy admonished into his cufflink.

"Yes, I did invite you...but...I thought you weren't interested." Crawford replied surprised.

"It is a woman's prerogative to change her mind, isn't it? So I changed my mind.*"*

"Do not do this! Stop it, Liz!"

Darcy couldn't see Crawford's eyes travel up and down Liz's perfect body and expensive attire, but he heard it in his voice when the man said, "You look different, Lizzy."

"Yes, well, with the death of Daddy, I decided to sell Longbourn and take the money and run. You look different, too, but I would know those blue eyes of yours anywhere."

Just as Darcy arrived on the other side of the roulette table to stare Liz down and get an eyeful of the man they had been tracking, Crawford took Liz's perfectly manicured hand in his and kissed it.

"Oh, I didn't know your father had died. I'm sorry for your loss. Why don't we move from the gaming table so we can speak privately? I'd like to know more."

Frustrated and panicking, Darcy ran his hand through his hair and spoke quietly but sternly into the cufflink. "Don't you dare leave this table, Liz!"

She ignored him, instead replying to Crawford in defiance of Darcy's order.

"What a wonderful idea, Henry, but what about your guest? Won't she miss you?" Liz looked around for Crawford's escort, who was cozying up to another man.

"Angelique? Trust me, she won't mind at all."

Angrily, Darcy ordered, "Sit your ass down. I mean it!"

Liz looked up to meet Darcy's angry mien. His dark, dilated pupils were as though daggers shooting out at her. She chuckled insolently.

Is she laughing at me? Darcy inwardly groaned.

Liz then smiled in that smile he had previously seen her give her sister. It was that fake mocking one. She took Crawford's offered hand and left the gaming table and him.

To suggest that Darcy was over-the-top angry with her was an understatement. He was livid. She was a foolish, headstrong woman who clearly didn't have any respect for him or his professional direction. It was quite possible she could get them both killed. His heart rate sped up exponentially as he discreetly followed the couple through the crowd to where they settled in a quiet place.

He lingered down a hallway not far from the restrooms, and thankfully, the wire transmitter had a long enough range so nothing was missed when Crawford asked Liz, "When did you fly in?"

"I arrived just this morning. Don't look so surprised Henry. Surely you knew how I felt about you?"

"What!" Darcy nearly screamed.

Liz continued to ignore him. She was hell bent on taking matters in her own hand. She could do this, wanted to do this, and knew just *how* to do this. Damn, she knew exactly what made Crawford tick and knew that by manipulating it, it would get them closer to her father.

Crawford looked astonished. "I had no idea you had feelings for me. Do you mean to say that you had been playing coy all that time at Longbourn?"

Liz artfully drank from her champagne flute, knowing that he watched her red lips cling to the glass. That brief respite permitted her time to focus and choose her words perfectly.

Darcy, too, clung. He clung to every word she spoke, growing more red-faced with each syllable.

"Coy? I don't know about coy, but I was certainly intrigued, especially when you cut my *Coelogyne ochracea* orchid and stole my sketchbook. I knew then that you were a man with depth and passion. Any man who can appreciate orchids and the impassioned, introspective sketches of a woman is a man who can win my heart."

"You thought...I...yes, it was a beautiful orchid that reminded me of you. The sketchbook was a piece of you that I had to have, expressive insight into that intelligent mind of yours."

"Fucking lying scumbag!"

Liz tried not to widen her eyes or flinch at Darcy's angry curse, and she wondered why he would think Crawford was lying?

"Thank you for finally telling me the truth, Henry. Honesty is so important to me. I believe in honesty, so I'll be honest with you. That day in my greenhouse, you tempted me with exotic travel to Monte Carlo and Morocco. It was Morocco, wasn't it?"

"Morocco? You never said anything about Morocco to me! Please stop this, Liz, please. I'm begging you," Darcy said.

"Well, Morocco has been put on hold for a little bit, but I leave in the morning for Seville." Crawford kissed Liz's hand again. "Will you join me for an excursion aboard the luxury trains bound for Andalusia, Spain?"

"No! I forbid it!" Darcy chastised.

"Yes! It sounds exciting. I always wanted to visit Spain!"

"Go to the restroom! Now!"

Utilizing Darcy's very effective means of discombobulating, she ran her red fingernail down Crawford's cheek. "Will you excuse me for a moment? I have to use the powder room. I won't be long. How about I meet you at the blackjack table in fifteen minutes?"

For the third time, Crawford kissed her hand. "Until then, Lizzy."

Once Liz was out of Crawford's vision, as soon as she turned the corner down the hall, Darcy grabbed her wrist and pulled her into an unused coat room. It was dark and filled with empty hangers and an upright vacuum. He wanted to scream at her the minute the door closed behind them. Instead, he dragged her deep within the closet and pressed her against the back wall. Leaning over her, he spoke forcefully.

"What are you doing? Have you gone mad?"

"No, this is good. He will lead us straight to Daddy. I'm not afraid."

"Clearly. And what was all that crap that you have feelings for him?" He mimicked her flirtatious manner. "'I knew then that you were a man with depth and passion.'"

"Gee, Darcy, you sound a little jealous. You know I don't have feelings for Crawford, but I had to make it believable, didn't I? You obviously bought it."

"And Morocco? Why didn't you tell me about that?"

"I forgot."

"You forgot? This seems to be a habit with you, Liz. What else have you forgotten?"

She couldn't help the smart ass remark that flew from her lips. "I forgot to tell you that I enjoy when you beg, and...oh yeah...I don't respond well to 'I forbid it.'"

"Then maybe you'll respond well to this."

He kissed her, but not with the expected sudden white-hot, slamming intensity. No, he gave her a smooth kiss so filled with longing and with such passionate yearning that he hoped there would be no doubt in her mind what he felt for her. He hoped this kiss and all the emotion behind it would offer her the clarity she desired.

His lips made love to her, molding to hers with a tenderness that lingered and consumed not just this intoxicating woman's breath, but her entire being. His tongue was neither insistent nor probing, it caressed and explored as it danced in perfect unison with hers.

It was a kiss unlike any Liz had ever received, and it left her breathless, melting in his strong arms.

When Darcy parted from her, his eyes locked on hers as his hand went to the microphone hidden on her gown. His fingers brushed against the exposed curve of her breast, lingering for just a moment before removing the mic. "Since I obviously can't control events, which you are determined to go through with, I have one request."

"Anything," she panted.

Yeah, I thought you'd feel that way after that kiss.

"Never take off your necklace, not even to sleep. I want to hear every breath, every word, and every confirmation that you are safe."

Liz nodded as he placed the microphone under the snake's diamond-encrusted head.

Darcy could hardly make out the flush upon her face, but it didn't matter; he was sure it was there. He felt the same way. This woman heated him to the core. She was the only fire to succeed in melting his ice.

The moment his eager lips descended on the pulse at her supple neck, he felt her blood rush and heart beat as fast as his. His lips burned with each suckle as they kissed and smoothed down to her delicate collar bone.

Their liaison in the pitch darkness of the closet was erotic and salacious, and it aroused her all the more. She tilted her head slightly away to give him greater access and brought her hand up to thread through his hair, holding him firmly to her aroused flesh. Each wet, delicious kiss he gave her seared her, branding her as his.

Her body responded with no conscious thought, and she purred in reply to the caress of his hand at the slit of her gown.

The palm of his hand slid up her bare thigh, and he moaned when her leg hiked up onto his hip in response.

Liz willingly gave him greater access to the treasure he sought. She wanted him to touch her there. She wanted *all* of him there.

She forgot all about the casino, the closet, the op. All she knew was that she never wanted anything more than to have hot sex with Fitzwilliam Darcy at that exact moment and most likely forever. Her heart and her body were fully engaged, and somewhere deep, she acknowledged that every fiber of her being was putty in his hands.

Darcy's tentative yet eager fingers confirmed that she wasn't wearing panties beneath the gown. He lifted his head, smiling wickedly. "Naughty, naughty girl," he whispered. His touch traveled to her apex, smoothing over her soft flesh, discovering her Brazilian wax. "Delightfully naughty."

Those two words opened a flood of heartfelt endearments into her ear as his fingers caressed and explored her folds, touching her with reverence and one sole purpose in mind: to bring her pleasure. When a single, long finger tenderly entered her slick heat, he whispered, "Oh God, Liz... you're so wet...just for me."

He was overwhelmed, inebriated by her with each slow dip of his finger in and out, feeling every curve and softness of her. Her warm breath upon his ear and the way her body responded to his ministrations as she rode the waves of pleasure caused his arousal to strain and clench. "You are so beautiful when you come. Come for me again, Liz. Only this time, don't hold back."

Darcy dropped the strap to the gown, exposing a breast to his hungry mouth. His tongue savored her taut, berried nipple in purposeful, unhurried licks that caused her body to tremble in his arms as his fingers masterfully continued to play her. The taste and scent of her sweet arousal drove him wild, and to hear "Fitzwilliam" emerge from those beautiful lips of hers caused his arousal to bulge further, straining the fabric of his trousers.

Unexpectedly, she released him into her hand.

The feel of her fingers surrounding his shaft was sublime ecstasy, and he couldn't hold back the groan he fought. Words flowed from his lips; he knew not what he was saying. "Promise me you'll remember this. Promise me you'll dream of how I make you quiver."

Liz panted into his ear. "I promise, oh God, I promise…yes…yes." All reason left her with each stroke she employed to his hardness. She needed to experience all those things her sister told her about, but it was more. She needed him *inside* her—physically, emotionally, and mentally.

His lips crashed against hers, kissing her deeply, his thumb circling and stroking her swollen pearl. She shattered hard holding onto him, stroking him faster with each electric spasm that shot through her.

She shifted her hip, rubbing his swollen head where his fingers vacated. It was more than Darcy could bear. The feel of her bare pubis, soft folds, and engorged nub rubbing, surrounding, and drenching him was the most erotic feeling he had ever had. All he wanted to do was slide into her. It was torture for him not to thrust into her with abandon. "I need you. I want you, Liz. Let me love you."

She shattered again from the currents of rapture every time his shaft brushed and pressed against her swollen apex of nerves. Holding onto her tightly, he moaned and rumbled. "I want to make love to you so much, baby. I always have—from the first time I saw you at Longbourn."

"Yes, oh God, yes. I need you. I'm yours." She nearly cried out as his throbbing tip dipped ever so slightly into her wetness.

The tight feeling, even before he could slide in any further, sent him over the edge, hard and fast. He pulled from her just in time and climaxed with such powerful intensity that his body shook from the explosion she had created.

They breathlessly clung to each other, both gasping in spent passion, their bodies trembling from the powerful erotic interlude. With palms cupping her cheeks, he kissed her lovingly. "My God, you're incredible."

"We're…we're incredible…together."

"Yes, we are, baby." He kissed her again, lingering upon her lips until he whispered, "I promise…to always protect you, Liz."

"I know."

Darcy righted her gown and, after removing the handkerchief from his pocket, carefully cleaned her leg of the evidence of their passion. He couldn't help himself, he kissed her one last time. "Please be careful."

"You'll never be far behind me, right?"

"Never. I'll never leave you."

~ ♠ ~

15
Regulation

Darcy sat in Liz's darkened hotel suite deep in thought, nursing the remainder of the glass of Jack Daniels Silver Label—100 proof. It had been quite a night for the two of them with emotions and fears running high. Nothing more was expressed beyond the uttered exchanges of lovemaking in the closet, and neither had since spoken of their audacious, explosive coupling. She emerged from behind the coatroom door as poised and perfect as when she entered. The only difference he had noted, besides the sparkle in her hazel eyes, was the flush to her face and neck. Otherwise, the mask she employed was as skillful as his own.

He now watched as Liz slept with the moonlight trespassing though the open window and a wayward breeze disturbing the curtains. His mind played over and again her subsequent reunion with Crawford—her meeting him at the blackjack table and his smarmy, obsequious mannerisms. Darcy's skin crawled every time he thought of that slime ball kissing her hand or touching her shoulder, but Liz had foolishly and bravely chosen this route. She willfully put herself in harm's way for the sake of her father.

Darcy shook his head, not understanding the dynamic between father and daughter. He knew her mother had abandoned her, but he hadn't before thought that, more than likely, Liz had abandoned her own dreams as a result, even so far as suppressing the spirit that truly defined her. Maybe, like him, she had denied her conscience and its promptings to flee for survival. He wondered if she was afraid of abandonment again and maybe that was why she chose to marry a man whom she didn't love. She was afraid of heartbreak.

All of it was speculation and only some of it made sense to him. For all of her assertions and *her* need for clarity and comprehension, she herself was as big an enigma as she thought *him* to be.

When that creep escorted Liz back to the hotel, Darcy couldn't help the jealousy coursing through his veins, particularly when Crawford stood before the door of her suite and chastely kissed her goodnight. At that precise moment, Darcy realized he needed to set aside his personal interests and emotions. He was running way too hot. This was a mission. Bennet, Liz, Crawford, and Al-Hanash made up a four-sided danger sign known as Operation Cancan.

It was at the moment when Crawford's lopsided lips descended upon Liz's that the Iceman returned for the duration.

It was three in the morning, and Darcy's Bluetooth beeped an incoming message. He pressed the button to listen to Charlie who spoke low. He could hear disco music in the background.

"Rick's declared you rogue, Darce, and Caroline is madder than hell. You never checked in with either of them about Operation Cancan, and all they know is that you are in Monaco pursuing Virginia Reel. Apparently, the agency is breathing down Obsidian's back. Listen, if you are in trouble, if Liz is in trouble, I want to help. I not only care about you, but I now have a vested interest in Jane's sister. Well, in Jane's happiness. Yeah, I know ... I've become emotionally engaged. Shoot me; call me foolish, but Jane has wiped out all recollection of Scandinavia.

"So with that said, we're flying out of Dulles in the morning for Capri. My father still has his summer home there. I'll be waiting to hear from you, and I won't take 'no' for an answer."

Darcy smirked ever so slightly at his friend's falling for the blonde. Who was he to cast stones? Had he not done the same? He didn't think it would come to his needing Charlie's assistance, but he was thankful nonetheless to know that his friend would be on this side of the Atlantic should they need him and his skill set. Then a thought occurred to him: *We? Did he say 'We're flying out'?*

He tapped the Bluetooth again for the next stored message. With this one, he knew what was coming. He braced himself.

Rick said evenly, "If you weren't my cousin, I would hunt you down and beat the shit out of you. You've gone off half-cocked—or maybe full cocked for that matter—around the world, playing James Bond to right a wrong. You have failed to contact either Caroline or me with your whereabouts and progress. It is not above me to track you, but I will if I have to. Consider yourself deemed rogue.

"Let me make myself perfectly clear on this Darcy: if you do not succeed in killing Al-Hanash and bring back Bennet to face justice, then Obsidian has no recourse but to deny your existence when the administration and the agency start looking for a scapegoat. You know what that means. You were a SEAL. It's been done before, and they'll do it again. Look, I love you. You are my cousin, but in the bigger scheme of things, the lives of three hundred million Americans make you expendable. In other words, don't fuck this up.

"Oh, and just so you know the full extent of what I'm going through in your absence, Caroline and I are through. Her jealousy over your foray from the dark, celibate side over this Bennet girl was more than I can handle. I should have known better than to pick up your sloppy seconds."

Darcy clicked the unit off, ignoring the Caroline remark. After all, it was expected. She was a lethal viper, and Rick would eventually become Rikki-Tikki-Tavi. The only thing that resounded with him through his cousin's entire diatribe was, "Don't fuck this up." He understood exactly the position he was in, and his cousin was correct.

His thoughts traveled back to Liz, who in five hours would be leaving for Nice to catch the train for Seville, and he would once again be hiding in the shadows: watching, listening, observing, and waiting. Only this time, he realized there was an additional element to his role. He would also be protecting. If he had to, he would give his life protecting her.

Darcy looked over to where she lay soundly sleeping. She hadn't heard him enter her suite in the dead of night. Adjusting the transmitter in his pocket, he listened to her calm, slow heartbeat through the necklace still resting around her neck. She wore nothing else, just the necklace. He sat riveted, polarized between reason and desire, but he couldn't deny how tempted he was to wake her and make love to her. The vision of her bare, voluptuous breasts' rise and fall with each gentle breath spellbound him. What she had done to him earlier that night was unprecedented in every way. Yes, Liz was a serpentine of perfection, the only kind he wanted to constrict his body and to snake around his heart, the only kind that made him respond. The kind he couldn't resist: the mythological creature of passion, seduction, and intelligence who hypnotizes with her charm, compelling him to lose his head. She'd succeeded in that, and he loved her with a passion equal to her own. *Damn!*

Darcy mused over the irony of life that brought them together. That, too, was unprecedented. In his entire tenure as an assassin, he never felt a modicum of emotion. Now, he found himself in love. She was an assassin, too, sneaking into his heart, shooting pangs of yearning and desire through him, disarming him with her wit and smile, leaving him quivering at her feet from just the touch of her lips. Only her kind of death-dealing had the power to destroy and melt the Iceman with the heat of her nearness, but the Iceman was needed now.

Slugging back the remainder of his whiskey, he shifted in the Queen Anne chair at the foot of Liz's bed. He was still hard with want of her—uncomfortably hard. He had yet to stop wanting, acknowledging that he would never stop, wishing to possess her body and soul. But not now. It would complicate everything. It would do neither of them any good at this juncture. The Iceman needed to stay focused, and so did she. Too many times now he had screwed up in regard to her. Now was not the time to do so again. She was depending upon his skill and his steady, detached focus. Real danger faced them both.

Liz stirred in the bed, rolling to her side. Her lips opened slightly, and so did her eyes. Even asleep, she had instinctively felt him watching her. Although it was dark and he was in shadow, she could tell he was lost in thought. His right hand clenched around the crystal glass, and every once in a while, he would turn his head to gaze at the moon outside the window. She watched Darcy for several minutes without his awareness. He was back to his familiar black apparel and motorcycle boots. She could see his tattoos, and she became flushed and heated. Memories of the closet came rushing back to her. They were so palpable that she still felt his hand on her, his tip entering her, and the craving inside her began again. Rapture in Darcy's arms was everything Jane had explained being with the right lover would be: explosive. In her soul, she knew only this man would be that lover.

Liz was amazed at how suddenly, how readily, she had shed "Lizzy."

Shocked by her own boldness and audacious behavior, for the first time in her life, she felt alive. He had done that, he had awoken her. And even though she knew nothing about him, neither his history nor his heart's desires, she knew unequivocally he was *her* heart's desire. She was falling in love with him.

Darcy's eyes bore into her open ones. He didn't know how long she laid there watching him. Neither said anything to the other, but both remained still and silent in the moonlight. The only thing that spoke was Liz's heart, not only when he heard it speed up through the microphone but also when she lifted the bed linen to him in invitation.

Liz, in the moonlight, nude, and glorious with only the diamond serpent necklace upon her porcelain skin, was exquisite, and she wanted *him*. It near killed him to restrain.

Rising, he pulled off his Bluetooth and walked to the bed. Both were acutely aware of each other's extreme arousal. It was clear to Liz that his erection needed satiation. The sight of which made her wet and ready for him. Her body was near lifting from the bed in invitation, straining to feel his lips upon her, suckling and nibbling her aroused nipples.

Darcy sat at the edge of the bed beside her and pulled the linen completely away from her, exposing her form to his starving, dilated eyes filled with desire.

She thought he looked ready to devour her, every nerve in her body humming: *yes, yes, devour me.*

With her back arching to meet his touch fully, his hand caressed over her willing body. His palm slowly brushed over her taut nipple, gliding languidly to the curve of her waist, smoothing over her hip and gently caressing down her shapely, bent leg.

She watched him close his eyes and witnessed pure pleasure infuse his expression as he appeared to commit every curve of her to his mind's eye. His touch alone sent ripples and shockwaves through her body.

Finally, when Darcy's hand reached her apex, his finger drew between her bare folds, and she separated her legs, encouraging him to dip into her wetness. Expecting his blissful ministrations to continue, she dropped her head back in ecstasy. Her long hair cascaded above the pillow; her moan filled the room. Already, she was on fire. The throbbing in her womanhood demanded what it wanted: him—all of him. It needed him, and she responded with slick readiness.

As suddenly as he had begun, Darcy removed his finger with a slow stroke up and over her swollen pearl.

Liz lifted her head and locked eyes with him. "Fitzwilliam, please—" But her plea was cut short when he placed his wet finger to her lips, replacing it with his mouth. It was a deep, sensual kiss filled with intensity as both tasted the sweet honey his finger deposited. His impassioned lips were so expressive that of all the things he had done to her, this was the most earth-shattering. Her heart burst in response, knowing unequivocally—because she could feel it—he was giving her the kiss of separation.

The feeling of their lips parting clearly affected them both, leaving them bereft. Darcy smoothed his index finger down her cheek and pulled the bed linen over her, seemingly tucking her in. He smiled contritely then stood looking down at her face, rosy with the heat of excitement and the burn of confusion. He had to do it, and it killed him to do so. The man who only hours before had whispered and moaned such things as "I need you" now stood donning his mask of detachment and indifference.

He had become the Iceman once again, and all expression, save his straining arousal, disappeared.

"Fitzwilliam...don't go...stay with me. Make love to me."

"No, Liz, it's better for both of us this way. It's too dangerous." He abruptly turned from her.

The last thing she saw, for the third time in their brief acquaintance, was his retreating back. Tonight's difference was that when he left, she cried at both his rejection and his departure.

For the first time in the past two days, Liz wished to retreat to the prudent Lizzy of old. There her heart was safe from the irrational, romantic notions that someone like the reckless Fitzwilliam Darcy had made her feel.

To the outside world, it had once been known as a prison, but to Thomas Bennet, it was still a prison. Having arrived blindfolded after a long boat journey on still waters, all he knew was that he was on an island... somewhere. The sound of the surf pounding below the stone wall of the room where Al Hanash kept him was relentless. It was not the soothing white noise that breaking waves often created, but fierce and tumultuous instead, rather like the tide and swell of self-loathing, fear, and thought patterns coursing and hammering throughout his body.

Before him sat two computer monitors staring back with lines filled of source code. Slumping back in his wood chair, Thomas stared through them. If only…there were lots of those "if only's," but he only focused on one in that moment. *If only I could contact the outside world. Think, Thomas…think,* he demanded of himself, tapping his temple in deep thought.

A black mouse ran across the baseboard at the corner of the room. It stopped and put its nose in the air to smell the meal resting on the table next to Thomas's right arm. Thomas might have been disgusting by the dish, but he was too damn hungry and thankful for it to give it up to the rodent. He'd never heard of *mokh* and was quite repulsed when Omar explained it to be goat's brain seasoned with cumin and lemon.

He thought of Lizzy's beef stew with potatoes and carrots, and his mouth watered. "Lizzy…Lizzy…are you safe? Is your sister safe? I pray so. Forgive me for all I have done."

The island where they held Thomas was considered uninhabited, with the exception of a great many birds in the nature preserve. It was declared an eco sanctuary and a safe breeding ground for the great Eleonora's falcons on their migratory pathway to Madagascar.

The locals on the mainland in Essaouira, Morocco had been told that the Ile de Mogador was forbidden; only they never knew why. Devlin Renaud had seen to that. He had chosen wisely in the selection of his compound. The ancient island's uninhabited outbuildings surrounding the centuries-old mosque was the perfect cover for Al-Hanash's lair. The spectacular views and easy access through his own heavily-controlled and fortified peaceful harbor of Mogador Bay were added bonuses. Renaud owned this corner of the globe where ancient traditions concealed his modern ways. Marrakech was his playground, and every local inhabitant, both in and out the Medina, nearly bowed down to his presence when he walked through the dry good stalls in the souk or enjoyed the Jemaa el Fna nightlife with his lovely wife, Sophia.

He stood on his bedroom's balcony overlooking the angry North Atlantic as it pounded the island below him. Sprays of water and mist jumped into the air, meeting the fierce wind the island was known for.

His cell phone rang. He noted the caller ID and snickered. *Dog.*

Promptly engaging the special satellite tracking feature on his phone he said, "Speak."

"Sir...it's me, Crawford."

"This is unexpected, *dog.* I did not anticipate hearing from you so soon."

"In truth, I did not expect to contact you so soon, but I realize that a man with your vision and great benevolence might forgive the unfortunate circumstances in Virginia. I have, after all, been very loyal to you these past couple of years." *And now that I have a traveling companion, my financial situation and predicament has changed,* he thought.

"So the dog is asking to come home, or are you seeking asylum from America's Central Intelligence Agency? Tell me, are they in pursuit of you as we speak?"

"No. I have covered my tracks well. I'm calling because I wish to apologize and offer my regret for Bennet's untimely death. Surely with his unexpected demise, I am no longer accountable for his change of mind in finishing the program, and therefore, as a businessman, you can understand my desire for payment for the time and energy I exhausted on Bennet."

Al-Hanash quirked an eyebrow. Usually, his feathers never became ruffled. As a general rule, nothing could be said or done in the business world that would cause him to reveal his inner thoughts, anger, or frustration. Many said he was born with a poker face—the epitome of indifference and control on the surface.

"You have heard that Bennet is dead? How did you come by this information?" he calmly asked.

"His daughter, Elizabeth. I have had a recent re-acquaintance with her where I am staying, and she has informed me of his unexpected death and the sale of their estate."

"Is she still in your company?"

Crawford didn't like the tone in his boss's voice. It had menace behind his evenness, so he lied. "Not at this moment, but we will be reuniting in the south of Spain."

"So you are slowly making your way to the island? Perhaps sewing your oats before you enter 'The Land of God'?"

"Yes, sewing my oats. At least I hope to…she is a virgin. That takes… you know, a lot of romancing and breaking of barriers." Crawford laughed uncomfortably.

"Ah, the land of milk and honey resides in a virgin's tight warmth. You refer to Bennet's daughter as the virgin?"

"Yes. Sir, Marrakech is my final destination. Perhaps we can meet there at the Café Arabe in two days, where you can pay me my due, and then I can be on my way?"

Omar stood to the side of his employer, witnessing a slow smile form upon Renaud's face. It was almost frightening…menacing.

"Yes, good. Bring her with you. I'd like to meet Mr. Thomas Bennet's daughter."

Crawford swallowed hard. "You want to meet her, sir? Can I ask why?"

"Because after you have soiled and dishonored her with your filth, I will further defile her before her father's eyes until he capitulates in finishing the code. You see, she has set a trap for you, you worthless dog. Most likely, the CIA has gotten to her, hoping you will lead them to her father. You would be of more use if you were castrated because a man is no good to me if he allows his cock to rule his reason and intelligence."

Crawford grew red-faced at the insult and stammered in confusion. "I…I don't understand, Mr. Renaud. Her father is dead."

"So she says, Crawford. She lies, and like a fool with his cock in his hand, you believed her." Renaud spoke firmly, his anger kept at bay with firm control. "I have Thomas Bennet imprisoned on Ile de Mogador. Yes, I will meet you in Marrakech. It will be a life for a life. Your life in exchange for hers, handed over to me."

He clicked the phone off, turning to Omar. "Did I not tell you, Omar? All dogs eventually come home. Only this one brings a bone with him."

"You will meet him in Marrakech then?"

Al-Hanash gave his trusted adviser a look of humor. "Let him think that. I owe him nothing. He failed and now demands money. He is a half-wit who thinks he can extort money from me. Me! I will squash him below my heel."

"You would not defile the girl, sir."

Renaud chuckled. "You have always been my conscience. I could not hurt my Sophia in that regard. I would, however, sell the girl to the highest bidder. That is business, not pleasure, and could easily line my pockets with at least one million Euros."

"She is a virgin?"

"At the moment. I want you to find Crawford. Kill him when he meets the girl in Spain, then bring her to me. I know you will succeed in finding him behind his ridiculous disguises. He is no doubt being trailed by the CIA, so be watchful."

"And what about Bennet?"

"What about him? He is already working on the code, is he not? If he suddenly has misgivings again, then he will no doubt cooperate after I hold your machete against his neck?"

Renaud pressed a series of buttons on his cell phone, glanced at the screen, then tossed it to Omar, who caught it.

"He is at the Nice train station most likely headed to Seville. He has a sick obsession with bullfighting." He shook his head and voiced his disgust, "Such cruel, senseless killing that only a dog would find enjoyment in watching."

~♠~

**16
Clarity**

The Spanish coast sped past with incredible speed, but it wasn't fast enough for Liz, not because she desired the thrill of the Ferrari, but because speed wasn't all she needed. She needed freedom, too. She couldn't wait to finally—hopefully—have some solitude at their final destination: Seville.

After three stops in northern Spain, transferring each time, she and Crawford were finally underway. But for the churning in her heart, her barely contained anger at the rejection by Darcy, and an extreme repulsion of Crawford, it was a very pretty train ride. Under different circumstances, she would have enjoyed it immensely. She shook her head in wonder. Again, she had to pinch herself. *Am I really here doing this?* It was thrilling, and she felt alive with a capital *A*.

Liz knew the Iceman was never far behind and listening. She had faith in that much. She instinctively knew he was close, hiding in plain sight. Thankfully, she hadn't laid eyes on him since the previous night when he set her body aflame and then abruptly left her to deal with her fall from cloud nine. Gravity sucked, particularly when it caused her tears to fall unchecked. Even the morning's chilled shower water raining down upon her failed to extinguish the memory of his burning touch or the craving sensation newly embedded under her skin. Would they always have such emotionally raw and explosive meetings? Probably. They were two of a kind.

Sitting side-by-side in the exclusive club class, Crawford took Liz's hand across the small table between them. She had been staring out the window far too long, and he hoped to regain her attention from the Balearic Sea below them. They were both playing a game now, both acting out a role until the final curtain: Marrakech. He was livid at her deception, but in the end, he felt it negligible. He would get what he wanted: her virginity *and* his money. Then he would take the cash and his freedom from Al-Hanash.

"Tell me about your father, Lizzy. You didn't share with me the details of his death."

Liz made her eyes well with tears. In truth, it wasn't very hard to do since her thoughts were just coming from that last kiss Darcy had given her. She focused on the pockmark between Crawford's eyes. "He died of a heart attack three days before my wedding."

"Dearest, dearest Lizzy."

"You can call me Liz." *Take that Darcy!*

"Liz, I am so sorry to hear that. So, you never married Bill?"

"No, you were right. You were so right. I should have listened to you when you told me he was gay. It seemed that Daddy's passing saved me from a very unhappy marriage and future."

"You and Thomas took good care of each other. I saw that. It was clear you were his little girl. He protected your innocence."

Liz looked at him strangely. *What a peculiar thing to say.* "I...um... suppose in a way."

"In a way, your father's death liberated you from the plantation and its many obligations. Selling was wise. I'm very glad you decided to take this trip with me. I hope to show you things you only dreamed about back at Longbourn. The excitement of the *corrida de toros* in Seville, the passion of the flamenco. Andalusia is seductively romantic. We can tango in the moonlight."

"I don't tango. I'm sorry, but I *won't* tango." *That's his dance.*

"Well, perhaps when we get to Marrakech, we will be dancing something altogether different. I understand that's one experience you'll need to work up to. I'm patient. I will respect your timidity."

Liz looked at him perplexed, again. *Is he implying sex? Of course he is, why else would he want me along for the trip?* "Yes, I am very timid in regard to that."

"I've wanted you for so long now. Back at Longbourn, you were all I could think of while I assisted your father. Your first time should be special, memorable, and under the crescent moon of exotic Marrakech is just the place. I'm truly flattered that I can be your first, Liz. Once we arrive in Morocco, I'll complete my business, and then you and I will take our time."

Oh. My. God. He thinks I am a virgin.

Two rows behind them, concealed behind a spread newspaper, Darcy chuckled, then cleared his throat. She knew that chuckle. It carried to her, and she blushed in anger.

"Fuck you," she said to Darcy through the necklace. *Oh no, that's right; you* don't *want me.*

"What did you say, Liz?" Crawford asked.

"I said is *that true?* I was all you could think of, Henry? Day and night?"

She couldn't hold back saying her piece to Darcy as she spoke to Crawford.

"I've had others profess the same thing, you know. So forgive me if I seem a bit skeptical. As you can attest, my record of choosing potential lovers leaves a lot to be desired. They all seem to lie and deceive me. It seems as though they deliberately want to hurt me, such as by crushing my heart below their motorcycle boot. Cruel bastards. I just don't know if I can allow anyone to take the liberties others have attempted, only to cast me away as though trash. You understand that don't you, Henry?"

"I would never use you, Liz." Of course, not only was he lying, but he also thought she was speaking of Bill Collins.

Darcy moved the newspaper he pretended to read and leaned into the window to get a clearer view of her. Her words, once again, stabbed at his heart. She made herself perfectly clear. She was mad as blazes at him for leaving her like he did last night.

He watched her place the palm of her hand on Crawford's cheek. "I know you would never use me, but I've heard that before, too, and I can tell you firsthand, Henry, it broke my heart."

Crawford laid it on thick. "I would never do that to you, and with open arms, I will show you what a *real* man is. That scum was a fool, Liz—not a real man at all, but a real coward who certainly didn't deserve to know you intimately."

"Yes, he is a lying, manipulative, son-of-a-bitch coward, and I'm sorry I ever laid eyes on him."

Crawford's gaze rested upon the snake around her neck. He had designs on the fine diamond prize Liz's hand consistently toyed with. "Did he give you that stunning necklace? I'm assuming it had special meaning since it appears to be quite expensive?"

"Yes, I suppose the only meaning I can derive from it is that he turned out to be a real snake in the grass." She laughed at her wit at Darcy's expense.

A newspaper ruffled, and she heard the whoosh of the closing train door. A quick looked revealed Darcy's retreating back. *That's it, run, or in your case, slither away. You're good at that. Snake.* Quite unexpectedly, she had developed a recent aversion to snakes, and to her mind, Darcy was now embedded within the reptilian classification he himself held in disdain.

~ ♠ ~

Darcy had retreated into the cover of darkness once the sun set and the high-speed train headed toward Madrid. It stopped and took on passengers in Tarragona before continuing the journey west.

He was well practiced at storing his emotions in that box where his scarred memories and pain were kept. Pandora had already done a number on him at Pemberley, but he had no intention of allowing her to do the same with regard to Liz. That was until he saw her exit the lavatory wearing a short black sheath dress and gold spike heels. Her hair was braided down her back, sleek, sexy, and long like her legs. Darcy's hand twitched remembering its touch upon them. His heart fluttered, and then it turned green at the realization that she had dressed for dinner… with Crawford.

Other men on the train noticed Liz, too. One in particular watched both her and Crawford keenly. Darcy had noticed him when he boarded in Tarragona. He was tall, dark skinned, and of Middle Eastern descent. Further, there was something familiar about him. Iceman stored it in the back of his mind, resolved to work out the details of the stranger's face and body structure later in the night while he stood watch over Liz's sleeping form. He would go through every op and every year of his life, processing thousands of faces through his brain like a rapid-fire slide show.

Darcy stood in the dark between the two rail cars, waiting for Liz to pass from one car to the next. The train traveled at breakneck speed, and the wind rushed with penetrating force between the sleek structures held tightly together. His feet were firmly planted on the metal platform.

The door opened, and she stepped onto the metal grate in those gold strappy shoes, and he grabbed her arm, pulling her into his body.

In steadying herself, she accidentally placed her right hand over the pistol holstered below his leather jacket. As if touching him burned her hand, Liz reacted as only a woman scorned would: she slapped him hard. "Get your hands off me!"

The powerful wind filled the small space where they stood fixed, almost embracing, as the train rocked violently on the tracks.

"No. I won't let go of you!" Darcy yanked at the hem of her dress. "Are you wearing this for...*him*...*Lizzy*? That's right. You're just a tease, another fickle woman like the rest of them."

"What if I am wearing it for *him*? You shouldn't care. It was *you* who rejected *me,* not the other way around. I'm hardly fickle, but you made it clear that you were not interested!"

"So you are getting back at me for trying to protect you? For having the sense to back away so I can remain objective and focused in spite of what is obviously happening between us? I'm trying to keep you safe while finding *your* father."

"Don't flatter yourself. *Nothing* is happening between us. Remember, I'm not a romantic. And don't lie to me by saying you chose not to sleep with me in order to *protect* me! That's the lamest excuse I've heard for protecting *yourself.* Your selfish actions only show you are a coward! You're afraid, Darcy. Admit it, you're afraid of me!"

"Yeah, I'm so afraid of you that I brought you with me to Europe, nearly made love to you countless times, and vowed to protect you. Not to mention, I bought you that diamond necklace. Come to think of it, I *am* afraid! I'm afraid of the fact that I did it all against my better judgment!"

Echoing the turbulence of the insults being hurled and the tempestuous emotions, the vicious wind continued to hammer them, only serving to heighten their anger at each other.

"Countless times? Against your better judgment? You didn't seem to think it was against your better judgment when we were in that closet! In fact, you said that you wanted me from the first time you saw me at Longbourn. Another lie, since the first time you saw me was at the dance studio! As I said, you are nothing more than a snake in the grass!"

Longbourn. That definitely was not a lie, and he was in the grass. That was a slip of the tongue in the erotic heat of the moment when he was about to slide into her. "So which is it, Liz. I lied about wanting you, or I lied about *not* wanting you? You seem to be a little confused about what *you* want!"

Liz attempted to look away the moment he exposed her confusion. She stuck out her lower lip, pouting in petulance.

He was right, and she knew it. She *was* confused. She wanted him, and she wanted to love him, wanted to believe in romance, experience life and adventure with him, and give her heart to him. More importantly, she desired for him to want the exact same thing. If only he would say it! If only he would say that he unequivocally wanted her because he cared for her. Maybe even…

Darcy set her back away from him. His hands gently clasped her biceps as his dark eyes grew darker, more venomous. His expression turned thunderous with his lips forming a thin, taught line as the train barreled at 150 mph on the tracks below their feet. She infuriated him in every way and pushed every single friggin' button. *God damn if he didn't love it!*

He growled out into the wind, "I'd have to be a snake charmer to tame the likes of you!" Then slammed his lips against hers with such ferocity that she couldn't help but to respond in heated anger. Their lips crashed, exploding like TNT. Their tongues dueled as though trying to destroy the other with their kiss.

They were clearly not immune to each other even after his rejection and their vitriolic words.

Liz suddenly pulled back and then slapped him again, hard. "I said… get your hands off me!"

He let go, quickly releasing both his hands, causing her to stumble against the connecting glass door to the dinner car.

"Go back to your new victim, princess. Have fun trying to fend off *his* eager hands. Dressed like that, I doubt you'll be successful, but perhaps he'll be able to offer greater clarity about *his* feelings for you than I can about mine. After all, he thought about your supposed virginity day and night."

~ ♠ ~

With two hours left on the journey before arrival in Seville, Darcy stayed awake the entire night staring at Liz in the darkened club car. As soon as everyone had fallen asleep and only the emergency floor lights remained illuminated in the darkened car, he changed seats to face her from the opposite aisle.

He sat patiently watching and waiting for anything unusual. At least he could still do that well. It seemed that Rick was right; he was determined to fuck up Operation Cancan.

The Beretta pistol in his shoulder holster felt uncomfortable, but besides the razor-sharp knife sheathed in the inside of his motorcycle boot, it was his best defense. He was still uneasy about the other observant man who had made it his business—and not so covertly Darcy thought—to keep watch on Crawford and Liz. As hard as the Iceman in him tried to identify the stranger, the connection evaded him, but one thing was for sure: the man was not *just* a fellow traveler on his way to Seville.

Darcy's eyes appeared closed as he rested back against the plush seat at the aisle. The lights of Andalusia and Cordoba passed by the train's windows in red and yellow blurs when the train sped through. Sleeping heads bobbed and rolled with the movement of the bullet train, and he feigned the same, only he was awake and focused. How could he not be? The woman he loved, not to mention repeatedly offended, sat only five or so feet from him, and he would protect her life until death.

He loved to watch her sleep. She was even more beautiful in the moonlight. Darcy vowed that when the op was over, he would repair whatever had begun to develop between them. Perhaps he could learn to trust again. Perhaps his heart was thawing no matter how hard he tried to remain frozen. He wondered what had happened to have made Liz so volatile and skeptical about love. *Was it her mother, too?*

Within the train's economy-class car two sections behind them, he noticed movement when the cars briefly aligned. He reached into his pocket and slowly pulled out his compact, portable night vision binoculars. It was the other observer stealthily making his way forward through the train.

Darcy rose and, with silent, deliberate movements, remained concealed against the seats beside the aisle, making his way to the door. Slipping out, he stationed himself in between the speeding cars, just as he had done when waiting for Liz earlier.

He calmed his heartbeat and regulated his breath as he patiently waited for the Arab to pass through the door to the platform. Disappearing and molding into the blackness, Darcy became part of the strength and metal of the train. Deadly still, he was shadow and steel—ready for the kill. Through the door's window, he watched the man withdraw a pistol and silencer from his black Sherwani suit jacket. Clearly, Darcy's intuition had been spot on, either Crawford or Liz was his planned target.

If only his intuition about all things Liz could be as astute as his professional prowess.

Omar did well with his specialized dexterity and honed observation skills. He had been with Devlin Renaud for six years now, and together, they had explored, expanded, and exceeded in all things related to terrorism and death dealing. Crawford was easy to spot, and he laughed at the infidel's attempt to disguise himself behind facial hair and black dye. An expensive suit and a different name on the passenger manifest certainly couldn't keep Omar from spotting him. What he didn't expect was the fact that the dog had blatantly and foolishly lied to Al-Hanash. The girl was with him. He remembered her from the kidnapping, confirmed by the repetitious television news reports.

Making the hit on the train would be easy, then he'd grab the girl and jump off as they neared the next stop. He had jumped from a slowing bullet train before. He could do it again.

Even in the darkness, Darcy could see the Arab's dark, deadly eyes. They appeared emotionless and focused on his task. A lariat cord hung from the man's jacket belt. There was something else the Iceman noted, which caused his heart to stop dead on the tracks. A diamond encrusted image upon the ring he wore flashed in the red and yellow lights of a passing town. It's design—a distinct cobra insignia—was the same snake crescent moon image of Lucy Steele's tattoo. Coincidence? He didn't think so.

With sudden blinding recognition, he remembered the boat chase in Cuba. That experience was another painful memory of defection he had boxed and stored, but it now came back in vivid recollection.

In a flash, he recalled the failed hit of the arms dealer in Operation Mambo and Lucy's betrayal. Now he remembered the face of the man who approached him. The pieces connected with a spark. The Arab was the one steering the speedboat intending to kill him. The ring and the tattoo confirmed to Darcy that Lucy wasn't a double agent in the Cuban government. She worked for the *arms dealer.*

The passenger car door opened, and he grabbed hold of the killer's wrist, twisting it and forcing the pistol he held to fall to the metal floor. The sounds of the harsh impact and skittering weapon against the floor were lost to the roar of the wind whistling through the space. Within the narrow confines of the four-foot platform, hand-to-hand combat ensued between the men with furious strikes and jabs. Hand chops, thrusts to the neck, and fists to the body landed and redirected.

The pistol slid off the platform into the dead of night as the train shook and vibrated on the tracks.

Darcy crouched forward with tremendous balance, secured his hand, and yanked at his adversary's leg with lightening speed. The Arab crashed backward onto the platform, his head hanging over the edge, mere feet above the rapidly passing track below.

In the split second Iceman took to draw his breath, his enemy raised his head, making violent contact with Darcy's forehead, forcing him backward. The Arab rose instantaneously to his feet. Battered and breathing heavily, both men stood toe-to-toe, eye-to-eye. One without his gun, and the other determined not to fire his, given that it had no silencer. In such close proximity to the occupied passenger cars, the sound would not go unnoticed by the travelers within.

Omar stared him down. Recognition occurred and he snickered. "You do not remember me?"

Darcy took a step back bracing himself for impact. "Oh, I remember you all right. Cuba."

"I will take great satisfaction in killing you. My employer has searched for you these many years."

"And who might he be?"

"Al-Hanash. You killed his lover, Lucia."

Darcy's face remained impassive, but inside was altogether different. *She was a cheater, too.*

His fierce roundhouse kick to his enemy's gut sent the man flying backward, nearly over the side of the train, but he braced himself with hands on both cars to keep from falling.

He charged at Darcy. His fists were deadly and unrelenting, one after another, after another. The two men were equally matched as they each continued to slam their opponent's body against the exterior end caps of the fast-moving train, attempting to kill each other.

It was only when Darcy was violently knocked to his back on the platform that he was able to grab the knife hidden within his boot.

Omar dove upon him intent on snapping his neck with lethal hands, but the Iceman was quicker, jabbing the knife under his opponent's ribs, twisting the blade upward with exacting precision.

"Give Lucy my regards," he panted in exhausted relief. With all his remaining strength from the prone position, he tossed the Arab's lifeless body up and over him, off the speeding bullet train out into the darkness.

Darcy sat still on the floor with elbows resting on bent knees and dropped his head to catch his breath and sort out what had just transpired. The rushing wind continued to whip around him in a competing roar against the sound of the train's whistle. He had a knot the size of a baseball forming on his head and a cut to his lip, but he was alive, and so was Liz. For that, he was thankful.

He shook his head astounded at the coincidence. Operation Cancan put him in hot pursuit of Al-Hanash, the very man he was sent to kill three years earlier as part of Operation Mambo in Cuba. That man, Devlin Renaud, had been Lucy's lover. In stark clarity, Darcy knew that had *that* hit been completed, Operation Virginia Reel would never have needed to be sanctioned.

Rising, he braced himself with one hand against the door frame and peered into the club car where he assumed Liz still lay sleeping. Shocked, he watched as she ran down the aisle toward him.

She had seen almost everything each time the two men passed across the windowed door in the course of their clash. Her legs trembled so violently that they almost gave out when she ran to Darcy. The passengers were still largely asleep or oblivious when Liz flew through the door into his arms.

This embrace was nothing like the one five hours earlier. Liz carefully wiped the blood from his lip with her thumb and held him up against her body, taking his weight upon her, thinking he needed her support.

"Are you okay? Is anything broken?"

"I don't think so, but man, my head hurts. I'm getting too old for this shit."

"Come with me." She took his hand, entwining her fingers with his just as he had done with hers so many times before, leading him to the exclusive lavatory in the club car.

As they passed, Darcy looked to Crawford who was still asleep by the window. He was clearly surprised the man had slept through the noise.

Liz smiled and whispered, "He said he had a headache, so I gave him three Dramamine from the plane. Who knew it would knock him out cold?"

Yes, you have skills, Liz Bennet.

Once the door latched behind them, he sat on the edge of the sink with Liz standing between his open legs in the small space of the washroom. Gone were the animosity and heated words. They seemed so unimportant in the grand scheme of everything.

He couldn't know it, but Liz now understood the full weight of his decision to remain focused. He afforded her more clarity in that one fight with the Arab than he had in his explanation for pulling back from her. She now understood the real danger and further understood the danger she had placed them in by agreeing to this ruse with Crawford.

"Your forehead needs attention." She proceeded to place cool compresses to his head, then took his hand, pressing it to the rolled wet paper towel. "Hold this here, and don't argue."

Darcy smirked at her take-charge attitude and obeyed.

"Did you kill him?"

"Yes."

Her care moved to his mouth where she carefully cleaned the split to his lip, causing him to wince from the pressure. "Don't be such a big baby. It's only a small cut. You kill a man with your bare hands, yet you wince from a little nursing?"

"Knife. I used my boot knife, and the cut hurts."

Who knew he even had a knife in his boot.

She stilled her hand in astonishment. "This *hurts*? *This* hurts? I survived a Brazilian wax, and you think *this* hurts? Some SEAL you are."

Darcy tried to smile, but it pained when he did. "Like I said, you have skills, Liz Bennet."

She went back to tending his cut with a smirk of her own.

He loved being cared for by her and would gladly act the wounded warrior time and again if for no other reason than to have her nurse him back to health.

"Who was he, and what did he want?" she asked, continuing to clean his lip.

He debated for a second and thought about lying but then thought better of it. Hadn't they lied enough to each other?

"He was sent by the man who has your father. My guess is it was to kill Crawford then take you as collateral in case your father isn't cooperating with finishing the software."

She tightened her lips and nodded. What she asked next surprised Darcy because the tone in her voice sounded almost resolved to the fact that her father was guilty of causing this situation. "What did my father really do, Darcy?"

"Well, he sold a top secret Department of Defense software program he is writing to a very evil man. This program could potentially be used against America by this terrorist or sold to another of our nation's enemies. It is a weapon that could change life as we know it, killing millions in the process."

"Daddy wouldn't do that. He loves our country. Besides, he's not a violent man in any way."

"I'm sorry, Liz, but he did do it, and Crawford convinced him to do so. Crawford is a terrorist who also works for the man we are tracking. Don't underestimate him and his charming ways. He's a deadly killer. The act he employs, which you have seen today, is for one purpose only."

She leaned into him and whispered with humor in her voice. "He thinks I'm a virgin."

"Is he correct in his assumption?" Hell, he *was* curious after all.

"No, Mr. Smartypants. Don't worry about Crawford and his intentions. I'm careful with him. As you can hear, I know how to handle him. This isn't anything new for me where he is concerned. I had a sixth sense about him and never trusted him around Daddy—or myself for that matter."

"Unfortunately, he is the only one to lead us to Al-Hanash in Morocco, otherwise I'd leave him on this train with a bullet in his head."

"It still doesn't answer why. Why would my father become a traitor? He is so proud of the Bennet legacy, the plantation, and our family's role in Mount Vernon."

Darcy smoothed a fallen tendril of her hair, tucking it behind her ear. "You tell me. Why would he need money?"

She dropped her hand from his lip, and began to pace inside the small confines of the lavatory, two steps away, two steps back and so on. He noticed how the fingers on her right hand tapped repeatedly against her thigh and how she furrowed her brow, working out the details in her mind. He knew the answer when he asked the question, having made the correct assumption when in his hide site preparing to eliminate Bennet.

Liz's mind was all over the place but kept coming back to the same conclusion: Longbourn. What she didn't expect was the immense guilt she felt for having coddled her father for far too long. In doing so, she had overlooked the extent of his obsession as nothing more than desire to preserve the family's legacy. She fed that obsession by acquiescing to his every whim, which didn't allow him to face reality. Maybe, just maybe, if she had listened and acted upon the urgings of her conscience, things would have been different.

Then there was the whole other subject of his insistence on her marrying Bill Collins. Sure, the ultimate decision was left in her hands, but he pushed the issue. Why did he do that if he knew he had money coming from the sale of the software? She was angry at his selfishness but was almost angrier at herself for ignoring the spirited Liz who should have said, "over my dead body." She had squashed that Liz down for too many years.

"What are you thinking, Liz? Are you feeling responsible for his decisions? Angry, even?"

Her head snapped up. "How did you know?"

"I make it my business to observe things. I know your expressions very well by now."

She came to stand between his legs again, bowing her head in silence, causing Darcy to lift her chin with his index finger. "Did he do it for Longbourn?"

Liz simply nodded with sadness behind her eyes.

"Why do you feel guilty for his actions? A man makes his own choice whether or not to go to the dark side. You didn't hold a gun to his head."

"No, but I should have realized the extent of his desperation. I feel responsible for having been his enabler since my mother left. Jane had the foresight to leave. I stayed and denied myself *everything* so he would be comfortable and at peace. I think I *created* the desperate man he became, fostering that notion that Longbourn was all he had. I nursed his obsession. Hell, I almost married a man I disliked in order to save Longbourn for Daddy."

Well, that answers that question, Darcy thought.

"Are you angry at him or yourself? I know anger at a parent, Liz. Shit, I'm still angry at *both* of my parents after thirteen years. So trust me when I say that I understand. And, if I am really honest with myself"—he swallowed hard, hating to admit what he'd locked away—"I'm more angry with myself for having stood by and watched, doing nothing to change the course of events. It changed everything about me and my life. I ran away and became the man you see today. In a way, I'm still running."

That's why he always leaves, Liz thought.

She took his bruised hand into hers, soothing his scraped knuckles with her thumb. This was only the second thing he'd shared about himself, and it was huge. She didn't want the moment to be lost. She wanted to understand him. This and only this was the clarity she needed. This was why Fitzwilliam Darcy moved seamlessly between two worlds as though he was born into wealthy society yet chose to live bad-ass and hard-edged.

"We seem to be more alike than we realized." It killed her to verbalize it, but she did. "The Lizzy Bennet of Longbourn is not the woman I want to be. She's not the woman I really am deep down inside."

"I can tell."

"Tell me, what happened with your parents?"

"Brace yourself because it's ugly. I had just come back to the stables after polo practice, riding up to the barn door as my father confronted my mother about her cheating with my best friend." He paused, taking a deep breath. "He shot her and then, in his heartbreak, shot himself."

Darcy looked away from her compassionate gaze. He was sure she didn't notice that his eyes grew glassy. No tears, just that telltale prelude of what surely would have followed under other circumstances and less reserve.

"It all happened right before my eyes, and I did nothing to stop it. I was a coward who hid in the shadows until right before he pulled the trigger, ending his own life."

He looked back at Liz, and he knew she understood how very similar they were. Silence ensued for long minutes as the train continued to rock. She continued to caress his knuckles, her eyes held steadfast to his.

"Thank you for sharing that with me. I know how difficult it must have been. I'm so sorry for your loss and your horrific pain." She lifted her hand to his cheek. "I am sure that had you not been immobilized by fear and shock, you would have reacted. Perhaps you and I can help each other get over our anger and regret. Perhaps we can help each other break free."

Iceman was threatening to re-emerge and put up his wall of defense. He just wanted to push back all those emotions and apparent truths, not to mention the guilt that her own revelations caused to surface. "Perhaps," was all he could reply.

Liz understood Darcy's need to retreat. After all, just about every moment she spent with his taciturn self, usually preceded his leaving. Now she understood. That was his defense mechanism, and this small glimpse into his soul was for her benefit only, meant to help her cope with her father's poor decisions and her own misguided guilt.

"What will you do with Daddy when we rescue him?"

Darcy smiled at her understanding. He liked her optimism in regard to her father's outcome. Although, it was unlikely they would find him alive once the source code was finished. He hated to say it, but she needed to hear it. "If he is still alive when we get to Marrakech, then I will bring him home to face justice."

He raised her hand to his lips and kissed her knuckles with such contrition. "I'm sorry, Liz. I'm sorry to tell you the truth about what he did. Most importantly, I'm sorry for causing you pain. I don't want to fight you any longer. If you're not scared off by what you saw just now, do you want to continue? Are we a team again—you and me?"

Liz was entirely affected by the look upon his face and his almost begging words. She did say that she liked begging, and she enjoyed that he remembered. She leaned into his hard body, wanting to move on from the guilt and anger and get lost in healing his wounds and her own. "Is that look your way of charming a snake, Fitzwilliam Darcy?"

He smoothed his right hand over her backside and pulled her in even closer. "No, Liz Bennet, this is." He kissed her softly, careful to avoid exacerbating the pain in his lip.

So much for his self-restraint and pulling back to keep from getting too attached to her.

His lips separated from hers, their eyes locked. When he admired the brilliance of her hazel greens, he groaned, "Aw, screw it," and kissed her ferociously.

Liz eagerly responded. Scorching hot mouths reclaimed each other in reconciliation as hands roamed and caressed. The moment Darcy's hand began its ascent on the back of Liz's bare thigh, her breathless treaty to stop left him hungry and bereft. He knit his brows.

She panted, "I need...I just need to see if you're hurt anywhere else before we leave this bathroom."

Her mischievous smile said so much, and he couldn't help but smirk in reply.

"As you wish." Already, her exploratory hands were rising his T-shirt above his stomach.

The tips of her fingers grazed over the sides of his waist when she pulled the black fabric higher and higher until she finally lifted it over his head.

Liz's hands traveled over his bare chest and broad shoulders. Her eyes drank in his beautiful physique. "Hmm...no bruises here," she seductively voiced while slowly depositing open, wet kisses, purposefully leaving a trail toward his firm pecs.

Darcy dropped his head back enjoying the feel of her mouth upon him.

The train speedily rocked around a sharp turn, causing the lights in the cars to flicker on and off until unexpectedly ceasing altogether.

They were in absolute darkness, but it didn't stop Liz from her provocative path. Her other four senses rose to the occasion. She enjoyed listening to his labored breath and feeling the rapid beat of his heart below her attentive lips. Her hand reveled in his smooth, hard abdomen as it traveled downward, seeking its treasure or, in this case, its prey.

Darcy couldn't see her, but he was totally taken by surprise when her tongue flicked and nibbled his erect nipple. "Liz…baby…" he moaned into the dark space.

She turned the faucet on in anticipation of his moans to come. Yeah, she knew there would be many.

He reached for the zipper to her dress but had no success because she abruptly repositioned his hand to rest on the sink's counter. Her tongue continued to languidly glide over his firm body, flicking and teasing. He tasted salty and sweet, and his scent was driving her wild.

She knew her teasing licks over his taut nipple were heightening his arousal. It was evident when she ran her hand over his erection, molding her palm to his girth, rubbing him with teasing delight. His need was apparently great, meeting her touch with slight grinds and pushes. Her own need was at its peak of restraint. A moment longer in this game she played, and she would be putty in *his* hands, but turnaround was fair play, and she was determined to give him as good as he gave in recompense for the night before.

It was salacious and erotic in the pitch dark as the train shook violently, almost as violently as his need to make love to her on the counter top, but he held back, letting Liz take the reins to her sexual freedom. Who was he to object? He was hers to do what she pleased. He'd do and be anything she wanted him to be, and sex slave was a great beginning.

Liz made quick work of unzipping his jeans, dropping them and his briefs to the floor. The moment her hand surrounded his hardness, he bit back the temptation to cry out in passion. Her strong grip was hot and determined to bring him to climax with each stroke. He never expected her curious, eager exploration, but when she cradled his tight balls in the palm of her hand, massaging him, he thought he would die. "Liz… please. Let me make love to you."

She said nothing, but squatted before him, taking him firmly in her right hand sliding up and down, her thumb stroking the bulging vein in his rigid shaft.

A wicked smile formed upon her lips when she purposefully, starting at his balls, gave him one long, slow, deliberate lick up his throbbing cock. After a flicking tease of her taut tongue upon his engorged tip, she dropped a sweet kiss, rose before him, licked her lips, and righted her dress.

In the dark, she could just make out Darcy's gorgeous, nude silhouette splayed against the sink counter. His impressive arousal was huge and ready to burst. He rumbled, "Liz?"

She smiled. "See you in Seville, big guy." And slipped out the bathroom door.

~♠~

17
Telephone

Jane stood on the terrace of the luxurious villa that seemed to hang precariously from the hillside on the island of Capri. Looking out at the crystalline turquoise waters of the Bay of Marina Grande and the Bay of Marina Piccola, she nearly squealed in excitement at the panoramic view of the Piazzetta. Hot pink fingernails held onto the ornate white railing as she leaned over, mindlessly defying death and the laws of gravity so she could see the lush gardens below.

She chuckled. Damn if she wasn't glad her father got kidnapped. *No, Jane Bennet, you did not just think that!*

Charlie was a mystery. His decision to travel to Capri was so spontaneous that even she was surprised by his insistence she join him. One thing was certain: she was having the time of her life and had absolutely no compunction when she called the museum to say, "I'm taking a short leave of absence."

Set against the blue backdrop of the bays beyond, the terracotta pots filled with vibrant red geraniums lining the terrace looked wildly exotic. The sun was high and brilliant, and Jane felt as if she were in paradise, even more so when Charlie exited the villa, holding a tray with a plate of Canestrini cookies and a bottle of chilled Limoncello di Capri.

In flip-flops and tan cargo pants, he looked relaxed and very much at home in his father's summer home as his long blond curls blew in the breeze. Jane took in the image of him approaching with an eager smile and an alluring flush to his cheeks. In her opinion, Charlie was more than a fabulous lover and a good-natured man. He possessed many of the same attributes as she did. Both loved to live life on the wild side, adored corny jokes, comics and cartoons, body surfing, and boating. He seemed to be her other half. Like a long lost twin, only one she wanted to screw night and day. As though an animated Kama Sutra, he knew tricks and positions that even she had never been exposed to, and she enjoyed delving into his pages—repeatedly.

"Do you like what you see, Jane?"

"It's beautiful. The stuff of dreams, really. I can't believe I'm here."

"I'm glad you came with me. Even if I didn't swear to Darcy to keep you safe, I would have asked you to come along anyway. We can take a flight around the island tomorrow in my dad's plane, or we can go out on the boat if you like. There are some great caves where we can go spelunking, and along the Mediterranean, there are even some small crystal-clear coves where we can skinny dip from the boat. I'll pack a picnic lunch for us." *There I can talk to you about my career. Maybe over dessert—chocolate. Women love chocolate. Hmm…melted chocolate…on me…with her mouth occupied. My confession won't even matter at that point, and she certainly won't be able to talk about it,* he added in his mind.

Charlie intended to tell her about his career. He just needed the right moment, the right circumstances to do so. Although he was an assassin, a hired gun for the CIA, he was never really very good at lying. He was just a proficient guy with a rifle. He liked Jane, believing her to be an honest and forthright girl. Therefore, he felt no guilt in desiring to be honest with her and explain exactly why they were in Capri and what his intentions were. Admittedly, he wanted her along for the thrill of it all. He was sure Darcy and Rick would say he had lost all reason, not to mention his professionalism, but he didn't give a crap. He was sure that a girl like Jane would grab Operation Cancan by the balls and kick ass, all the while laughing as though it were the adventure of a lifetime. Could he trust her? Hell yeah, he could trust her. After all, her father's and sister's lives lay in the balance.

"Skinny dipping? That sounds incredible, Charlie. I have yet to go anywhere where I can feel free enough to do that. Although, there was this gay beach on Long Island, but the thrill would have been lost on sunbathers who wouldn't care…or notice for that matter."

"You can sunbathe here if you like. It's pretty secluded, and I sure as hell won't mind and would definitely notice." Charlie wiggled his eyebrows in encouragement, and with that simple suggestion, Jane pulled the string to her bikini top, and off it came.

Taking his ice-filled glass, he poured the lemony liqueur, then held the cool glass between her full breasts, enjoying the image of her nipples hardening from the chill. Almost immediately, his lips began to suck. Shortly after, he gave in to the sweet indulgence of pouring the limoncello onto her breasts, licking and tasting. Yes, it was only a matter of minutes before both were completely nude and covered with sticky limoncello, sucking, screwing, and moaning on the terrace with only the sunlight and geraniums as witnesses.

Jane heard her cell phone ring in the kitchen where she'd left it. Her head snapped up. Torn from her moans and oncoming orgasm by concern that she may be missing Liz's call, she quickly rose from Charlie's splayed body and ran to the phone.

"Lizzy?" she panted into the phone.

Liz spoke low into the cell phone that Darcy had given her in Monte Carlo. "Yeah, it's me. Listen, I don't have much time. Crawford went to check us into the hotel."

"Crawford? Why are you with Crawford?"

"It's a long story. Look, I'm in Seville on a black op. Darcy is here, too. Although he's staying in the shadow, he hears everything through the snake."

"What about his snake? I'm not sure I understand what you are saying. An op? He's in the shadow? What the hell does that mean? I thought you were going to Monte Carlo, and now you are in Spain?"

Liz looked around her suspiciously. "Jane, stop. Just listen for a minute. You need to take care of yourself, and you need to know about Daddy. He's in a lot of trouble. He could be…he could be dead already, and Darcy killed an Arab with his boot knife at close range during a fight on the bullet train. The Arab was going to take me, too."

Standing in the kitchen flush and naked, Jane's hand went to her heart. "I'm sure Daddy is safe, and don't worry about me. I'm safe, too. I'm in Capri with Charlie sharing some limoncello. What do you mean Darcy killed a man with a boot knife, Lizzy? Oh. My. God. You're becoming a spy! Better yet, a Bond girl!"

"Shut up, I am not! And what are you doing in Capri?"

"Did you sleep with him yet?" Jane asked with a huge grin.

"Crawford? Eww…"

"No, not Crawford! You mentioned a snake. Is it one of those candida-canibis ones? I'm talking about Darcy, your hot, CIA, motorcycle God."

"What! Darcy's much hotter in a tuxedo playing roulette, and no, I didn't sleep with him. I'll ask you again more slowly this time: What. Are. You. Doing. In. Capri?"

Charlie walked up behind Jane with a still-swollen member bouncing in front of him. He leaned in, kissing her neck, and she turned with excitement to tell him, "They're in Seville. Darcy killed an Arab on a train. They haven't had sex yet, but his snake has been doing some talking to her. You're sticky, mmm …" She licked his chest, holding the phone away from her ear for a moment.

"Jane, are you listening to me? Hello? What are you doing in Capri, and why is Charlie sticky?" Liz asked firmly.

"I have no idea why we are here, Lizzy." She grabbed Charlie's erection in her hand. "But I know what I'd like to be doing while here. Look, take care and be safe. I have no doubt that you're in good, not to mention talented hands. Call me later. I promise I'll be more focused then."

There was a click of Jane's disconnection. "Jane…Jane…Shit! She hung up!"

~ ♠ ~

Even at that early hour, it wasn't too early in the morning for Darcy to be sitting in the American Bar of the Hotel Alphonso XIII nursing a Glenfiddich. The bar just opened, and while waiting for Crawford to finish checking-in, he had just been privy to the most delightful one-sided phone conversation coming through Liz's necklace.

Hotter in a tux. He couldn't help but smirk as he brought the rocks glass to his lips.

The trendy bar was fashioned in chrome, decorated with gold beveled mirrors and sleek paneling. He sat there on one of the chic barstools with a huge knot on his head and a cut lip. His eyes drank in the curve of Liz's form standing on the other side of the lobby. He felt strangely liberated today, as though the windows of his soul have been opened and the breeze was blowing through. She did that from the first moment he had laid eyes on her. Every time he was in her presence, she continued to do that, and it was his sharing of the biggest piece of himself with her that was truly liberating. He wanted to fly.

Darcy continued to be in awe of her, and it wasn't just how she made him feel or how she looked. It was the whole of Liz Bennet. He could clearly see that she was reaching beyond her tame existence by jumping with two feet into his dangerous world in spite of her fear. He loved how she looked at everything with a glass-half-full perspective, and how her wit carried her through scary, unfamiliar moments. It was clear that Liz wasn't afraid of speed or adventure and had the innate ability to live in two worlds—just like he did. Hell, it was written on the pages of her sketchbook. Only like him, she had never listened to her inner voice encouraging her to fly, run, live, and be free until now.

As Crawford stood within his line of vision at the concierge counter, Liz examined a display case with her back to him. Darcy picked up his cell phone, calling her as soon as she hung up from the call with her sister. It wasn't the first time he'd broken protocol, and even though he vowed not to do it, he couldn't help it. She looked so beautiful in that lovely yellow sundress he had first seen her wearing three weeks earlier at Longbourn. Set against the exotic Moorish mosaic gracing the walls of the lobby and the red backdrop of the case, she dazzled like the morning sunlight streaming through the front windows of the hotel. Liz looked resplendent.

"Hello?" she tentatively greeted.

"What's in the display case, beautiful?"

"Vases and crystal," she whispered, surreptitiously looking over her shoulder at Crawford. "Why are you calling me?"

"To tell you that was very naughty what you did to me on the train. You made for a very uncomfortable trip."

"Aww, poor baby. Maybe next time you'll finish what *you* start."

Darcy licked the whiskey from his lips. "You know, I can see through your dress, and I just wanted to tell you that one day my tongue is going to slide up those long legs of yours."

"Stop it!" she hissed.

"Don't you want to hear how much my lips are desiring to kiss every inch of your body?"

"I'm not kidding. You're embarrassing me!"

Darcy chuckled. "You shouldn't have called Jane, not very covert, Agent Bennet. You have a burner phone, but she does not."

"A what?"

"A throw-away phone."

"Oh. I was worried about her."

"As soon as you are able, take your phone apart, and throw the pieces away in different locations."

"Okay. Are we done here? Can I hang up now?"

He saw Liz's fingers bounce against her thigh. "No." He really just wanted to hear her voice and completely loved getting her frazzled.

"But he's almost done." She covertly looked over her shoulder again.

"No, he's not. I can see him looking down the concierge's dress. So about my tongue under *your* dress, on your thigh, tasting your…"

"Yes?" *Oh God, my first phone-sex conversation,* she internally panted.

"Just giving you something to imagine when you try to get some information from Crawford about Marrakech. Who is he meeting? Will you be in the Medina, or will the meeting take place in the Souk? Stuff like that will help me if we get separated. And remember, try to remain in public, less chance of his eager hands. Stay where I can see you. I don't want to lose you."

"You won't lose me."

"No, I definitely won't. Are you afraid, Liz? We do not have to do this. I can pull you out at anytime. You just say the word."

Liz grew very quiet for a moment and then said softly, "No, I can do this. I can do anything so long as I know that you've got my back."

"I do. I'm committed." Darcy meant it in every way.

"Listen, how's…how's your head?"

"Swollen,"

"And your lip?"

"Lonely."

She blushed, suddenly understanding his innuendo. "I meant your battle scars."

"I know what you meant, but that's not what I meant."

Crawford's voice came from behind her. "Are you ready to go to our rooms, Liz?"

"Good bye, Lakmé. See you later." Darcy disconnected the call.

He followed behind Crawford and Liz until she was safely settled into her suite. He then placed the long overdue call to his cousin back in DC.

~ ♠ ~

Rick sat in the dance studio's office, watching Caroline shimmy and shake with one of her students, a fellow named Jared who was far more preoccupied with watching the ass of the FedEx deliveryman than any asset belonging to the female spitting cobra with whom he danced.

Obsidian's director chuckled. *Bitch.* He would fire that finely-toned ass in a minute if she didn't do such a damn good job in Obsidian. He should have known better. He should have never crapped where he ate. Moreover, he should have trusted Darcy's judgment about Caroline, and more importantly, he should never have slept with his cousin's ex-fling.

Now that she was out of his bed, Rick was starting to think clearly again, realizing her machinations to further herself and get what she wanted within his organization, not to mention the studio, which Obsidian funded. That previous slip of Bertram's tongue about a mole made things all too clear. He would have to think on that, think on how he would deal with that unexpected intel.

Having been played for the ultimate fool, he now understood Darcy's opinion of most women. Caroline fit the description of the deadliest kind of viper. After all, her forked tongue certainly did a number on him. He swore that in time, he would get over her completely. Watching her through the office window, he controlled the rage building within him, and when his cell phone vibrated upon the desk, he was thankful for the distraction. The caller ID indicated Darcy's international number.

"It's about time. Where are you?"

"Just arrived in Seville. Still on the target. Still with the girl. He's heading to Marrakech in two days."

"Good, keep me abreast as things unfold. Did you know that Charlie was leaving for vacation with the other Bennet sister?"

Darcy lied. "No. He most likely wanted to get away from you breathing down his neck. Am I still on your shit list? Are you still threatening to denounce me if this op fails?"

Rick snickered. Of course he wouldn't do that, and his cousin knew it. "It all depends on what else you have for me."

"Remember Cuba? Operation Mambo? Renaud?"

"Please don't remind me. I had to eat crow for months when Homeland Security called me before a Senate hearing. Until Operation Virginia Reel, that was our only failed hit, not to mention one of my best agents betrayed us."

"Not to mention she was the woman I had been sleeping with for six months. I see you're starting to understand women a little better. Anyway, Devlin Renaud is Al-Hanash. I may end up finishing Operation Mambo after all."

Rick's eyebrow shot up. "You've got to be kidding?"

"There's more. Steele was Renaud's lover. Apparently, he's been searching for me since I put that bullet in her head."

Rick swiveled the chair to face the wall and shot a rubber band against the red brick surface.

"I'll be damned. Another lying, cheating woman."

Darcy chuckled. "Boy, Caroline did a number on you, huh? You're beginning to sound like me."

"That's never good."

"Yeah, well, I'm hoping to change my woman-hating ways."

"You obviously have inspiration."

"You might say that."

"Did you sleep with her yet?"

"You know better than to ask that. The Iceman doesn't kiss and tell, even to you."

Rick didn't see that Caroline stood listening by the office's open door.

"Does she know about Obsidian? Does she know what you do for a living?"

"One thing at a time, Rick. I want to keep her beside me, not scare her away."

"I wouldn't want to be in your shoes when she finds out that you were hired to kill her father. If you want my advice, have your little international romance. Sleep with her, kill Al-Hanash, bring Bennet home, and be done with the whole thing. You once understood that mixing business with pleasure wasn't a good idea. I'm on the same page now."

"Man, she really did screw you up."

Rick shot another rubber band onto the wall. "Call me when you get to Marrakech. Be careful Darcy." He clicked the phone off just as Caroline entered the room.

Her red hair, pulled into a high ponytail, swung behind her as she nonchalantly sauntered in. Rick ignored her and began to pack files into his briefcase, then opened the metal drawers of the desk, removing surveillance gear and his covert travel equipment.

"Going somewhere?"

He didn't look up. "What's it to you?"

"I am still an agent in this organization and still have a vested interest in every op. Just because you and I are no longer romantically involved does not mean you can shut me out."

Rick turned, seething but in control. Of late, his anger had been pushed to the point of eruption far too many times. When faced with Caroline's pouty lips and feigned concern, he fought back his vitriol. He would rather have his eyes gouged out than admit thinking himself in love with her and, therefore, left heart-broken.

"Caroline, you and I were never romantic. You were my cousin's sloppy seconds, his leftover whore. I now fully comprehend why he kicked you to the curb. You're a shrew."

He continued to pack his black-op bags, pulling from the closet an emergency travel kit containing clothing and toiletries for an extended trip to warm climates.

"You're being irrational, not to mention jealous," she proclaimed with an indignant huff.

"I'm hardly the jealous one. Your comparisons and sick obsession with Darcy, not as a man of character and worth but as a lover, have reached their threshold with me. I get it; you want what I don't have, but obviously, he does. That's fine, but don't expect me to continue to overlook the fact that I can't *measure* up to him. I won't allow myself to be used any longer. Darcy has long moved on from you, and now so have I."

Measure up is right. "Yeah, he's moved on with a traitor's daughter. She's most likely leading him into a deadly trap, if you ask me."

"Don't go there again. I'm warning you. My generosity with you has nearly run out."

"I'm sorry, Rick, but it's true. He's lost focus. She is no good for him."

"No good for him because she is not you, right?"

She didn't answer his question.

"Just wait until she finds out what he does at Obsidian. Miss Goody-Two-Shoes won't want him then, won't ever understand this world of ours. She could never cope with the kind of life he leads: the last-minute, prolonged travel, the women who fall all over him, the danger around every corner, not to mention the lonely nights."

Rick turned to stare her down. "Don't go there, Caroline. I can hear the machination in your tone. If you cross him…if you interfere in his relationship with this woman, he will, I have no doubt, kill you just as he killed Lucy Steele, and if he doesn't do it, I will."

She looked away, hating that he could read her so well. She hated that he was so very good at this game of espionage and duplicity, and she hated the Bennet woman for obviously succeeding with Darcy where she failed to time and again. Good God, she would do anything to experience just one more night in his embrace. Never in all her years and many conquests had she ever met a man who possessed so much virility and prowess in the bedroom. Nine inches…nine thick inches that he put to very good use. Caroline nearly swooned just remembering what he could do with it.

Rick turned his back to her and began to dial in the numbers to the safe hidden behind the painting of Vettriano's *Dancer in Emerald.*

"What are you doing?"

"What does it look like I'm doing? I'm packing to leave the country."

He fanned through a thick wad of Euros and placed them in his black leather billfold. Next, sorting through the five different alias passports and matching credit cards he had on hand, he chose those for Hank Tilney and James Morland. He shoved them into the inside pocket of his grey suit.

"Where are you going?"

"That's none of your concern."

With a stone-cold expression, Rick grabbed his gear and bags and headed toward the office door, halting for a moment at the threshold. He turned to Caroline. "If you really consider yourself part of this team, you might try *helping* Darcy rather than *hindering* him with that venomous tongue and jealousy of yours."

He departed, leaving her mouth agape. As soon as he exited the dance studio, he called KLM Airways to book a flight to Marrakech. His cousin was going to need him.

~ ♠ ~

In Liz's opinion, the Hotel Alphonso XIII was more exotic than the Hotel de Paris in Monte Carlo, but hell, all of it was exciting and much better than lifeless Longbourn any day of the week. The luxury accommodation's ornate moldings, inlays, mosaics, and marbled pillars conveyed the many traditions of Spain. It all bespoke Andalusian, Moorish, and pure Spanish styles. All three cultures embodied in perfect harmony within the hotel.

Her large room, although at the bottom of the offerings, was fresh and airy, decorated in Moorish-style featuring floor to ceiling windows and a small balcony. Everything about it was appealing, except the fact that Crawford's room was on the other side of the connecting door.

He came up behind her as she took in the full measure of the view of the hotel's famous courtyard garden, holding precariously onto the wrought iron railing to look down. If not for the fact that her father could be dead and Crawford was with her, this was the best and most exciting time of her life.

She nearly jumped from her skin when he surprised her by snaking his hand around her waist.

"Careful, careful, Liz. We can't have anything happen to you now." He pulled her backward, close against his body. "Do you like what you see?" He whispered beside her ear. "And feel?"

Darcy tightened his fist as he listened from his room one floor above. The last two words sent him into simultaneous hyper-alert in fear for her and in jealous frenzy.

"I…umm…I'm not ready for that, Henry. Perhaps when we get to Marrakech. Will we be staying in the Medina?"

He released her, thoughtfully repeating, "Marrakech…no not the Medina. I said I would be patient, but I do hope the Andalusian spirit will release some of your inhibitions. If you would reconsider dancing with me this evening, I am sure you'll be more than ready. The passion of watching flamenco or dancing the tango at an outdoor square is bound to heat your blood. You'll see. Tonight you will want to be mine."

Liz was petrified by his intentions. The fact that at that very moment his finger ran down the side of her breast sent the wrong type of chills down her body. She was coming to regret her hasty decision to play covert CIA agent. Darcy was right. She had neither the skills nor the mettle to pull off what was needed. Yet she didn't want to disappoint him, let alone her father. Knowing that he heard every conversation through the necklace, she would have faith.

Crawford's fingers toyed with the diamond necklace. His lust for both her and the expensive jewelry was apparent when he spoke. "It's a beautifully erotic piece of jewelry. Did you know the Chinese believe that if you were born in the year of the snake, then you are not only a highly passionate individual but also someone who would sacrifice themselves for the sake of their family? And yes, while they are highly proficient schemers, they also are quite beguiling. Did I mention they are liars? Snakes are capable of all kinds of lies—white lies, true lies…"

Fuck! Neither Liz nor Crawford heard the door slam behind Darcy when he sped toward the stairwell down the hall from his room. His feet couldn't move fast enough as he flew down the steps, leaping over reversing handrails toward Liz.

Crawford ran his finger across her pink lips. "Snakes are most capable of deadly lies, which always lead to deadly consequences."

She didn't know anything about the Chinese calendar, but it seemed fitting to lie, "It's…it's a good thing that I was born in the year of the Dragon, then."

Darcy was outside her door before Crawford began his next sentence.

"Ah, the mightiest of all the signs. I hope you are right. I would hate any kind of treachery and deception or have to exact revenge for it. I don't take kindly to a woman's manipulation. I enjoy when a chic plays coy as much as the next man, but a cock-tease is an entirely different matter."

Liz bravely put her hand on her hip and snorted a laugh. "Yeah, me, sheltered Lizzy, traveled alone to Europe so I could play games with you. Not likely, Henry. I came because I like you. I always have." Her heart pounded so thunderously in her chest that she was sure Darcy could hear it through the necklace.

"We shall see," he replied.

"I suppose you will. You know, I was thinking that I *would* like to go dancing with you tonight. Perhaps a tango may just be the thing to break free from the old Lizzy and her reticence."

Crawford's vibrant blue eyes flashed in delight as that crooked smile of his grew in satisfaction.

Darcy heard her offer through the microphone. He felt the same type of ownership over that dance as she did, and the dark spirit of jealousy shrouded him, but he forced himself to remember that Liz was only playing a part. At this moment, it meant her survival.

This is what he wanted after all. Wasn't it? Separation—no emotional ties. But he blew that plan to hell when he kissed her on the train, allowing her to do what she did to him, nearly making love to her in the lavatory.

His expression grew dark and severe. It was the face of an assassin.

Wearing a white linen shirt and grey trousers, he practically blended into the marble pillar in the hallway without drawing notice as he stealthily observed Crawford leave Liz's room to enter his own. A hand remained poised and still on the aimed Beretta, ready to take him down if necessary. Only when Crawford's door closed behind him did Iceman remove his finger from the trigger and finally breathe. He remained concealed opposite Liz's door until she and Crawford left for a luncheon of the famously spicy chorizo sausages downstairs.

Liz was only left alone with Crawford in the restaurant for fifteen minutes while Darcy thoroughly searched the scum's suite for anything that could lead the way to Marrakech, Al-Hanash's compound, and possibly end Liz's necessary participation in this dangerous charade.

There was nothing he wanted to do more than to make his signature kill shot to Crawford's head and leave him in Spain as he and Liz both jammed to "Shoot to Thrill" on their way to Marrakech.

~ ♠ ~

18
Tango

Although *la siesta* in Spain had been relaxed by the government, many businesses and local inhabitants still maintained its long tradition. Three people made good use of their time until later that night when they found their way through the darkened narrow streets toward the park to tango under the stars.

Under the pretense of resting, Liz remained within her suite, avoiding Crawford. She sat on the balcony overlooking the garden below, drinking a sparkling water and listening to the birdsong.

Darcy sat beside the elevator on her hotel floor, pretending to read a GQ España magazine. He remained attentive, should Crawford decide to leave his suite.

Unsure just where he hid, Liz did something completely unexpected, she spoke to him through the necklace, knowing he was somewhere on the other side listening. It actually comforted her to share herself and her life with him. She could see neither his expressions nor what she assumed would be his condemnation of her lifelong practice of safe, sacrificial denial.

Darcy heard every word she spoke, clinging to every thought she shared as she opened her soul to him.

"So, I bet you are still wondering why I came along with you. Sometimes, I wonder, too, and I have to admit that I'm pretty frightened by it, not just by the experience, but also by my willingness to be so carefree and reckless. I know it took a lot for you to recognize how your experiences changed you, and I think that if I were honest with myself, I could say the same. For many years, my conscience and logical self have been in a battle for dominance. I've wanted to run for a long time. I wanted to live more like Jane does. I have secretly wanted to experience life in all its fullness and not remain at Longbourn. That's my father's dream and vision for his life, not mine, but I love him, and well, I pity him, too. I know it may seem that I'm aloof about the danger he is in, but I'm not really. I'm actually petrified for him, but as you astutely pointed out, I am terribly angry with him, also.

"Did you know I am a kindergarten teacher? I love my little students and try to teach them that they should be creative and imaginative and not to be afraid of anything. I was probably that age when my mother would take me into her greenhouse where she taught me all about orchids, which I still cultivate. She used to sketch, too. I guess I picked up her creative outlets. Drawing is kind of an escape for me. As you heard in the casino, Crawford took my sketchbook. That's kind of embarrassing because my inner thoughts and feelings are on those pages. Guess I will have to start a new one—or not since I am now living out my dreams of adventure with you. Thank you for that. I might be scared, but I'm definitely exhilarated.

"So, what else can I tell you about me? I love opera. You know that already. I love classical music, particularly Chopin, but I really like rock, although I don't listen to it that much. It gets in the way of Daddy's creativity, and I never seem to have expendable cash to go on hunts for old cassettes to play in my Jeep." She snorted a laugh. "Maybe I should have played rock at Longbourn before my father started bringing his work home and making poor decisions. Let's see…what else? I've only had three boyfriends and one fiancé in my life, and you know how I fared with the latter. Oh, I have two left feet and a fascination with snakes, which you apparently have an aversion to. And for the record, I am not a viper. I'm anything but, and I hope in time you'll come to see that about me."

As though he could see her, Liz blushed when she added quietly, "I have never been in love, well, not un—"

Quickly, she cut her sentence short. "Now, what about you? You perplex me, Fitzwilliam Darcy. I know I've only known you for three days, but I know nothing about you other than what you have shared. Do you like being in the CIA? Where is your home? Are you an only child? Have *you* ever been in love? Maybe when all this is over and I decide to take back my life, you and I can get to know each other better. Perhaps we both possess something the other needs."

Liz skirted the issue of her feelings for him. In fact, she was hoping to get better acquainted with him in every possible way—sooner rather than later. She couldn't deny what her heart was telling her, and that was very dangerous in and of itself. Even though she hardly knew the man, she had fallen madly and, yes, deeply in love with him.

In the hallway, Darcy's mind whirled at her revelations. He longed to answer every question, but alas, she could not hear his inner thoughts, thoughts that were compelling him to trust again. Yes, before this was over he would tell her everything, he resolved.

I'm not in the CIA. I am an assassin contracted by the CIA, and I am quitting when this operation is over. I'm a Virginian, like you, but my home will be wherever you are. My sister, Georgiana, will love you as I do. I have only been truly in love once in my life—with you. Yes, Liz, you are right. You make up all the missing pieces of my life, and together, we can complete each other. Together, we will have adventures and make love, listening to Chopin in the moonlight. I'll teach you to ride horses at Pemberley, and you'll teach me how to grow orchids. We'll swim naked in the pond beside Longbourn and go speed boating down the Potomac while listening to rock music.

Pemberley? Horseback riding? Did I just think that?

Darcy rose from the chair and walked to Crawford's room. Hearing the snores from within, he stealthily picked the lock and slid in. The creep lay flat on his back wearing only white Fruit of the Loom underwear. Sound asleep, his mouth hung open, and his arms lay spread out. For once, Darcy deeply regretted his observation skills and near faultless memory.

Locating Crawford's cell phone, he placed a tiny call tracer and bug device within the unit and exited the suite but not before noting the connecting door to Liz's room. *Hopefully, this will end tonight.*

~♠~

The knock at Liz's hotel suite door startled her awake. She had dozed off as the sun set beyond the garden, thereby loosing track of time. Travel, adventure, and danger were beginning to take their toll on her. She rose and wiped the fog of sleep from her eyes as she walked to open the door, suddenly worried that it was Crawford.

"Senorita Bennet?" inquired the tall, slender woman standing in the doorway.

"Yes?"

"I was asked to deliver these items to you from an admirer." The saleswoman handed Liz a large white box with a red bow wrapped around it. It was from the hotel's exclusive women's boutique in the lobby. There was also a smaller box, which appeared to be shoes.

Liz surreptitiously peered into the handle bag draped over the woman's wrist. Within was even a smaller box from the hotel's luxury jeweler.

"Did this admirer leave a name?"

"No." She smiled wistfully. "He was extremely handsome and tall. Black eyes the color of onyx. Hair…oh, his hair …" Five fingers fidgeted in the air, and Liz understood what the saleswoman meant. *Yeah, his hair.*

"Thank you." *Yes, Fitzwilliam Darcy is a god, isn't he?*

The moment the door closed, Liz tore into the box as though a child at Christmas. She withdrew from the white tissue a sexy, spaghetti-strap, red dress with a bare back and asymmetrical skirt trimmed by a flounce of fabric. It was formfitting, slinky, and simple, but it was clearly meant to seduce. But seduce *whom* was the question? Clearly, Darcy meant him, but was he not stoking Crawford's embers as well?

The new shoes were ruby in color, strappy, and high. And within the jewelry box were nestled incredible earrings adorned with rubies at the center of a two-tiered cluster of diamonds. The display label tucked within the satin lining stated the pair contained 9.75 carats of VVS1-rated diamonds, and they complemented the snake necklace beautifully. Liz chuckled to herself. *Will there be clothing and jewelry at every one of our destinations? Perhaps a bracelet to complete the ensemble? God, he's so good to me. Why?*

A simple note lay folded at the bottom of the dress box: *Will you tango with me tonight?*

An hour later, Crawford knocked on her door. The game had begun.

"Come in," she called from the bathroom.

He entered, sauntering to the open balcony in all his slick reptilian style. Primed and ready to go, he assumed it was going to be his night.

When Liz entered into the room, that annoying crooked smirk of his almost made her run and hide. Lust seemed to drip from his every pore. Clearly, she would have preferred Darcy's admiring gaze and the smile that he'd given her the night they had gone to the casino.

"You look sexy, Liz. Wow! You're one hot number tonight. I guess you are ready to burn the floor with me." Crawford unconsciously licked his lips.

"Thank you." She lied. "I bought it especially."

It made her flesh crawl at how he examined every detail of the image she presented. Her hair was pulled into a low, smooth bun, and tucked within the curve of coiled locks clung a full red carnation. The new earrings caught the light and sparkled in conjunction with her ever-present snake necklace.

Crawford approached to kiss her, clearly tempted by her siren red lips where his gaze had affixed, but he refrained, instead kissing her hand.

Torn between repulsion and laughter, she remained stone-faced—Iceman-like—as she took in the man's ridiculous appearance of newly-dyed black hair and a Spanish mustache and goatee. The black shirt he wore was mostly open down the front, revealing a lackluster build covered with curling blond chest hair. It took all her control not to laugh at the contrasting color upon his head. *Jackass.*

"You have new earrings."

Of course he would notice. She knew he would.

"They match your necklace." He couldn't help refraining from toying with the snake again, running his fingers along the inset diamonds as if caressing Liz's body. He stroked it possessively, holding the head of the gem reptile and repeatedly rubbing the rubies.

One floor above, Darcy's ear-canal amplifier painfully pierced when Crawford's touch interfered and abruptly cut off the necklace's microphone transmission.

"Fuck!" seemed to be a word that he had come to use repeatedly during Operation Cancan. He now had no means of listening to Liz.

When Liz and Crawford exited the hotel, Darcy wasn't far behind. As they traversed the darkened side streets of Seville, he walked in the shadow, careful that the white dress shirt he wore would not catch the illumination from the street lamps.

The three made their way to a regularly held outdoor tango dance gathering within Maria Luisa Park. Liz felt the magic and excitement in the air the closer she drew near to the sounds of the seductive music filling the night air. If only she were on the arm of another man, but she would look forward to his promise of a dance. *Is he always going to break protocol where I am concerned? It appears so.*

Glowing lanterns hung from extended cords above the dance floor where couples clung, embracing and demonstrating their footwork under the lights. It was romantic, and Liz felt her blood stir from the palpable emotion displayed in the body language and expressions of the dancers.

Crawford and she settled at one of the many tables surrounding the dance floor.

"Can I get you a drink, Liz?"

"Yes, please…a red wine."

She didn't drink wine. In fact, apart from her monthly beer with Jane at the Hard Rock, the champagne in Monte Carlo was the only other time she recalled drinking. However, on this night, she *needed* a drink.

Darcy sat beside the musicians with a clear view of the dance floor and her. It was obvious to her that he made no point in concealing himself once they arrived at the outdoor dance square. Her eyes couldn't help but continually stray to his impressive manner of dress. He wore a sharp, European-styled black suit and a dress shirt open at the collar. His hair was styled with a small amount of gel, which highlighted the curls at his neck, giving alluring waves to the hair resting at his forehead. She tapped her fingers on her leg, not from nerves, but from the unsettling desire to run them through his locks.

He caught her eye and gave her a half smile indicating…what? She couldn't be sure. Hello? Approval? Playfulness? Whatever it was, it jump-started her heartbeat, but she didn't smile back. She winked instead.

Unbeknownst to her, at that small flirtatious gesture, his heartbeat increased as well.

Darcy watched as Liz crossed her legs, the skirt hiking up slightly, revealing their smoothness. The dress he chose for her fit perfectly, and he delighted that already he was able to determine her size and hidden style awaiting emergence.

Following behind Liz and Crawford on the way to the park had been torturous. She had the most perfect backside, and all he could think about was holding it while she sat upon him, straddling his body. This game of cat and mouse they were playing needed to stop. Their mutual teasing foreplay and pulling back was taking its toll on both of them, and he knew without a doubt that they couldn't contain the heat any longer. They were ready to explode with want of the other.

Before Crawford even made his way back to Liz with her drink, she was asked to dance by another patron. Darcy's observant acumen noted how every male eye present had affixed with lustful approval on her as soon as she entered the square of the park. Her shapely, toned body and the way the dress clung to the curves of her waist, hips, and breasts couldn't help but inflame any man's libido. But he knew, she had dressed for *him* that night.

The way she walked and moved on the dance floor seemed to be a provocative accompaniment to the beat of the staccato music. Each foot's placement seemed a deliberate movement to the plucking of the guitar. She had an air about her tonight that she hadn't had before, and Darcy realized it immediately. Liz seemed uninhibited, challenging, and confident – even in spite of her self-proclaimed two left feet. Perhaps it was the baring of her soul to him through the necklace, or was it the dress? Maybe it was the passionate music. Whatever it was, he knew the long-suppressed Liz was now fully released.

It was a hot, still Andalusian night as Crawford and Darcy sat at opposite sides of the dance floor watching Liz learn and step to the tango. Her footwork looked just fine to Darcy, and her full breasts looked just fine to Crawford. Both envisioned her in their arms, and both imagined making love to her. Only one of the two imagined doing so for the rest of his life because his intense physical response had been brought on by so much more than just his libido.

Her dance partner, an older, sophisticated man was patient, taking the time to show her the basic turning moves and small "gancho" kicks. She learned quickly, allowing herself to give into his lead. She wasn't intimidated by the dance, and the fact that her partner had remained in proper frame added to her comfort.

Partner after partner sought Liz, never giving her an opportunity to recover after each dance, and it seemed to Crawford that the gods were conspiring against him. There was no way he could keep her to himself, and it infuriated him. Rather than make a scene, he had to relinquish her from his arms time after time, having twice only had the opportunity to dance with her. Livid, he drank heavily, stewing in his unrequited desire. Unwilling to consider dancing with another, his elevated ego saw every other woman as a dog and not worth his time to dance with. He was there to seduce only one woman, and she was in everyone else's arms that night.

After sixty minutes, he was extremely intoxicated. In what would be his final trip to the bar, he failed to notice the tall, black-suited man who broke into Liz's dance.

With a tap to the shoulder of her partner—a partner who cared more about the size of her chest than the beauty of her fine eyes—Darcy cut in.

Gone was the proper dance frame when his fingers brushed her shoulder, sliding down her bare back. He pulled her close against his body, his hand wrapping around her waist, their mouths breathlessly panting, only two inches apart.

The music changed, and the slow, seductive pluck of the violin began the "Assassin's Tango" as their legs moved across the floor, brushing against each other with electricity.

Liz's skin grew hot and flushed from perspiration and the intensity of the dance and those dark eyes of his locking with hers. Darcy's firm hold upon her burned as though a scorching iron, branding her flushed skin, leaving its mark deep below her flesh.

Theirs was not a tango of conflict with each other or of predator and prey. It was a dance of longing and complex expression performed to the hypnotizing, sensual repetitive beat. Liz's body was pliant and willing in his arms. She followed his every lead, mimicking his kicks and turning at his deft prompts upon her waist. Each time their legs hooked with each other, it was erotically charged.

Darcy rested his head upon hers in their tight embrace as he gently rocked them provocatively to the music. The melancholic violin orchestrated their unfulfilled longing for each other. When the bow slid across the strings, rhythms spoke of their yearning, their passions, and their secrets.

Liz remembered her "corte" instruction, and each time she leaned forward as though the sensual music pulled her into his arms and strong body, she imagined them making love. Because of Darcy and what she felt for him, their intimate tango evolved, and her body responded and moved of its own accord. Their hold upon each other never separated as their feet stepped and glided with precision. She brazenly lifted her foot, smoothing her calf behind his. In turns, their bodies remained close with hands clasped.

Without inhibition, her hips swayed, prompting her foot to create figure eight movements on the floor. Each glide of red sandal swept in seductive movement, dramatically meeting his own footwork. Throughout the dance, their senses and emotions sought a fulfillment that could not progress on the dance floor.

When again, Darcy guided her forward into him, she raised her bent leg to his hip. Her hand clasped to the back of his head, holding him fixed to her as his hand smoothed down her bare thigh. It rested in the crook of her folded leg, tugging it slightly higher. She gazed into his dark and dilated eyes filled with want and passion, which spoke the same thing that the erectness of her nipples did when pressed against his chest.

He smirked, looking to where Crawford stood at the bar with his back toward them and, overcome with intense emotion, whispered, "Come with me."

Breathless by the power of their unspoken yet expressed desire, she said nothing, only nodded.

Entwining his hand with hers, they left the dance floor into the shadow and darkness of the park, traversing the expansive gardens.

"Your microphone is broken," Darcy said.

"Oh, is that why you're taking me into the park?"

"No."

She could feel the heat rolling from his body, and when they reached the stone gazebo pavilion beside the pond, she didn't need verbal confirmation of Darcy's intentions. The second they were concealed in the shadow of darkness, he pressed her against the only wall of the structure and kissed her deeply, almost violently. His lips were hot and aggressive, as were hers. His hands were all over her body, as were hers upon him.

"God, you're so beautiful. I love how you move in my arms," he panted between scorching kisses that dropped to her neck where he suckled and licked, savoring her scent and the taste of her salty, moist flesh upon his tongue.

Her hands ran under his suit jacket, pushing it from his broad shoulders to the ground. "I thought you wanted distance."

"I lied. I can't keep away from you. I need you too much."

His arms shirked from his shoulder holster, landing it atop the discarded jacket.

With lips grazing her collar bone, he dropped the thin straps of the dress, baring Liz's breasts to his needy hands and starving eyes. His palms cupped her, his thumbs brushing desire against her taut peaks. She responded, arching her back, offering herself to his descending lips.

His suckles and nibbles released any last restraint within her. She cried out into the midnight air, her dress dropping to the stone floor of the gazebo. With the release of a ribbon, her red, silky panty fell away.

She stood naked before him, provocatively perched on bright red stilettos, free and wanton in the moonlight

Tonight, she thought nothing of restriction or reserve, only of the dangerous thrill of this freedom, the collision of bodies, heart and heat, and the craving that had never ceased to course through her blood since the first time he held her. The tango had brought it all to the surface. It had been the first flare of their passion for each other. Now it fueled and ignited their ultimate combustion. Everything in between had been tinder, feeding this burning, growing, raging fire.

The feel of Darcy's hand sliding over her hip to her bare, smooth apex was intoxicating, and when the tip of his finger taunted and slowly dipped into her core, she begged him unabashedly. "Make love to me. Oh God, Fitzwilliam, make love to me."

"I have every intention of making love to you, princess. I want to show you how I feel about you."

She ripped his shirt open, sending it to the floor amidst flying buttons. Needing an anchor, her left hand clutched his tattooed bicep when his finger began its erotic exploration, seeking her sensitive center of climax as his thumb brushed and rubbed over her throbbing nub.

His mouth consumed hers, swallowing moans and cries of ecstasy when her body began to spiral and shudder uncontrollably in his arms from his talented fingers.

She needed him. She needed to feel him inside her, so she quickly dropped his trousers and briefs. Her hand surrounded his rock-hard and hot cock, and she wanted to beg again. His tip was so swollen that it felt even larger than she recalled from the dark casino closet and the train's lavatory. Instinctively, her hand took control, sliding up and down his smooth shaft, causing him to fill the air around them with deep cries of passion.

Their brazen public coupling, the black sky, the danger of discovery, the deep heavy breathing, and the escaping moans of pleasure all added to the eroticism of the moment. It was torrid and steamy, so urgently aggressive and physically charged that they both loved it.

With Liz's released inhibitions, she broke their kiss and squatted before him.

Darcy gazed down at her beautiful body and the perfectly divided curve of her backside perched above red stilettos. The sweat glistening the path between her full breasts, the red carnation fixed within her dark hair, and the dazzling diamond earrings sparkling in the moonlight added to what was, without a doubt, the most erotic moment of his life. But it was the sight of Liz's cherry lips surrounding his enflamed erection that nearly caused him to burst. Seeing her mouth filled with him and feeling her covetous sucking as her lips slid up and down in wet glides was more than he could bear.

He threw back his head in ecstasy. "Baby…oh God…wait…I need to be in you. Now."

As soon as Liz rose, he urgently lifted her against the wall, wrapping her legs around him while keeping his hands firmly clasped on the smooth curves of her backside.

Both cried out as he slid her body down upon his straining erection and thrusted upward, filling her completely. His extraordinary size touched her in places that had never experienced pleasure before.

Her hands thread through Darcy's hair, weaving within his thick, dark curls as she gave herself up to his masterful strength and control with utter abandon. Leaning backward, she arched from the wall with his strong hands supporting her. Sweat from the heat they generated continued to run between her breasts.

His lips left hers bereft when his tongue traveled slowly down her delectable neck and chest until meeting its treasure. Firm, upright nipples were met by scorching lips and nibbling teeth. Steamy vapor from deep, panting breaths surrounded their slick bodies, hardening her rigid tips even more. Electric currents shot to her apex with each lap of Darcy's ardent tongue as he loved her with deepening, raging thrusts.

Every touch, lick, whisper, and pounding of heart and body sent Liz to heaven and back. Each spasm of mind-blowing, blinding ecstasy tore through her, never allowing her reprieve from the repeated explosions. She soared with each desirously invasive thrust, climaxing again and again. Gravity didn't exist, only the heady experience of the rapture he generated within her.

When Darcy bent his legs to slide from her, ecstasy became palpable regret, and she felt the loss so deeply that her sex pulsated in unbroken ecstasy even after his withdrawal from her.

Liz needed to touch him, to hold the power setting her fully aflame. He was throbbing with arousal and coated with her honey when she once again took him in her hand. She gazed into her lover's dilated pupils, riveted to her own, and then he kissed her fervently, lovingly. It was a kiss of love, without a doubt, and she knew it. She felt the emotion on Darcy's mouth, feeling the unspoken words of amor on his lips. They were the same words upon hers, the same intention as her unyielding touch. They were the same proclamations as in his moans of connection and reawakening, which she accepted lovingly, absorbing them with her consuming kiss.

He turned her to face the railing of the gazebo. Standing behind her, together they looked out at the water before them. With the moonlight illuminating their nude bodies, he nibbled her neck and cupped her breasts, brushing her nipples with his thumbs. "You are so beautiful." He rubbed his erection against her backside. "Feel what you do to me? All I want to do is make love to you, feel myself inside you, and make you mine."

She took one of his hands, smoothing it down her belly to her swollen apex. Toying with his finger, she guided him to her folds and rubbed the tip of his long middle finger over her engorged nub. "See what you do to me? I've never felt this way before. I can't stop coming from your embrace. I need to have you inside me."

Bending her over slightly, Darcy rubbed his smooth shaft mercilessly against her sex. "Good. Because when I'm inside you, I feel complete."

He whispered softly and clearly into her ear so that she wouldn't miss a single word of what he was about to say. With the feel of his cock rubbing, teasing, and sliding against her wet sex, he said, "I love you, Liz. I love you so much. I can't be without you." and slid into her in a slow, measured erotic torment, which drove her mad.

Feeling his tip surrounded by her, he continued to whisper, "I adore you, and I need you."

He glided into her smoothly, feeling the soft walls of her passage clench him with spasms of delight. "You've conquered me and melted my frozen heart."

With every inch of penetration, Darcy stripped himself bare to her. Finally seated to the hilt and reveling in the moist heat of the woman he adored, he gave her final victory over him. "You bring me to life, princess. I'm yours."

The moment her hands joined his, one on the railing before them and the other at the curve of her waist, she spoke with a quiet truth. "I feel the same."

Darcy slowly pulled out his shaft, leaving only his near-bursting tip toying with her rim. Then he thrust into her with vigorous intensity, releasing the last remaining vestiges of the Iceman. With each deep, penetrating plunge, he felt the shedding of thirteen years of guilt and anger. Her love had set him free.

When the ultimate pressure built in them both like the release of the tightest of coils, together they came crashing with uncontrolled cries amidst explosive shaking tremors. He remained sheathed inside her, wrapping his arms around her waist, hugging her even closer to his body.

Dropping tender kisses to her neck and shoulders, he trembled as his seed continued to spill into her. "I have to hear it, Liz. Tell me what you feel for me."

She leaned her head back against his and closed her eyes. Vowing into the darkness, she spoke softly. "I...love you, Fitzwilliam." She didn't see his smile in the darkness, but she felt the tightening of his hold around her waist.

Darcy could tell that her legs were quivering and about to give way from the intensity of their lovemaking. He held her tightly to him and pledged, "I've got you, babe, and I'm never going to let you go."

~♠~

19
Knaves, Knives
& a Baretta

L iz and Darcy had been gone too long. Time, location, and circumstances were forgotten when caught up in the heat of the dance and
the intensity of their lovemaking. Only the two of them existed, and they
just admitted that they loved each other.

Liz couldn't stop smiling as she slipped her dress back on, and Darcy
suddenly turned quietly shy. It was the first time he had ever said the
words "I love you" to a woman, and he was a little overwhelmed by the
extent of what they felt for each other, not to mention what they had
allowed to happen in a public park.

"Liz?" He didn't need to continue his sentence when she moved into
his embrace, staying there, listening to the rapid beat of his heart. She
didn't wonder what he was going to say. His tight embrace told her
everything she needed to know. Neither of them had regrets.

He alternated between kissing and resting his head on hers. "We have
to get back, baby."

"Not yet, just a minute longer."

Although Darcy couldn't see him, he was sure that Crawford had
mostly likely begun to search for Liz by now. No doubt he was drunk
and ready to claim her for himself.

Crawford's thoughts unknowingly confirmed Darcy's speculation as
he searched the park, obsessively playing over in his mind what he would

do to Liz when he found her. He gave no thought to what constituted rape or not. His only intent was to take her virginity, giving her the ride of her life before turning her over to Devlin Renaud.

His cell phone rang, and he stopped along a path beside the pond twenty yards away from the gazebo.

Alerting Darcy to Crawford's proximity, the receiver beeped in his right ear, and he immediately scrambled for the cell phone within his jacket's inside pocket.

"What is it? What's the trouble?" Liz asked.

Darcy placed his index finger over her lips, moving her backwards into the shadow of the gazebo, indicating for her to remain hidden there. He pressed a button on his cell phone to begin a trace of Crawford's call. Listening to the conversation unfold, he secured the shoulder holster over his arm and promptly screwed the newly acquired silencer to the tip of his Beretta. As quickly as the Iceman had been banished while furiously making love to Liz, he was called forth in protection of her.

Noting that there was no caller ID, Crawford said nothing when he pressed the talk button.

"So I see that you are still alive, Crawford," Al-Hanash said in his distinctly accented voice. Only this time, it was filled with undisguised disdain and venom. It was clear that his thick-scaled exterior had begun to shed.

"Is there a reason you were expecting otherwise, Mr. Renaud? We have a meeting scheduled after all. The girl for my money, and I assure you that I will be coming for my money."

Renaud laughed. "You are overconfident as usual. Do you think me such a fool as to make deals with a dog? You failed me. Punishment awaits you. By your apparent good fortune of escaping Omar's blade and his unexpected silence, I can only assume that either you killed him or whoever is following you did."

"No one is following me, sir. I am sure of it. I have been very careful. It is just the girl and me."

Through the trees, Darcy observed Crawford looking around in fear.

"You are a bigger fool than I thought. Of course you are being followed. The woman has made you weak, unfocused. You have mixed business with the personal needs of your obsessions. Tell me: have you deflowered the Bennet woman yet?"

"Tonight." Foolish in his drunkenness and without thinking, he added, "If I can find her. She seems to have disappeared."

"Disappeared or has she been taken? You forget that I have already claimed her as my property. For your sake, I hope you find her. Here is our new arrangement: 5:00 pm tomorrow in the Jemaa el Fna, food stall number twelve. The woman, unspoiled, in exchange for your life. If you defy me, I will come for you myself. If you are followed, I will kill you on the spot. My eyes will be everywhere within the Medina, and I will know if you betray me. If you defile her, I will cut off your dick and shove it down your throat. Don't bother running because you know I will find you wherever you are."

"But...but...my money. You owe me!"

"There will be no money. Does your life not have value enough? Number twelve. If you and the girl are not there, I will unleash all hell to find you." Crawford and Darcy heard nothing more than the click of Renaud's call ending.

Crawford looked around wildly. His eyes darted from person to tree, looking for anyone or anything familiar or suspicious. Uncharacteristically, he was nervous. Omar was not a man who was bested easily. The Arab was fierce and extremely strong. His presence alone was intimidating. If someone had murdered him, then that someone was powerful in his own right, more powerful than he could ever be.

He knew he had better find Liz and bring her back to Marrakech with him, or he was a dead man. Certainly, his life was more important than having sex with her, but then again, Renaud said nothing about her pleasuring him in other ways.

There was only one pathway leading from the gazebo, and Crawford was on it. Liz and Darcy were trapped from an unseen escape. Darcy whispered into her ear. "Stay silent and hidden in the shadow, and no matter what happens, do not be afraid or scream." Liz nodded, and he winked at her before moving stealthily in the darkness to the steps of the gazebo. Raising his arms, he fluidly lifted himself up into the eaves of the wood cupola where he stretched and lay in wait for Crawford to enter.

Darcy knew what he was going to do. After all, he was a highly skilled assassin. There was no need for Crawford any longer, and the snake's diabolical plans for Liz left only one particularly fitting end. That one phone call had given Darcy all the information they needed: time, date, and location. One less scum-sucking bastard in the equation was a logical means to the end. His only regret was that Liz would have to witness Crawford's death. He didn't intend on executing his kill shot. He absolutely preferred to beat the ever-living crap out of this scum. Crawford didn't deserve the expense of a brass bullet.

Crawford's eyes spanned the gazebo before him. He spotted Liz hiding in the shadow, tipped off by the glimmer of her necklace and diamond earrings just as the moon exited from behind a cloud. He smiled wickedly. *Yeah, great place for a blow job.*

His first step up into the gazebo coincided with his words, "Are you playing coy, Liz, or are you just a cock tease after all?"

He didn't expect the force of Darcy's custom-made Ferragamos to come down in one fell swoop to his chest, sending him flying backward from the gazebo onto the grass, nearly knocking the wind from him.

Darcy stood in the moonlight before the man. Cool and calm, the Iceman was ready to kill with his bare hands. He could see fear register upon the terrorist's face, but it was quickly replaced by a survival instinct.

Crawford's blue eyes flashed before he charged Darcy, forcing both men to fall heavily to the ground.

Instantly rising to their feet, they separated, assuming attack positions, re-balancing with hands raised and ready. Crawford analyzed the full measure of his unknown opponent. The realization came quickly that this must be the man who had killed Omar.

"So you're the one following me! Who are you?"

"Your worst nightmare come true."

Darcy's fierce strike connected solidly with Crawford's upper right jaw, the impact making the man stagger backward, the force loosening a tooth.

The terrorist surged forward with wildness in his eyes. Inebriated, his fists as well as his advancing kicks were ineffective, failing to connect.

Easily dodging then retaliating with fearsome strength and controlled accuracy, Darcy's assault enclosed his adversary amidst the surrounding trees.

Slipping into the shadow behind a broad trunk, Crawford took a moment's reprieve to regroup and quickly evaluate his options. He was no match for the stranger; his street-fighting skills were only average in comparison to his opponent's obvious military training.

He called out from behind the tree. "My employer will pay handsomely for the girl and her virginity. We can split the money fifty-fifty."

"Fuck you, asshole. She's one hundred percent mine. You'll have to kill me first, and even if you did, she'd probably cut off your balls."

Crawford laughed in spite of the loosened, bloody tooth. He quickly withdrew two small clinch pick knives hidden inside his belt buckle. With the intention of unnerving his opponent, he burst from behind his impromptu barricade, viciously brandishing the deadly small knives before his face as he advanced menacingly.

Darcy ducked and bobbed away from Crawford's wildly flailing arms.

The former SEAL responded with a series of roundhouse kicks, attempting to dislodge the deadly weapons from his enemy, but in a split-moment's assault, the right-hand knife connected with his arm, cutting it and drawing blood through the pure white shirt.

Liz stifled her scream.

It wasn't until Crawford got around Darcy that he made a beeline for the steps of the gazebo. It happened fast, faster than Liz could absorb, when a bullet entered the back of Crawford's head. He lay dead, stretched out over the steps on his stomach.

Technically, the bullet hole was right between his eyes. Damn, Darcy was good at what he did. Even from behind, he was able to execute his signature kill shot.

Fear immobilized Liz. Her arms continued to clutch Darcy's now wrinkled suit jacket as she watched in silent astonishment how the man she loved holstered his pistol.

Above Crawford's dead body, Darcy held out his hand to her, but her eyes locked upon the cut to his arm. His calming words washed over her. "It's okay, Liz. You're okay, and I am, too. It is just a flesh wound. Take my hand. It's just one step over him. You can do this."

Liz stepped carefully over the body, holding tightly onto Darcy's hand. When she cleared the steps, she fell into his waiting arms. She didn't cry. She was too dazed by what had happened.

With his free hand, he wrapped his Bluetooth around his ear, and then he kissed Liz's head. "We have to get out of here quickly." He smiled down at her serious expression. "Are you with me, Agent Bennet?"

"Yes."

Once his suit jacket was back on, he draped his arm around her shoulders as they quickly made their way through the park to the nearest thoroughfare. His right thumb busily tapped into his cell phone, calling up the tracking coordinates from Crawford's phone call: Ile de Mogador, Morocco.

Noting a row of sleek motorcycles parked in front of a restaurant, he removed his specially-made universal key. He straddled a black and silver Suzuki, then held out his hand to Liz. "Get on and hold tight, baby. We have to get to Marrakech. Don't be afraid."

She looked at the small seat on the sport bike with doubt. "I don't think we'll both fit."

Darcy mischievously smirked, disarming the fear he knew was at the core of her hesitancy. "Don't you want to be pressed against me?"

Oh yeah, she thought.

There wasn't time for discussion. Liz understood what was happening. Darcy had just killed a man in public, and he was now stealing a motorcycle. She climbed behind him, hanging on for dear life as the growl of the bike's exhaust filled the air and the back tire spun as it burned rubber.

As the bike weaved and sped through the busy street, Darcy pressed his Bluetooth, placing his first call to Charlie. He could hear through the unit the beat of dance club music booming behind his friend's shout of "Yello."

"You're up, buddy. Cancan needs you. How quickly can you fly your father's plane to Seville? We need immediate extraction."

Liz thought, *Cancan, what the heck is Cancan?*

"I could be there in two, two and a half hours. I just have to wake Rocco to fly us. Are you safe? Is Liz safe?"

"We're on the run with just our passports and the clothes on our backs. We can't go back to the hotel, so bring us both a change of clothing. We're flying to Marrakech. I'll explain the rest when I see you."

"I'm bringing Jane, Darce. She knows everything."

"Everything?"

"Everything."

"Fine. Bring her. We will be waiting for you at Moron Alb Airport." He would worry about Charlie's loose lips and pillow talk later. It had disaster written all over it if Liz found out from Jane about Obsidian before he had the chance to tell her. "Where are you now?"

"A little hot spot for dancing. Leonardo DiCaprio just arrived, and I can't get my girl away from him."

"Well, just tell Jane that her sister needs her. That should get her unglued." Darcy disconnected, yelling over his shoulder to Liz. "You okay?"

Unexpectedly, she laughed in his ear.

The motorcycle hugged the pavement as he expertly navigated through the late-night Seville traffic, picking up speed and changing lanes until forced to stop for a red light.

Liz looked drop-dead gorgeous in that red dress and stiletto heels with her arms wrapped tightly around his waist. The light changed, and he gassed the throttle.

She didn't know what possessed her, but she boldly let go of him with her right arm and released her hair from the bun at the back of her head. The red carnation bounced onto the road below the wheels of the bike, and her hair blew out in the wind just as in her sketch.

In Darcy's peripheral vision, he could see what she had done, and he smiled. No, "Shoot to Thrill" wouldn't be the song. It was more like "Welcome to the Jungle" by Guns and Roses as the bike sped up and her hair flew from its velocity. Like the song, she was his serpentine and going to be just fine. In fact, he was certain she was actually enjoying herself.

He pressed the Bluetooth twice, and Rick answered.

"Where are you?" Darcy said.

"Walking to Le Comptoir in Marrakech for a late night cocktail."

"Well, that's a mighty good thing since that's where I am headed."

"Yeah, I figured you'd end up here soon. I'm just getting my bearings, casing the Medina, asking questions."

"Don't bother. I need you to contact Caroline. She needs to get to Marrakech before five tomorrow evening. I know where Renaud is going to be, and I have a plan to get inside his stronghold so we can get Bennet out."

"Oh no…We are not putting the bitch in the field."

"Tough shit. We *are* putting her in the field. She's the only one who can get inside. Her skills, Rick, think about her skills. Caroline is like the bride from *Kill Bill*. We need those skills."

"Yeah, skills that can silently pull a man's balls up through his throat before he knows what hit him. I should know. Hell, you should know."

"That's exactly why we need her in Marrakech. Charlie's en route from Italy, so we are all mobilized."

"Where's Al-Hanash's compound?"

"The Island of Mogador off the Moroccan coast of Essaouira."

"What happened with Crawford?"

"Dead…couldn't be helped. I'm not much of a pistol man, but damn if that Beretta isn't as accurate as my SR25 rifle. I'll call you with the details when I'm on the plane. Right now, we're on the run."

"And the Bennet woman?"

"She's sitting behind me with her beautiful arms wrapped around my waist on a Suzuki GSX-R600. 599cc's burning my balls, and her hand is only five inches higher."

"Those bikes aren't made for two. You're in love with her, you stupid fool."

Darcy smiled, and before disconnecting the call, he replied, "You're damn straight I am. I'm head over heels in love with her, and she fits me and the bike just perfectly."

Liz caught that and smiled. Apart from Crawford's messy demise and her father's unknown fate, this was the best damned time—not to mention sex—of her life. Well, maybe she didn't mind Crawford's demise so much. The snake had it coming.

Before entwining his fingers with Liz's at his bare stomach where his shirt was missing its buttons, Darcy tapped the Bluetooth four times, placing his last call for the night. This one went to Knightley, who was occupied in his bed with a voluptuous blonde lying naked on his chest.

"What the fuck, man? It's late."

"You said anytime, baldie. Now's the time. I need your help."

"Did you find the guy you were looking for?"

"Yeah, and we've got to leave Seville without looking back. Can you get down here and take care of our belongings? My gear can't fall into the wrong hands, if you know what I mean. We were at The Alphonso, rooms 211 and 311."

"Sure, I'll fly down now. My employer keeps a plane fueled and ready to roll at a moment's notice."

"No, I need your boat."

"I'm hoping it's the fog of sleep causing me to hear you ask for my boat."

"You heard me correctly."

"No boat."

"Yes boat."

"Darcy, man, that's a grand prix powerboat, the winner of the Cowes to Monte Carlo."

"Exactly why I need *it* and *you* to come to Marrakech after your stop in Seville." Darcy could hear Knightley swearing on the other end. "After this, we're even," he added to sweeten the deal.

"Even?"

"Yeah, I'll have no need to call in favors once this is over."

"Famous last words."

"Call me when you get to the port at Essaouira."

~ ♠ ~

The dance studio was locked and appeared empty. Caroline sat in the middle of the wood floor wearing her black leather catsuit considering how everyone was on board with Darcy—all except her. She didn't like the feeling of abandonment and isolation systematically imposed by her fellow Obsidian members, but truth was, she had chosen a different path long before Obsidian was assigned to her. Charlie had called to mention his flying from Capri to Marrakech. Rick had left the country, and here she was sitting alone in the dark practicing, not the dance art of the mambo or the hustle, but the art of a ninja master.

With legs crossed and eyes closed, she breathed deeply, slowing her heartbeat. She was good at this. In her opinion, it was the best thing she did, well besides doing Darcy, but that was an entirely different thing. That *sped up* her heart rate. Trying hard to eradicate the memory of him was proving more difficult than even her ninja mind-control skills could master.

In the complete darkness of the room, even her reflection in the mirror opposite could not be seen. Caroline became one with her environment. Feeling the cool metal of the ninja bo staff, which lay beside her on the polished wood floor, she wrapped her hand around six feet of death-wielding venom. She somersaulted, then rose, lifting the stick over her shoulder with the blade pointed downward. The weapon, with its unique, pointed four-edged blade was specially designed just for her.

Acting as one with the staff, she executed deadly rotations, jabs, twirls, and thrusts with precise hand, wrist, and body movements. Her lethal back-and-forth lunges were long and masterfully controlled.

After ten minutes of continual strikes, overhead sweeps, and blocking hits, she flung the staff into the balls of the male dummy at the far end of the studio. The bo's pointed end stabbed him like a vasectomy cut as the six-foot staff bobbed up and down like a hard cock in a stiff breeze. Caroline's face remained frozen steel, hidden behind a half mask. The surrounding space was so dark that not even the cherry-red sheen of her lips—the lips of a red spitting cobra—could be seen below the mask's bottom edge.

She broke into a run toward the eastern wall beside the office window. Becoming a lethal scorpion, her long legs ascended the wall as though propelled by something other than human strength. Once she reached the horizontal beams above the dance floor, she balanced in stillness, perched and spread-eagled in a perfect split between two beams.

With hands pressed together before her, she stilled, meditating before entwining her fingers together to practice the ancient form of finger-weaving exercises to control her mental attitude and calm her nerves.

Her cell phone rang below, disturbing the peace. *Shit.*

Grabbing the low beam, Caroline executed a series of turns and swings and landed silently, fixing on both feet. All she could see was the illumination of her iPhone as it vibrated on the floor. After three effortless no-handed cartwheels across the floor, she picked up the phone without even a modicum of shortness of breath.

Seeing who the caller was, she answered in Japanese. "Konnichiwa."

"Get your gear. You're going out into the field," Rick said.

"Why?"

"I thought that's what you wanted. Don't all lethal animals need to feed? You must be starving since I left. No one in town to sink your razor-sharp fangs into."

"Ha, ha. I'll have you know that I ate dinner already, and he did nothing for me or my appetite. I'm working off my frustration now. Rick, don't be like this. You're sounding more and more like Darcy."

"With good reason. I don't care to hear the details of your latest meal ticket, Caroline. You need to get on the next plane to Marrakech. Darcy needs us. He's identified Al-Hanash and has a location scouted on him for tomorrow at five. You're integral to Cancan's success."

"Is the Bennet woman still with him?"

"Yes. Not that it's any of your business, but they got married in Spain." Rick smirked on the other end. He couldn't help lying. He was just as adept at it as Darcy. Perhaps this was just what the shrew needed to hear to get off his cousin's back. "Caroline…are you there?"

Removing the hair-clip she wore, she released flaming locks down her back. From within the clip, slid out two titanium Ninja stars. Caroline flicked her wrists, sending the five-pointed blades across the room, straight into the dummy's heart.

"Yes, I'm here. Married you say? Hope she knows what she's in for. He is not all that easy to handle and certainly untamed."

"I suppose that is why you shamelessly keep holding on. Look, I didn't call to discuss my cousin's attributes. I called to tell you that you need to meet me at Riad Salam in the old Medina as quickly as you can get here."

"Right. I'm there."

"And, Caroline, bring your toys, particularly that hair clip of yours."

She chuckled. "Oh, Ricky, you know me so well."

Four days had passed since they locked Bennet inside the concrete room. Four long days of nerve-wracking stress from the stalling and personal disapprobation at his foolish decision. What a mess he had created. He looked to the wood desk beside his cot and chuckled at the irony. There resting on the worn, scuffed surface was a book: *Crime and Punishment.* He normally loved irony, but not in this case. Angry at his persistent conscience, he internally screamed, *All right, all right already – I did wrong!*

He hoped that Lizzy had survived the gunfire and went on to marry Bill Collins. Her husband would protect her, saving Longbourn, too. She was lucky to have a man like Bill for a husband. Maybe not seeing it now, her sacrifice in marrying him was small in comparison to the sacrifice that he, himself, had made. He had sacrificed his soul when he sold it to the devil in order to save Longbourn, a legacy he was leaving to her and Jane. *Thank God I have you, Lizzy. You always do the right thing.*

Four days of pretending to finish the source code wasn't without merit. He managed to do one thing. With the tools and hardware from one of the computers, he built a small homing device that emitted a silent SOS signal to anyone with an American government or military-issued IP address within a ten-mile radius. He was sure someone would be coming to rescue him.

The door to his cell unbolted, and Renaud stepped into the small space. The man looked over the computer monitors at Bennet's spectacled eyes. The slight man before him was in disarray. His hair was chaotic, and he had heavy bags under his eyes. He sat typing away on the keyboard.

"Are you finished yet, Mr. Bennet? I have business awaiting me upon completion, and right now, the only thing that stands between me and $500 million is your procrastination."

"I'm...I'm...not procrastinating. This takes time, and there is very little means of experimenting on its actual effectiveness once deployed. I don't have an internet connection or a cell phone."

Renaud chuckled. "Do not mistake me for a fool. You will have to work around those obstacles, or simply put, I will kill your daughter when she arrives tomorrow evening."

"Lizzy? Jane? One of them is coming here?" Bennet's small hands shook. *My God!*

Renaud walked to the window and looked out at the rough North Atlantic beyond the perimeter of the island. Two of his best men guarded that wall with their Russian AK47s, another sixty guarded the island's cliffs and beaches, not to mention those in his employ who continually patrolled the waters. And then there was the added security provided by the sharks feeding on the trash that the compound dumped to lure them into the local waterway. A prisoner within these walls could never escape undetected, let alone survive. It was impenetrable from within and without.

Although surprised by Bennet's information, he spoke as though unfazed. "Ah, so you have *two* daughters? Well, I believe it only takes one knife to one throat in order to guarantee your expeditiousness."

"Please. Please don't hurt my girls. I'll work harder, faster. I promise. Just don't hurt my girls."

~♠~

20
Skills

L iz and Darcy stood on the tarmac as Charlie's Cessna turboprop taxied to a stop. Draped with Darcy's black suit jacket over her shoulders, Liz's fingers tapped the side of her thigh, causing him to grasp them in his hand.

"Why are you nervous?"

"How do you know I am nervous?"

"Liz, I just made love to you. Do you think I would do that without noticing these small details about you?" *Besides, I'm trained to notice everything.*

She looked up to him with a quizzical brow. "I don't know. You tell me. We know so little about each other's history."

"That's called our back story. Those are details we will come to know and understand over time."

"Over time?" *Is he implying...forever?*

"Yeah, over time, as in *the future*. I meant what I said in the gazebo." He leaned down to her ear and whispered, "In case you didn't hear me the first time, I am in love with you. Crazy, mad love. Liz, *future* means *forever*."

She didn't have time to reply or even see the sincerity in his ink-filled irises. Jane was running down the aircraft's steps, waving her arms in the air. Looking like the party girl she was, her hair was slicked back, and her bubble-gum-pink lip gloss matched her fingernails perfectly. The little sparkly sheath dress she wore concealed nothing. She was all legs and breasts.

"Lizzy!"

Liz broke into a run, and the two sisters collided with tears and laughter. Jane pulled back, looking her up and down. It was clear that Liz had done well on her own merit out in the big world of international espionage with Darcy. Sure, the red dress was dynamite, but the earrings and snake necklace were explosive.

Jane raised an eyebrow. "I approve. Are you wearing the red panties I bought you?"

"No, I'm not wearing underwear. I tore them by accident when I dismounted the motorcycle."

Jane hooked her arm with her sister's. "Oh my. Does your biker god know?"

"Sure, they're in his pants pocket."

"Did you...did you, you know?"

Liz only smiled and nodded, but Jane thought she read her sister's lips correctly when she mouthed the word, "Snake."

Darcy was all seriousness once again, greeting Jane and Charlie with a simple nod and clipped tone to his voice. "Hi. Thanks for coming on such short notice. Let's get in the air before our passports are flagged."

Charlie looked at the blood-soaked, poorly-patched cut to Darcy's arm. "Playing with knives again?"

"Just a scratch. My nurse says I'm a big baby, so I can't complain even if I wanted to."

Taking in Darcy's open shirt, Charlie smiled wryly. "What happened to the buttons on your shirt?"

"None of your business."

As the women walked toward the Cessna's steps, Jane kept her arm tightly hooked with Liz's. She spoke softly. "Are you glad you...you know...with him?"

"Definitely."

"Was it everything I said it would be?"

"Most definitely. I retract my former statement that sex is overrated."

"Is he your knight? Lizzy, do you love him?"

Liz surreptitiously looked over her shoulder at the man ascending the steps behind her. Darcy noticed, slightly smiled, and winked at her, causing her to snap her head forward quickly. He had protected her. He was saving her father. He was funny and filled with all kinds of passion and energy. He loved opera and the fine things in life, yet he wasn't afraid to live dangerously. He treated her as his equal, and his confidence in her abilities gave her the strength to break free from Lizzy of Longbourn. In everything, Darcy had shown her respect and gentleness, in spite of his Iceman persona. Even when walking away from what had been developing between them, his rationale was honest and forthright. Poorly executed, yes, but his intentions were never meant to hurt her. Furthermore, he had wounds and scars that had changed his life, just like her.

Liz replied softly. "Yeah, Jane. I do. I love him more than I ever thought I could love someone. He's everything my heart needed."

"Does he, you know…the same?"

"He does. He told me so."

Jane nodded, knowing then that the secrets she held would remain just that. There was no sense in causing pain by telling her sister what Charlie had confided about them working for an assassination organization. It was Darcy's responsibility to tell her sister he was a hired hit man. She certainly wasn't going to tell Liz that he had been sent to kill their father. Judging from the rosy look upon Liz's face and the gorgeous diamond necklace and earrings, not to mention the way she kept looking back at the man while he climbed the steps, it was clear that Liz had arrived at that elusive place of happiness. Jane wasn't about to send her back to the Lizzy of old, who hid away and denied herself the life she was meant to have.

Instead, Jane replied, "You should travel more. It agrees with you."

Dressed in a pale-blue, embroidered Moroccan shirt and brown trousers, Rick met the four weary travelers at the Riad Salam hotel located in the old part of the city within the Medina. It was still dark at four-thirty in the morning when they stood before the gated hotel. Liz and Jane were in awe, not only of the exotic location but also at the sound of the adhan emanating from the ancient mosque down the narrow street. The Islamic morning call to prayer filled the air around them.

Rick rushed them into the traditional Moorish hotel, escorting them toward their reserved rooms through the open-air courtyard enclosed by Arabesque wood screen panels. The hotel's staff was otherwise occupied by hastening to prayer.

Lavish furnishings of linen and silk decorated the interior of the hotel, and the scent of jasmine hung in a heady exotic aroma. Leather poufs and hand-woven floor mats created a fantastical scene as though taken from one of the exotic stories within *One Thousand and One Nights*.

Rick explained to the women that Morocco was ninety-nine percent Muslim and that they would hear the call of the muezzin five times daily. He also explained the important things every Westerner should understand, particularly about their dress.

He looked Jane up and down, and she smiled broadly at his insinuation. She liked what she saw, too. Refined ginger was always her favorite flavor. "What's the matter, Rick? Don't you like my dress?"

"What dress? That's about the size of a band aid."

"It covers, well, most of me." Jane giggled.

"And your hair, blondie, better keep a scarf on it in this part of the world if you don't want all the men groping you."

"Which men in particular are you referring to? Anyone I know?"

Charlie recognized the flirtatious tones in both their manners, and his arm instinctively went around Jane.

Rick smiled at the move. He had no intention of picking up one of his friend's women. He'd been devoured and spit out once already, and he wasn't keen on repeating history, but Charlie couldn't know that.

Before shown their accommodations, the men made plans to meet in ten minutes over Moroccan coffee up on the rooftop terrace. Caroline was scheduled to arrive in about two hours, and Obsidian needed to have a plan of attack fully formulated with the intel Darcy had assembled.

Elegant and decorated in muted greens and yellow gold, Liz and Darcy's suite bespoke of a rich and alluring culture. Concealed behind sheer panels that hung from the archway leading to the sleeping area, the bed was covered with rose petals. On a settee, the riad staff had laid out traditional clothing for the couple. The fireplace was lit, and mint tea and Moroccan pastries had already been placed on the small, bone-inlaid table in the sitting area.

Darcy could see the fatigue settling in Liz's eyes. Although she didn't get ill and did attempt to sleep on the plane from Seville to Marrakech, he knew it wasn't enough. No matter how much she snuggled against him—God how he loved that—he could tell her obvious newfound sense of adventure was taking a toll on her.

Liz admired every detail of the beautiful suite, smoothing her hand over the inlaid table. Dreamily she said, "It's incredible, so exotic."

This was Moroccan history of days gone by. Yet unlike Longbourn, it didn't hold onto the death of generations before. The ancient Medina spoke of life alongside the vibrant, modern Gueliz section of Marrakech, both filled with passionate colors and energy.

In a ceramic vase beside the entrance, five long stems of purple orchids popped out in colorful contrast against the yellow wall. She approached the oblong flowers, admiring them with a gentle touch to a bloom.

And Darcy admired her as she did so. "*Orchis mascula,*" he confirmed.

Playfully she replied, "Its tuber is called the Adam and Eve root. They say witches make love potions from them." She looked over her shoulder at him standing with his hands in his pockets. "How do you know so much about orchids?"

"They were my mother's favorite. Like you, she had a greenhouse, and as a child, I spent hours playing at her feet, listening to Mozart and Puccini. That was before I found out I preferred a smelly horse stable, a polo mallet, and ultimately, rock music." He smiled fondly in recollection. "To think Led Zeppelin's 'Black Dog' enticed me away from Mozart's 'Jupiter.'"

"I like Led Zeppelin, but I never really had the opportunity to enjoy them fully. Daddy always listens to classical at home, and I have old cassette players in the Jeep and greenhouse, not CD players. Did your mother also teach you to dance?"

"Ah, I knew you would get around to asking that sooner or later. No. She didn't teach me but forced me to take dance lessons in preparation for all the cotillions she was sure I would attend, where every gold digger was waiting to hook their claws into me."

"You're from money?"

"Don't hold that against me. I'm from Leesburg."

"Northern Virginia? You're a Virginian?"

"Yes." *And if you stay with me forever, I'll make Pemberley a happy home for us. Pemberley? Yeah, Pemberley. Stay with me, and together, we can banish the ghosts.*

Liz walked through billowing drapes between the private sanctuary and the spacious terrace. A luxurious, completely private, blue and yellow mosaic-tiled dipping pool in the shape of an onion-domed minaret was before her, tempting her. Within the inviting water floated more strewn rose petals. She unconsciously bit her lip. Oh, she had plans for that pool. Yes, she did.

Darcy came behind her, wrapping his arms around her waist. He kissed the curve of her ear, feeling as though they had been a couple for years. He had never felt so at peace and so sure of the fact that *this* woman wouldn't betray or hurt him. Sure he was a little nervous. This was a big step for him, but he was willing to take the chance, and that said something significant.

"I have to go. Please try to relax and get some sleep. Tonight will be high-octane, not to mention dangerous. You'll need to be well rested," he said.

"I'll try, but I do want to catch up with Jane."

"That's fine, but Liz…" He turned her by the shoulders. His dark eyes narrowed, his expression serious. "…do *not* leave this riad under any circumstances. Going out unchaperoned could be dangerous. I'm *begging* you to listen to me this time."

"Begging?" She flirtatiously ran her finger down his white shirt. "You know I like begging."

"Yes, I know, but I am also *forbidding* you."

She didn't argue, now understanding the scope of the danger they were in. "You have my word. Will you be gone long?"

"I'm not sure. I promise that we will have some time together this evening before I leave for the island to get your father."

"Thank you. You're risking your life for a man you don't know, for a man who clearly didn't care for the lives of others."

Darcy took both of her hands in his. "I'm doing it for you, you know, not because of my job or your father, but because of you and how I feel about you." He wanted to tell her the truth about how he accepted the assignment to eliminate her father and how he couldn't go through with it the moment he saw her with the sun shining down upon her face. He would tell her soon, when the time was right. Now was not that time.

"Thank you," she repeated humbly. "Don't be too long."

"I have something for you in my absence."

Liz raised a curious eyebrow when he reached behind his back waistband.

He withdrew a 9mm pistol. "It's one of Rick's. Keep it safe; keep it hidden, and shoot with the intention to kill. Do you know how to shoot?"

She shook her head, and he pulled back the slide to chamber a bullet round.

Handing the pistol into her unsure hand, he said, "Keep your finger off the trigger until you're ready to fire. Are you okay with this?"

"Yeah, I guess I have to be."

"It could save your life if I can't get to you. I'm sure you and Jane will be safe, but it's just a little insurance policy. Besides, it makes *me* feel better, so humor me." He looked at his watch. "I gotta go, baby."

Darcy's kiss, his first since the gazebo, was gentle and filled with sweet tenderness. His lips caressed and molded around hers as his hands cupped her face. He was making love to her, and she gave it back with the same emotion. Liz knew then that when he said *forever,* he meant it.

Their lips parted, but their eyes remained locked like that night two weeks ago at the dance studio. She could see he was affected by the kiss. After dropping another to the tip of her nose, he turned and left the room. It was the first time his departure didn't cause her frustrated bewilderment. She knew he would be coming back and why.

Two conversations unfolded at the same time in different locations of the riad. One between two beloved sisters sitting cross legged on embroidered floor cushions in the middle of Darcy and Liz's suite, and the other took place on the roof as the morning sun broke over the Medina's rooftops.

Both women were too wound up for sleep.

"Liz, I'm sorry I cut you off when you called. You should know that I *did* try to call you back, but there was no answer. I'm not *so* one-track minded."

Liz snorted. "Yes, you are."

"No, really. I just knew you were in good hands." Jane waggled her eyebrows, and Liz chuckled.

"You didn't actually tell me what you were doing in Capri."

"Having fun, of course. We went cave-diving and skinny-dipping. Charlie took me shopping and clubbing. Oh, Liz, I didn't think I could be this happy. He's everything a man ought to be: strong, playful, fun-loving, responsible, and let's not forget rich. He can be serious, too, and believe it or not, he's deeply introspective and philosophical. Who would have thunk it?"

"So you like him? I mean really like him beyond the good sex."

"Who said good? It's fan-bloody-tastic! And, yes, I really, really like him.

"Which brings us to you, my dear sister. Based on the look upon your face and that never-ending smile, I'm not going to pry you for details, but I can't help but wonder what else it is that you're smiling about. You've fallen in love. You've had great sex, but there's more, isn't there?" Of course Jane knew her sister was having the time of her life, but she wanted to hear Liz tell her.

"It's this whole trip, Jane. I can literally feel the blood rushing through my veins. In the Ferrari and on the motorcycle, the danger didn't frighten me so long as Darcy was there with me. It's as though I'm finally living. I did things I never thought that I would do: flew in an airplane, tangoed in the moonlight, played roulette in Monte Carlo, wore diamonds and an evening gown, rode on a bullet train. I even had erotic, exhibitionist sex in a gazebo."

Liz swept her arm wide. "Look at this place. I'm not in Kansas anymore. This is *Morocco* for goodness' sake, and I'm Scheherazade in *One Thousand and One Nights*. Darcy did this. When he agreed to take me along, he forced open that door I hid myself behind a long time ago. I feel free to fly, and he's right there with me."

Jane leaned back and popped a small fig in her mouth, listening to that long-lost, much-missed sister expound on her adventure. She said nothing, just laid there giving free reign to Liz's excitement as it poured out. No sister could have been as happy as Jane at that moment. Her sister had broken free from prison.

"And that dipping pool, did you see that? Oh. My. God." Liz asked in awe.

"Tell me about the necklace and the earrings that you refuse to remove or let me even touch for that matter."

Liz's eyes continued to sparkle as she revealed the secret of the hidden microphone and how Darcy told her to never remove the necklace so that he would always know that she was safe. Even though the microphone was now broken, she still wouldn't remove it.

"So what now, Liz? What happens when we go home and you return to Longbourn?"

Liz grew serious. "I never said I was returning to Longbourn."

"Well then, where are you going to go? I mean, you are welcome at my place, but the loft is really small for the two of us. After a month, you and I will be killing each other. I love ya,' but you know I dig my space."

"I guess I haven't thought that far in advance. I'm not sure if I can go back to the life Daddy wants for me, let alone be that person he molded me into. I'm free now. I like this person. I like who I am when I'm with Darcy." She became reflective for a moment, adding, "I understand now why Mom left. She felt trapped. While I can't condone *how* she did it, I do forgive her. Staying with Daddy is like a cancer."

"I wouldn't go that far, but I am glad to hear that you understand the reasons both Mom and I left."

"I'll consider my future carefully. Besides, we don't know what will happen with Daddy, let alone tonight." Liz somberly added, "For all we know, we could be stranded here or worse …"

"Don't think like that. These guys know what they are doing. It's what they do for a living after all. Creep around in the middle of the night, kill evil men, and then slip out unnoticed." *Oops.*

Liz snorted a laugh. "I don't know about that, but Darcy does have skills."

Jane cocked an eyebrow. "Skills?"

"Yeah, skills—all kind of skills, the best kind of skills."

"That snake thing?"

"Hmm…yeah…skills."

~ ♠ ~

Rick stirred his strong Moroccan coffee. "So what's the plan, Darcy? Our window is small here. Five o'clock only gives us eleven hours."

"It's simple really. Renaud wants Liz. Frankly, I don't blame him."

Rick and Charlie looked at each other. *Oh yeah, he's a goner.*

"But he doesn't know what she looks like. He and Crawford planned a meeting in the souk at five this evening. That's why we need Caroline."

"You want her to take Liz's place?"

"It's the only way to get someone inside the compound. Caroline has the ability to create silent havoc and kill off the inside perimeter while we breach the island from the water in the dead of night."

"Scouting?" Charlie asked.

"We'll need a fishing boat to take us out today and a telescopic camera to do some recon to see what we are up against. It'll give us an idea of how tight security is at the sea wall. That will be where Rocco comes in later, Charlie. This is a direct action strike: seize, destroy, and recover."

"So we are going to sky dive in, infiltrate, hit, and run? How are we getting off the island after we have secured Bennet?"

"Parachuting in, boating out. I've arranged for a SEAL buddy and his powerboat to meet us in Essaouira. It'll be the same protocol as Operation Kazatsky when we breached Russia's airspace and dropped into the Black Sea undetected. Only that was a high-altitude free fall. Remember that? Man, that was a blast. On this one, we're dropping in from low altitude."

Behind them, they didn't hear Caroline ascend the steps to the terrace until she said, "I doubt the little woman will let you do that anymore, Rambo. My guess is now that she has the ring, she'll soon have you tied to a nine-to-five desk job, sell the Harley, and laser off your tattoos. Before long, you'll be out of shape with a passel of children and eating at Chuck E. Cheese."

Everyone looked up to see the woman slithering toward them like a black mamba snake in her tailored, black business suit with neat pencil skirt and black pumps. Her red hair was pulled into a tight chignon, secured by her favorite lethal clip. Coiled around her wrist was one of her special toys: a thin, gold expanding garrote made to crush a man's neck in seconds.

Darcy couldn't help think for a moment how she looked so much like a CIA agent—sticking out like a sore thumb while hoping not to be discovered. Could it be that his powers of observation were working overtime? *CIA?*

"Excuse me, Medusa? Are you implying something with that spitting tongue of yours?"

Rick kicked him under the table. The two men held each other's glare. All Darcy understood from the gleam in his cousin's eyes was "Don't go there."

Gripping a thin, lightweight titanium briefcase in hand, Caroline approached the table and nodded. "Boys."

She was all business. This was serious stuff to her, not because a misguided man or the lives of a nation hung in the balance and not because she wanted to assist Darcy in bringing down Al-Hanash. Caroline's liquid venom dripped because this was *her* moment to shine in the field. Every moment of her duplicity had earned this reward. She was now an active field operative for Obsidian, and it was because of her skill, not because she obtained it on her back. It had been a long time since she last experienced the thrill of the kill.

Taking a seat on one of the plush, white sofas under the canopy, she leaned back and crossed her tanned, long legs, which seemed to glisten in the rising sunlight. She was beautiful, and she knew it.

The Berber waiter dressed in traditional salwar kameez shirt and pants couldn't take his eyes from her as he poured mint tea. Moroccans loved red-headed women almost as much as they loved blondes. Obsidian's agents waited for his departure before continuing their planning.

Diplomatic, cool, and collected when it came to business, Rick cleared his throat to break the tension. For a moment, he was able to forget that the woman before him was evil personified, but damn, he hated to admit that he was still in love with her.

"Thank you for coming so quickly, Caroline. You're the star of our show tonight, so I'm glad you were able to arrive in time for the intel briefing."

"You asked. I'm here. Simple as that. You know me, Rick. I'm committed to Obsidian in every way. So what is it that you will have me do with my little ninja toys?"

Darcy laid the plan out for her. "At five this evening, Rick will make contact with Al-Hanash. We know him as Devlin Renaud."

"Renaud of Operation Mambo?" Caroline was shocked.

"Yes, apparently his organization has grown substantially over these last three years. The CIA couldn't have been more wrong about the ideology of Al-Hanash. He's not some religious zealot. He's a terrorist for profit and profit alone. Anyway, his plan is to sell Liz's virginity on the human trafficking market."

Caroline couldn't help herself; she laughed – almost cackled really. "Virginity? You showed him, didn't you?"

Rick kicked Darcy again.

"Whatever, Medusa. You will be posing as Liz to get inside his compound. The minute we touchdown in the water, you'll begin your systematic dismantling inside the prison walls and locate Bennet. We will be sniping from the outside as my man Knightley joins us from the water after taking out whoever will stand in our way of escape. Rocco and the plane will be waiting with Liz and Jane in Tangier where he will transport us all back to Capri."

"Do we know this Knightley well enough to trust him? After all, we trusted Lucy Steele, and look what she did to us. If I remember correctly, a boat was involved in that debacle as well."

"Don't you worry about him. The only thing you need to know is that if you touch his head, he will kill you on the spot. That's no joke. That's a fact. He'll tear out your windpipe with his bare hands."

"Ooh, he sounds rough."

Rick noted the gleam in Caroline's eye, and he didn't like it.

Still acting the behind-the-scenes agent, she opened her briefcase and took out a pen and pad. "I was thinking, Rick, it's time we change the name of the operation. Clearly, we are not in France any longer. Cancan is obsolete. Perhaps we can name it something Arabic. What do they dance in Morocco? The shikat? The belly dance? Rambo, you would know. What shall we name it?"

Steel chairs screeched on the concrete as all three men pushed away from the table. They left, ignoring her insistence that they return. Instead, they went to Rick's suite to prepare for their day of scouting.

They didn't give a shit what they called the operation as long as they all survived. For Darcy, he had too much at stake. Worrying about a stupid dance name was the least of his problems should this go to hell in a hand basket.

~♠~

21
Snake Charmers

Try as he might, the Iceman couldn't detach himself from Liz. Before leaving for the quick flight to Essaouira at the coast, he checked on her three times, twice finding her sound asleep, curled in a ball in the center of their bed. When he returned before leaving for Caroline's hand-off to Al-Hanash at five o'clock, Liz was at the spa with her sister, and he was elated. She had finally listened to him and didn't take matters into her own hands. She was safe, and he could breathe easy before heading to the Jemaa el Fna.

~♠~

The marketplace within the Medina's old quarter was filled with activity as the sun set as a backdrop to the vibrant colors and pungent aromas rising from each food stall. Situated on one side of the square was the busy souk market of household and exotic wares of clothing and rugs. Metal buckets of colorful spices piled into pointed peaks of vivid display to entice the shopper. A few local women dressed in traditional hijab bartered with peddlers as a myriad of female tourists scoured for treasures among the many incredible offerings of Moroccan lamps, serving dishes, and carpets.

Darcy lay prone on one of the rooftops surrounding the square's courtyard. His rifle rested poised and aimed on the man he recognized from years earlier: Devlin Renaud. His scope's image was the same as it was that fateful day outside of Cuba. The face never changed, only the location. Flattened below a huge satellite dish, the sharpshooter had only room enough for the barrel and scope of his rifle to take in the scene below.

Stylishly attired in a navy blue suit and red tie, Renaud sat at a small bistro table for two, fronting stall number twelve. He was the only patron dressed in such fine western apparel. Drinking orange juice, he watched the snake charmer no more than five feet before him working magic with the cobra and a viper coiled on the ancient stone pavers. As the charmer's musical horn pierced the evening sky, Darcy couldn't help but smile ever so slightly at the irony of the scene. Snake, Al-Hanash, *the snake*, was clearly enthralled with the charmer, particularly when the peasant picked up one of Africa's most lethal vipers, the puff adder, and displayed it before Renaud's face. Both charmer and terrorist laughed at the danger.

Through the aperture of his scope, Darcy located five men pretending not to be who they really were: Renaud's armed guards. One lay like him on the rooftop below the mosque. Two stood beside the neighboring food stall, and another watched from within the medicine shop. The last sat smoking a hookah at the table beside Renaud.

The Iceman observed as Rick, dressed equally fine in an impeccable charcoal suit with yellow tie, pulled back the chair opposite Renaud and sat down. Man, he was smooth. His words, manner, and debonair polish bespoke a confidence perfect for the front-man role he assumed. Rick may have been lethal in his own right, but *this* was what he did best.

Rick signaled the waiter to bring him a glass of orange juice, and Darcy noted the wary expression that immediately shrouded Renaud's face. With microphone and earpiece in place, he listened as the two equally-matched powerful men sat opposite each other, giving the appearance of civilized cultured friends. To the average man, no one would suspect Rick to be the dangerous killer that he was. Darcy had seen it first hand when his cousin snapped the neck of one of Gaddafi's soldiers with one hand, then laughed as his victim fell in a heap to the ground.

"And who might you be?" Al-Hanash inquired as he sized up Rick.

Rick noted the pinky ring. *Yes, it's our target.* A subtle nod indicated confirmation to Darcy.

"I am the man who has come to do business with you. I believe you had a meeting scheduled with a mutual acquaintance of ours."

"My business was with Crawford. Where is he?"

Rick sipped his orange juice and looked out at the courtyard toward where Caroline, dressed in traditional black abaya and headscarf, stood beside Charlie. "Crawford? Dead, of course. Would I be here if he were not?"

Renaud eyed him up and down. "You are CIA?"

Rick laughed. "Hardly. I'm what you might call an opportunist. I saw an opening, and I took it. Your friend enjoyed his drink and his talk a little more than you would have liked, but don't get me wrong, I certainly appreciated the information and the woman."

"You have the woman?"

"Again, would I be here in Marrakech if I did not? Trust me, Morocco is the last place I would like to be. The heat from the Sahara locks up my trigger finger. Ah well, I always did prefer to use a jagged knife anyway."

"It seems my deal with Crawford has changed hands, Mr....Mr...."

"Tilney. Hank Tilney."

"Tell me, Mr. Tilney, have you spoiled the woman? If so, the deal is off."

"Let's just say that although I am *ginger* myself, I don't prefer red-headed women, something I understand is highly sought after in this part of the world."

Impressed, Renaud raised an eyebrow.

"There are many in Northern Africa and the Middle East who would pay handsomely for a redheaded virgin. Why not sell her yourself now that you understand her significant value in the market? Surely it would be wiser for you to do so than to become involved with Al-Hanash. In doing so, it could mean your life."

"Because you are well known and trusted by your contacts who would pay well above my asking price. I'm only a simple businessman who has become involved in something beyond my circle or expertise. I am aware that her value is well over a million Euros, but I ask only two hundred thousand in exchange for the girl. I am how shall I say...in need of quick cash."

Rick took a Russian monocular from his pocket, handed it to Renaud, and pointed across the courtyard. "There, to the left of the magician."

Al-Hanash liked what he saw. Indeed, even his manly appetite wanted a taste. Sophia was untouchable for all these eight months of her pregnancy. Perhaps, he could use the girl without penetration and still sell her virginity. Business was business, but lust was something else entirely. He noted the red hair peeking out from the headscarf. She was gorgeous with porcelain skin and ice-blue eyes and imagined what her body looked like below the black dress. He would find out. The Bennet woman was worth the money, and he knew he could most likely triple his outlay once he was through with her.

Besides, the man who had acted as his conscience lay dead somewhere in Spain. Omar's religious beliefs had kept Renaud's base instincts in line during the many years of their friendship. Perhaps his death was a sign to deny himself no longer. He knew that for all his external refinement, he still had an unquenchable thirst for bondage, dominance, and sadomasochism.

Yes, he wanted the girl for business *and* pleasure. "Done. Bring her to me, and I will wire you the money."

"Now, you don't really expect me to believe that you will keep your end of the deal do you? I may be many things, but I'm no fool."

"Well then, I will provide you with an alternative choice. It is simple really. I can kill you and your associate over there with a snap to my fingers, taking the girl anyway, and then you get nothing. Would that be more to your liking?"

Rick raised his left arm high, signaling Charlie to bring over Caroline. Once she was relinquished and Darcy's Swiss account number provided to Al-Hanash, all parties, including the Iceman, parted ways just as the darkness began to settle upon the Jemaa el Fna.

Liz's day had been one of sisterly bonding and refreshment. The luxury hotel had gone above and beyond catering to them. She was well rested and prepared for what the night had in store. Only one thing was missing: Darcy. This was the longest she had been separated from him since they embarked on this journey together. Even when they were physically apart, she had always felt his presence through the necklace. It had given her comfort, but today, she felt a void, and worry was never far from her mind.

In the blackness of night, the call of the adhan carried to the narrow streets of Marrakech and to Liz, who was concealed behind the opaque curtains on the balcony. She bathed in the exotic dipping pool, silhouetted by Moroccan lamplights at its perimeter.

The MP3 player emitted the tender melody of Rimsky-Korsakov's "Scheherazade" violin solo, representing the alluring storyteller herself. The movement wrapped around Liz, relaxing her as well as her enamored observer, creating a fantastical sensation of *The Arabian Nights*.

Beside the open French doors leading to the romantically-lit balcony, Darcy stood watching Liz. With eyes closed, she floated on her back surrounded by rose petals within the softly illuminated watery depths. He didn't notice the blue and yellow mosaic tiling within. He only had eyes for the woman he loved, who was the exotic feature. Tired as he was, his eyes were grateful, and his body came alive at the sensuous vision with long hair floating all around her.

Languidly, Liz spread her legs wide to move in the pool. Her bare apex bid him enter, but he held back. He wanted this night to be different for them, desiring to enclose her in his arms and cover her with his body. He yearned to make love to her in the cool silk sheets and run his tongue up her soft thighs as she thread her hands through his hair. More than anything, he wanted to fall asleep afterward with her wrapped within his embrace.

Sensing his eyes upon her, Liz opened her own and met his smoldering gaze, which told her so much. She rose in the cool water and then dived down, coming back up before the stairs to exit.

Darcy watched her seductively slow ascent from the pool as water droplets cascaded down her perfect body, some clinging, others gliding. Because their first coupling was in the dark, he had yet to see her curves illuminated by either incandescence or candlelight. The candlelit lamps cast a sensual radiance upon her glistening skin. She looked like a goddess. In that millisecond, he committed every contour of her body to his mind's eye.

He was fully aroused when he approached Liz, holding out an open towel for her entrance. Once enclosed and wrapped in his strong embrace, he nervously said, "Hi."

"Hi." Liz was nervous, too.

He lifted her chin with his finger. His lips hovered over hers until depositing a sweet kiss, which grew ardent within seconds.

When their lips parted Liz spoke the words, "I missed you," which brought Darcy's lips back down upon hers fiercely.

Her fingers thread upward into his locks, holding him to her until their mouths separated again. "I missed you more," he murmured.

"How long before you leave again?" she asked wanting to beg him to never leave.

"Three hours."

"Make love to me, Fitzwilliam."

Darcy kissed her again, then swept her into his arms, carrying her toward the bed. With each step through the suite, surrounded by the emotional music, kisses grew deeper until he laid her upon the bed.

She watched in spellbound appreciation as he disrobed, baring his magnificent body to her hungry eyes. When, with both hands at the bottom of his T-shirt, he uncovered his sculpted torso in one movement up and over his head, she thought she'd die at his sexiness. His tattoos, broad bare chest, and the black hair under his arms and below his navel caused her heart to pound in anxious anticipation. His black jeans dropped to the floor and her womanhood fluttered.

She opened the towel, inviting him to join her. Part of her wanted to forego any foreplay, just wanting to feel him inside her, reaching that place only he had the power to bring her. The other part of her wanted to feel his handprint burn her, his tongue stroke her, and his talented fingers explore her.

Darcy sat on the bed at her side, his right hand caressing her slender leg the same way he did that night in Monaco when he kissed her good-bye. Only this time, her hand caressed him as well, stroking him with matched tempo as his finger dipped in and out of her heat.

Liz reveled in the passionate look upon his face, which appeared over-whelmed by her ministrations as though lost in the moment. With her cradling grasp to his hot tip, he dropped his head back releasing a throaty moan. His fingers tickled her deep within, finding that electrifying spot.

She couldn't help her own moans of delight as her core lifted, meeting his stroking hand, riding the tide of escalating rapture. Lacking Darcy's control, she peaked too soon, crashing in white heat, her body shudder-ing from his ministrations.

Liz gazed into his darkened pupils, and he smiled mischievously.

"Do you remember what I told you on the phone?" he asked.

Breathlessly, she barely managed, "Something…something about my thighs and your tongue."

Darcy started low with her perfectly painted toes, suckling and licking, driving her crazy with burning desire. She didn't know feet could be so erotic, but he made it so. His tongue slid higher, making circles over her ankle then languidly gliding up the side of her knee. She bent and opened her leg giving him greater access.

Oh God, she silently screamed, unaware that the crease of her knee was an erogenous zone, but he did that to her. Eagerly his tongue slid up the inside of her thigh as she writhed in anticipation and need.

That first long, slow lick to her slick, parted sex caused her to arch her back with a passionate cry of ecstasy filling the bedroom.

It was the first time any man had done this to her, and she thought she would burst into flames when he turned his mouth sideways, kissing her sex. Similar to the kiss he gave her mouth this morning, he was making love to her apex, kissing her in the same manner, French kissing her pearl as though it was her tongue.

It was earth shattering, so erotic that her deep pants, writhing body, and throated screams caused Darcy to flick his tongue faster. Liz dug her hands into his curls as his tongue danced and explored in the same way it did whenever their mouths met in intense yearning.

The feeling of his finger entering her combined with the pressure of his tongue shot currents of electricity through her in another explosive orgasm. All Liz could think was how she wanted him inside her, quenching her need. She needed him body and soul.

Darcy thrilled watching her ride the tide of climax before rising to lay his body upon hers. He was straining hard from the taste and feel of this magnificent woman below his mouth. All he wanted to do was let her know how much he loved her. Every part of his body wanted every part of hers to feel the love he had to give.

Tenderly, he smoothed the damp hair from her face, looked deeply into her hazel eyes, then kissed her again, slowly.

She tasted herself on his lips and tongue, and it drove her wild. Her hand smoothed down his back and tight backside, pressing him against her to let him know exactly what she wanted.

Darcy smiled wickedly when she wrapped her leg around his, flipping him onto his back. He adored this unleashed vixen in her. It was clear Liz was so wild with craving that she needed to give in to the impulsive dominant rush she felt. With eager hands, he cupped her breasts, pinching those hardened, succulent nipples he had once had the pleasure of tasting.

Running her hands through her wet hair, she arched, moaning from each alternating brush and pinch. The intoxicating image of the highly aroused woman he loved straddling his body was his near undoing.

Liz leaned forward to kiss him, sliding along his arousal, her folds kissing his shaft with a wet glide.

"I love you, Fitzwilliam. I think I've loved you from the first moment I met you."

He kissed her with scorching pent-up emotion. There would be no more foreplay. In the heat of the kiss, she drove down upon him, filling herself with all of him. Darcy's mind cried out, *Oh God, Liz,* but her mouth continued to capture his breath, making impassioned words impossible.

She rode him in slow, delicious minutes of moving and rocking seductively, teasing him as he tilted his pelvis upward, pushing into her. Liz teasingly slid from him, leaving only his tip sheathed in sweet torment only to glide back down with deliberate control.

She loved this—loved the ability to show him her love the same way he had shown her. Darcy's hands held tightly to her hips as she moved, grinding her hips down upon him. The look of ardent rapture upon his face heightened her arousal, and her body trembled in response, her pace quickening.

Darcy's hands clutched the supple curves of her backside, reveling in her vigorous, back-and-forth movements, and he cried out in sheer mind-blowing torment. "Yes! Oh baby, yes!"

The pressure in them built to fever pitch, until he could stand it no more. He flipped Liz on her back and thrust into her with abandon.

Their slick bodies clung to each other as hands entwined above Liz's head. Her sheath clenched him tightly with each thrust to the hilt of his cock and stroke of his pubic bone against her pearl. Each powerful movement caused sparks to course through her body again and again. Lightning and rolling waves of thunderous sensation meeting and exploding.

His pants and moans met her cries of ecstasy, soaring her weightless until their bodies crashed and collided, his own orgasm tearing him apart with powerful wracking shudders of explosion.

Gravity welcomed them as they lay spent, clinging to each other. He stayed lying upon her with his head tucked in the crook of her neck. Between deep breaths, he dropped kisses to her perspired skin, feeling liberated from his emotional constraints. "I love you. I love you. I love you."

Liz whispered back. "I know."

He shifted his weight to face her on their shared pillow. His breath was laden with intensity. "You asked me a question yesterday...about being in love."

She nodded, running a hand down his back.

"I've never been in love before. You're the only woman I've ever felt that I wanted to spend the rest of my life protecting and loving. Someone I can share everything with—particularly myself, the *real* Fitzwilliam Darcy."

Liz brushed the disheveled hair from his forehead. She just listened, allowing him to pour out his heart.

"I've been deceived and hurt by so many women, Liz, and I shut myself off because of it. It's been easier not to feel *anything*, but you changed that. You brought me back to life."

She leaned in and kissed his lips in ardent assurance. "*I* won't hurt you. You have my word. I will never deceive you or betray you. I will never lie to you or cause you pain. Only promise me that you won't break *my* heart in return, because I don't think I could bear it."

Here was the window, that long-dreaded opening that his conscience demanded, but he faltered, ignoring it, denying its very existence. He could have told her then about the sketchbook and everything else of importance, but he couldn't break the magical spell cast by their love-making. Darcy wanted to savor this moment, this feeling, forever.

He held her tightly to him as her hand continued to smooth over the planes of his back. He vowed, "I'll spend the rest of my life protecting you from heartache. Trust me, baby. I won't hurt you, and I'll sure as hell never leave you. You're stuck with me."

Liz was at peace with that. That was the reassurance she needed.

Darcy felt he should have said more, so much more. He knew that what he concealed had the potential of breaking her heart but swore he would tell her everything, just not right now. He needed to feel all her love.

When exhaustion finally took hold of them, they slept soundly, holding each other in slumber for the first time as though it were the last time. Unlike every night for the past thirteen years, Darcy dreamt in color and light.

~ ♠ ~

With the drapes pulled back, exposing the balcony to the moonlight, Liz stood looking out at the illuminated old quarter of Marrakech, hating that the time had arrived for Darcy to leave for the airport.

Behind her, Darcy packed his gear, humming Puccini's "Nessun Dorma." She couldn't see him finger the sketchbook and then put it back in the bag, only to take it out again. He didn't want to leave with things unsaid, having given her his assurance of love and unfailing commitment. Upon their awakening, he had slowly and tenderly made love to her again and felt sure she would understand what he was about to tell her.

He loved her too much to continue lying to her – or rather, concealing the truth. Holding the sketchbook, Darcy walked to the railing where she stood wearing only his black T-shirt. He was ready to lay bare his heart and conscience for her censure or forgiveness.

Liz looked up at him. "Are you nervous about tonight?"

"No. It's part of survival. This is what I did in a SEAL team. You have to disconnect your fears during acts of battle when it's in service to your country."

"I suppose you do. I can't help but be nervous *for you*. If anything happens to you, I'll never forgive myself or my father for putting you in this situation."

"It's not your guilt to be had." Darcy nervously stuttered and turned to face her. "Liz…I…um …need to tell you something before I leave. It's important, and I'm more nervous about telling you what I have to than I am about the outcome of tonight."

She looked down at the book in his hands, and he noted the recognition upon her face. "I…" He cleared his throat. "This is hard for me, so please let me say it all. I have loved you from the moment I first saw you at *Longbourn, not* the dance studio. *That* was a coincidental meeting.

"At first, I only observed your arrival to the estate. You were in the Jeep, driving fast down the dirt road, listening to the 'Flower Duet.'" I became intrigued by the woman whose hair blew so wildly around her."

She started to say something, but he placed his index finger gently upon her lips. "Please let me finish.

"I'll never forget the date. It was June 24 at 11:05 in the morning, and *that* day was the *first* time I gazed upon your beautiful face. It was you who caused my heart to come alive. You pulled open the curtains to your father's study window and greeted the sunshine with your own radiance."

His thumb brushed the edges of the sketchbook back and forth in nervousness as his memory poured out the details long imprinted on his mind. "I remember every detail of that moment. You were wearing your yellow sundress, the same one you wore in the hotel in Seville. Your lips were the most alluring shade of pink, and your silky hair cascaded down over your shoulders. Liz, it was me who took your sketchbook from the greenhouse, and it was me who cut the *Coelogyne ochracea*, not Crawford. I wanted a piece of you to remind me of the goodness and purity of life that it called to mind after a very long time. Your sketches spoke to me of a woman whose soul was crying out and searching as much as my own was. *Volat, libertas, animus* were words I could relate to personally."

Liz furrowed her brow. "That's how you knew of the greenhouse. You…you were at Longbourn. I don't understand. Why were you at Longbourn? Was it part of your CIA security detail?"

"Yes and no."

She could see Darcy swallow hard. It clearly was difficult for him, so she placed her hand upon his where he still clutched the book. Strangely and surprisingly, she wasn't upset about the orchid or the book, especially given that it signified her most intimate, private escape. His taking, let alone viewing it, would normally have been considered the greatest violation of privacy. Instead, she found herself curious about his confession and trepidation. The book was negligible; his feelings and obvious torment weren't.

Darcy felt comforted by the reassurance of her hand. "Liz…I work *with* the CIA, not actually *for* them. The organization I work for is named Obsidian, and what I do for them is specialized and dangerous with skills I learned as a SEAL. The CIA pays us a lot of money to enter into a civilian contract and use those skills in the nation's interest."

"Are you and the others hired mercenaries?" He looked surprised by her question. *Such a smart woman to know what a civilian contractor did.*

"No." He swallowed hard. "We are hired *assassins*, and the first time I saw you was through the scope of my rifle. I was at Longbourn…to kill your father."

The attentive, compassionate expression upon Liz's face darkened. She withdrew her hand from his grasp. Darcy reached for her but was too late. She was already withdrawing from him. Her hand flew to her mouth, and she stepped backward. The chasm of distance and understanding grew between them with her every retreating step.

~♠~

22
Prisons

Liz ran from Darcy, and he ran after her. Withdrawn entirely from his explanation, she found herself sitting on the bed as though a little girl, covering her ears and shaking her head from side to side.

"No, no. How could I have been so foolish? No!" Feeling like some stupid Katy Perry song, she awoke to find her knight a deceitful user.

Darcy squatted before her as his brave new world of honesty and emotion came crashing down around him. "Please, Liz. Let me explain."

"No! You used me! You said you would *never* use me, and I foolishly led you right to my father just so you can finish your job! I was nothing to you but an eager lay in the line of business. Evil business at that! You took advantage of me!"

He reached for her hands.

"Don't touch me!"

Strong, formidable Iceman was reduced to nothing but pieces of a shattered heart lying on the floor at her bare feet. The woman he loved rendered him powerless by her accusations. What remained of his heart clenched as each sentence of venom expelled from her mouth. He expected this from the very beginning. The viperous woman in her had emerged.

"I'm begging you. Please…listen to me. It's not like that, baby." He pled, reaching for her hands.

"It is like that! You are going to kill my father! You lied to me, and I fell right into your trap. Leave, Darcy, just leave. This is all my fault. I never should have convinced you to take me with you. I never should have attempted to be someone whom I clearly am not. I was right; romance and adventure are highly overrated. I knew it! I knew you would be just like everyone else! I don't want to hear anything else you have to say."

Darcy stood. He recognized the danger in where her mind was taking her. He clearly understood her emotional retreat and the self-blame. After all, he had spent many years becoming the Iceman. He didn't want the same thing to happen to her.

"I won't leave, and I won't let you push me away either. You are doing the exact thing I did years ago. This is *not* your fault – neither your father's actions nor where we are now, and obviously what I do for a living hasn't kept you from falling in love. The person you clearly are *not* is the one you shut away in that decrepit house of yours, pretending that you aren't romantic or free willed or free spirited! You will hear what I have to say, Liz, if for no other reason than to keep your promise to me."

"I promised you nothing!"

"You promised me everything. You promised me your heart and never to cause *me* pain. It pains me that you would shut me down without hearing me out!"

Darcy knew that if she failed to see reason, this first true love would be the last time he would feel anything for anyone ever again, and it most likely would have the same effect on her. He knelt before her, shamelessly begging for her to hear his explanation. Taking her hand, holding it tightly, he refused to let go as she tried in vain to pull it from his grasp.

"Please, Liz. Please listen to me."

Liz turned her face, staring vacantly at a Moroccan lamp. She was trying to shut down emotionally, but damn if her heart wasn't betraying her. She *did* love him—fiercely—and couldn't deny the many reasons why she had fallen for him so hard, so fast.

Darcy persisted. "Before you judge me and think the worst of me, before you say we're through, let me explain."

Glancing back at his contrite expression, she finally nodded tightly.

"From the start, I had misgivings about your father's assassination, but I accepted the job because the lives of our entire nation were at stake if your father finished the source code. Later, after *I* chose not to go through with it, I discovered that the hit was a convenient political posturing tool for the CIA and the president.

"The night of the hit, I saw you and your father together in his study. I knew firsthand what witnessing a parent's death would do to you, and I couldn't do it. I froze. Baby, I loved you from the moment I saw you, and I couldn't cause you the same pain I have lived with all these years. That night, I decided to resign my position with Obsidian. Just ask Rick; he'll tell you. The next night, I saw you at the studio and left town after our dance. You know we felt something when we tangoed. It was more than an attraction. It was a deep connection filled with understanding. You can't deny that. You can't tell me that you didn't feel the same way."

She looked down to their clasped hands and bit her lip, shaking her head, giving him leave to continue in his confession.

"I was afraid, and you were getting married. I came to your wedding for the sole purpose of seeing you one last time. I imagined that it was *me* standing there waiting for you in the gazebo."

Liz looked up, touched by his pleading sincerity and the love conveyed in his dark orbs. She could swear tears threatened to come forth in them but felt sure he had too much pride to cry. Her heart was shattering.

She couldn't imagine this man as a stone-cold killer, but he *was* here on official business. He said so. Their eyes locked as she repeated in her mind the words he just spoke. I *chose not to go through with it.*

Darcy's hold upon her softened, and his thumb brushed against hers. "When everything happened with your father's kidnapping, I knew I had to protect you both. That day, I discovered the CIA had sent one of their own men to eliminate him…on your wedding day! Liz, I'm not going after your father to *kill* him. I'm going after him to *save* him and perhaps broker a deal with the CIA for his safety while bringing him in to face proper justice, legal justice. I want to set you free from the guilt and that self-imposed prison you have obviously been living in since your mother left. I want to help you restore Longbourn and experience life with you. More importantly, I want to love you as you should be loved."

At those last words, tears streamed down Liz's face. Did he really care *that* much? Was he telling the truth? What was she really upset about—his not being forthright from the start or his being an assassin sent to kill her father? Perhaps it was just the reality that she had known so little about him and had already given him her heart in its entirety after years of protecting herself from that ever happening. Whatever it was, she could tell he was both earnest in his explanation and his unreserved love.

Darcy rose from his knees to sit beside her on the bed. She wept, and he pulled her tightly into him, surrounding her with his strong arms.

Liz didn't fight him. She welcomed his embrace.

He kissed her head. "Shh. It's going to be okay. We're going to be okay."

Between sniffles, with her face pressed to his chest, she said, "You lied to me."

"I didn't lie. I just didn't say."

"That's semantics, Fitzwilliam."

He smiled. *Yeah, we're going to be okay.*

"I'm sorry. I know I should have told you sooner. I just…I was afraid. Please forgive me?" he asked.

"Only if you tell me why you do what you do."

Darcy sighed and paused, continuing to hold her to him. When he began his explanation, his voice was dispassionate. "With the exception of your father, the CIA contracts Obsidian to kill those who are only the lowest scum of the earth, people the government wants to eliminate, those proven would deliberately hurt the innocent. My tenure as a sharp-shooter began solely for revenge, to become the best at what I do so that it would never be discovered when the time came for me to kill the one man who destroyed my parents and my life. Every villain who ended up on the receiving end of my bullet represented that man."

Liz gazed up at him in astonishment. He certainly had her attention now, and she remained silent.

"He was my best friend, a ward of my family since we were small children. In college, he had an affair with my mother, which broke my father's heart, provoking his murderous jealous rage. When my parents were not even cold in their grave, he kidnapped my little sister, keeping her locked in a dark closet for two weeks while he demanded ransom. Once returned safely, she was taken from my care. He's in prison now and will be released in eight months."

Liz's hand went to Darcy's cheek, causing his expression to soften from the Iceman cold, which had grown while he spoke. "And now? Are you still motivated by revenge? Will you still kill him?"

It wasn't meant to be manipulative or meant to hold sway over her.

It was simply the God's honest truth when he said, "So long as you're beside me, I can begin to heal and forgive. I have no desire to kill George Wickham any longer, and I'm through with running. This operation is my last. I'm going to retire my rifle."

"Then I forgive you, but surely, you must see the truth of what you told me about my father and his decision to venture into the dark side. It holds true for your mother as well. This man, Wickham, didn't force her to make the decisions she did and certainly didn't cause your father's violent reaction. Wickham is, however, responsible for his actions against your sister, and it is for that crime he is in prison for his punishment."

Darcy knew she was right. In his pain, he had sought to assume the role of judge, jury, and executioner for all the things that his mother's infidelity had instigated. He sought final retribution and justice toward Wickham, all with one brass bullet. Liz confirmed all the things his conscience told him of late.

"Now let me ask you, Liz. Why did you stay at Longbourn, hiding inside a life where you were clearly unhappy?"

She had never admitted to anyone those thoughts she kept secret, and it pained her to admit them aloud. However, to Darcy, she would only tell the truth. He had been honest knowing how she would react, and she owed him that same trust.

"What I rationalized as remaining for the sake of my father was for my own protection. Caring for Longbourn and for my father was a safe haven where I felt I would be protected from silly romantic notions and unrealistic expectations of love.

"Because of my mother's actions, I...I was afraid to open myself up to real love because I knew that, at any given moment, my heart could be broken when it all came crashing down. I believed I would rather have never loved at all than to experience love and loss. I saw what it did to Daddy. I know now that *Longbourn* wasn't the prison, it was just the place where I locked away my heart, until you set me free."

Her words were his thoughts. He had felt the exact same way.

"Tell me about your father. You need to get that out."

She sighed and bit her lip before answering with a stutter. "Because... because of my fear of abandonment, I allowed him to manipulate my love for him. I *allowed* him to take advantage of that love and trap me the same way he did my mother." Liz sniffled, swiping at her tears with her fingers. "He made me feel guilty if I considered leaving, and of course, I let him make me feel that way."

Darcy wiped her tears with his thumbs. "It was wrong of him to do that, but you're stronger now. You don't have to go back to that. Are you still afraid to love?"

Liz nodded. "I'm afraid you'll hurt me. I'm afraid now that I've given you my heart, you'll walk away like my mother did."

"It's no different than the advice I gave you in the Ferrari. Remember? If you allow yourself the fear, then you will never experience the thrill of anything. Like me, put aside your trepidation, and let's experience what it is like to love with our whole hearts."

He cupped her cheeks in his hands and fervently kissed her.

When their lips parted, she said, "Hold me until you go. Please don't let go of me."

"Liz, I'm never going to let go of you. I'm never going to hurt you again. I love you with all my heart. I'm committed."

~ ♠ ~

Caroline stood in the concrete cell on the west side of the prison. It was clear that care had been given in preparing the room for her arrival, obvious by the red satin bedspread on the cot below the barred window and the assortment of finger foods on the table. There were no utensils or anything else that could be used to facilitate her escape, however. She was surprised that she hadn't been drugged given so many women who were to be sold on the human trafficking market generally were. Having long developed a resistance to most drugs, that would have been a fruitless effort. As part of her ninja training, she had deliberately exposed herself to some of the worst drugs and debilitating toxins in order to avoid falling victim. Charlie often joked that it was a shame the three men of Obsidian couldn't have been so fortunate when exposed to the Caroline Bingley toxin.

Her mind continued to plan as she took in her surroundings and what she had learned about her captor upon her arrival. In another situation, she would have found Devlin Renaud extremely attractive. With long lashes framing his dark eyes, he looked exotic and was definitely someone she preferred to sleep with rather than kill. She could tell by his perusal when he removed her abaya that he liked what he saw, too.

She felt confident that the black, scoop-neck workout bra, and matching lycra shorts she wore hidden below the Islamic dress left nothing to his imagination. It took everything in her power not to smirk when Al-Hanash inspected her goods. Instead, she feigned tears of fear and pleas of mercy. When he patted and smoothed over every part of her body, she noticed how his pupils dilated. Oh yes, he wanted her for himself, and it was expressed when he promised his return later in the night.

By the look in his eyes alone, Caroline realized that Renaud's cool, slippery control could easily be manipulated by the snake charmer in her, but she would have to wait for that. Whichever came first, the boys breaching the perimeter or Renaud's attempt to breach hers, it didn't matter, she was inside and lethal, but timing was everything.

She slightly pressed the tip of her index finger into her ear canal, triggering the receiver and minuscule microphone transmitter hidden in the snap of her bra top. The voices of the team still in the air awaiting their parachute drop into the Atlantic had yet to come through, but she would know when they touched water. That would be her signal.

Her mission was specific: take out security within the compound, find and secure the target, Bennet, and await extraction. Finding the target had already been accomplished. Rick's cell phone picked up a faint SOS homing signal coming from the island when they scouted on the fishing boat that afternoon. Given the target's profession, they were going on faith. It must be Bennet at the east end of the compound.

In Caroline's estimation, they locked her up with two henchmen on the other side of the door for six hours. Two more guards stood on the rocky shoreline outside her window. Peeking her head out the window, she stifled a chuckle when one of the two men scratched his nuts. Beyond him, she noted that the surf in the Atlantic was mild, not because she could see it in the dark, but because the crashing waves against the rocky shoreline and the large spray of salt water had ceased. She was thankful; because, if the boys were not on time and the surf became rough, this whole plan could go belly up. Earlier, before the dark of night became pitch, she had noted the shark fins. Snakes hated sharks. A chill went up her spine, and she hoped the Knightley guy would be able to divert them with chum thrown from the boat.

Truth be told, she was having the time of her life. She had worked hard to get where she was now and feeling quite self-satisfied that this challenging and fulfilling operation hinged on her prowess and training.

Two thousand feet in the air above the island, Rick, Darcy, and Charlie stood by the open door of the Cessna as the air whistled and rushed within the cabin of the plane. In stark contrast to the white leather seats and luxury cabin, the three military-toughened warriors stood with camo painted faces, wearing skin-tight black diving suits and parachute packs. Their gear, waterproof rifles, pistols, rope, and whatever else they thought they would need, was strapped to the front and back of their bodies. They were ready to jump.

Thankfully, the ancient mosque on Ile de Mogador acted as a small lighthouse, so achieving their drop zone wouldn't be too difficult. The wind was low, and the night was clear, perfect conditions for an unsanctioned direct military action.

Over the speaker system, Charlie piped in the crazy metal music that always got him pumped whenever he was about to free fall or skydive. Even though this was low altitude, he was revved and ready to go as Godsmack jammed to their song "Awake."

From the cockpit, they barely heard Knightley's voice come over the secure radio. "Leapfrog, this is Cobra. Do you read? Over."

Rick pressed the button on the hand-held microphone, "We read you, Cobra. We're coming into jump coordinates. ETA, five minutes. Over."

"Great. I'm in position, knee-deep in fish guts and surrounded by sharks, so let's get the hell underway. Tell Iceman he's ruining my $300,000 boat. Over."

"Will do. On my signal move into the southern perimeter and begin eliminating the targets from your location. Over."

Turning to his cousin and friend, Rick gave a thumbs up and shouted above the loud music. "Ready to jump?"

Charlie, with his broad, happy smile shouted back, "Fuck yeah!"

Darcy, on the other hand, had his Iceman face set in place, giving only a single nod. He was ready to kick some ass and take back Liz's father.

One after the other, they dropped from the Cessna into the black of night.

It was only minutes until Caroline heard Rick over the microphone in her ear.

"Leapfrog is down," was all he said before Darcy, Charlie, and he began to swim the Atlantic Ocean to the shoreline.

The short, stocky sentry standing outside Caroline's door heard retching from inside her cell. When her moans and cries grew louder, he slid back the cover to the peep hole, peering in to observe her kneeling on the stone floor, hunched over the commode. *Shit!* He was loath to go in. His orders were emphatic. However, the last thing he needed was for the goods to be spoiled in any way on his watch. Al-Hanash's punishments were brutal.

Opening the door, but blocking Caroline's view or escape to it, he approached her cautiously, nudging her with the butt of his rifle. "You there. What is wrong with you? Get up." He didn't know what hit him when in one swift move the woman grabbed his rifle, spinning it around and swinging it hard against his skull.

In less than a second, he had been knocked out. The noise from the crack and his heavy thud to the floor alerted the second guard, who ran through the open door.

Caroline swiftly removed a shuriken ninja star from her hair clip and flung it into the center of his forehead, dropping him dead. That was *her* signature kill shot, and she smiled smugly.

She left the guns where they lay; her skills were more deadly than any AK-47 could ever be. Like the living shadow her ninja form became, she exited the cell and invisibly began her deadly assault, silently picking off one guard after another where they were stationed at each corner and hallway of the prison. She employed her expandable garrote coil bracelet causing burly men in camouflage to meet their demise when the thin gold weapon crushed their necks from behind.

That was the way of the ninja: secretive, silent, and deadly.

Within her ear canal, she heard Rick's whispered one-word orders to Darcy and Charlie as they found their hide sites along the fortress's perimeter and water's edge, and just like them, she continued her quiet lethal attack.

With stealth and slithering movement, she became her environment, oftentimes imitating the sounds of the mice scampering along the floor in deliberate subterfuge.

Near the far end of the eastern hall where Bennet's signal emanated, four armed guards stood watch.

Caroline deftly climbed the wall, crouching in the beams above the ancient structure's passageway. Like an inch worm, her sleek body looped, slid, and inched forward along a long beam until she lay unnoticed, suspended directly above the guards as though part of the wood beam itself. Concealed in shadow, she slowly pulled an expandable razor chain whip from her waistband. After carefully tucking her ponytail into her top, she rotated her body and draped her legs at the knees over two beams.

Deep within her ear, she could hear the muffled sound of the bullets exiting Rick's rifle. That was all, just the bullets, one after the other. She knew the boys were hitting their targets in the dead of night. They were without question the best at what they did. It would be just a matter of minutes before they breached the compound.

Caroline didn't know that Darcy had already scaled the east wall where the rusty old canons lay pointing out to the ocean or that Rick had breached the west entrance and that he was now using his pistol. She couldn't see Knightley within the boat picking off guards one by one on the south face of the small island. Her brother had charged the north and was, at that moment, strangling one of Al-Hanash's henchmen. His hands were as deadly as her venom.

Bent upside down hanging by her knees from the wood beams, she stilled her breath then attacked.

As though the deadly razor chain was an extension of her arm, it circled and whipped the surrounding air like a serpentine striking in the shadow. In four fatal and swift fluid movements, it sliced four jugulars, leaving their bodies quivering in death upon the stone floor.

Releasing her legs, she flipped in the air, landing on her feet cat-like, silent and ready to strike again.

She peered around a corner, her eye fixing on the one man between her and Bennet's door. Her expression was as stone-faced and emotionless as the Iceman until she decided to use a different modus operandi, one not of a ninja master, but one of a viperous woman whose predatory sexual appeal and allurement was deadly in its own right. Reaching her hand into each bra cup, she lifted her breasts up so that her nipples were nearly showing. Boldly, she sauntered to the leering guard who was so thunderstruck by her beauty and flaming red hair that he failed to realize she was the enemy.

"Hi, handsome," she purred, approaching the door with an alluring smile. "The men thought you might like a little fun on your lonely sentry duty." Caroline leaned into his ear, noting the beads of perspiration forming on his forehead. She whispered, "Is that a pistol in your pocket?" Her red-painted fingernail traced his bottom lip, and she watched his eyes follow her finger when it slid down her cleavage toward the bottom of her bra.

His eyes remained fixated on her mounds. So much so that he didn't even notice when she withdrew the underwire of her bra, which was, in fact, a narrow dagger.

She thrust the dagger into his throat. The gurgling noise emanating from the stab didn't affect her in the least. In fact, she was quite proud. She was, after all, an accomplished woman, and she knew of no other woman who possessed such thorough proficiency as a ninja master and skilled Obsidian field agent, not to mention the fact that she had no conscience whatsoever.

Stealthily moving through the narrow passages of the prison, Darcy calculated Caroline's deadly destruction by each body he quickly stepped over. He stopped counting after twenty. Man, she was good in the field, but he would never admit that to her.

He, too, dressed in black and still wet from the swim ashore, blended into the shadows, making his way toward the homing signal at the far eastern end of the prison. With each step closer, he could hear a man's voice echo down the stone hallway.

To Caroline's back, Renaud said, "I should have known by the glint in your eye you were not as you appeared."

She turned to face her captor—her other target—as he walked toward her with a pistol drawn. Clearly, he had been woken up. Gone was the stylish, well-dressed, poised man always in control. In his place stood a man on the edge, unkempt with clothes haphazardly donned, and a mien that resembled frustration. Not only had his prison been breached but so had his composure.

"You are very good at what you do, Miss Bennet...or whoever you are."

Caroline feigned to examine her fingernails, replying as though bored with the whole thing. "No, I am not Miss Bennet, and yes, I am *very* good at what I do. Were you not thinking with your *dick*, you might have guessed I was a little more than the innocent virgin you wanted to violate. You do realize that's a hazard in your profession, no?"

He knew she was right. Didn't he blame Crawford of the same thing? "You are here for the programmer. It would appear that I have been betrayed by Crawford, useless dog. It is so hard to find trustworthy associates these days. Perhaps you would consider…"

The words died upon his lips, and his gun dropped to the floor when, from behind, Darcy grabbed Renaud's neck with his arm.

Iceman kicked the pistol toward Caroline. "Medusa."

"Rambo. You're late."

As he secured Al-Hanash within the tight grip of an elbow lock, the fierce grasp of his hand held the terrorist's wrist at his back. Darcy coldly asked Caroline, "Do you want to take care of this scum, or shall I? Quite frankly, I have a personal score I'd like to settle with him."

She sauntered up to Renaud, standing toe-to-toe with his tautly secured body as her tightening fingers smoothed over his nuts until she clasp them within the palm of her hand. "You can have him. I've tortured him enough already. Nothing worth messing with anyway. I'll get Bennet. Hold him still while I look for the key."

She patted down Renaud's body in the same fashion as he did hers, their eyes remaining locked in her search. His anger obviously held at bay behind a veneer of control.

There was no key, but she tauntingly winked at him, then searched the guard lying dead on the floor beside the door. Still nothing.

In one swift move, Caroline released the ornate hair clip, allowing her long, flaming tresses to cascade down her shoulders. On the back of the clip rested C4 explosive putty.

As she went to work on blowing the lock to the cell where they held Bennet, Darcy dragged Renaud's uncooperative body to a nearby cell. With a powerful kick, Darcy pummeled the door open wide, forcing his captive within.

Both men heard Caroline speak to Bennet through the door. "Mr. Bennet, clear away from the door. Find shelter. I'm going to blow it open."

Darcy released his hold on Al-Hanash. It was personal now, and Operation Mambo would finally be finished.

In contrast with Renaud's tan dress trousers and mis-buttoned dress shirt, Iceman's dark, raw masculinity raged from his body.

Al-Hanash looked up into the black eyes of a man who seethed with only one purpose: revenge. He knew that vengeance was the most powerful weapon in any man's fighting arsenal. Many claimed it was control and energy, but he knew from the scars in his own life that revenge was the motivation that transformed warriors into death-dealers of the worst kind. The man before him seemed twice his size. His expression was as lethal as his own. Both men postured an attack, circling the other defensively, ready to pounce once they laid ground.

Al-Hanash baited overconfidently, "You cannot best me. American special forces have not the training I possess."

Darcy laughed. "Yet a 120-pound woman with a ponytail *did* best you."

"What is it you wanted to discuss?"

"Betrayal, Cuba…Oh, and my taking your life. I plan on doing that in about…" He looked at his SEAL watch, "one minute and twenty-five seconds."

Renaud moved in closer to where Darcy positioned himself. "Such an exact science. How can you be so sure you can kill me that quickly?"

"Because that was how long it took for me to kill your man in Spain. Oh, and Lucy Steele, of course."

Recognition dawned on Al-Hanash. "Ah, my Lucia…I have searched a long time for you John Willoughby."

"Willoughby? My name is not Willoughby." *Is that the name she told him?*

Renaud tsked and shook his head. He ran his hand through his unkempt hair. "Then yes, it is appropriate to discuss betrayal. I should have known that she would protect you even in the end. I long suspected her attachment to you." He laughed. "You killed a woman who loved you! Now that is poetic justice."

Darcy looked at his watch again, and before Al-Hanash could even react, Iceman drew the pistol from his holster evenly declaring, "Time's up, asshole." Then he fired two rounds between the terrorist's eyes. One for the CIA and one for him.

Of course, he would have loved to beat the crap out of the man who had turned and used Lucy, abducted Liz's father, ran guns to other terrorist organizations, intended trafficking a young woman, and was planning to sell a deadly weapon to the highest bidder. However, with Renaud's admission of Lucy's true feelings, Darcy realized that anger, remorse, and infinite resentment no longer had a place in his heart. There were only two things that resided in that space now: Liz and redemption. He wasn't in the vengeance business any longer.

~♠~

23
Apprehension

When the door blew open, Bennet was met by a beautiful redhead and a face-painted, ominous-looking soldier whose eyes were as dark as his camouflage and clothing. As far as he knew, the United States Military had rescued him. It was not because he was so valuable. It was because he knew unequivocally that he was a security risk and in a heap of trouble—prison-type trouble.

His small hands shook almost as much as his voice. "Thank God you have come! I never doubted you would find me. My daughters...my daughters may be imprisoned here as well. Please, we have to find them."

While securing her hair back into a ponytail, Caroline replied to Bennet in her usual all-business, reptilian-cold voice. "Your daughters are safe."

Darcy said nothing. He couldn't help staring down with censure at the slight man trembling before him, a man who not only put the lives of millions of people in jeopardy but also both his daughters. He was a boa constrictor who preyed upon his daughter's loving heart for his own selfish needs, strangling and suffocating her free spirit. Darcy understood what life was like for Liz at Longbourn and how this man attempted to substitute his ex-wife with his daughter. Forcing her into a loveless marriage for his selfish agenda was the icing on the cake. The Iceman's heart clenched, frozen toward the man who would one day become his father-in-law. *Father-in-law? Yeah, that's right.*

Touching the Bluetooth, he declared to Rick and the other team members, "Target dead, Virginia Reel secured, proceeding to extraction point. Over."

Taking Bennet's arm in his grasp, his voice was cold. "Are you hurt?"

"No. No sir. I am not hurt."

Darcy took note of the computer hardware on the makeshift desk. "Is the program near completion?"

"Yes. It is, but the code contains built-in inaccuracies that would have to be changed by a secured password in order to be initiated."

Iceman dropped his grasp of Bennet, picked up the AK-47 from the downed guard, flicked on the automatic fire and emptied one hundred rounds into the computer screens and hardware upon the wood desk in twenty seconds. Everything was blown to bits with the exception of what was in Bennet's mind, but the source code was lost forever.

Together, the three silently made their way to the southern point of the compound. Each step toward their extraction location required them to step over dead bodies lying as if speed bumps in their path.

Once through the perimeter doors of the prison, Rick and Charlie met them, looking none the worse for wear. Other than a simple acknowledgment of confirmed identification by Rick, Bennet met Obsidian stone silence.

Of course under other circumstances, Charlie wanted to say, "Your daughter Jane is terrific, Mr. Bennet." But he didn't. He was a different man when on an active op and he remained in soldier mode.

Without a doubt, Darcy was tempted to take Bennet to task, but the Iceman covered him like the Arctic.

And although the misinformed Caroline of a day ago would have wanted to blow the lid on Darcy's impromptu marriage to the Bennet woman, which she was sure would result in a tongue lashing by the traitor father, she strangely held back.

Everyone remained silent and deadly, especially once they climbed into the waiting powerboat.

It was a tight fit for all of them, but the boat was so fast that it wouldn't take very long to reach Tangier where the plane waited with the Bennet sisters to reunite with their father.

Caroline had been the first to enter the boat, placing herself on the white leather co-pilot seat. She'd had an exciting day, but damn if she wasn't exhausted, not to mention she was sure she had a splinter in her abs from sliding on the wooden beam. She swiveled seductively in the chair toward the man beside her. "You must be Knightley?"

Even in the pitch black night, she could see the man beside her: powerful body, huge biceps, and broad shoulders, not to mention the fact that she always had a thing for bald men. Oh, she liked what she saw.

He liked what he saw, too. Her hair coming lose in the wind did things to him. Like Charlie, he'd been around the world, enjoying ladies in every country, but there was just something about a wild redhead, particularly one with finely honed ninja skills. However, he knew her history, and Knightley lived by a code of friendship and loyalty.

"John Knightley, in the flesh. You must be Medusa, the viperous man killer who can castrate men with just the whip or slither of your forked tongue."

"So you've heard about me?" Caroline inquired, leaning back with her elbows propped up against the side of the boat, a position she strategically employed to push her breasts forward.

Knightley wholeheartedly approved of the position, too. Hell, he was a man, after all. His code said nothing about looking, only touching.

Standing behind the wheel, he pushed the boat's throttle forward all the way. The mist from the watercraft's wake and the battering wind caused everyone's hair to whip backward, all except his, of course.

Both Rick and Darcy overtly watched the interaction between the two, both understanding exactly where the viper hoped it would go. Darcy cocked an eyebrow at Rick, motioning with his head to Caroline and Knightley.

Rick shrugged. "I don't give a shit." But he really did. No matter how hard he tried, he couldn't truly turn off what he felt for her. Seeing her flirt with another man was more than he could bear.

Knightley replied playfully to Caroline. "Of course I've heard about you, Caroline. Your reputation precedes you, not all of it bad either."

Let's see what he's made of. Caroline stood, held onto the top of the windshield, and stepped into his personal space. In a slow, suggestive movement, she ran the palm of her hand over his bald head.

He swiftly grabbed her hand. "Normally, I would kill you on the spot for that, but seeing that you are Rick's girl and Darcy's former fling, I'll show them some respect."

She laughed nervously, hating the fact that he knew her history and that he clearly had no intention of pursuing a liaison, even if she had made her intentions clear.

Rick suddenly rose, stepping through the others who sat watching the soap opera unfold. He swooped his arm around Caroline's waist and pulled her into his hard chest.

She feigned objection but secretly reveled in his demonstrative show of ownership. Perhaps he should have done this a long time ago. He definitely caused her discomfiture. She made a crude, sarcastic joke in her uncomfortable circumstance. "It might be safer for you if you just piss a circle around me."

"I'm not afraid of your acerbic tongue, Caroline, but Knightley is right. You *are* my girl, and staking my claim of ownership to your heart requires a little more than marking it with a circle of urine. Besides, you know piss is a powerful snake repellent."

She rested her hands on his shoulders, gazing straight into his eyes. The wind whipped around them, blowing his hair straight back with ferocity. He had the most sincere expression on his face, and she couldn't help but acknowledge that she cared for him differently than she had any other man before, even Darcy. Of course, he lacked Darcy's physical attributes, but toward her, Rick always displayed more emotion and honesty. In that moment, she felt bad for having treated him so disrespectfully.

"So you forgive me then?" she asked. "You have put aside your petty jealousy?"

"Only if you have put aside your unhealthy obsession with my cousin." Rick's eyes bore down to hers.

Caroline laughed, attracting Darcy's attention. "Yes, Ricky, I'm through with Darcy. What would I want with a married man? Lizzy Bennet can now be on the receiving end of that stone-cold, arrogant attitude."

Rick smirked. *Gotcha!*

It didn't seem to matter that Rick and Caroline's lips had crashed down on each other and that tongues were dueling for dominate control. Darcy barely noticed Rick's hand grab her backside.

At her declaration, he suddenly stopped his removal of camo face paint, abruptly stood, and stepped toward them, wrenching their kiss apart. His expression was fierce. "Caroline, did you just say that I'm married to Liz Bennet?" Then he noticed his cousin's quick wink.

"Aren't you?"

"Yeah. That's right. I'm fiercely in love with her." It was the truth, after all.

She looked away from him, met by Rick's piercing mien.

Beside Charlie at the stern of the boat, Bennet sat oblivious to anyone and everything, concentrating on the pounding of the speedboat against the waters of the bay beside Essaouira. He lifted his chin into the air to feel the wake's misting spray upon his face and hoped, above all things, that his daughters had no idea what he had done. Nothing could be worse than to lose their respect as well as Longbourn. He needed his Lizzy Bear. She would understand and forgive him. She would take care of him.

Once Darcy sat back down and continued the removal of the camouflage, Rick demanded of Caroline a confession to something he knew she had been harboring. "Are you going to tell Bertram to shove it up his ass when we get back to DC?"

"What…what are you talking about?"

"You are working for him as a CIA mole in Obsidian. You don't think I know you've been feeding him information?"

"How did you find out?"

"Because the jackass let it slip that he had an informant, and you're the only one I know to be ambitious enough to consider it."

"Yet you said nothing."

"I had to let this play out to be sure. How long have you been an agency operative."

"Years. They recruited me out of college. I used to be a field agent until he assigned me to Obsidian."

Rick shook his head. "I can't believe we didn't see it. I can't believe Charlie didn't see it."

"Well, I'm good at what I do, Ricky. Aren't you mad at me then?"

"Hell yeah, I'm pissed at you. Just because I forgive you your delusional behavior about Darcy doesn't mean you are off the hook for having deceived Obsidian. You betrayed your brother and friends by reporting our inside operations back to that bloviating, bumbling fool. If nothing else, I at least thought you loyal to us. You've disappointed me, and I have lost all faith in you as a respected agent."

Embarrassed by the stinging truth of his accusations, Caroline couldn't meet his eyes. Yes, even she was disappointed in herself. "You're right. I'm sorry."

Rick's head pulled back in shock, and he looked at her. "What did you say?"

"I said, I'm sorry. You're right. I was wrong. Can you ever forgive me?"

"I'll forgive you if you help me with this deal I made with Bertram over Bennet's prosecution. The best way for you to prove your loyalty not only to *me* but also to Obsidian is to help Darcy and Liz."

She looked away from his searing gaze. He was doing it again, reading every one of her thoughts and burrowing down into her soul. Damn, she hated being so transparent to him. She sighed. *Damn!* "Will you make me a permanent field agent? Teach me to sharp-shoot?"

"Yes."

"Deal. I'll see to it that whatever deal you made with Bertram sticks."

~ ♠ ~

Two non-commercial planes had touched down at Tangier's international airport. One carried Rocco and the women, and the other, a Gulfstream Learjet, which sat waiting beside one of the private hangers, had flown in two men. That plane was known as a rendition aircraft, and anyone in the business of transporting international prisoners knew what that meant: the CIA had come to get their prisoner.

As Rick had previously arranged, a trusted "associate" of Bertram's met the team at the marina in Tangier to drive them to the airport in a beat up van. The city, port, and dirt roads were all deserted at this late hour when even the vultures slept. Obsidian would be undetected in the blackness of early morning.

Although the Director of Obsidian already had two victories this evening—Caroline and Operation Cancan—he hoped three times would be the charm. In exchange for Bennet, he had brokered a deal with the agency and, hopefully, Darcy's expected wrath wouldn't cause a rift between the cousins. But a man's got to do what a man's got to do to save not only America but also the reputation of Obsidian.

Unbeknownst to the others, it had already been decided. Bennet would be turned over to the CIA so he could face charges, and Obsidian had to agree to their absolute secrecy and anonymity of their involvement in his apprehension. That was to be expected and was normal protocol of every op completed by them. Obsidian always remained anonymous and in the shadow, never associated with the agency. The CIA would publicly take sole credit for the fall of Al-Hanash and the quelling of a planned act of terror. The exchange, as part of the brokered deal, was that Bertram had promised Rick that Bennet would get off with only house arrest plus lose his job at the Department of Defense. Even though it killed Rick to do so, it was for Darcy and Liz's sole benefit, but there was a caveat that had to be imposed on both Charlie and Darcy. All connection with the Bennet family had to be severed until the dust, press, accolades, and speculation settled. When the press moved on to another scandal or fifteen-minute fame-seeking new story, then they could pursue their romantic intentions.

The tarmac was inactive and dark; not even the lights from the Cessna's cabin lit the fuselage. The CIA's rendition transport also sat in a shroud of darkness, its mission so covert that only Rick knew of its existence.

As the van neared, Darcy could barely see Liz and Jane waiting at the bottom of the steps of the Cessna. His heart rate calmed, not sped up. Liz's assurance of love and trust had become a balm to him, and he found himself feeling proud and redeemed by being able to deliver her father to her alive and safe. He was prepared to do whatever else was necessary to be worthy of her love and trust.

As both sisters continued to observe the van's headlights approach, Jane inquired, "Did you decide what to do, Sissy?"

"I'm not going back. I'm going with Darcy. Where...I don't know, but wherever it is, I want to be with him. What about you?"

"Back to life in Georgetown and the museum. Oh, and did I tell you that I'll be getting free dance lessons for as long as I want them at the Bingley Dance Studio? That's not counting the private home lessons perfecting the horizontal mambo."

Both sisters chuckled until Liz grew serious. "Jane, for the first time in my life, I feel whole. Thank you for encouraging me and always being the voice of reason and support. If it weren't for you and Darcy, I might very well be married to Bill right now."

Jane put her arm around her baby sister, hugging her close. Both continued to gaze out at the oncoming van. "What are big sisters for? I knew the real you was still in there, Liz. You just needed to break free. I missed my headstrong, impertinent, and fun-loving sister who so dearly loves to laugh. I'm proud of you."

"Me, too."

"Liz, will you forgive Dad? You need to forgive him, you know."

"In time. One thing at a time."

"Will you forgive me?"

"Whatever for?"

"For saddling you with life at Longbourn. I shirked a responsibility that should have been born as a team, together."

Liz squeezed her sister closer. "Yes. I forgive you, Janie."

When the van stopped twenty feet from where the women stood, from the front seat, Darcy saw Liz clearly. She looked beautiful wearing black leggings with a Moroccan embroidered turquoise and white tunic. On her feet, she wore a simple pair of babouche slippers. A long, neat braid lay draped over her shoulder. She smiled brightly, and he wondered momentarily if she was happy to see *him* or if the smile was for her father.

Another man also noted her radiant smile. Bennet, however, was sure it was for him. His daughters waited for him. Both women appeared different, not just in attire, but in the way they held themselves. Jane had changed her look. Gone was the frivolous trendy style she usually donned. Instead she wore a long, black and tan Moroccan caftan dress with flat shoes. However, it was his Lizzy's appearance that caused him to frown. He noticed the dangling chandelier earrings, diamond serpent necklace, and black leggings. His eyes took in the kohl and lipstick and then rested upon the henna tattoo on her hand. *Where is Bill?*

The door to the van slid open, and two of Bennet's rescuers exited. He watched as Jane ran into the blond soldier's arms, hugging and kissing. Unhappy with the intensity of said kiss, he frowned.

The man "Fitzwilliam" stood before him at the back of the van, commanding with a sneer to his lips, "Up, Bennet. Your rescue ends here. Time to face punishment."

As he took Bennet's bicep into the palm of his hand, the brute who rescued him exited the van with his diving suit peeled down.

Liz ran directly toward his bare-chested body with open arms. They stood motionless on the tarmac just holding each other. Their bodies clung to each other; her head pressed against his strong chest as he held her tightly to him, kissing her dark locks.

That was the image Bennet saw when he exited the van. In the darkness, he didn't even notice Bertram and another CIA agent descend the steps from the Learjet on the other side of the runway.

He couldn't help himself from calling out. "Elizabeth Bennet!" And all turned toward him, including Darcy and Liz. "Who is this man, and where is your fiancé? Aren't you even glad to see your father?"

Liz entwined her fingers with Darcy's, and together they walked to her father. Darcy watched as she seemed to slip into a persona he was unfamiliar with. Her contrite, acquiescing demeanor was one he had never witnessed, but he knew this was what she had spoken of earlier in the evening.

She kissed Bennet in greeting and apologetically said, "I'm sorry, Daddy. Of course I'm happy that you are safe. Are you hurt?"

"No, I'm fine. Thank goodness I sent out a homing beacon. See, your father is always thinking. It's a good thing I took action as soon as I had arrived in that prison."

His comment was a bucket of cold water, startling her from the accommodating pass she was normally inclined to give him due to his usual nerves and depression.

"Yes, good thing. However, thanks to *these* brave people and particularly this man here, neither you, Jane, nor I were killed *because* of your actions. These honorable people put *their* lives on the line to save us and America while you almost destroyed it! What were you thinking, Dad?"

Bennet took a double take. "My...my...actions? Anything I did Lizzy Bear was for you and your sister. I did it for Longbourn! As for your safety, you were supposed to be married and protected by Bill Collins."

Jane came to stand beside Liz and snorted a laugh. "That's a joke, Dad. You strong-armed and guilted Liz into marrying a gay man who only wanted to use her to get to Longbourn."

"Gay? That is not true! He promised me that he loved you and would protect you from the world."

Liz quieted her voice, looked down at her feet, and tightened her grip on Darcy's hand. She was seeking the strength within her. "Yes, it *is* true. He had no interest in a wife, only a bed and breakfast, but that is beside the point. What you did, Dad, not only betrayed our country and put the lives of every American at risk, but also *hurt* me and Jane. You put *our* lives in jeopardy to save a stupid house! It was selfish and misguided. I'm so angry with you. I don't even think I can forgive you for what you have done."

She looked straight into her father's eyes, raising her voice in confidence. "As for protecting me, Darcy is the only man whom I trust to protect me. He saved me in every possible way and has promised his *true* love—unconditional love. Do you even know what that is?"

Gazing into Darcy's eyes, she smiled, and his return of that smile encouraged her to continue. This was her fight, and she needed to purge the old Lizzy all on her own.

Bennet's jaw dropped, his heart and spirit deflated by the unexpected accusations of his favorite daughter whom he had always expected to be a woman of docility and amiability in all things. He hardly recognized the outspoken young woman before him. Where was the forgiveness and understanding he had counted on? He was no longer his Lizzy Bear's "Daddy." She had reduced him to Jane's moniker of "Dad."

He spat out his own accusations from amidst his wounds. "Love? What does a war-mongering soldier like him know about love? Look at him; he's not the man for you with his tattoos and stern expression. Save you? Based on your manner of dress and the way you're holding onto each other, I'd say that he's ruined you! Look at you, Lizzy, you look—"

Darcy couldn't help it. Really, he couldn't. His right hook came out of nowhere, making contact with Bennet's chin.

Liz didn't flinch from the sight of her lover punching her father. Instead, she looked at the man's stumbling body and said matter of factly, "Consider Darcy's punch my slap to your face for your continued selfishness and your intolerable insult. I'm no longer a child, and I'm certainly not Mom."

Jane stood beside her sister with her hand tightly clasped over her mouth in utter shock, but not dismay. Her father had long had it coming, and she was grateful that it was not only Liz's knight in shining armor who came to her defense but that she defended herself as well. That was the bigger victory—one that was long overdue.

Within seconds, Bertram slipped the handcuffs onto the criminal's wrists. "Thomas Bennet, you are under arrest for treason to the United States of America and conspiracy to sell a weapon of mass destruction to enemies of the state," Bertram declared as he continued to Mirandize the traitor.

As soon as Bennet's arm was clasped and he was being escorted toward the rendition aircraft, the other CIA agent came to stand before Liz and Jane. "If you ladies will follow me, we will need to take your testimony, placing you under the protection of Homeland Security and the Central Intelligence Agency."

Darcy held tightly to Liz's hand, attempting to stop her departure with the CIA. His broad chest overshadowed the smaller man before him. He knew how things worked once one entered into so-called protection of the feds. Their life would become a living hell with no freedom and no escape from the incessant probing. He'd be damned if he would allow Liz to be forced back into any kind of prison, whether it had bars or not.

Rick approached. "Let go of her, Darcy. This was the deal I made with Bertram."

He snapped at his cousin. "What? She stays with me. She's not involved in her father's traitorous actions!"

"No, but this was the arrangement Obsidian made. He gave his word that Bennet's name will be kept from the press and that he won't serve prison time, but you and Charlie must keep away while the CIA and the president take the spotlight for having brought down Al-Hanash and an un-named terrorist's plot. Obsidian cannot be seen anywhere near this. If Bertram gets one whiff of our continued involvement with the women, then they will throw us to the dogs as obstructionists and rogue civilian contractors. We cannot afford to give him ammunition that will bring our organization down. You know this. We exist solely for cloak and dagger. Put a spotlight on what we do, and we are finished."

"I told you, Rick…this op was my last. I'm out. I'm no longer Obsidian, and neither you nor the feds are going to keep me from Liz."

"Come, miss," the agent repeated.

Darcy yelled. "Give us a minute, would ya'?"

Both men backed away as the dark, ominous expression of the Iceman overtook the face of the man before them.

"Fitzwilliam, it's okay. I understand," Liz said, trying not to let the tremble of her lip become obvious to him.

"They are playing a game with us, Liz. This is politics."

She rested her tattooed hand on Darcy's cheek. Her warm palm soothed him when she spoke like the pragmatist she was. "Whether we can be together now or later won't change the fact that I love you and I always will. We *will* be together. I'll be waiting for you."

Darcy nodded, grasping her fingers. He kissed her palm. "I love you, baby." Then he enclosed her hand within his, making a fist together as their lips met tenderly.

They rested their foreheads against each other's and spoke quietly, oblivious to the stares around them. He admired the henna artistry on her hand and wrist. It was a lacy, floral design of orchids along the length of a snake. "This is beautiful. What does it mean?"

"It means I'm yours."

Overcome with emotion, he closed his eyes. Two weeks ago, he never imagined he'd find himself in the position of trusting a woman, let alone loving one deeply.

Composing himself, he asked, "We had a damn great time, didn't we?"

"The best of my life."

"I don't even know your cell phone number."

"Neither do I. I don't have one."

"We'll have to remedy that. Take care of yourself. If you need me for anything, *anything* at all, phone the dance studio, and speak to Caroline. Apparently, she thinks we are married."

Liz raised an eyebrow. "Really?"

"You sound intrigued by that prospect."

"Perhaps. I'll let you know when I see you again."

"I'll hold you to that, you know."

She chuckled nervously in reply. *Was that a proposal?* "Where will you go after here?"

Darcy smiled thoughtfully. "After Capri, to Pemberley. I'm going home."

"I hope you find peace there. Perhaps, this separation is for the best. Both of us need to become reacquainted with ourselves as well as put to rest the dysfunction in our childhood homes."

Their kiss good-bye felt all too familiar and resembled, in both heartache and bitter sweetness, the one they shared when he said good-bye that night in Monte Carlo. Lips and arms clung to each other as their tongues spoke volumes of words that could not be expressed in mixed company.

When their lips parted, Darcy noticed the tears brimming in her beautiful hazel eyes. Even in the dark, he could see they had turned vibrant green. His thumb brushed her cheek as it had done many times before.

Off to their side, Charlie kissed Jane after whispering to her he would see her at the dance studio for "lessons" in a couple of weeks. He had a job to do in South Carolina. Operation Shag was still a go, and he doubted Knightley would be joining the team before September. He was surprised that Knightley accepted Rick's offer, willing to give up the high life in Monte Carlo for a career with Obsidian. But in truth, nothing truly surprised Charlie any longer, not even Darcy's punch to Bennet's face.

Darcy entwined both his hands with Liz's, and only when her steps took her from his reach did their hands separate. He was sure his heart broke for the second time in his life the minute their fingers slid apart and she turned her back to him.

Rick couldn't help but feel moved when he witnessed his cousin standing with his hand over his heart, watching the woman he loved ascend the steps into the CIA's Learjet.

When Liz turned to blow him a kiss, Caroline knew Darcy had found true love, and she fought to conceal her envy.

24
Salvation

Almost at the North Carolina border, Darcy stood waiting on one side of a bulletproof glass window. On the other side, two armed correctional officers watched prisoners of the Halifax Correctional Unit #23 speak with their visitors on yellow telephones clinging to the dividing walls of each stall.

Darcy had ridden his vintage Harley four hours south for this long-overdue visit with George Wickham. At Pemberley, he was determined to clean out the cobwebs and start afresh, determined to be the best man he could be for Liz when they finally came together. Three long, painful, yet renewing weeks had passed since their good-bye in Tangier, and with no green light on the horizon for their reunion, he continued his mission to banish the ghosts and the horrific scars. Those memories no longer had a place in his life. For her, he vowed to think only of the past as its remembrance gave him pleasure. She had inspired that in him.

A new beginning and renewal at Pemberley had begun. Gone were the white linen sheets covering up the long-hidden past, and gone was the temptation to curse his mother's photographs. Fresh light permeated the house that had once been a loving home and that would be again. Darcy was sure his family would begin again. He and Liz would be together soon. Of course it was never far from his mind that they had, in fact, had unprotected sex, twice. Was it too much to hope for? *One step at a time,* he chastised himself.

The biggest change to Pemberley was made to the stables. Ten days prior to Mrs. Reynolds's expected arrival, Mr. Reynolds had come from Asheville. Together, they filled the tack room, prepared the stalls and pastures, and purchased horses for polo training and sale. Five days ago, after a long hiatus of thirteen years, Darcy mounted the back of a one-year-old chestnut thoroughbred named Lakmé for what turned out to be the most liberating ride of his life.

Other changes had also occurred since his heart-wrenching good-bye to Liz in Tangier. The president and the CIA had their media victory while Obsidian laid low, welcoming Knightley to replace the departed Iceman. Charlie defiantly continued to give dance lessons to Jane under the guise of her being a new student, an act that even Caroline did not condemn. Apparently, some of her tough, scaly skin had shed in the advent of her renewed relationship with Rick. Perhaps she was learning to become a little romantic and a little less toxic. According to Rick, she actually uttered the *L* word. Granted, it was after three mojitos, but she said it nonetheless, and he was happy.

Now, before meeting with the man who had altered the direction of his life, Darcy removed his leather jacket, revealing a light blue Ted Baker T-shirt. The serene color exemplified his new persona of optimism for the future. He was definitely a different man from the beaten boy who once before sat on this side of the window facing his sworn enemy.

Wearing orange prison coveralls, Wickham was escorted into the visitor room and directed to where Darcy sat. Recognition was immediate as he expected it would be. What he didn't expect was the genuine smile upon his nemesis's face. It disarmed him immediately.

Wickham had aged physically and not particularly well in comparison to Darcy. Gone was the youthful, powerful man whose fitness and agility once made him an incredible horseman and lothario. Facing him stood a smaller, thinner, gentler man, a man who looked to have tasted humble pie and learned to appreciate it. To Darcy's observant eye, the physical weakness of Wickham was inconsequential. The man appeared inwardly stronger—in a good way.

The prisoner had found a purpose greater than his own.

Both men picked up the receiver to begin, one toward redemption and the other toward forgiveness.

Nervously, Wickham cleared his throat before speaking. "Will, this is unexpected." He furrowed his brow in curiosity. "Why are you here?"

"I'm not really sure why I came. I understand your parole hearing is coming up soon."

"Yes. God willing, I'll be released soon. Although, I'll never truly be free, will I? I'll live forever with what I have done and how my actions put into motion events that were irrevocable. I suppose that will be my continued penance."

Darcy was surprised to say the least. "I...I...just wanted to tell you that I won't stand in the way of your release. I've written my letter to the parole board. You've done your time."

"Thank you for that. Listen, I never had the opportunity following our last visit to apologize to you. At the time, I was young and stupid and filled with greed and jealousy. I'm sorry for the malicious things I said to you. I hope you can find it in your heart to forgive me."

Darcy thought of his confession to Liz that night in Marrakech. She had heard him out. Yes, he would hear Wickham's confession.

"I can if you just tell me why. Why did you hurt my family after all that my father did for you? You were my brother in every sense, and you betrayed me. What you did to Georgiana was reprehensible."

Wickham hung his head, having a difficult time maintaining eye contact with his once best friend. "I'm sorry. I guess I wanted to be you and have all the things that you had, not just the money, but the wealth of real familial love, a family's legacy, a mother, father, and sister who adored me, the reputation of having the best and being the best. No matter how hard I tried, you were still the better polo player, better look- ing, more cultured, and you had Emma Woodhouse. I never told you, but I was in love with her, yet she only wanted you."

"No, I never knew. Is that why you...and my mother?"

"Yes. I felt I had finally bested you because I took someone from you." He ran his hand over his brow. "I'm sorry for her death, and I'm sorry that my selfish actions took both your parents' lives, effectively taking yours from you. I'm sorry for traumatizing Georgiana."

Wickham bowed his head. *This* was the truly difficult confession. This was so much harder than the confession he made to the priest five years ago, but since then, he had a lot of time to think about the things he did. He always knew he had done wrong, and now as a penitent man, he vowed never to deny his conscience again. As Van Gogh said, "a conscience is a man's compass." As the priest said, "it is innate, the voice of God placed within us all."

Darcy leaned forward. "Georgiana doesn't remember that time. So rest easy about her trauma. She is happy. In fact, she will be getting married next summer." He grinned recalling her excitement when she and Justin arrived in Virginia two days ago. They were both over the moon.

"I'm glad. I wish her every happiness," Wickham replied, feeling relieved by the information.

Darcy needed to know why the man before him had changed. Was it prison life, the solitude, the loss of freedom, or was it something more? "George, if you don't mind my asking, what helped you feel contrition?"

"I've had a lot of time to search my soul, Will, time to think about what I had done, and then one day, a priest came to the prison. We talked, and over months, I found God and forgiveness. It might sound trite, but the love of the Almighty has given me peace and a new life."

"No, it's not trite…not at all. I guess, whether it is God or something else, a new beginning, a new life, a better life awaits if we are open and ready for it."

"Are *you* happy? Have you found what will bring you peace?"

"Yeah, and she was heaven sent, too."

Both men, unsure where the conversation could go from there, grew uncomfortable until Darcy stood. "Good luck to you, George. If it helps you at all, know that I do forgive you."

Wickham smiled, and both men hung up. The burdens of the past had lifted so that they both were finally free to truly begin life again, renewed.

As she had done every day since her return to Longbourn three weeks earlier, Liz stood beside the weather-beaten mailbox at the end of the dusty road, about to remove the envelopes.

The postman had just completed his delivery of *her* mail, which was always sure to come from Darcy. He was diligent and thoughtful, each day sending her something to let her know he was thinking of her: a cell phone, a new sketchbook, love letters, a manual on motorcycle riding, and a cassette of Puccini's greatest arias for her greenhouse. He also began her education in exposing her to his favorite rock bands and, over the weeks, sent her various cassettes from his old collection: The Eagles, Bad Company, Led Zeppelin, and a myriad of others she could play in her Jeep. Each gift, he lovingly packaged, and they arrived one after the next, day after day. Rain or shine, she ran down the road through mud or dust, tracking the mailman's delivery in anticipation of her lover's latest thoughtful reminder that he was still there—waiting.

Her return to Longbourn was a constant challenge to maintain her independence and free spirit against her father's continued neediness and occasional *attempt* at manipulation. She no longer placated him, nor did she gloss over the severity of his actions. She stood up to him and took back control of everything in her life. Inevitably, the subject turned to placing part of Longbourn's acreage up for sale. Stances were formed, words exchanged, and a battle ensued, but Liz's reasoning won out time and again.

Unavoidably, her father slipped in and out of depression. His world had crumbled with his misguided trespass toward the dark side, and in stark comparison, her world had been restored, the result of her journey into the light of living.

The new reality for him was hard to face, having lost his daughter's respect. That was the greatest punishment of all. She told him so with a little regret, but without reserve. On one rare occasion, he admitted to her how much he enjoyed when the boisterous and fearless little girl Lizzy had once been resurfaced. It was then that they began to share enthusiastic discussions of books, music of all kinds, people, and delighting in the ridiculous together.

Predictably though, Thomas Bennet's conviction and house arrest only fostered his need for constant companionship. However, his loneliness in his isolation was expected by his daughters, and neither was willing to give in to his guilt tripping.

Liz's determination and restlessness encouraged her to escape the house as much as possible. The monthly lunch dates with Jane became weekly events; sleepovers became more frequent, and swimming in Longbourn's pond took place every morning, not to mention the restoration and enjoyment of the old tire swing. Dare she divulge her and Jane's visit to the Ink Spot a week ago and the smaller rendition of her henna tattoo now permanently inked upon her hip? And her bravest new adventure of all: the visits to Al's Chopper Shop where she was learning how to ride a motorcycle. She smiled at the thought of what Darcy would think.

From the back pocket of her denim shorts, Liz's new mobile phone vibrated against her bottom, alerting her to an incoming text message. She smiled gleefully. It was the second text that day.

It read: "My tongue…your thighs"

She texted back: "Naughty boy…miss u too"

And she did, more than she ever thought imaginable. Once she succeeded in melting his Iceman persona, Darcy revealed himself to be her soul mate in every way: the yang to her ying, the jelly to her peanut butter, cookies to her milk. Every day without him was bland and ho-hum. Metaphorically, chorizo sausages now replaced broiled chicken. She no longer had the palate for the ordinary, dull, safe life attempting to suck her back in at Longbourn.

She removed the stack of letters from the shaky mailbox, which suddenly shifted to the left when she shut the metal door. *Damn!* She was going to have to fix that, too. *Nah, it'll wait. I have other things to do today.*

Like her endless days of the past three weeks, today's mail was equally uneventful. Strangely, nothing from Darcy was included, only bills and one letter from a lawyer that looked imposing. That letter was quickly employed as a fan in similar fashion to the one from the State Historic Preservation Office weeks earlier. She waved it back and forth before her face. It was a stinkin' hot, dog day of August.

Strolling past Bennet Oak, now aptly renamed by Jane as "The Scene of the Crime," Liz smiled in remembrance of Darcy's hard body slamming against hers, throwing her to the ground beneath him. She chose not to remember the horrors of that day. Besides, in truth, she thought of Darcy in just about everything. Just like in those love songs that always seemed to be on her mother's old transistor radio whenever she went for a swim, they sung of longing. Yeah, she longed for and missed everything about him. From the way he unconsciously cracked his pinky knuckle when he was pondering a strategy and his random humming of a tune when he thought she wasn't listening, to the simple, affectionate brushing of his thumb against her cheek. Yeah, she missed him to pieces.

The late-morning sunlight reflected off the antique glass of her greenhouse. It was still Liz's haven, still her quiet slice of heaven and a place that strangely held many memories of Darcy. Apart from their first embrace that dark night when she convinced him to take her to Europe, most of her thoughts were about *his* memories: his mother, his finding of the sketchbook, his love of orchids and learning opera within Pemberley's greenhouse. One day down the road, when she finally leaves Longbourn, she will revive that greenhouse, and together, they will make their own memories and family, if that is what he wants. It was definitely what *she* wanted.

Liz switched on the cooling oscillating fan and settled herself on the stool beside her cassette player. She placed the stack of mail, including the lawyer's letter, atop yesterday's ignored, unopened letter from Aunt Elinor and the confiscated volume of *Crime and Punishment*. The lowered play button on the boom box began Edvard Grieg's adagio "Piano Concerto in A Minor," filling the hot house with its melancholic lyrical movement.

She closed her eyes, allowing the strings to transport her to a place she imagined in her mind's eye: Pemberley. The adagio's singular piano note descended like a large raindrop. The notes following were the ripples it created, building into flowing waters. Darcy was like that large raindrop. Meeting him began the ripples of living. Running with him was the torrent of life that had awaited her.

The lawyer's letter sat staring at her until she snatched it up, tore it open, and began reading. Something *had* come from Darcy today. Liz knit her brows. Absorbing every word, her jaw dropped. She lowered the letter to her lap and then picked it up again, reading through for a second time, disbelieving its contents.

The sum of two million dollars had been set aside in a trust for the exclusive use in the renovation and restoration of the plantation. Longbourn Plantation Trust had been established with the primary trustee as Elizabeth Bennet and the secondary trustee being Jane Bennet.

Overwhelmed, her breath caught, knowing instinctively that this was Darcy's doing. This was an incredible expression of his love, his restoring of her family's legacy so terribly tarnished by her father's actions.

Picking up a cheery, hot pink misting water bottle, Liz walked through the greenhouse, showering her beloved floral friends as she pondered the letter and what to do about it. Drawing the shade blinds over the glass roof, she made her decision. *To hell with the CIA.*

Thirty minutes later, she found herself holding Jane's cowgirl hat in her left hand, standing in her father's study, dressed in her yellow floral sundress, tan cowboy boots, and her "most alluring shade of pink" lipstick. With her hair cascading down around her shoulders and a radiant, golden tan, she felt and looked like summer-kissed freshness, pure femininity, and enchanting seductress all in one.

Bennet looked up from his desk, donned his black eyeglasses, and narrowed his eyes. "I always loved that dress on you, Lizzy dear. It's very feminine, much better than those denim shorts you've been wearing."

"Thanks. Although I love my cutoff jeans, I love this dress, too... for sentimental reasons. I...um need to talk to you about something important. Do you have a minute?" *As if he had other things to do.*

"Of course. Are you having trouble fixing that window frame again?"

"No. Nothing like that. I've left the window frame for you to fix while I am gone. I'm...I'm...going on a little trip up to Leesburg. I won't be gone long, but I just wanted you to know that I've called Jane, and she has agreed to look in on you twice a week, bring you groceries and even allowing you to beat her pants off at a game of chess or dominos. You're on your own, which means cooking, dishes, and the lot. You should know that she's pretty adamant that she won't be doing it for you."

He hung his head in defeat. His daughter didn't need to tell him who was in Leesburg or why she was going there. He was quick to ask, "You really like him, don't you? You're going to him, aren't you?"

"I am. I love him."

"He is a lucky man to have your affection. Why wouldn't you care for him? He has done all the things that I failed to do."

"That's not it at all, Dad. I don't love him because I need a *father's* unconditional love and encouragement. I love him because he is everything I ever dreamed of finding in a mate. He makes me feel alive and fearless, cherished and respected. He encourages me to be myself. He's my equal. Fitzwilliam and I are so similar. We complement each other perfectly. I *already* have a father's love, now I have a partner's love as well."

"You do have my love, Lizzy. I regret so many things, but the thing I regret the most is treating you like I treated your mother—so disrespectfully. I know coming back to Longbourn has been difficult for you, and in many ways, I am still acting as the father I have always been, but please know, I am trying to change. I didn't realize until these last three weeks just how much I missed my spirited little Lizzy and how my selfish behavior stifled you into becoming someone you are not."

Liz walked to his side of the desk, kneeling on the floor beside him. He choked out, "Can you ever forgive me and respect me again?"

"I already have forgiven you, and in truth, I'm equally responsible. I hid and denied the promptings of my soul for many years. I made that choice, and I could have said no."

"Lizzy, my Lizzy…" Bennet became choked up. "I didn't know about Bill. Please believe me. My only hope was that you would be cared for."

"I believe you, Dad."

Father and daughter hugged, and tears brimmed within their eyes until Liz pulled away, wiped her tears, and attempted to smile brightly. "Now for some good news. It seems that the man I love has gone and done something unfathomable."

What she was about to say seemed so unreal, so fantastic that she could hardly believe it as the words came out. "As of today, we no longer have to worry about selling land to finance the restoration of Longbourn."

"What is it? What has he done?"

"He has set up a trust with funds for the complete restoration of Longbourn Plantation House."

Bennet slowly leaned back in his chair, covering his lips with his fingers, holding back a smile. Astonished, he almost hesitated to ask the amount, already feeling completely beholden to a man he knew nothing about and had grossly insulted. "How…how much has he given you?"

Liz, too, covered her lips to stifle a giggle, her eyes sparkling with joy. "Two million dollars."

"Good Lord…good Lord. You must go to him. Thank him in person. How can we ever repay him for what he has done?"

"He won't want thanks or repayment. He won't want you to worry about anything. Together, we will preserve the Bennet legacy. As soon as we come back to Longbourn, we'll begin construction and get some historic contractors and professional landscapers. We'll even do some of the work ourselves for the fun of it."

"We?"

"Sure. Don't you want to meet the man who will hopefully be your son-in-law properly? My guess is that Darcy will love taking a hammer to that ugly sunroom." *Yeah, his hands are as big as his heart…among other—stop that, Liz.*

Reminiscent of other times, she bent and kissed her father's cheek. "I love you, and I'll see you soon."

"I love you, too, kitten."

She stood at the doorway of the study and looked back at her father's broad smile. It seemed as though the weight of the world had been lifted from his slight shoulders. "Oh, and if you think of it, will you care for my orchids while I am gone? They were so neglected last month and could really use some extra attention."

"I'd love to. I used to have quite a green thumb. It'll be good to get back in that greenhouse. I may even do a little gardening and start that vegetable patch I always meant to plant in the west field. You know, even though you stole and hid *Crime and Punishment*, I remember one line in particular. 'I know that you don't believe it, but indeed, life will bring you through. You will live it down in time. What you need now is fresh air, fresh air, fresh air'!"

Minutes later, feeling as renewed as her father, Liz sat in the front seat of her Jeep, enjoying the radiant sun upon her face and the slight breeze in her hair. Confident that she had made the right decision to go to Darcy, she clicked the seatbelt and started the engine. She felt the Lizzy of old disappear in the cloud of dust created as she sped away.

~ ♠ ~

Liz's GPS directed her to the formidable wrought iron gated entry of Pemberley, its large *P* stopping the Jeep dead in its tracks. All she could see beyond the impressive entrance was a long, narrow road covered by stately arched trees. She was part petrified and part humored when she leaned out of the driver's side to press the intercom button for admittance into the estate.

"Hello?" A young woman's voice said on the scratchy other end.

"Um…hi…I'm here to see Fitzwilliam."

The woman chuckled. "Fitzwilliam?"

Liz couldn't see Georgiana's gleeful smile on the other side nor her waving both Mrs. Reynolds and Justin toward the intercom while mouthing, "It's her!"

Liz continued warily, "Yes. Fitzwilliam Darcy? This *is* Pemberley, right?"

"Yeah, it is. Follow the road to the end." With that, she buzzed Liz through as the huge gates separated in welcome.

Liz's heart rate sped up, and with each quarter mile down the picturesque road, she became more nervous. Her fingers tapped the steering wheel, not to the melody or words of "O mio babbino caro," but in anxiety.

The grounds of Pemberley were spectacular. Surrounding the green, lush fields were deep woods establishing the circumference of the estate. To the left of the drive was a small lake with a lovely foot bridge suspended over the still waters. To her right, two horses and a colt grazed. As the two miles came to an abrupt end, there stood a magnificent country estate built of stone, which was easily twice the size of Longbourn Plantation House. Apart from Mount Vernon itself, she had never seen a home in such perfect harmony with nature, each complementing the other in stately, peaceful beauty. Like the day she looked out at the Mediterranean, Liz was in awe.

She parked the Jeep at the far edge of the circular drive and cut the engine, discarding her cowgirl hat on the front seat. Before climbing out, she checked her lipstick and hair in the visor mirror, unaware that the woman who she had spoken with watched her keenly from the library's window. *So this is Liz. I like. I like.*

Cowboy boots crunched the gravel as she walked to the front entrance door. A tentative finger rung the doorbell.

Inside the house, four of the five residents came running as Georgiana opened the door.

Liz's heart sank. Before her stood a gorgeous, tall blonde with riveting blue eyes. Her smile in greeting was warm and felt familiar. Her slender, athletic body was pleasing, and Liz couldn't help it when her own smile slowly faded, thinking that her curvy self had been replaced in just three short weeks.

"Hi. You must be the girl looking for Fitz. Please come in," the blonde said.

"Fitz? Oh…right."

Liz stepped into a massive, light-infused marble foyer and her eyes immediately fixed upon the large staircase before her. She was more than a wee bit intimidated. Somehow, her arrival wasn't quite going how she planned, gone was the hoped for running straight into Darcy's arms, lips crashing, promises made. She certainly didn't imagine being greeted by the Greek goddess Aphrodite. *Who is this woman?*

"I'm Liz, a friend of Fitzwilliam's. Is he here?"

Georgiana couldn't help but laugh. "God, I haven't heard him called that since Mrs. Reynolds yelled at him for tracking horse manure into the kitchen when I was six. I'm sorry; where are my manners? I'm Georgiana, Fitz's sister."

Liz exhaled, visibly sighing in relief. She blurted, "Oh, thank God. I thought you were his girlfriend."

"We'll leave that role to you. The way he talks about you, one might think you were already married."

Liz blushed.

Mr. and Mrs. Reynolds approached from midway down the foyer, and Justin followed, exiting the library where he and Georgiana had been spying on Liz in the Jeep. All were ecstatic to meet her as solicitous introductions were made.

Sure, Liz was really happy to meet them, too, but damn if she just didn't want to see Darcy, immediately. It had felt like the longest three weeks of her life. She had things to say, thanks to give, and kisses to administer.

"We have no idea what you did, but you have our esteemed gratitude for turning around the Man of Steel. Since his trip to Europe, he's a different man. I've never seen him smile so much!" Justin said. "Who knew he even had a smile?"

And so it went for seven long minutes: "You're so pretty." "He's bought horses, hoping to train them for UVA's polo team." "Never thought we would be back at Pemberley." "He can't stop talking about you." "The black is gone." "Did you know he's a CIA agent?"

Well apparently, he wasn't going to tell them the *whole* truth…after all, some habits die hard.

Liz bore it all graciously until finally she said, "I'm really happy to meet you all as well, but please, is he here? It has been a long time since I've seen him, and I'm rather anxious."

Georgiana grinned. "Sure. He's here. He is in the stable. I'll walk out with you and point the way."

Together, they walked down the front steps onto the circular drive. When the two women finally stood beside the vibrant pink azalea bushes,

Georgiana unexpectedly pulled Liz into a tight hug.

"Thank you, Liz. You saved my brother from a lifetime of anger and mistrust. I never thought he would find love. He loves you so much."

Liz didn't know what to do with her arms, so she simply chose to hug the young woman back. "No thanks necessary. He saved me, too, and I love him just as much. If it weren't for Fitzwilliam, I shudder to think what my future would have become."

Georgiana had tears brimming in her eyes when she pulled back from Liz. "Just walk through this field, and you'll see the stables around back."

"Thanks, Georgiana."

"Call me Gigi. Fitz hates it, but I love it, and I can't think of any better name for my future sister to call me."

"Thanks, Gigi." *Future sister? Yeah.*

She walked over to the Jeep, reached in, and then with a smile of anticipation, settled the cowgirl hat on her head. She was going to the stable to see her Harley biker god turned cowboy!

A verdant green pasture welcomed each footstep as she drew closer to the red barn, where rock music emanated from the open double doors. Immediately recognizing the band from one of the cassettes Darcy had sent her, she knew the Outlaws song that floated in the hot summer air.

Liz playfully kicked up the dust with her cowboy boots as she approached the barn. Strangely, she suddenly felt quite at home in this unfamiliar place he had once described as a haven for death.

Perhaps she felt at peace and ease at Pemberley because he was there, and wherever he was, well…that was where home would be.

She walked silently to the entrance of the barn and listened to Darcy from somewhere within singing at the top of his lungs to the lyrics of "There Goes Another Love Song." He had a damn great singing voice and was obviously having a good time. The music was energizing and filled the barn with joy and frivolity. It was clear to her that he was happy, obviously having found *his* peace, not only at his childhood home but in this barn as well. Clearly, being back with horses and doing what he loved had helped to restore the Fitzwilliam Darcy of Pemberley he was always meant to be.

Liz continued to move slowly down the row of stalls housing magnificent horses and two motorcycles until finally she reached Darcy. Tending to a brown horse, he sat with his back to the opening of the stall. She couldn't make out what he was doing, but she enjoyed the view of his well-worn cowboy work boots, collar length hair, white T-shirt, and that perfect blue-jeaned backside perched on an upside down bucket. His body rocked to the music as he sang at full volume. His tattooed, muscular bicep flexed with each movement of his arm. Man, her heart sped up crazy fast. Of all Darcy's personas, this one was definitely the sexiest. He was raw masculinity. Yeah, cowboy suited him perfectly. Every pore of his hard body sizzled hot, hot, hot! And every beat of her heart said mine, mine, mine!

Quietly, she hid behind a wooden post and began texting him, covertly observing his reaction as though a top-level assassin. After all, Darcy had always insisted that she had skills. He trained her well.

His cell phone beeped in the back pocket of his stone-washed Levi's, and she stifled a chuckle when his hand snaked around his body to remove it.

Her first text read: "What are u doing?"

"Picking the hooves of my new horse."

"Can we go riding?"

"On the horse?"

"LOL. Yes, the brown one with white blaze."

Liz watched as he looked up from his iPhone to gaze at the horse. She texted again immediately. "Or I can ride u...vigorously."

"OMG, yes! When?"

"U have hay in your hair, Fitzwilliam."

Darcy's hand flew to his hair, and he brushed hay from the curls at the top of his head. When it fell before him, he abruptly stood, knocking over the bucket with his boot, startling the horse. He turned to see Liz leaning against the post by the stall's opening, looking as fresh and innocent as summer daisies. Sun-kissed, she looked resplendent in that yellow sundress, cowboy boots, and hat. She took his breath away.

His heart fluttered rapidly just like it did when he saw her wearing that black evening gown in Monte Carlo. She didn't need Versace or diamonds. Wholesome cowgirl suited her just fine at Pemberley.

Liz smirked, tipping her hat back with a pink fingernail. "Hi, cowboy. I like your blue jeans."

Darcy rushed to her, sweeping her up within his tight embrace. With hands and arms reacquainting and caressing, they kissed almost violently, making up for three weeks of starvation. She clung to him, and after she released the expressive dam within her, a magnitude of emotions came rushing forth. Unchecked tears rolled down her cheeks as a flood of happiness surged. She was in the one place where she truly felt herself: home within his arms.

Standing where his parents' betrayed vows had tragically come to an end, Darcy's lips grazed hers, softly declaring, "God, how I missed you."

She dreamily replied, "I missed you so much that I couldn't abide by the CIA's moratorium any longer. I never wish to be parted from you from this day forward."

Still holding her in his embrace, he leaned back, knitting his brows. "You mean that? Is this your reply to our conversation at the airport? You're not teasing me, are you?"

Liz cocked an eyebrow. "I thought you had an aversion to snakes? Didn't you once tell me most women were vipers of one type or another? Now you want to spend forever with me. Really?"

"What are you talking about? I always wanted to spend forever with you. You're my elusive serpentine." Punctuated by sweet, quick kisses to her lips, he added, "Intelligent, seductive, graceful, passionate, and dangerous to my heart. Marry me, baby. Say you'll be mine."

Not replying to his uncharacteristic effusions and tender proposal, she smiled and, with sparkling eyes, mischievously queried, "Did I mention that I got a tattoo?"

He laughed looking at her skeptically. "You did not."

"I did. Do you want to see it?"

"Of course, but are you trying to avoid answering my question?"

"No. I'd like to answer it."

Liz stepped back and, making sure she had his utmost attention, slowly and seductively, raised one side of the skirt of her dress.

He raised a curious eyebrow, not about to stop her.

When she pulled down one side of her panties, Darcy unconsciously licked his lips. For sure, he *definitely* wasn't going to deter her, even if they were in the middle of the stable.

"Here is my answer." Vibrant *Coelogyne ochracea* orchids, *their* orchid, caressed a snake. Clearly rendered within its black and white skin, in lettering of tribal design was the name "Darcy."

She simply said, "Remember? I'm yours. You did promise forever, right?"

~♠~

Epilogue

Thousands of people sat riveted in the open-air darkness of the ancient Roman Arena di Verona in Tuscany, Italy. It was an unusually balmy October night for the opera house's final production of the season.

The extravagant gold sets and elaborate costumes depicting ancient China held experienced opera lovers from all over the world spellbound as they anticipated the spectacular finale of Puccini's *Turandot*. The color and passion of the soprano's voice carried into the midnight air as audience and players watched Prince Calaf, on bended knee, await the icy Princess Turandot's answer. Had the prince won her love and hand in marriage, or was she able to guess his name, and if so, would he be put to death?

Liz had never seen this opera, and gripped Darcy's hand tightly. They sat so close to the orchestra pit that she could almost feel the tension of the prince, the chorus, and the king as Turandot began her emotion-filled proclamation.

Darcy smiled as he watched his new wife literally sitting on the edge of her seat in anticipation. The diva's powerful crescendo seemed to shoot straight into Liz's soul, and when the princess held out her arms in loving welcome to the prince, proclaiming his name to be "Love," Darcy was sure he saw tears in her eyes. Hell, he almost had tears in his own. He was so damn happy that he could hardly contain it.

He leaned over to her and whispered in her ear. "I love you, Mrs. Darcy."

Turning her head toward him, she planted a little kiss on his ready lips, then smoothed the back of her index finger down his cheek. Her radiant smile undid him.

He remembered asking himself almost four months earlier, while sitting beside her in the Ferrari on the way to Monte Carlo, if it could get any better than that. From the moment Liz said yes to his marriage proposal, every day had been the best day of his life—a life she had given back to him.

The chorus surrounded the couple on the stage, delivering in collective unison the prince's previously delivered "Nessun Dorma."

Liz and Darcy continued to applaud as the cast took their bows. Even as the exterior spotlights came on and the crowd began to depart the ancient arena, they remained in their seats. It was a beautiful star-filled night, and they weren't in any rush to leave amidst the throngs of people. This was their honeymoon, and they had no desire to be anywhere other than together.

Their motorcycle, parked outside the eastern exit, would wait undisturbed until their departure when they would travel back through the winding and dangerous hills to their love nest on Lake Garda.

"Oh my God! That performance was incredible! Her proclamation blew me away! " Liz exclaimed enthusiastically, her eyes sparkling in the moonlight and dimmed peripheral lights.

"Now you know why it is my favorite. I'm a sucker for a happy ending."

"I thought you said *Lakmé* was your favorite opera?"

"I lied. I knew *Lakmé* was *your* favorite."

"Were you trying to impress me then even when you seemed so detached and solemn, playing Mr. Tough Guy Iceman denying that anything was growing between us?"

Darcy toyed with her wedding gift, a diamond and white gold, serpent coil bracelet, specially designed to match her necklace and earrings. He raised his eyebrows, inquiring, "Didn't it work? I mean, when *exactly* did you know that you were in love with me?"

Liz adjusted her husband's red silk tie as she contemplated a proper response. He looked so damn sexy at that moment with his questioning brow and sensitive look. Forever banished was that brooding, severe mien he used to wear. She was pretty sure that as soon as the last opera-goer left the parking lot, her husband and that motorcycle were in for a good hard ride, even before they hit the road. Panties were a thing of the past on their honeymoon, and it wouldn't be the first time the red dress she wore had seen outdoor action.

"Hmm…When did I know that I was in love with you?" She ran her hand through his wavy locks and guided his lips toward her. "I cannot fix on the hour or the spot or the look or the words, which laid the foundation. Baby, I was in the middle before I knew I had begun."

~♠~

Acknowledgements

My heartfelt appreciation and undying love goes out to my husband who has encouraged me every step of the way to pursue my dream of writing. Patient, generous, and loving, he is my Mr. Darcy.

To my parents whose support and faith in my ability to bring my stories to the public continues to guide me through those times when my confidence abandons me. Their 60-year marriage is the muse to my romance writing.

A special thank you to Jakki Leatherberry, editor supremo and an all around awesome gal. I couldn't have done it without your tolerant and diligent vacuuming of my split infinitives and comma obsession. You rock! To Sarah and Sharlotte, who were with DoC from the very beginning, sharing their expertise and helping to bring the story to life. Thank you both!

To you the reader, in appreciation for allowing me to come into your life and whisk you away. I love you all!

And to the two ladies to whom this book is dedicated: Sheryl, your sisterly friendship confirms to me that angels aren't just in heaven. They walk among us, having been heaven sent. And to Pamela, your strength and dignity in difficult times are an inspiration to me. Your friendship is a true blessing.

About the Author

Cat Gardiner loves to take you around the world in her novels, places you may never have been with music that maybe you've never heard. A member of Romance Writers of America and her local chapter TARA, she enjoys writing across the spectrum of Pride and Prejudice inspired romance novels. From the comedic Christmas, Chick Lit *Lucky 13* to bad boy biker Darcy in the romantic adventure *Denial of Conscience,* these contemporary novels will appeal to many of her Mr. Darcy lovers.

"I love an adventure! So my storytelling uses fresh innovation to bring the reader on a multi-tiered journey. Using sights and sounds with Spotify music playlists, blogs, and inspirational image Pinterest boards, the reader becomes immersed. Books should be an escape to a time, place, or world where you can lose yourself."

Married 22 years to her best friend, they are the proud parents of the smartest honor student in the world - their orange tabby, Ollie. Although they live in Florida, they will always be proud native New Yorkers no matter how far away they are.

Catgardiner.blogspot.com * facebook.com/cat.t.gardiner_ *
* Denial of Conscience Facebook Novel Page *
twitter.com/VPPressNovels

Check out other Austen-inspired books published by Vanity & Pride Press

Lucky 13
by Cat Gardiner
Winner of Austenesque Reviews Favorite Modern Adaptation for 2014: "What a phenomenal read!! The attention to detail and the clever way the author immersed her audience in the story was such a terrific experience!"

A Contemporary Austen-Inspired, Pride and Prejudice Novel - New York City advertising executive, Elizabeth Bennet is determined to find a respectable date to take to Christmas dinner with her insane family. So, what's a girl to do with only 26 days remaining? She and her best friend embark on a mad-cap dating blitz. Speed dating and blind dates become a source of frustration when one man continually shows up, hell-bent on either annoying her or capturing her heart. Fitzwilliam Darcy, wealthy, hunky, part time New York City firefighter is Elizabeth's new client, one of thirteen men chosen for a fundraising, beefcake calendar.

Sparks fly and ignite as misunderstandings abound. Sit back and laugh for an unforgettable, hot, holiday season in the Big Apple.

Dearest Friends
by Pamela Lynne
"Dearest Friends is one of those rare stories that quickly grabs hold of the reader and never lets go; it is a thrilling ride filled with danger, seduction, romance and humor. I never wanted it to end."

A heartwarming, Pride and Prejudice Regency Variation – Fitzwilliam Darcy and Elizabeth Bennet have both experienced betrayals that have caused them to reconsider many of their preconceived notions of life and love. When they see each other again in London, they bond over a shared grief and begin a courtship in spite of Mr. Bennet's insistence she marry another. They are supported by an unlikely group of friends and as they follow Darcy and Elizabeth on their road to happiness, connections are formed that will change their lives forever.

Made in the USA
San Bernardino, CA
10 July 2015